An Officer and a Gentleman

Book 5 in the
Soldier of the Queen Series

By

Griff Hosker

An Officer and a Gentleman

Published by Sword Books Ltd 2025

SWORD BOOKS

Copyright ©Griff Hosker First Edition 2025

The author has asserted their moral right under the Copyright, Designs and Patents Act, 1988, to be identified as the author of this work.
All Rights reserved. No part of this publication may be reproduced, copied, stored in a retrieval system, or transmitted, in any form or by any means, without the prior written consent of the copyright holder, nor be otherwise circulated in any form of binding or cover other than that in which it is published and without a similar condition being imposed on the subsequent purchaser.
A CIP catalogue record for this title is available from the British Library.

Dedicated to Richard Wilkinson, a real gentleman, a fine educator and a good friend. I shall miss you.

Contents

Contents..4
Prologue..6
Part One..9
Chapter 1..10
Chapter 2..22
Chapter 3..36
Chapter 4..50
Chapter 5..60
Chapter 6..71
Chapter 7..83
Chapter 8..94
Chapter 9..106
Chapter 10..118
Chapter 11..133
Chapter 12..143
Part Two...159
Chapter 13..159
Chapter 14..171
Chapter 15..184
Part Three..200
Chapter 16..200
Chapter 17..213
Chapter 18..224
Chapter 19..234
Chapter 20..246
Chapter 21..258
Epilogue...270
Glossary...272
Historical Background..273
Other books by Griff Hosker..................................275

Some of the characters in the book

Captain Archie Dunn
Second Lieutenant Griff Roberts
Sergeant Major Bob Leonard
Sergeant Stan Shaw
Sergeant Abn Hamed - commander of the cooks and garrison at Fort Farafra
Corporal Charlie Atkinson
Corporal Tom Higgins
Bugler Wally Wilson
Trooper Paul Cartwright – batman
Trooper Bill Burton – batman
Trooper Geoff Bates
Trooper Michael Peters
Trooper Bill Foulkes
Trooper Simon Flynn
Trooper Roy Hunter
Trooper Ben Bentinck
Trooper Alan Dale

Prologue

Egypt

I had survived my first four months in the desert. I had led men in battle and I had buried one of them. I would not call myself a veteran but I no longer had the pallid skin of an Englishman from the north west of England. I had the tanned skin of a warrior who rode a camel while wearing a keffiyeh in the oven of the African desert. Second Lieutenant Griff Roberts had begun his military career and while I could never hope to emulate the deeds of my illustrious father, Jack, a hero of Rorke's Drift, Tel El Kebir and Omdurman, I knew that I was well thought of and that was enough for me.

The fort at Farafra was now home. We were miles from the nearest help and the caravans that brought us our food and ammunition were a lifeline. They also brought something we had not enjoyed at first; they brought letters. They meant we could send letters home. Of course, the letters had a long journey. They had to go from here to Faiyum and thence along the railway to Cairo. From there it would be a ship to England and then the British Post Office. I had sent one letter when I had taken the survivors of the Ottoman attack in the desert to take the train. I did not expect a reply from my father and aunt any time soon. I was, therefore, surprised when a month after I had sent the letter there was mail for me when the relief caravan arrived. The letter was not from home but from Lucinda Cowley, one of the survivors. We had got on and I know that I was smitten but Lucinda had seemed to me a very practical young woman who had her heart set on becoming an archaeologist. It was a lofty ambition. The letter surprised me. She had written it in Alexandria while they had waited for a ship to take them to England. That she had thought to write to me was touching enough but the tone of the letter was so friendly that I re-read it many times to see if I had made a mistake. She said that she had enjoyed my company and wished to maintain the correspondence. That sentence alone set my pulse racing. She said that she and her guardian would live at the family home in Grasmere until he could secure a position at a university or a college teaching archaeology. She would let me know when they made the move and gave me the address in Grasmere. It was the salutation at the end which made me smile so much that I had to force myself to become serious when I faced my men. She also said that she would write to my father when in England, I had given her his address, and tell him how I fared. That letter would get home before any missive that I might send. At the end she wrote, *'all my love, Lucinda'*. I had not had many friends growing up. When I had been at Sandhurst I had made three friends but they were posted across the globe and we did not write. I now had a young lady to whom I could correspond. How had that happened?

Paul Cartwright was my batman. I had been reluctant to have one at first just as he had been reluctant to be a soldier but I now relied on him and he seemed to enjoy the life at the fort. When he had brought me the letter he had smiled, "A letter for you, Sir, and from the perfume, a young lady. Perhaps Miss Lucinda?" After I had read it many times, he had knocked on the door and said, "A cup of tea, Sir? Freshly made."

"Thank you, Cartwright." I placed the letter on the cabinet next to the bed. It was one of the three pieces of furniture in the tiny room: a bed, a chair and the small bedside cabinet made from a packing case. My clothes hung from a spear that we had taken which, placed horizontally, filled a convenient gap between two walls.

Cartwright handed me my tea and I saw his eyes flick to the letter and then the smile. I felt embarrassed. I don't know why. "Miss Cowley wrote to thank us for saving them, Cartwright. Thoughtful eh?"

He nodded, "She struck me as a thoughtful young lady who measured all that she said and did." Cartwright had been a gentleman's gentleman and had moved in far loftier circles than I had. My only experience of such people had been an unhappy one. The Blue Bloods as we called them from Sandhurst had driven one of the cadets to suicide.

I looked up at Cartwright. I valued his opinion, "Her letter was..." I hesitated as I sought the words, "friendly."

"And that she wrote from, where was it," He glanced at the top of the letter, "Alexandria, implies that you are much on her mind. Sir, the caravan will be leaving in the morning. You have time to write the reply." He smiled, "It would be the proper thing to do, Sir, if you don't mind me saying so."

He was right. I bit my lower lip, "But what would I say? I have never written to a young lady."

"Nor have I, Sir, but it seems to me that if you write to her the way that you spoke to her when we rode to the railway then that would be the correct tone. Neither she nor her guardian objected to the manner of your speech."

I grinned, "Cartwright, you are a genius."

"I am just doing my job, Sir, but one last piece of advice."

"Yes?"

"I think you have the salutation, eh? The young lady has invited informality." I flushed. He had read the last part. "I would put your title below your Christian name. After all she addressed you that way, did she not?"

After he had gone I knew that he was right. I went to the office. I was adjutant and had to write most of the reports. The office was empty. I lit the lamp and took a sheet of paper. After dipping the nib into the ink and shaking off the excess on blotting paper, I began to write, '*Dearest Lucinda*'. I was being too personal and I was going to tear the paper up and start again. I shook my head. My heart had directed my pen and I would continue in the same vein. I wrote and filled the two sheets. I wrote the address on the envelope and then sealed it. It was done. If no reply came then I would know I had been too bold. It might take months for a reply to come and I would need to be patient. My life had changed.

An Officer and a Gentleman

Part One

The Desert

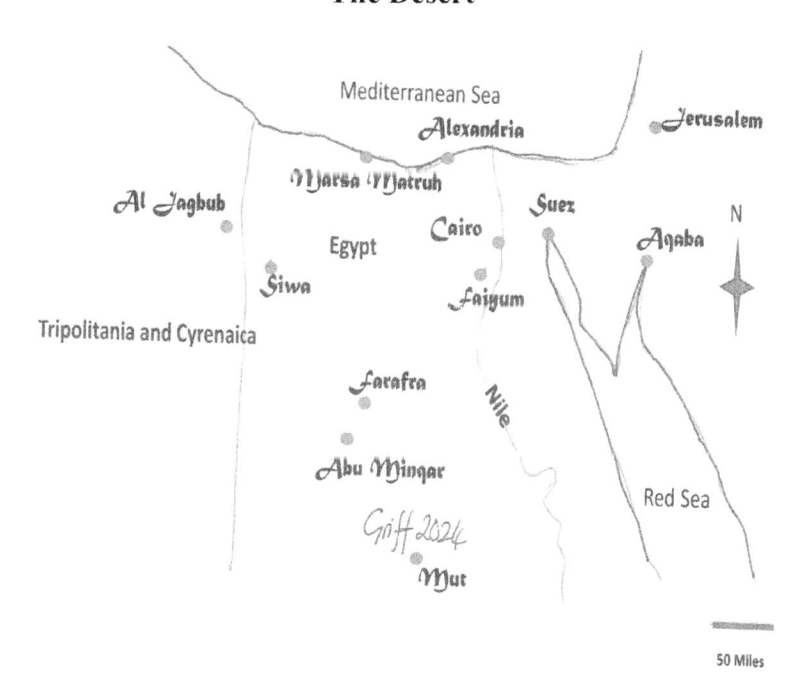

Chapter 1

Fort Farafra

Patience was a necessity in the desert. Each day was almost identical to the previous one. Every third day I would lead a patrol into the desert to ensure that the caravans that plied the desert were safe. On the days when we were in the fort we trained and I did the paperwork. It was an ordered, though largely dull, life.

The day that the caravan headed back to the railway, carrying my letter, Captain Dunn summoned me to the office. "Take a seat, Griff." He tapped the official looking document that lay on the desk. "This came from Cairo; you can read it at your leisure but I will give you the gist of it now." He shook his head, "You can tell that Kitchener is no longer in command. It says that thanks to losses in South Africa and the demands of India there will be no relief for us. Instead of a six-month tour of duty it is more likely to be a year."

My heart sank. I had hoped to be able to travel back and see Lucinda. My dreams the previous night had been amorous ones and I had fantasised about courting her. If it was a year then she would meet some young man who was more of her class than I was. I had seen a light flickering in the dark only to have it doused. I forced myself to keep a stoic expression. "The men may not like it, Sir."

"I am damned sure that they won't but we are all soldiers. Even worse is that the brass don't seem to take the threat from the Ottomans very seriously. Englishmen were killed at the dig and yet it is being ignored."

"Our hands are tied then Sir?"

He smiled, "They appear to be but nowhere does it say that we cannot police the border rigorously. Thanks to our patrols the bandits appear to be leaving the caravans alone. I think that Sergeant Major Leonard and Sergeant Shaw are more than capable of taking a couple of troopers to escort the caravans who head to Abu Minqar and Mut. We can concentrate on extended patrols to Siwa and the border." He shook his head, "And there is more bad news, Major Lowery and his Egyptians have been withdrawn from Siwa. The sergeant in charge of the caravan told me that, apparently, the officer liked to drink. When the Turks came across the border he was drunk and that was why they got past him. Half of his men deserted. He has been sent back to England to face charges and the rest of the unit disbanded. We are the only British force between here and the Turks. The coast has the Royal Navy to keep it safe but we are it as far as the desert is concerned."

I brightened. Throwing myself into work would help me to put thoughts of Lucinda and other young men, from my mind. "And we have a name too, Sir, to put to the man who led the raid."

"Name?"

"Yes, Sir, remember, that dying Turk said Captain Mustapha."

"Ah, yes, but how does that help?"

"I am not sure it helps but the Turk said that he was an aggressive officer. I cannot see him sitting on his side of the border, can you? If we see no signs of Turks then we know that he is no longer in the area but if we come across their trail then we can expect trouble."

He smiled, "I am a navigator, Griff. I love the challenge of finding my way across this sea of sand but you are a warrior. You are like your father and that is what makes us a good team."

"Will we tell the men. Sir?"

He nodded, "I think it is only right, don't you? You have a good eye for such things. Watch the chaps when I tell them and let me know if any are particularly unhappy."

"Sir."

Bugler Wilson sounded the bugle for assembly. Sergeant Major Leonard barked, "Get a move on you slovenly shower." The words were said without venom. Old habits died hard. When they were lined up he said, "Attention!"

They all snapped to attention.

"Stand easy." The men relaxed a little. The parade ground could be like an oven but it was early enough and there was enough shade to be relatively pleasant. Captain Dunn would not keep them long. He held the message from Cairo in his hand and he tapped it, "Orders from Cairo." He smiled, "They brought the rum and the supplies, this is the payment." I saw smiles appear on the faces of most of the troopers. "We are to continue our patrols and to keep the land between here and the border safe. Nothing new there, eh? What is new, however, and somewhat more unpalatable is that we will not be relieved. The Boer War has cost the British Army many soldiers and the ones who were due to replace us and give us three months in England are now needed elsewhere." He paused to let the words sink in and I scanned the faces but saw no anger, just resignation. "It means that this pleasant weather of winter will be replaced by the hot sun of summer before we can hope to get back to England. Anyway, I just thought I would let you know. Sergeant Major, this will be a make do and mend morning. I would like to see all non-commissioned officers and officers in my office."

"Sir." The men were dismissed and dispersed. Make and mend days were always welcome.

The office was pleasantly cool, "Burton, make a pot of tea and then join the others, I am sure there are tasks to keep you occupied."

"There always are, Sir."

The office was crowded when the four NCOs arrived. Burton brought in the huge pot of tea, the mugs, sugar and tinned milk. "Thank you, Burton, we can serve ourselves."

"Sir." He left.

An Officer and a Gentleman

"Gentlemen, help yourselves."

The four poured their tea and made it suit their own taste. Sergeant Major Leonard waited until the rest of us had poured our tea and then took his. It was not out of politeness; he liked his stronger than the rest of us. He took four spoons of sugar. He liked it sweet.

"You may smoke if you wish." Those who had the habit did so. "I am sorry about the bad news but I thought it best to give all of you the information at the same time." He waited but they were all old soldiers who knew better than to voice an opinion without being asked. "What do you think about it?"

Bob Leonard was the oldest soldier in the troop as well as the most experienced. He had twenty years in the army. "Well, Sir, for me it makes no odds. This is my last year and then I can retire to England. I have a place picked out already and I can grow flowers and a few veggies and bore the life out of the blokes in the pub. I would not be travelling back to England before retiring in any case. This saves me a few bob. I don't spend much and this posting suits me." He picked up his mug and topped it up, "Now some of these young lads might have a different opinion."

Stan Shaw shook his head, "I am with the sergeant major on this matter. Cairo has no lure for me and the thought of ten days on a boat to get back to England does not appeal."

I saw corporals Higgins and Atkinson nod in agreement. The captain looked questioningly at the Egyptian, "Sergeant?"

"Effendi, for me and my men it is different. We have families back in Cairo and Alexandria. Some of my men have families at Faiyum. We work here for pay. It would be pleasant to get back home but we can wait. If any of my men need to get home because of an emergency then we can arrange it."

The Egyptians were responsible for the fort. Even if we left they would still be here. Our presence meant that they could take leave if they wished. Most preferred the life at the fort rather than at home. Like Sergeant Major Leonard, they all husbanded their pay.

"Good. I have asked Lieutenant Roberts to keep an ear to the ground. We don't want any malcontents. I ask you to do the same. Any trouble then let me know." They nodded, "Now, the

An Officer and a Gentleman

matter of patrols. The lieutenant and I are both worried about the Turks. Cairo does not appear to be. We are forbidden to cross the border. However, we can be as aggressive as we like on this side. What we plan is for Sergeant Major Leonard and four chosen men to remain at the fort to be available to escort caravans safely on the road south. The rest of the troop will be divided equally between the lieutenant and me. We will each take ten days to patrol to the border and then return. It will mean there is always an officer in the fort but we will have men in the desert."

He paused again and this time there was a response. Once more it was the sergeant major. "Sir that is three hundred miles. It will mean a round trip of six hundred miles. Sixty miles a day is asking a lot."

He smiled, "If it takes longer then it is not a problem, Sarn't Major. However long it takes the other half have an easy time while they are away."

Stan put up his hand and Captain Dunn smiled, "Just come out with it Shaw."

"And if there is trouble, Sir, then that patrol would have no help, would it?"

There was silence and Captain Dunn said, "No, but I think this troop has shown that we have the measure of any enemies we might encounter. When Lieutenant Roberts sent the Turks packing the last time he was outnumbered but it was they who ran." He stood and went to the map, "In a perfect world there would be a fort at Siwa. The business in South Africa means that will not happen. Lieutenant Roberts and I are both sensible chaps. We will make measured decisions. It is in neither of our interests to jeopardise this troop. Any more questions?"

Corporal Higgins said, "How about more camels, Sir? Long patrols will take it out of them and we will need a pack camel for such along patrol."

"Good point. I will make a request. Now, let us choose our men. Sergeant Major, who do you want?"

He had clearly thought about it and he said, immediately, "Troopers Bentinck, Dale and Peters."

"Lieutenant?"

I was more guarded in my selection. I knew the captain would want the bugler and he and Tom Higgins seemed to get on well. I went with the men from the Carnic, "Sergeant Shaw, Corporal Atkinson, Troopers Cartwright, Hunter and Bates."

He had been writing the names down, "Good. They seem balanced. I will leave with my patrol tomorrow. When I return I will send my report to Cairo and ask for the extra camels. By then I should have a clearer picture of the scale of the problem. This afternoon have the men check their equipment, draw ammo and make sure the camels are in tip top condition."

I went with Shaw and Atkinson. The glare and heat of the sun hit us the moment we left the shade of the office. Wrapping his keffiyeh around his head Stan Shaw said, "Thanks for picking us, Sir. We both appreciate it."

I shrugged, "I didn't like to break up a successful team. Sergeant, you tell the men. I will speak to Cartwright."

My batman had expressed doubts to me about serving here in the desert. While he had done nothing to let me down I wanted the air cleared before we left for the border. He and the other batman, Bill Burton were washing the captain's shirt and mine. We had dhobi wallers but they were perfectionists. The shirts would be washed, starched and ironed fit for us to attend a gentleman's club.

"You have no need to do this Cartwright."

Burton laughed, "It is one of his few pleasures in life, Sir. It makes him think he is back in England."

"Well, I do miss it, Sir. Dressing the young master for a dinner always made me proud. If we were in a regiment I could do this for regimental dinners but here…"

"Then we shall see if we can have a troop dinner, I will speak to the captain." I felt guilty for I said it facetiously but Cartwright's reaction told me that he thought it was a grand idea.

"Splendid, Sir. Capital."

I saw Burton roll his eyes. "I shall just go and hang this up. See you later, Paul. Sir."

We were alone in the dhobi area and I said, "How do you feel about no leave, Cartwright?"

"Nothing in England for me, Sir, I have no family and, to be honest my memories of England are not the best."

"Do you still regret joining the army?"

"Oh, no, Sir. The alternative does not bear thinking about. I could have taken a job in a hotel but…" he shook his head, "dealing with women and the like. Not for me. I have grown used to his life Sir. Like I just said there are many things I miss but here I feel like we are making a difference. Until we rescued the archaeologists I was not so sure but when we escorted the survivors I knew that but for us they might all have been dead. The men in the caravans owed their lives to us too. If I was still a gentleman's gentleman that would never have happened. No matter what I did in my job I would not make a difference. Forget my whining, Sir. I was just feeling sorry for myself."

I believed him. "Good. Now we have ten days in the fort and then we go on a long patrol to the border and back. You are a sensible fellow. Work out what we need to take. There will be just six of us and we shall need to be self-sufficient."

Pleased to be given something to tax his mind he grinned, "Righto, Sir!"

That evening as we all dined together, there was no separate officer's mess, I mentioned Cartwright's idea. Archie was bemused by it. "I can see what he means. At sea eating is all very formal and I hear that regular battalions also make a point of dressing up regularly but that is what makes us unique, Griff, we don't do things the normal way. I think it gives us the edge when it comes to fighting. We may be small in number but our enemies can't predict what we are going to do." He was dismissing the idea.

I told him about the change my father had experienced. "He went from red, woollen uniforms with high colours and unsuitable headgear to this sort of thing. How they managed to fight in those red uniforms…I wore it once, in England and in winter. It was just for fun but I was melting… in winter."

"You are right, Griff, and I think that this is the future."

It was strange the effect that the letter had on me. The next day, when the captain and his men had left us and I was in charge I did not feel, as I had on previous occasions, as though the weight of the world was on my shoulders. I found myself dealing with the problems that arose in a calmer manner. As usual, with Archie gone, I was more isolated and left alone with my own thoughts. When I ate the men spoke to me but they were more engrossed in their own lives, the games of dominoes, the wood carving and the other hobbies they engaged in. The NCOs were a tight bunch and I think Sergeant Major Leonard regarded them as the sons he would never sire. Even Cartwright kept to himself. It allowed me to sit in the cool of the evening and fantasise about Lucinda. I imagined a future with her. It was just fantasy and I could let my imagination run riot and it did. The effect was that I rose bright and eager for the day having had pleasant dreams while I slept.

The first caravan passed through the oasis four days after Captain Dunn had left. We did not recognise the caravan master but word must have spread amongst the merchants that the British soldiers at Farafra would escort them. They never asked for assistance. I think they feared if we did that we might charge them but they made a point of coming to the fort to ask our permission to water their camels and they usually made us a gift, normally of dates or figs.

After we had eaten Sergeant Major Leonard and I walked to the tower overlooking the gates. From there we had a good view of the camp. "All set for the morning, Sergeant Major?"

"Yes Sir. It will be a little easier with fewer men and the last few patrols have been without incident."

"You are too wise a bird to take that for granted though, eh Bob?"

When there were no men around I used his Christian name and he did not seem to mind despite my youth. He chuckled, "No, Sir. The minute you think it is easy is your last in this world. I have good lads with me, it is why I chose them. One good thing is that we have done this route so often that if there was anything odd we would spot it straight away."

He was right. The ancient caravan trails that had been barely discernible to us when we had first come to the desert now seemed so clear that they were like the turnpikes back in England. The bones of dead animals were like the mile markers on the roads and the occasional piece of vegetation was like a signpost.

"Will you be alright until we return, Sir?"

"I think so. I have a mind to have the men clear the ditch. That last storm blew in more sand and the stakes are less effective."

He laughed, "They will love that."

The caravans always left before dawn to take advantage of the cool. In the middle of the day they would rest. I rose with the patrol to see them off. Cartwright was always a good batman and he rose with me. The two of us were the first at breakfast as the Egyptian bugle sounded reveille. It meant I had finished by the time my men were beginning to eat. While Cartwright took our plates and mugs to wash I stood, "No drilling today." There were smiles but they were wise enough not to actually cheer, "Instead we will don fatigues and clear the ditch." Their faces fell.

I laboured with the men. We had spades and shovels. The sand we removed we packed against the base of the walls. Vegetation was removed and where the spiky thorn branches had been broken they were replaced. That was a messy and sometimes painful job. By noon we had cleared most of the ditch around three walls.

"Sergeant Shaw, when we have eaten I will take Cartwright and we will fetch more thorns."

"I can get Corporal Atkinson to take Flynn and get that done, Sir."

I shook my head, "I have the gloves. I will manage it, Sergeant." One of the things my father had insisted I buy, when we had gone to the outfitters in Liverpool before I had left was a pair of hide gloves. As he had told me they were useful not only for doing what I would be doing in the afternoon, desert gardening, they were also handy when riding a camel. They afforded protection. Thus far I had not had to use my sword but the Turks we had fought all carried them and I knew that one day the gloves might save me from a wound. As well as the gloves Cartwright and I took two of the Turkish swords we had taken at the battle of the archaeologists' camp. They were two short ones and we could use them like machetes. With keffiyeh wrapped around our heads we headed towards, not the oasis, but the stand of thorn bushes that grew half a mile from the fort. I guessed that the water which fed the oasis came close enough to the surface for the hardy thorn bushes to suck up enough water to survive.

They also acted as a sort of wind break and the sand piled up on one side of the bushes.

I knew exactly what we needed. We wanted straight branches that were at least two feet in length. In a perfect world they would be three feet long but beggars could not be choosers. Cartwright and I worked our way through hacking the best branches. The gloves would be needed when it came time to collect them. We had brought thick twine to bind them. I quite enjoyed the work. My father had worked at Pritchard's in St. Helens when he had been a young man and had done physical labour. I had not. The rhythm of hacking the base of the branch and moving on to seek the next one was satisfying and the pile of branches grew.

We had quite a few but we still had time for more and I pointed to another stand, just forty yards away, "We will find a few more from over there and then call it a day."

"Yes, Sir." Paul's weary voice told me that he had hoped we would have enough already. While I liked the labour Cartwright did not.

Leaving our collection we trudged through the sand to the next stand. As we neared it I said, "Stand still, Cartwright."

He stopped and looked around, fearfully, "What is it sir? Snake? Scorpion?"

"No, something worse, the sign of man." What I had seen were the footprints of boots. They might have been our Egyptians but they were not for close by were the dog-ends from cigarettes, Turkish cigarettes. I walked over to peer at them. I saw, over to one side, the remains of a cigar. I had read 'The Moonstone' by Wilkie Collins and I had been fascinated by the idea of a mystery. Here I had my own mystery and I used logic to make sense of what I saw. Cartwright had obeyed me and not moved. I looked at the footprints and the dog-ends. The cigar was to one side and the boot prints there were longer and narrower. I deduced that it was an officer. The other prints were more jumbled but, it seemed to me that there were four or five men. Without disturbing the prints I headed down into the wadi that ran just beyond it. I found the camel prints and the holes where the tether stakes had been planted. It confirmed six camels. I headed back to Cartwright.

"Sir, what is it?"

I pointed, "Men smoked here and watched the fort." Cartwright turned. The fort was clearly visible as was the oasis beyond. "They had camels that they hid in the wadi. Follow me."

He was not yet a soldier and he didn't really understand the implications of what I had said, "What about the thorn branches, Sir?"

"We will have to make do with what we have. This is more important." I did not head back the way we had come but followed the wadi. There I saw signs of men walking. They were harder to see than at the thorn bushes for there were no cigarette ends. When we reached the end of the wadi I saw that we were just two hundred yards from the walls. One of the Egyptian guards gave a friendly wave. The rocks that were at the end ended my hunt for tracks.

"Let us collect our stakes and head back. I have seen enough."

We planted the stakes and then, as the time for the evening meal approached we returned to the fort. As the men went to wash up I said, "Shaw, fetch Sergeant Hamed."

"Trouble, Sir?"

"Could be." When I reached the office I took a fresh sheet of paper and then wrote down my thoughts. I was halfway through when the two sergeants appeared. "Take a seat." I leaned back, "I have found evidence that there were men watching the fort." The Egyptian sergeant frowned. He took pride in his work and if men had got close enough to the fort for me to find evidence then they had not been doing their job properly. "Sergeant Hamed, they were hidden in the wadi. I found where they smoked their cigarettes and cigar. Your face tells me that they were not your men."

"The were not, Lieutenant."

"Then they were Turks and they were scouting us out. Until the rest return we are vulnerable. I want either you or me on duty at night, Sergeant Hamed."

"I will stand the watch tonight."

I nodded, "Shaw, tomorrow I want you to take Bates and ride a five-mile circle to the north and west. Find their route. They clearly did not come down the trail or the sentries would have seen them, even at night. If we know their route then we can watch for them."

They both nodded and then Sergeant Hamed said, "When do you think they watched, Lieutenant?"

"Since the rain and as the sand had not blown over the dog-ends and boot marks then it has to have been in the last two nights. We had that sandstorm the day before that."

"I will speak to my men."

I finished writing down my thoughts and left the unfinished report on the desk. I washed up and went to eat. As I was eating Sergeant Hamed came over. "Sir, I have spoken with my men. The night the caravan arrived, Ahmed, he was on duty on the wall furthest from the oasis, says he smelled cigar smoke. He thought it was from the oasis or perhaps one of your men had smoked one." He shook his head, "The man has the brain of a chicken whose head has been removed, but he is honest."

I pushed away the plate and spoke my thoughts aloud. I saw my men and the two sergeants listening, "That all makes sense. The Turks used the arrival of the caravan to disguise their presence." Strange camels always made our camels a little restless. They had been restless on the night in question. We had put it down to the caravan. "From now on, Sergeant Hamed, I want your men to report anything they hear, see or smell, no matter how inconsequential it appears."

"Sir."

I finished my report and left it on the desk.

That night as I lay in my bed I did not fantasise about Lucinda. Like my father, the writer, I had a fertile imagination. I put myself in the Turks' position. They must have seen Captain Dunn's patrol leave. If they saw the caravan arrive then they might have seen Sergeant Major Leonard leave. What if they were scouting out the defences? From what I knew of their officer, Captain Mustapha, he was a hawk and a hawk took its chances as soon as they appeared. We were in danger.

Chapter 2

I was a little relieved when the sergeant told me that he and his men had heard and seen nothing. After breakfast I sent out Shaw and Flynn and then, with Lee Enfields at the ready, led my men to the thorn bushes. Charlie Atkinson picked up the cigar butt. "Sir."

"Yes, Corporal?"

"This is not a cheap cigar."

"How do you know?"

"When we went back to England I visited a tobacconists in Alexandria. I wanted some nice cigars for my dad to smoke at Christmas."

I remembered the cigars my uncle had produced after dinner when we had enjoyed a Christmas at his house before he was killed. I nodded, "Go on."

"Well the chap there, I knew he was trying to get me to spend as much possible and he tried to sell me the best. You can see the wrapper is still there on this cigar." I had not seen it and I berated myself. It was evidence and I had ignored it. "Well, that tells me that this is expensive. Can you see how thick it is? There is still a good couple of inches left to smoke. Most men would nip it out and smoke it later on. The man who smoked this is not bothered about cost."

I knelt and looked at the boot print. I had known it was an officer's boot but now I studied the outline a little more. This was a good boot and while the other boots showed their hobnails the print on this one was smooth.

"Well done, Atkinson." I did not know what this told us but it was all grist to the mill. There was no such thing as useless information. There was just knowledge you had not needed…yet.

When Sergeant Shaw returned it was with more disturbing news, "Sir, we found the camel trail. There were six camels and they used the trail yesterday morning."

"You are sure?" That meant that while we had been clearing the ditch the watchers were still there.

"The camel dung had not dried out." One thing we were experts in was camel dung. When it was dry enough we used it for fires when we camped in the desert.

"Right. Until the others return we are on full alert. The gates remain closed during the day. Have as much water brought in as we can and fill the barrels."

"Sir."

We had a well but I wanted to be as prepared as we could be.

"I want the men to keep their weapons loaded and close to hand. If the alarm is sounded I want the walls manned as quickly as we can."

"Sir." The sergeant added, "Surely if they were scouting they would have to get back to Al Jagbub. The captain would see them."

"Unless they were already in the desert. They could be on their way here now. Think about it, Sergeant. The attack on the archaeologists was a few weeks ago. They have had time to plan. We were waiting for the relief column and assumed that the garrison at Siwa was still there. There could be an army out there."

"An army, Sir?"

I nodded, "I don't think for one moment that there is but the desert is big enough to hide one. The attack on the camp was not an act of war but it was aggressive. Whoever commands, this Captain Mustapha or another, may well have his own agenda. We will be vigilant."

"Sir."

I took a nap after the evening meal and then wrapped up against the cold as I prepared for a night watch. Sergeant Shaw and Corporal Atkinson offered to watch instead but I declined their offer. "We will need you to be alert tomorrow. I am just an officer and lead a life of luxury, eh?"

I knew most of the Egyptians and I walked the walls and spoke to each one before I took my position at the top of the guard tower that loomed over the rest. There was one sentry there and the two of us watched the desert. There was movement. Animals hunted at night. Knowing that there might be enemies out there, however, focussed our senses. It was not a watch for anything but one for the sound of a boot on a stone; the smell of cigarettes or humans; the glint of moonlight on metal.

When dawn came we had seen nothing and while that was good in one way, I had lost a night of sleep to no good purpose although it had been good to see, hear and smell what the garrison had. I was ready for my breakfast and the cooks had made a pot of strong coffee for me. The Egyptians preferred it to tea. I normally enjoyed my tea in the morning but the coffee would keep me awake. After a filling breakfast I went to the office to complete the paperwork. I had ordered, the night before, for two patrols to leave the fort. They would just scout out the land a couple of miles to the north and west. It was a risk because it left us perilously short of men but I thought it was worth it. They came back with the news that there was nothing to be seen and no more signs had appeared.

By the time we ate our evening meal I was exhausted. I had been awake for more than twenty-four hours and tension made a man even more tired. "Sir, turn in early, eh? Sergeant Hamed is on duty tonight and he will keep a good watch." I didn't answer Cartwright immediately. "Sir, you will be no good to anyone if you are over tired."

He was right, "Very well, Cartwright, and thank you. I never knew my mother but you do a damned good impression of one."

I almost collapsed into the bed and for the third night in a row I did not fantasise about Lucinda. I was too weary.

It was Cartwright who shook me awake, "Sir, trouble." I was out of bed in an instant. My batman held my tunic for me to don and he spoke as he dressed me. "Sergeant Hamed reported the smell of men and camels from the north."

"Sergeant Shaw?"

"He has the men already heading to the walls, Sir."

It did not take long to dress and I grabbed my Lee Enfield. My two pistols were already loaded and with ammunition pouches that were full I was prepared.

There was silence as I left my room and entered the square. I glanced up and saw the shadows that were the defenders. I hurried up the stairs to the main gate. Sergeant Shaw was there. He pointed to the north and sniffed. I nodded. I signed for him to go to the north west tower and for Sergeant Hamed to go to the north east. That left me with Cartwright and two Egyptian soldiers on the main gate. I turned to look at the highest tower. Corporal Atkinson and Flynn would be there. That I did not see them was comforting. The only problem as I saw it was that there were no sentries patrolling. The Turks might be suspicious. It could not be helped. We did not have enough men to risk sentries being picked off by sharpshooters. I stood and looked into the dark. Had I done all that was needed? The men had plenty of magazines. There was water strategically placed along the fighting platform. The ditches had been cleared and fresh stakes implanted. What had I not foreseen? The one thing we could not plan for was an assault by artillery. We had asked for a small six pounder but, as with the replacements, Cairo said that guns were needed for other theatres. We were forgotten.

The shadows moved. I did not need to alert my men; I saw my NCO's tap men on the shoulder and point. Tucked behind the embrasures my men had a good view of the outside. If they poked their rifles over then it would give away our presence. Our weapons remained hidden. I saw that the shadows moved in groups of three and only one group moved at a time. It was like a long shadow moving, almost undulating, from the wadi. These were commanded by an officer who knew what he was doing. They were using classic skirmisher tactics. One group ran while another group covered them. I now had a decision to make. When did I give the order to fire? Too soon and we would not drop enough. Too late and they might make the ditch. To remove them from there we would have to expose ourselves. We had placed a ring of white painted stones one hundred and fifty yards from the ditch. They could be seen in the dark. The Lee Enfield had an effective range of five hundred and fifty yards. I decided that the white stones would be the time to give the order to fire. We had men all around the walls but the rear walls had the sparsest number. We had to outgun our attackers somewhere. If this attacker had sense then they would attack where we least expected it.

I counted the shadows, there were forty of them. If we had a full complement then we could have repelled them easily. As it was we had half their numbers. My first order would be the most important one. I saw that more than half of the shadows had reached the white stones. I made out the rifles. "Open Fire!" I hoped that the simple command would give us an edge. I had not told them to present and take aim. I trusted that they would all have a bullet up the spout and be able to raise their weapon and fire within a heartbeat of the order. My rifle was aimed at a shadow towards the rear, beyond the white stones. I knew that the Egyptians would fire at the closest target. Some of the attackers might be hit by more than one bullet. We needed as many men to be hit as we could.

The voice that gave the command to fire was a European one. I heard it through the bang and crack of Lee Enfields. I put the thought to the back of my mind but I was intrigued. The shadow at which I had aimed fell. I switched targets. As I had predicted the soldiers from the garrison were hitting fewer men than the handful of troopers. It was to be expected. They were largely cooks and dhobi wallers. The sergeant was the only real soldier amongst them. The shadows rose and a wall of flame rippled through the dark. I heard bullets ricochet off the walls of the fort and there was a cry as someone was hit. It might not have been a bullet. It could have been a piece of stone. As if to prove the point, as I leaned over to shoot at the shadow pointing forward a bullet pinged in front of me. A piece of stone sliced across my cheek. I had cut myself more badly when I used to shave but it was a warning. Men naturally ducked when they were fired upon and, in that ducking, the shadows made forty yards.

Desperate times called for equally drastic orders, "On my command I want a mad minute!" I had warned everyone about the possibility of such an order. If we had not had such a reliable weapon and as much ammunition as we had then it would have been impossible. "Fire!" I stood and loaded and reloaded as fast as I could. Sergeant Instructor Snoxall had taught me well. The air was filled with the sound of cracking guns. There was not as much smoke with the Lee Enfield as there had been when my father had first fought in Africa but the air was filled with the smell. "Cease fire!"

I looked and saw that there were fifteen shadows that were not moving. The European voice gave a command. It was a command to fire. The enemy were using guns that only fired one bullet at a time and the desultory popping seemed tame in comparison to the roar we had made with the mad minute. Bullets pinged off the walls and men, me included, ducked. I heard the command to withdraw and shouted, "Open fire!" The shadows were moving back to the wadi. Whoever commanded had seen the folly of trying to attack a wall that had such firepower upon it.

I aimed carefully and hit another shadow but the man I hit was helped by a comrade and when they reached the wadi I shouted, "Cease fire!"

Sergeant Shaw shouted, "Sound off!"

"Here, Sergeant," Corporal Atkinson was alive and unhurt.

"Here, Sergeant," Trooper Hunter's voice carried from the far tower.

"Here, Sergeant," Trooper Baters waved a cheery hand from my right.

I turned to my batman, "Are you alive, Cartwright?"

"Yes, Sir."

"Then answer."

"Here, Sergeant!"

"All present and accounted for, Lieutenant."

"Thank you. Sergent Hamed."

The sergeant did the same but it was as the replies came in that we discovered one man had died and two others were wounded.

Cartwright acted as the medical orderly and I said, "Cartwright, make the mess into a sick bay. Do what you can for them."

"Yes, Sir."

We needed a doctor and that had been something else we had been promised. The South African War's ripples still affected us.

I was left with the two Egyptian soldiers. I took my water bottle and drank. I pointed to theirs, "Drink, the night is not over."

"Yes, Effendi."

When I heard the sound of camel's hooves disappearing north I knew that the attack was over but only a fool would relax. The hooves could be a trap and if we went to investigate we might find ourselves ambushed. As we waited for dawn I reflected on the attack. Why an attack on the fort? They had sent too few men to guarantee victory. They had to have been led by a man who thought he had the measure of a depleted fort. We knew from the stubs and dung that they had watched us. They would have seen the Egyptians and might have underestimated their quality. They would have seen almost two thirds of the troopers leave and had gambled. If it had succeeded then the two returning patrols would have walked into a fort held by the enemy. Someone was trying to make a name for himself.

When the sun rose in the east I sent for Sergeant Shaw and Sergeant Hamed. "Well done, to both of you and your men. That was stoutly done. Sergeant Hamed, I want half of your men on watch. The other half can get food ready. Full bellies are what we need. Sergeant Shaw, Cartwright apart, we will see what remains of those who chose to attack us."

"Sir." Sergeant Hamed looked pleased.

"Sir." Sergeant Shaw added, "And you gave the right commands, Sir. In the dark I could have mistaken you for your dad."

It was the best compliment I could have had. I left my Lee Enfield at the gate and drew my service revolver.

When we reached the gate Sergeant Shaw said, "Fix bayonets."

The two Egyptians held open the door to allow us to leave and then slammed it shut behind us. Sergeant Shaw was on the extreme left and Charlie Atkinson the right. All my men held their Lee Enfields and were ready to fire or stab. We approached the bodies as though they were cobras. I saw that the nearest body to me was dead. The bullet hole in his chest had puddled a large pool of blood. Where there was doubt my men used their bayonets to flick over the body or to poke it. The fifteen were all dead.

"We will take their weapons and search their bodies later. Let us just make sure that they have all gone."

We moved beyond the thorn bushes as though the enemy was still there. I saw that they had gone.

"Sir."

"Yes, Flynn."

"There is blood here. They took wounded away."

An Officer and a Gentleman

Charlie Atkinson triumphantly held up the half a cigar. He blew on the end and it glowed, "Same chap was here again and he likes his cigars. He had a quick puff before they left."

"They had camels, Sir. Their dung is all around."

"Right, let's get back to the bodies. I want them searched. Take all their weapons and any paperwork. This was an act of war and we need to let Cairo know."

"And the bodies, Sir? Burn them?"

I shook my head, "We will bury them and mark their graves. I think you would want your family to know where you were buried, eh, Sergeant?"

We had enough evidence to point the finger at the garrison across the border at Al Jagbub. I put it all in a manilla envelope. I wrote half the report while the graves were dug. Leaving just my men on watch in the fort, Sergeant Hamed said the right words over the fifteen Turks and one Egyptian who had died in the action. I had the men fire their rifles as a mark of respect. They had been our enemies but they had been brave men. I had the report finished by lunchtime. Cartwright reported that the wounds were not life threatening but they meant that the garrison was now three men down. Until the captain and the sergeant major returned there would be more work for everyone.

I held an officer's call after we had eaten lunch. I had come to a decision while eating and looking at the strained faces of both troopers and garrison troops.

"Until the sergeant major and his patrol return we are dangerously short-handed. We need to let Cairo know the situation but that will have to wait until the captain returns. We have, by my estimate, two or more days until Sergeant Major Leonard returns and five days until the captain makes it back. I want to divide each twenty-four hours into eight-hour blocks. The two sergeants and myself will command each block." I held up a piece of paper. "Cartwright will continue to act as a doctor. The rest of the men I have divided up. Sergeant Hamed, can you handle the midnight to eight a.m. slot?"

"Sir."

"Stan, four p.m. until midnight?"

"Sir."

"Charlie, you will be with me. We have the day shift."

"Sir."

I took a breath, "I intend to use the daylight to scout around the fort. Scheherazade is the best camel and…"

Stan shook his head, "That is too risky, Sir. You said it yourself. Hunker down for a couple of days and wait until the lads return."

"I cannot leave us blind, Sergeant. I will be careful but I want to know if an enemy is up to something. Captain Dunn never expected an attack. He would not have implemented such a patrol regime if he had. Anyway, this is not a debating club. I have given the orders and they will be obeyed."

It was not bravado that made me ride out in the early afternoon. We had almost been caught napping and but for the luck of finding the stubs and the vigilance of my men it could have all ended badly. Nor did I think that we were in immediate danger for the enemy had to get back across the border, but I would sleep better knowing I had done all that I could.

I deliberately went out while it was still relatively hot. I wanted to catch any watchers while they rested from the noon day sun. I rode, first, to the north east. I found nothing and so I returned to the wadi. I plodded along it and followed the clear sign of the flight of the Turks. I was about to turn around when Scheherazade suddenly raised her head. She made not a sound but I knew the animal well and that meant she had sensed something. I drew my Lee Enfield and chambered a round. I did not use my voice to command her but by heels and she moved off. She went slowly as though she knew there was danger. The wadi was a dried-up riverbed. I had heard from the archaeologists that in ancient times more of the desert had been farmed and that the climate, they said, was different. Rivers twisted and turned and so did the wadi.

I saw the smoke from the two Turks' cigarettes before I saw them and I had my Lee Enfield levelled with my arm resting on my camel's hump as I turned the bend. Their horses neighed and that alerted them. I fired one shot and a Turk spun around. The other was remarkably agile and he raced to vault onto his horse. He grabbed the reins of the other and galloped off. I fired a second shot but Scheherazade was moving and my bullet merely plucked his sleeve. I made my camel sit and dismounted. I

An Officer and a Gentleman

covered the Turk with my rifle but he was dying. The .303 had hit him from a range of less than fifty feet and torn a huge hole in him. His eyes were open. He was a tough man. I saw that he had a pack of cigarettes. I took one and placed it in his lips. I lit it for him and he smiled his thanks.

I said, "Your friend has gone."

He shook his head, "He was not my friend. If he was he would have shot you."

I nodded, "And the officer," I took a guess, "the German, is he your friend, too?"

He coughed and blood came from his mouth. He did not have long to live, "Von Kleist? He is a butcher and likes..." The cigarette fell from his mouth and his head lolled to the side.

"Go to God." I took his papers and then used the spade I carried on my saddle. I dug his grave and, after wrapping him in his cloak, covered his body with sand. I found a couple of large rocks and laid them on the top. Then I took his rifle and after smashing the stock rammed the barrel into the earth and placed his headgear there as a marker. I had done all that I could.

I arrived back at the fort an hour later. I wrote down all that I had discovered. That the Germans were acting as advisors was not a surprise. They had their own African Empire. Unlike the British one, it did not extend the length of Africa but they had ambitions and if they could help the Turks then who knew what the result might be.

I gave my NCOs the information I had gathered. Stan looked at me, "So tomorrow, Sir?"

I knew what he was asking and I shook my head, "They are gone for the moment and there is nothing to be gained from a solo patrol. It is clear the two men were left to watch for us. They may return but we can wait for Captain Dunn to decide what to do about them,"

I saw relief on the faces around the table.

It was not long after the sun was at its peak that Sergeant Major Leonard returned. I greeted him at the gate, "Riding at noon, Sergeant Major?"

"We had an early start and were just a mile or so away. It has been a hot ride, Sir."

"Any problems Sergeant Major?"

An Officer and a Gentleman

Shaking his head he said, "Talking to the people at Abu Minqar it seems, Sir, that our patrols have deterred the bandits. They are raiding across the border where they are less than vigilant. I think we can expect more caravans using this route rather than others."

"Good."

"And here, Sir?" He glanced around and frowned when he saw the fresh marks left by bullets on the tower.

"Get washed up, Sergeant Major. I will have Cartwright make a brew and I can tell you in the cool of the office."

"Sir."

"Cartwright, a pot of tea. It is for the sergeant major."

My batman grinned, "Extra spoon of tea it is then, Sir." Making tea was something Cartwright was comfortable with.

Telling the sergeant major and using my notes helped me. I would add some details to the final report I would send to Cairo. I realised that I had not included my speculation about the purpose of the two horsemen watching the wadi. He absent mindedly took out his pipe and then began to put it away. "No, you can smoke Sergeant Major."

He smiled as he began to fill it, "Thank you, Sir. It helps me to think." I drank some of my tea and waited until the pipe was going and he waved his hand before his face to disperse the smoke. "It all seems a little aggressive, Sir. I mean, it is an act of war."

"Think about it, Sergeant Major. We are now the last western outpost. Siwa did not do much. If they had been effectively led then the archaeologists would not have been attacked. The trouble is we don't know enough about whichever Bey is in command. Remember it was not that long ago that the Ottomans ruled Egypt. If there is an aggressive Bey then he may see his chance to gain power because of the weaknesses here."

"You said the soldier confirmed it was a German officer who led them, Sir?"

"It was a bit of a trick but yes, I did."

"That makes sense, Sir." He smiled as he tamped down on the ash in his pipe and said, "I have been out here a long time, Sir, probably as long as your father. I remember the old days and what the Ottoman army was like. As I recall they brought in a

German, Colmar von der Goltz or something. Anyway, Sir, he retrained the Turkish Army and used German officers to do so." He waved his pipe in the air, "A bit like we did with the Egyptian army. It made a difference. They soundly defeated the Greeks in their last little war. Who knows, the Bey may have retained German officers."

I nodded. I had not known those facts. "We need Captain Dunn."

"We do indeed, Sir, this is too big a job for the men we have here."

"The trouble is, Sergeant Major, the fort can't take any more men. We are full as it is."

"Tents, Sir, we could use tents. This is a good oasis and there is plenty of water. Camels and horses could be protected by a pen. It might not be too pleasant for the lads living under canvas but we are British soldiers. It is what we used to do." He smiled and tapped out the ash from his pipe, "I bet your dad spent more time under canvas than in a fort?"

I nodded, "The only time he was in a fort was towards the end of his time, Fort Desolation."

"Well, if that is all, Sir. I will make sure the lads from patrol have sorted their gear out."

"Of course."

He stood, "We are lucky here, Lieutenant. We have a good bunch of soldiers. As far as I can see there are no bad eggs."

He was right.

Two days later, as the sun was getting lower in the western sky Captain Dunn and a weary patrol rode in. The sentry in the tower had spotted their dust and we ensured that there was food ready. As he rode in the sharp-eyed captain said, "Lieutenant, I saw some fresh graves…"

"Yes, Sir, we have had a bit of excitement while you were away."

He nodded. "Is everything written down?"

"Yes, Sir."

"And is there urgency about your report?"

"No, Sir, it can wait until you have bathed and we have eaten."

"Good because that was a tough patrol."

An Officer and a Gentleman

I felt guilty that I had not fully informed the captain about the attack for it was clear, as the men ate, that the tale was being told already. Captain Dunn had a mind as sharp as a tack and he said, "I can see that this report is a little more important than you implied, Griff, let us retire to the office and you can tell me all. I have a bottle of whisky that I think might ease the telling." We stood and he said, "Burton, fetch my bottle of whisky and two glasses to the office."

"Sir."

"Sergeant Major Leonard, I think you may splice the mainbrace tonight. I authorise a double ration of rum."

The men cheered and Bob Leonard said, "Now don't abuse this kind offer. Thank you, Sir."

As we headed to the office he pointed at the walls, "I saw the fresh bullet marks when we returned to the fort."

"Yes, Sir."

I waited until Burton had brought the whisky and the glasses and left before I began. I took the manilla folder and began to read the events as they had occurred. The captain finished one glass of whisky and had started on the second before I had finished half of mine. He nodded towards my half-filled glass, "Have a drink. That was a good report. Clear and well presented." He held up his refilled glass, "Cheers."

"Cheers." It was a peaty malt, the captain's favourite kind. It burned a little as it went down and I made sure I just sipped it.

"Now, my report. We did not cross the border but I saw that their fort was rammed with soldiers. There were tents outside its walls and they had horses as well as camels. To me it looked like a battalion. They had artillery." He emptied his glass. I saw him looking at the bottle. He made a decision and pushed the empty glass away. "In light of your report I do not see the need for a patrol to ride the border. All it does is increase the chances that they might ambush us. We need Cairo to act." I saw him looking at the map on the wall. He was thinking. I sipped my whisky. I would not have a second. For one thing I was not used to it and for another it was the captain's and he clearly viewed it as a treasure to be savoured. He would enjoy it more than me. "I want you to go, tomorrow to Cairo, with your report. See General Pemberton and make it clear what the danger is."

"Sir, surely, it would come better from you. After all I am just a lieutenant."

"I have been remiss. You should never have had to take on this responsibility. You did well but I am in command. No, you go and take Cartwright with you. We will just continue to protect the caravans until you return."

I was dubious and said so, "Do you think I can convince him and the other brass, Sir?"

He tapped the manilla folder, "This report was well written and cogently argued. General Pemberton is no fool and he will understand it better if the author is there."

"Sir."

"Take your best uniform too."

"Best, Sir?"

"I mean all your uniforms, best and dress. The general has a wife and daughter. There may be an opportunity for a gallant young officer to dress in his finery and impress them." He shrugged, "It can't hurt. When I was last there I was invited to dine but all I had were my fatigues. I could tell I did not win any friends. If it was me I would take them. Take a spare camel for your clothes."

"Sir."

"Oh and," he tapped the half empty whisky bottle, "If you get the chance another couple of bottles eh?"

"Sir."

Chapter 3

Cartwright was delighted to be travelling to Cairo. I did not think he would have been happy to have to endure the crossing of the desert but it was the inclusion of my dress uniform that excited him. He would put up with the nights sleeping in the open knowing that when we reached Cairo there would be baths and fans as well as irons. He would be able to be a gentleman's gentleman once more. He was like a chatterbox all the way to Faiyum. It was mainly about dressing his young gentleman for hunt balls and the like. He was excited about the prospect of me wearing my dress uniform. "Red is such a smart colour and yours has never seen daylight, Sir. There will be no fading. I will be able to put a crease in your trousers so sharp that you could cut bread with it."

"Cartwright, the captain only suggested I might bring it in case it was needed. It will probably stay in my bag."

He was not put out, "No matter, Sir. I will be ready."

The ride across the desert was somehow soothing for there was a rhythm to it. You rose early and breakfasted when it was cool and wrapped, not against the cold, but the sun and rode the camels that seemed like galleons across the sea of sand. A camel has a good pace but it does not seem fast, not unless you are charging. Even Cartwright seemed at ease, now, on the back of his camel. I made notes on my map as we rode. To a desert virgin the desert all looked the same but we had learned to identify features and give them our own names. Stan Shaw had called the rocks we passed to the north of us as granddad's teeth. There was another lump of rock that rose we had named Camel's Hump. To us they were the markers that gave us a sense of where we were. At night we ensured that there were neither snakes nor spiders close to our beds. We always lit a fire even if we were not cooking food and we always hobbled our camels. It was all second nature to us. We spotted the flag flying over Faiyum and I was pleased with the speed at which we had travelled.

We reached Faiyum after the last train had departed. There was a garrison there. They were Egyptians with British officers.

An Officer and a Gentleman

To Cartwright's delight we were given a room and the use of a bath. Captain Mainwaring was quite happy to look after our animals for us, "Leave your desert mufti here too, Lieutenant. I shall get my dhobi wallers to clean it for you. You don't want to look like a native on the train do you?"

"Where is the major?"

The garrison there was commanded by a major. They had a major, captain and two lieutenants to command the one hundred and twenty men. They would be the ones to come to our aid if we summoned them.

"Called to Alexandria. Some sort of conference about the way we treat the Egyptians." He leaned in, "Some damned fools of British officers went hunting along the Nile and when the locals objected shot a couple of them. There is a little more unrest along the river than there used to be." He smiled, "We, here at Faiyum and you at Farafra, know the value of keeping good relations. The leading merchant, Ismail, has spoken well of how he values your escorting of his caravans. I didn't know that was part of your remit."

"It isn't but as it keeps that part of the desert safer it seems prudent to continue."

"You make my point well, Lieutenant."

The garrison at Faiyum was just that; a detachment to guard the railway. The British officers and sergeants all dressed as though in England. Their only concession was that the fatigues they wore were tropical issue. Things had moved on since the Zulu Wars. The had a telegraph office and I sent a telegram to Headquarters in Cairo to tell them of our imminent arrival.

I confess that the hot bath and a good shave made me feel like a different man. Cartwright and Burton apart the rest of the troop grew beards. The two batmen endured dry shaves. Cartwright shaved off my beard but left a moustache which he groomed and oiled when I was dressed. He too had changed uniform and when we strode to the station there was a spring in his step. The station was busy as we were taking the first train to Cairo. The advantage in the train we were taking lay not only in the early arrival in Cairo but also the fact that it would be cooler travelling. The garrison commander had procured us two first class tickets and whilst that was not the style that one might

An Officer and a Gentleman

expect in England the seats were comfortable and it was far less crowded. We purchased fruit at the station and Cartwright had some sandwiches made up in the mess. He was a changed man away from Farafra.

We were not the only First-Class passengers but our uniforms ensured we had a compartment to ourselves. We were able to talk. "How long will we stay in Cairo, Sir?"

"Not sure, Cartwright. I suppose it will depend on the general. We may have to cool our heels and wait for an appointment. After all I am a lowly second lieutenant. On the other hand he may simply take the report and send us straight back." I saw the disappointment on my batman's face. "You want a longer stay in Cairo, Cartwright?"

"Well, Sir, when we arrived in Cairo all I saw was what could be viewed from the train. I should have liked to have seen the pyramids. I mean, they are an ancient wonder."

I nodded, "If we have time then we can be tourists but remember, Cartwright, while we are here others are doing our duties."

"I know, Sir, but the lads do not begrudge us this time." He hesitated and then continued, "They know that you saved them when we were attacked. You were cool under fire and did not make a bad decision. I have not been a soldier for long but such things are important to ordinary soldiers."

I did not feel comfortable when I was complimented and I changed the subject. "Anyway, there are other matters for us. We need either a doctor or more medical supplies. We can't continue with you as an unpaid sick bay attendant."

"I don't mind the duty, Sir, except that it takes me away from my duty to you."

I suddenly realised that I had no idea what day of the week it was, "What day is it today, Cartwright? Saturday?"

"No, Sir, Friday."

I wondered if the general would work at the weekend. I did not fancy waiting in some dusty barracks over the weekend. I wanted to give my report and have done with it. I knew that men's lives depended on me impressing on the army the need for more soldiers.

An Officer and a Gentleman

We watched the land change from the window. We had almost left the desert at Faiyum and we saw the fertile lands closer to the river. Here people worked and there was more greenery. Egypt was a huge land but it was only by the river that it could be called populated. Trains were still unusual enough for us to be waved at as we passed, especially by children.

The other advantage of the first train of the day was that it tended to arrive on time and we pulled into the crowded station. There would be many heading for the train to Alexandria. Faiyum was on a branch line. The ones hastening to make a connection scurried off like ants. We had time and were amongst the last to disembark. As we headed towards the ticket collector I saw a uniform and when we had passed the barrier a corporal snapped to attention, "Lieutenant Roberts?"

"Yes Corporal."

"I am your driver, Corporal Lowe." He hefted my bag on his shoulder, "If you would like to follow me, Sir." He was obviously used to this duty and the crowds for he barrelled his way through like a prop forward. There was a horseless carriage parked outside and two urchins were sitting on the bonnet. "Hey, get off or…" The two boys scurried off giggling. The corporal shook his head, "Good job your train was on time, Sir, if not then Gawd knows what I would have come back to."

He and Cartwright secured our bags on the luggage rack behind the two seats for the passengers and Cartwright sat next to the driver. There was no top and we would bake. I had the rear to myself. As we left the station, the corporal honking his horn to clear a path I asked, "Where are we staying?"

"The general has a house, Sir. You and your batman are to stay with him."

"Is that usual, Corporal?"

He glanced around to look at me, "It happens more than you might think, Sir, but you are the first men I have taken from the Faiyum train. I normally meet officers from Alexandria. It might be something to do with the big party they are holding tomorrow, Sir."

"Party?"

"Yes sir, the general's daughter turns twenty-one and they are having a ball. I hope you have brought your dress uniform." I could not see his face but I knew that Cartwright would be beaming.

Inside I groaned, "A ball, Corporal?"

"Yes, Sir, the house is a grand one with a ballroom. It belonged to some English merchant who made a fortune and then left to enjoy life in England. As there is not a large garrison in Cairo these days, what with that bit of bother in South Africa, well, Sir, there are plenty of young ladies who will be there and they need partners."

Cartwright said, in the silence that followed, "Can you dance, Sir?"

Aunt Sarah had taught me the waltz and the polka but that was all and as I had never danced in public I began to think of excuses not to embarrass myself. "A little, Cartwright."

"Don't worry, Sir, I can polish your steps as well as your boots." I could hear, in his voice, that he was delighted about all of this.

The house was not in the centre of Cairo and was surrounded by a high wall. There were sentries at the gates. The car pulled up and an Egyptian Major Domo approached us, "Lieutenant Roberts, the general is at the residency. He said for you to freshen up. If you would follow me we have a room for you and your servant." His English was flawless. He could have been a butler in an English country house.

I might have been offended by the title of servant but Cartwright was not. He happily shouldered his bag as another servant took mine from the corporal.

"Thank you, Corporal Lowe."

"You are welcome, Sir. I normally bring desk bound officers. It was nice to carry a real soldier."

The house was cool. I saw fans in the ceiling lazily circulating the air. The house had been well built and the cool floors were a mark of the thoughtful design. I did not expect much as we headed through a labyrinth of corridors but the room was well apportioned. There was a large bed and a cot. The cot looked out of place. "I am afraid there is no bathroom in these quarters, Lieutenant, but there is one down the corridor. Until tomorrow you will be the only one using it." He gave a smile, "Tomorrow we shall be packed to the rafters."

When the door was closed Cartwright immediately began to unpack my clothes and hang them. "I shall check out the facilities, Sir, and procure an iron." He was in his element. This was the sort of house he had worked in back in England. He worked efficiently and when he was satisfied he put away his own clothes. "Shan't be a jiff, Sir." He left me alone. I felt at a loose end. I saw that there was a desk and some writing paper. I went over and saw that there was a pen and a pot of ink. I would be able to send a letter home. Even as I was writing to my father I was also thinking about writing one to Lucinda. Would it seem impertinent? Then I remembered she had asked me to write. I used just one sheet of paper for the letter home but two for the letter to Lucinda. When Cartwright returned I hurriedly sealed both and addressed them.

"Sorry for the delay, Sir. I have found an iron but it is in the laundry room. I shall have to take your dress uniform there." He gathered them together. "The bathroom is next door, Sir. If you would like me to run a bath for you?"

"Perhaps later, Cartwright."

"Righto, Sir." He went off humming a cheerful ditty. I had never seen my batman so happy.

I left the room and headed back down the corridor to explore the house. It was the soldier in me. I was scouting. The house was busy. Everyone appeared engaged in the business of preparing for party. Servants were moving tables and chairs. Others were busy cleaning. When I reached the ballroom I heard an imperious female voice, "No, Mustapha, further to the right. No, my right."

I peered in the door and saw two ladies. One was clearly the wife of the general. She looked the right age and as the other one looked to be a young woman I took her for the daughter. Two servants were up a pair of ladders and had some bunting they were trying to attach. I was about to slip away when one of the servants saw me and smiled. His look attracted the attention of the young lady who turned and saw me. Her face lit into a smile.

"You must be Lieutenant Roberts. Mama, our first guest has arrived."

Mrs Pemberton turned. When she had been a young woman she must have been stunning. Even now, with flecks of grey in her hair she still looked beautiful. I saw that she and her daughter shared many features. She was also gracious. The imperious tone disappeared as she came towards me and proffered a hand for me to kiss, "Welcome, Lieutenant. I should have been told that you had arrived."

I did not know what to say. I was tongue tied.

"I am Emmeline Pemberton, Lieutenant." The young woman held out her hand. Did I shake it or kiss it? I chose the latter action and knew it was the right thing to do when the mother and daughter both smiled.

"And I am forgetting my manners, Lieutenant I am Caroline Pemberton. Is your room satisfactory? I know it is a little small but we have many guests arriving later today and tomorrow."

Before I could answer the young lady burst out, "It is my birthday and we have fireworks planned."

I smiled, "My driver told me and yes, Mrs Pemberton, the room is more than adequate. I am used to humbler quarters."

Her eyes softened, "Ah, yes, you are at the outpost in the desert. It will be most interesting to hear your stories at dinner tonight. We lead a dull life here in Cairo." Just then I heard the front door open and male voices. "This will be my husband, the general."

Emmeline said, "Must you go? I would like to talk more to you, Lieutenant."

"Emmeline, we have too much to do as it is. Your father wishes to talk business. There will be time tonight to talk."

I was dismissed. I gave a slight bow and turned.

General Pemberton was in the hall and when he saw me he smiled. "Good, the train was on time. Come to my office. Mehmet, bring us some sherry."

He turned and I followed him. When we reached the office he sat and I said, "Sir, I have my written report. Should I go back and get it?"

He shook his head, "Time enough for that on Monday." He waited until the sherry arrived. After the servant left he raised his glass and said, "Cheers."

"Cheers, Sir."

"Now give me the gist of the report. When I was told that an officer was travelling all the way from Farfara I knew it was important. I was just surprised that it was not the commanding officer," he looked at an open file, "Captain Dunn?"

"Yes, Sir. I was surprised too but I was ordered and here I am."

"Right, Roberts. On with your tale."

Thanks to the many drafts of the report I had the structure in my head and I began with the attack on the archaeologists. I ended with the discovery that there was a German officer involved.

When I finished he poured himself another sherry. I had barely touched mine, "Come on, Lieutenant, I don't like to drink alone." I emptied the glass and he refilled it. "I was told that the attack on the archaeologists was bandits."

I shook my head, "No, Sir, they were regular troops. They had modern weapons and wore uniforms."

He nodded and looked out of the window, "Egypt is a backwater now, you know? We have to keep a presence here because of the Suez Canal. The border and the desert…" he waved a hand, "still we can't have British soldiers killed. I will have to get the resident to have a word with the Turkish ambassador. Perhaps it is just a rogue unit. The Turks are not like the British Army you know."

I felt obliged to do all that I could to impress on the general the dangers we were in. "Sir, we need more men. We have a handful and the desert is huge."

He smiled and I saw that he would do nothing. "There are many who believe we don't need a garrison at Farafra. Faiyum, now that needs protection. There is a railway there but the caravan trails…" He nodded, "Let me have your written report and I will give it to my intelligence people. There may be lessons to learn. And you, Lieutenant, can enjoy a pleasant few days here. It is clear that you have earned the leave. Tomorrow, there will be a party and I am sure that your presence will be appreciated. We have many people from the residency attending and there will be a smattering of officers. None will have enjoyed as much action as you." There was a knock at the door. "Come."

The officer who came in was a lieutenant but he was in his late thirties. He had flecks of grey and a paunch but his tanned skin told me that he had served for a long time in the tropics. "General, Mr Lockhart from the residency is here to see you with the guest list."

"Very well. Horace, go with the lieutenant and fetch his report."

"Yes, Sir."

The pale faced gentleman who entered the room was clearly a diplomat and I was ignored as he entered the room with a sheaf of papers in his hand. The lieutenant closed the door and held out his hand, "Lieutenant Horace Jamieson, aide to the general and you must be Lieutenant Griff Roberts."

I was not sure of the protocol and so I said, "Yes, Lieutenant."

He laughed, "It is Horace. We can't have us using titles. Life is too short." He smiled, "As you can see I am a little old still to be a lieutenant. No ambition but I like the uniform and, to be truthful, I am not suited for any other life than the army. Your room is this way I believe."

"Yes."

"Now what is life like in the desert? It does not appeal to me in the least but I would be interested to know how real soldiers live."

In the time it took to get to my room I gave him a picture of life. Cartwright had returned and was hanging up my dress uniform. I picked up the manilla envelope and handed it to the lieutenant who said, "A gong will sound for lunch. Your chap can go to the kitchen. The dining room is off the ballroom. They do a very pleasant lunch here, Griff, I am sure you will enjoy it."

I felt deflated

I sat on the bed and Cartwright asked, "Something wrong, Sir?"

"It was a waste of time coming here, Cartwright. For all the good I have done I might as well have stayed at Farafra where I feel I can be useful."

"Don't give up, Sir. It is early days."

He whistled as he polished my best boots. Sergeant Major Leonard would have been impressed by the shine he attained. When the gong sounded Cartwright insisted on adjusting my tie and straightening my jacket. "Right then, Sir, off we go."

An Officer and a Gentleman

He escorted me down to the dining hall and then walked smartly towards the servant's quarters. He was in his element. There were just four people seated at the table which would have held twenty or more easily. The lieutenant stood as I entered and gestured at the seat next to him which was opposite the two ladies. The general waved a servant over, "We have an indifferent white here to accompany the soup. We have better wine for tonight, of course."

I hated every moment of the meal for it was like being back in Sandhurst and wondering if I was doing everything right. The soup course was easy as there was just a soup spoon but did one dunk the bread as we did at home and in the fort? I was glad I did not make that faux pas. They buttered their bread and ate it with the soup. At least when I was eating I did not have to talk and both the ladies were keen to chat about life in the desert. When the dessert came and went I was relieved. I would be able to head back to my room. My hopes were dashed and I was fated to have to remain. There was coffee in the drawing room and even more interrogation. This time I could not use the excuse of a full mouth. It was only when Lieutenant Jamieson said that they had paperwork that was needed to be signed. I was not sure if I was included but I took the opportunity to bow, thank Mrs Pemberton for the meal and head back to the room. Cartwright was there.

"Nice people here, Sir. Not quite as refined as those in my last position but good hearted. Did you enjoy the meal?"

I scowled, "The food might have been better than I am used to but I would rather have been back in the mess enjoying goat stew and beans."

He raised his eyebrows, "Miss Pemberton seems a pretty young thing, Sir. Surely she is easier on the eye than Sergeant Major Leonard?"

I did not answer immediately. I was reflecting on his words. He was right. She was not just pretty, she was stunningly beautiful and yet I had not felt attracted to her. It was in that moment I knew that Lucinda was more than a girl for me to write to. I had felt comfortable with Lucinda from the first moment. As pleasant as Miss Pemberton was, she was not Lucinda.

"Let us go for a stroll, Cartwright. The heat of the noonday sun has passed and there looks to be some shade."

"Very well, Sir."

We left the house and the two sentries came to attention as we did so. We just wandered down the road. This was, it was clear, a largely European area. There were few Egyptians and the ones we saw dressed in the European manner. We came to a busy road and I saw, to our right, the distant pyramids and to our left the road leading to the busier sections of the town. The pyramids were inviting but seemed too far to walk. I had said it was cooler but not by much. Just then a horse and a small carriage pulled up.

The driver said, "Taxi Effendi?"

He spoke in English and I saw his eyebrows rise as I said, in Arabic, "How much to take us to the pyramids and let us have a look around?"

"I will give you a good price, Effendi."

I smiled. Whatever price he gave I would be able to get it reduced. My father had taught me well. We agreed a price and entered the carriage. I say carriage but it was clearly home-made. However, there was a canvas awning which kept the worst of the sun from us and that was better than the horseless carriage we had used for the station. Once he knew I could understand his language the man chattered away. I think his English was limited to numbers and the normal interactions of a taxi driver. He seemed happy to tell us about the pyramids although I took some of his exaggerations with a pinch of salt. I could not see a million men building them. Having said that they were most impressive. When we left the carriage, the driver promising to wait, we were assailed by locals trying to get us to rent camels. I smiled. This was not a busman's holiday and I was happy to walk. Close up to the edifices I saw the wear and tear of time but they were astounding. To think that they were thousands of years old made my head reel. It was as we were walking back to the carriage that I realised I would have enjoyed the visit far more with Lucinda. She would have an archaeologist's eyes and be able to point out details that were hidden from me.

The driver took us back to the general's house. I gave him a good tip for he had gone out of his way to be helpful and the cost was reasonable. Cartwright was keen to get back to the room so that I could bathe and he could prepare my uniform. At lunch Horace had confided in me that they liked to dress for dinner and be more formal. As we walked through the hall and headed up the stairs to our room there seemed to be more people about. I realised that these were guests for the party. They were of a higher status than me. It was quite clear that the quarters we were using, whilst more than adequate, were reserved for people of little importance. Cartwright fussed over me. I was surprised he did not come into the bathroom to scrub my back. I think he wanted to. He gave me a good shave and oiled my moustache. He wanted to oil my hair but I drew the line there. The shoes were given a good polish as were the buttons. He had just finished when the gong sounded.

"I will walk you down, Sir. I am to dine with the other servants. I was told that there would be more here tonight. It will be interesting, I think."

There was a line of guests and I joined it. The couple before me were European and not in uniform. The man turned and nodded. He had an expensive dinner suit and his wife had jewelled fingers and a necklace with what looked to me to be diamonds and rubies. She smiled and said, "What a handsome young officer. A smart uniform. Reginald."

For all his expensive clothes the man had a flat Yorkshire accent, "Yes, my dear. It is good that we have such young men keeping our Empire safe."

I could not help but think of my Uncle Billy. Had he lived he would have got on well with the likes of this businessman. The line was moving slowly and when I reached the head I found out why. I recognised Lord Kitchener. I had seen his picture, not only in the newspapers but my father had a photograph of him too.

"May I introduce, Lord Kitchener, Second Lieutenant Roberts from the fort at Farafra."

I shook his hand and his eyes narrowed, "Roberts? The name rings a bell. Was your father a soldier? Lost a hand or an arm or something?"

"Yes Lord Kitchener and I would like to thank you for securing me a place at Sandhurst."

His face cracked into a smile, "That is it. And you are in the desert now, with the unit I created."

"Yes, Sir, I am."

He turned to the general, "Rearrange the seating, Gervaise, I wish to sit next to this young man. Looking at the other guests I doubt that their conversation will be half as interesting."

The general did not look happy but nodded, "Mehmet, a word."

While the general spoke to his servant Lord Kitchener said, "And how is your father?"

"He had another adventure in Persia, my lord, and now writes books. He seems happy to do so."

He smiled, "Good. I always liked him. Your father and others like him are what made the empire. Their children still keep it safe."

"All arranged, Herbert." From the use of Christian names it was clear that the two men were friends.

Mehmet, said, "Lieutenant Roberts."

I followed him and found myself seated next to the Yorkshireman's wife. There was an empty space next to me close to the head of the table. I saw that Emmeline had a scowl upon her face and she was pouting. Mehmet guided a skeletal looking man next to her. He looked like an official from the residency and I guessed I had been chosen to sit next to her. I smiled and said, "Good evening, Miss Pemberton. You look lovely tonight."

My flattery turned the scowl to a smile and she said, "And you look so dashing in your uniform."

Our conversation was ended when the general, his wife and Lord Kitchener joined us.

I confess I enjoyed the evening meal far more than the lunch. For one thing the questions from his lordship were easier to answer than the ones at lunchtime. I barely tasted the food for I realised, early on, that Lord Kitchener was genuinely interested in the fort. I learned that he had recently left South Africa and was on his way to India to become Commander in Chief there. He was to reorganise the Indian army. He quickly moved on to me and he remembered Captain Dunn. I was honest with him and told him about the archaeologists and the attack on the fort. I also mentioned the German officer.

We were close enough to General Pemberton for Lord Kitchener to say, "Gervaise, this business with the Turks, what do you plan to do about it?"

The general looked uncomfortable and said, "I hardly think the dinner table is the place for such conversations, My Lord." The fact he was more formal spoke volumes.

"As I am taking a ship from Suez tomorrow evening, then I think an early morning meeting is called for. Seven a m eh?"

"Yes, Lord Kitchener."

He looked at me and I smiled, "Then I will be having a lie in, My Lord."

He laughed, "A proper soldier."

The rest of the meal was spent with him asking me about life in the fort. I know that many people, especially later in his career, had a low opinion of Lord Kitchener but I found him a soldier's soldier. He understood soldiering and what made a good soldier. I was saved from after dinner pleasantries when Lord Kitchener, after brandy and cigars said, "Well Gervaise, Caroline, that was a splendid dinner but the lieutenant and I have an early morning meeting. I think we shall retire."

I saw the disappointment on not only Mrs Pemberton's face but also Emmeline's. However, Lord Kitchener had spoken and they donned smiles as the two of us bowed and then marched from the room. He said, "We have to endure such thing, Roberts, but we don't have to enjoy them. See you bright eyed and bushy tailed in the morning, eh?"

Cartwright was in the room and making up his bed, "An early finish, Sir. I did not expect you for an hour or so."

"I was saved by Lord Kitchener, Cartwright. I have a meeting at seven so let us rise by six, eh?"

"Yes, Sir." He could not keep the disappointment from his voice. His young gentleman would have caroused for far longer.

Chapter 4

I headed downstairs at five to seven and reached the general's office just as the clock in the hall chimed seven. Horace opened the door. He was somewhat bleary eyed. I saw that the general had not yet arrived but Lord Kitchener was seated behind the desk, "Ah, come in Roberts. Prompt, I like that. The general, it seems, is still at his toilet. Cut along, Jamieson and get breakfast sorted for us."

"Sir." He rolled his eyes as he passed me. This was clearly not a time of day he was accustomed to.

"I thought we could eat while we talked. I have a carriage waiting to take me to the railway station." I sat. He patted the manilla envelope, "I have read the reports. They make for interesting reading." Lord Kitcher took a pen and a sheet of paper, "Now before the general arrives, what is it that you and Captain Dunn need?"

I said, "Men, Sir. We need at least another fifteen."

He wrote it down, "With camels, I presume."

"Yes, sir, and remounts."

"Go on."

I decided to be bold and ask for the moon. "A Maxim and its crew would ensure that the garrison could hold off attacks." He nodded, "A doctor or some sort of medical orderly."

He frowned but wrote it down.

"Anything else?"

"Materially no, sir. We have ammo and we have good camels but…"

Just then the door opened and General Pemberton entered, "Sorry I am late, Herbert, but…"

He got no further, "Sir down, Gervaise. I have begun making a list. You were saying, Roberts?"

"The rest is policy, Sir. I know that a state of war does not exist but the Ottomans have been aggressive. Captain Dunn and I would just like the opportunity to cross the border if we have to. To be honest, Sir, as you know the border in the desert is not a clear-cut thing…"

He smiled, "I know and I agree."

There was a knock at the door and the lieutenant stood there with a line of servants, "Breakfast, My Lord."

Lord Kitchener rubbed his hands, "Bring it in and we will serve ourselves."

The servants placed the food on a second table that Horace had already cleared. When the servants left the four of us chose our food and poured ourselves tea.

Lord Kitchener tasted the tea, "You have a good chap in the kitchen, Gervaise. This is proper tea. Now I have to be away in an hour and we have no more time to waste." The general was being criticised for his late arrival and he knew it. The new Commander in Chief of the Indian Army spoke between mouthfuls. He read from the list. "We need twenty-five men. These chaps will function better if they have leave. All of that is simple enough. I want the new men there within a fortnight. They will be fully equipped with camels and tents. Now as for the carte blanche the lieutenant seems to want. I don't think we can go so far as that, Roberts. Sorry. I agree with you but let us just say that so long as you don't actually attack any Turkish forts then you can aggressively pursue any enemies who threaten the peace of Egypt. How is that?"

It was better than I might have hoped, "Thank you, Sir, that is all we ask."

Kitchener had finished eating. He was a fast eater and he wiped his mouth, "One more thing, young Roberts here deserves a medal for his actions, however there was no senior officer present and I know how the army works. However, it is in my hands to promote." He reached over to shake my hand, "You are now First Lieutenant Roberts backdated to," he glanced at the report I had given him, "to the start of the month." He picked up his hat and went over to the general, "Thank you, Gervaise, this was far more enjoyable a visit than I anticipated. I am pleased, Lieutenant Roberts, that the initiative I began in the Sudan is yielding such good results and fine officers." He turned to look at the general, "I know that it will now have the full support of Cairo, eh, Gervaise?"

The general gave a smile that came from his lips and not his eyes. He was not happy, "Yes, Herbert. Enjoy India. I will walk you to your carriage."

Horace smiled and shook my hand, "Well done, young man. I can see more promotion in your stars."

When the general returned I waited for a reprimand but none was forthcoming. "I might argue with others, Roberts, but Lord Kitchener is a force of nature. You shall have all that you need and I will see that your pips are ready for your man to sew on."

"Thank you, Sir."

"Now, Jamieson, you and I just need to fill out this shopping list. The Maxim is easy enough." He looked at me, "Does it have to be British soldiers?"

"No, Sir, Egyptians are fine. In my experience they are good soldiers."

"Good. A doctor, Jamieson?"

"Slightly trickier but not insurmountable."

"I fear the twenty-five men and their camels might be harder to find."

"Sir, they don't need to be experienced. We have good NCOs and we can train men. There might be volunteers…"

That made both men smile, "In that case," said the general, "I think we can help you. Raw men we have."

We spent an hour going through the fine details but by the end I was happy. As I left the general said, "And now, First Lieutenant Roberts, it is time for you to do a favour for me."

"A favour, Sir? Of course."

"My daughter has taken a shine to you. I would like you to make a fuss of her tonight at her party. She wishes, quite rightly, to be the belle of the ball for it is her birthday and her event. Dance with her and flatter her. She will forget you once you leave for my daughter is a butterfly but as she is my youngest I can deny her nothing."

I did not relish the task. "Yes, Sir, I will do my best." It was for the troop and I would steel myself to playing a part.

"Good fellow."

Cartwright was delighted with the promotion which he thought was no more than I deserved. "The thing is, Cartwright, I am not sure that my dancing will be up to muster."

"That is not a problem, Sir, I taught my young gentleman how to dance and we have the rest of the day. Now then, Sir, the hold…" I think that had he chosen to be one, Cartwright would have been a good teacher. He had discipline and he had the correct manner. He was a natural and despite my clumsiness he managed to polish me up. Aunt Sarah had made a good start with me but Cartwright understood the sort of partner I would have at the ball.

At lunch I began my flattery of Miss Emmeline and I saw both the general and his wife nod their approval. In many ways I thought it was deceitful but the general had said his daughter was a butterfly who would forget me as soon as I departed. Increasingly I found myself comparing her to Lucinda. The archaeologist's daughter won every time.

Dinner was, perforce, earlier, because of the ball. The same guests were there as had been present the previous evening. This time I was seated between Miss Emmeline and the Yorkshireman. To Emmeline's chagrin the Yorkshireman bombarded with me questions about Lord Kitchener. He had seen, the previous night, that his lordship had been interested in me and that made me interesting to him. I had to keep switching my attention between the two. I have no idea what I ate because I just wanted the meal to be over. Once we had eaten then we could get through the ball and the party. I had steeled myself to be patient. It would be like a night watch. No matter how long it lasted, eventually it would pass. They had a small orchestra and they were playing waltzes and polkas already.

Cartwright found himself co-opted into the proceedings and was placed in charge of the punch. Once more he was in his element. He had brought his best uniform and he was a credit to the troop. He descended before I did, "Good luck, Sir. You will be fine, I am sure of it."

I found the ballroom almost deserted. The guests were yet to arrive in numbers. The general, his wife and Miss Emmeline were at the door to the ballroom to greet the guests. I stood with Horace in close attendance in case the general wished either of us to perform some function.

"Will there be many officers coming, Horace?"

"A few but they are the ones from Cairo. Most of them will be my age. There will be officers from supply, intelligence, transport and the like. The only ones who have seen active service will be those on their way back from South Africa or on their way there." He leaned in and said, "It is why Miss Emmeline has been so attentive. She has met the other officers before. You are something new. You have young blood coursing through your veins and you are easier on the eye than old fogeys like me."

I laughed, "Surely, you can't be old."

"In years? No but in my ways, I am."

The guests who arrived showed that they had been out here for some time. The men were tanned but the ladies and their daughters had the pale faces of English women who shelter from the sun. Lucinda's skin had been bronzed by the desert. There were a few young men who arrived with their parents and they were smartly dressed but none wore a uniform. The ballroom began to fill up. Cartwright was in his element and the smile never left his face. The orchestra took a small comfort break and the room was filled with the buzz of conversation. I kept glancing over as the new guests wandered over to have a ladle of punch poured into a glass. I was looking in that direction when I heard, "And this is Oberst Klaus von Kleist."

My head whipped around. I saw a man with Arabic features and next to him wearing an Imperial German uniform was a German colonel. I did not jump to conclusions. There might be many von Kleists in the German army. I said to Horace, "Who is the Turk?"

"A Turkish diplomat, he is the equivalent of an ambassador. The situation here is difficult as this was the Ottoman Empire until the Egyptians revolted and we took over the protection of the land. Why do you ask?"

"Do you remember I said the Turks who attacked the fort were led by a German?"

"Him?"

"That is the name I was given by the Turkish soldier. He has the tanned skin of one who has been in the desert."

Horace nodded, "Say nothing. When I get the chance I will let the general know."

"But he is probably the man responsible for the attack. Men died."

Horace's expression changed and he became more serious, "Griff, the general has to play politics. Great Britain does not

An Officer and a Gentleman

wish to make an enemy of either the Ottoman or German Empire. God knows we have enough enemies as it is. The general will smile and the diplomat will smile. It is the way of the world. You are a soldier and have the luxury of knowing who your enemies are. Here we do not."

I nodded. He was right and I would have to play my part too.

I had planned on ignoring the German but he saw me and came over. I saw that he had medals on his chest and, as he and the diplomat neared me, I saw a duelling scar. It marked him as a Prussian. He clicked his heels and bobbed his head, "Two soldiers, do you mind if I talk to you gentlemen. I am out of my depth here." His English was flawless.

The diplomat said, "I will see if they have something other than punch. I will see you later, Oberst."

I knew that an Oberst outranked me and so I came to attention and said, "Sir."

Horace held out his hand, "The name is Lieutenant Horace Jamieson and this is Lieutenant Griff Roberts."

We shook hands. The German never took his eyes from me. He had the cold eyes of a cobra. "I can see, Lieutenant Roberts that you are the soldier."

Horace laughed, "And I am not, Colonel?"

The German turned, "I think, Lieutenant, that you are an aide. They are valuable but not as valuable as a soldier and you, Lieutenant Roberts, look to be a soldier. You look familiar. Have we met?"

In that moment I knew that he was the German. He had to have scouted out the fort and if he had used binoculars would have seen me. That he had drawn attention to himself was interesting. Why? I played the game, "I do not think so, Sir. I am based at small desert outpost. The work is dull and routine. I think I would remember meeting a distinguished officer like yourself."

If I needed confirmation I had it when he took a cigar from a case. I recognised the band. Horace said, "I am sorry, Colonel, but in deference to the ladies all smoking is not permitted here in the ballroom. There is a smoking area through the French windows."

He clicked his heels, "Then I will join the others who have the habit. We will talk more, a little later, Lieutenant."

As he strode away I said, "He is the same man. I know it."

Horace nodded, "And I think that you are right but do nothing." The orchestra began to play and I saw a couple of the guests start to dance.

Just then a pair of officers entered and I recognised one. After they had been introduced to the general and his wife one led the other over to me, "Griff Roberts, isn't it? The 1st Desert Group as I recall." He smiled, "It was such a rum name it sort of stuck in the old noggin."

As soon as he spoke I recognised the accent and the man, "Robert Kilbride." We shook hands. "Is Donal coming?"

He shook his head, "Donal died at Mafeking. This is another brother office, Captain Seymour."

I shook his hand and he said, "Pleased to meet you. 1st Desert Group? I have never heard of it."

I smiled, "Few people have. We are a troop based in the desert. Lord Kitchener set us up. We keep the desert safe for travellers." I turned back to Robert, "On your way home?"

He nodded, "Yes, we lost men and the captain and I are being sent home to train the Second Battalion. This is just a diversion while we wait for our ship."

We chatted about the war and I learned how Donal had died. The losses of which they spoke put the death of Trooper Davis into perspective. They had lost men to bullets and disease.

The general came over, "Lieutenant, don't you have something to do?" I saw Miss Emmeline and she was staring at me.

"Of course, General. If you would excuse me." Somehow the death of a man I had known, albeit, briefly, on the ship sailing to Egypt made the task of dancing with the young woman easier. Donal would never dance again. He would not hold a beautiful young woman in his arms and drink in the heady perfume. I danced and smiled as though Emmeline Pemberton was the most precious woman on the planet. I was thinking of Lucinda but I smiled at the general's daughter. As we whirled around the floor the clouds that appeared came when I passed the German officer who seemed to be constantly watching me.

An Officer and a Gentleman

Emmeline laughed and smiled as we sped around the floor. Paul's lessons had paid off. I was not embarrassed by either my steps or my hold. Emmeline was a good dancer and held her head at just the right angle. The fact that she was able to beam at everyone as she passed was a bonus. Eventually even she tired of the dancing and needed a break. I led her to the punch bowl.

Cartwright poured us two glasses, "If you don't mind me saying so, Miss, you make a lovely couple."

She squeezed my arm as she sipped the punch, "We do, don't we?" She emptied the glass and held it out for a second.

Cartwright said, "Careful, Miss, it is quite strong."

She was not listening. She leaned in to me and said, "I shall have to speak to my father and get you a posting to Cairo. Wouldn't that be splendid?"

I forced the smile knowing that it would never happen. "It would indeed."

We danced until the trickle of guests heading for their carriages became a torrent. When the orchestra stopped there were just the houseguests who remained. I had not seen the German officer leave. I took Miss Emmeline's hand and kissed the back of it. "A most delightful evening and one I shall cherish when I journey back to my fort."

Her face clouded over, "No! Father, I would have you command the lieutenant to stay here in Cairo."

The general shook his head, "The lieutenant must get the train back to Faiyum on Monday. Tomorrow will be his last day here."

"Then he must take me to the pyramids. I will enjoy the company of someone who is not withered and old."

I think the insult was aimed at Horace. He merely smiled and said, "A splendid idea. I shall have a carriage ready to take us."

She scowled, "Us?"

He nodded, "Well, yes, Miss Emmeline. It is my day off and I have yet to see them. I understand that Lieutenant Roberts can speak Arabic fluently. We shall both learn much, eh?"

Mrs Pemberton took her daughter's arm, "And after a busy day today, you need your beauty sleep my dear. Thank you, Lieutenant Roberts. You have been a most attentive partner." There was warmth in both her face and her eyes.

Left with the general and Horace I said, "The German officer, General Pemberton, I am convinced that he was the one who led the attack on the fort."

To my surprise the general nodded, "I wondered why the Ottomans sent their most senior diplomat. They are playing a game. They think to taunt us. Your arrival here is timely, Lieutenant. I think the sooner we get those men to you the better. I think there will be more attacks across the border. Lord Kitchener may have been right but we do not need to be more aggressive. We just need to have sufficient numbers to discourage such attacks. I think within a short time we can allow you and Captain Dunn to have a leave, eh? Why, we might even hand the fort over to the Egyptians. From what you say they are well led. I will have new orders for Captain Dunn ready for you before you leave on Monday."

This was lip service. He had to obey Kitchener but once the man who had created our unit was in India then he could gradually wind down the troop. The leave home would be the first stage.

Horace said, "It will be an early start, Lieutenant. The first train leaves at six and that means you will be leaving here by five."

I nodded, "The fine bed and the food have been appreciated, General, but I am a soldier. It is back to duty for me."

There were just four of us in the carriage. Horace sat with the driver and Cartwright and I sat in the back with Miss Emmeline. That she wanted us to be alone was clear. When she thought no one was looking she held my hand. Cartwright was wise to it and kept turning around to ask questions. She began to cast hateful glances at my batman who just smiled.

Cartwright and I had been there already but I did not mind a second visit. The alternative was to have the attentions of the general's daughter in the grand house. The outdoors were more suitable for there she would have to behave properly. After we had walked around them she spied the camels. She decided that she wanted to ride one. Horace tried to dissuade her but to no avail. The Arab attempted to charge us a fortune but I whittled him down. I chose the four camels that we would ride. I made sure that Emmeline had the smallest and the oldest. The Arab was smiling as she and Horace were helped to mount the animals. When they rose Emmeline squealed.

"Do you need help, Effendi?"

I smiled. Even Cartwright knew what to do and the two of us mounted and then we both rode the animals in a circle to show them that we were the masters. I told the two novices what to do and we set off to walk around the pyramids on the camels. We saw far more than when we had walked. Horace looked to be really uncomfortable and I had Cartwright ride next to him.

For the first time since I had met her, the general's daughter spoke to me about things other than herself, "You look very assured on the back of that camel, Lieutenant."

"I spend most days on the back of one. Normally I have a cloak and a keffiyeh."

She looked disappointed, "You do not wear your uniform and sword?"

"I wear a uniform, Miss Emmeline but it is a drab khaki and the sword is not as much use as a pistol or a rifle."

"A rifle? Do officers use rifles?"

"Good ones do."

She looked up at me, "You like the desert don't you?"

I was surprised, "Like is the wrong word. I am used to it and confident when I am travelling through it but no one likes the desert. It has to be fought. You can never tame it but you can understand its moods."

She sighed, "And that is why you will not accept a posting to Cairo."

"What you have to understand, Miss Emmeline, is that I command men who need me. Here in Cairo I would not be able to make a difference. In the desert I can."

We headed back and as we neared the car she said, "Will you write to me? I should like that."

I smiled, "I will but I should warn you that we only have supplies once every three months. That is a long time between letters."

"Three months!" I nodded, "It will enliven my dull life. Please write and I shall write to you, too."

My life was getting more complicated day by day.

Chapter 5

The general's wife gave Cartwright and I a hamper. It was filled with food and treats and I was touched by the gesture. Emmeline boldly kissed me and then dared her father to reprimand her. He gave a sad smile. He knew what she did not. I had been obeying orders. I think Horace had enjoyed my company for he drove us to the station in a carriage and chattered the whole way. He handed Cartwright two bottles of whisky to put into the hamper. "A little something from the general and me." He shook my hand, "You have enlivened my life, Griff. You take care and I shall keep an eye out for a book written by your father."

I handed him the two letters I had written whilst staying with the general. One was addressed to my father and the other to Lucinda. "Horace, could you put these with the mail that goes to England? They will reach there more quickly that way."

"Of course." He looked at the two addresses and he raised his eyebrows. He said nothing. He was a gentleman. He merely nodded and waved goodbye and we headed to the platform.

Once again we managed a compartment to ourselves and we chatted on the journey back to Faiyum. "I enjoyed that, Sir, but I will be glad to get back the fort. It sounds daft, and I never thought I would say it, but I missed the place and the lads. They are good blokes. Still, it was nice to be in civilised surroundings again and I do like to use an iron and put a good crease in a pair of trousers."

"I know what you mean." I looked at him, "Cartwright, do you remember the German officer at the ball?"

"Nasty looking chap with a scar, stank of cigars?" I nodded, "Yes, Sir, why?"

"I think he was the one who led the attack on the fort and I have the impression he is not finished with us."

"If I had known that, Sir, I would have slipped something into his punch."

I laughed, "No you wouldn't, Paul, it isn't your way and it isn't the British way. We will deal with Oberst von Kleist, but on our terms." It was clear to me that the German had not finished

An Officer and a Gentleman

with us. There was no reason why he should. We were a small outpost and yet we controlled a large area. If he and the Turks could eliminate us then unrest might cause the Egyptian Government some problems. The Ottoman Empire had not enjoyed handing Egypt over to another nation. They would not risk war with the British Empire but they might like to poison the minds of the Egyptians. I knew that some British officers had behaved in a high-handed manner closer to Cairo and the river. That they were fools and not typical of the rest of us was immaterial. The last thing we needed was an Egyptian revolution.

When we left the train and headed for the garrison the heat hit us immediately. With the windows open we had enjoyed a breeze on the journey from Cairo but out in the sun it was brutal. I was pleased to see that the camels had been well looked after, and after we had changed we left immediately. There was little point in waiting until the next morning. It was the middle of the afternoon when we departed and we rode for a couple of hours after dark. The camels were fresh and we had eaten well from the hamper.

We camped at the small oasis we normally used. It was almost like a halfway house. The camping prepared us better for life in the fort. Cartwright lit a fire and I filled the pot from the pool. We then let the camels drink. The water was not the best but boiling it made it drinkable and besides, it was for cooking. Cartwright took the camels to drink and I stirred the pot. The days might be like furnaces but the nights could be as cold as a winter's day in England. The fire and hot food were necessary. Whilst I did not expect trouble I was prepared for it and when Cartwright took over the cooking duties I laid a few simple traps to alert us to any danger.

As we ate I said, "Back to the desert, eh Cartwright?"

He looked around nervously, "I still prefer the fort, Sir. At least there I know there are no snakes, scorpions or spiders." He shuddered, "Horrible things."

A relief caravan could take days to reach our fort but we knew the route and we left before dawn. The result was that we made the journey in a day less than the caravan with the new troopers would take. We made good time and, it was late afternoon, when we saw the flag flying from the tower at the fort, it felt like we were coming home. I confess that I was worried until we saw the flag. The German officer at the ball had been a warning. I had feared that we might be attacked while I was in Cairo.

As we entered through the main gate, I saw that Sergeant Major Leonard was not there and that meant another caravan had been escorted. I gave a bottle of the whisky to Cartwright, "The NCOs and other ranks can have a drink on the general."

"They will appreciate that, Sir." It would only be a couple of glasses each but it was a good malt we had been given.

I shook my cloak as I took it off and patted down my tunic. I handed the cloak to Cartwright and two of the garrison took the camels. I entered the cool of the office.

Captain Dunn was eager for my news. Burton must have been forewarned for he brought a pot of tea as I entered the office, "Welcome back, Lieutenant." I took off my cloak and he saw the new pip, "Congratulations, Sir. First Lieutenant, eh?" He stood and held out his hand. We shook hands

"Thank you, Burton." The batman left us and I handed the second bottle of whisky to Archie. "A present from the general."

"And you have your promotion but I hope there is more good news."

"There is but first a drink of tea. I am parched." The tea was good, Burton knew how make a good brew. My thirst slaked I told him all finishing up with the news about the German officer.

"So, General Kitchener thinks there will be another attack?"

I nodded and told him what I had learned. After dinner, on Sunday night, he had given me a lesson in diplomacy. I now knew that the Germans were becoming more ambitious in Africa and using the Ottomans was a way of testing British resolve and probing for weaknesses. If we did not defend the western part of Egypt then it would be gobbled up by the Turks. They would ferment unrest and hope that the British Empire had enough troubles not to contest the gobbling.

"And when do we get these reinforcements?"

"Within the next couple of weeks but they will need training. They will not be desert soldiers." I added the caution because

British soldiers, as I had discovered, took time to adapt to both the desert and the way we fought.

"Then we shall promote Atkinson and Shaw. If we make Shaw the troop sergeant major then Atkinson can be troop sergeant."

"What about Bob Leonard?"

"He has less than six months to go before he retires. He will be happy to train up Shaw and, when they arrive, he can whip the new men into shape."

I refilled my mug, "And then?"

"And then we can be a little more aggressive."

"What about a corporal? I mean we have Higgins but…"

He looked at the list of men's names posted on the wall. "Wally Wilson. I know he is the bugler but we need an NCO more than a bugler. He can combine both." He shook his head, "A bugler is unnecessary although when your father led us the bugle saved us, once…" He looked thoughtful as he remembered an incident from the time he had served with my father. I knew what he was thinking. My father had told me all the stories, good and bad. I said nothing and did not disturb his train of thought. Such memories were important. He smiled and looked back at me, "I daresay word will race around the fort. We shall chat while we eat. I fear that the informal nature of our fort will change when we have more men. A small price to pay, eh?"

"Sir."

There was more good news as the sergeant major managed to return just before we ate. He had enjoyed a peaceful escort duty and had raced back to the fort.

There was a lively buzz to the mess that night. The word of our reinforcements had spread, as the captain had known it would, and it put everyone into a good mood. I also think that they were pleased that Cartwright and I were back. Bob Leonard waved his knife around, "If we have more men we will have to think about the eating arrangements, Sir."

I drank some of my tea to empty my mouth, "When they come they will bring a marquee as well as the tents for the new men."

Archie chewed thoughtfully, "We will have to use the land between the fort and the oasis."

"And if we do that, Sir, bearing in mind the night attack, we will need to make it a defensive position." The general had a library in the grand house and there was a book about the Roman legions. I said, "The Romans, when they marched, put up a palisade and dug a ditch each day. We could do what they did but only have to do it once. Some of those thorn trees need copsing and we could use their branches and intertwine smaller branches. The ditches are easy to dig."

"Yes, Sir, but we are giving more work to the garrison. They would have more to watch."

Captain Dunn leaned back, "Sergeant Shaw is correct. I think that we will have to help Sergeant Hamed and the garrison. We will have four men on watch each night." He looked at me, "How many NCOs and officers are coming?"

"The doctor will be the only officer and there will be a sergeant and a corporal. The rest will all be troopers."

"Cartwright and Burton can double up and the doctor can have their quarters. There are seven officers and NCOs." He smiled, "A convenient number. We all have one duty a week."

"Except when we are on patrol and if that is to be aggressive, Sir, then it will mean numbers. Those left in the fort will have to be alert."

Captain Dunn grinned. He had already thought of that. "And when we are on patrol we can house all the men in the fort."

That brought nods and to build on the good mood Archie said, "And Sergeant Shaw you are now promoted to Troop Sergeant, with immediate effect." I saw that Bob Leonard was pleased not to mention the others. "And Corporal Atkinson is now a sergeant." He nodded to Wally Wilson, "And you, Bugler, are now a corporal. Put the bugle in its case. When the new men arrive we will send a report back requesting back pay. I know that you may have to wait for some time for the back pay but…"

Sergeant Shaw said, "And as there is bugger all to spend it on here, Sir, that doesn't really matter."

I knew that they would all sort out their own stripes. Bob Leonard would have spares to give to Stan. Without his bugle Wilson could now have a side arm. We had captured ones and ammunition. The troop was in good shape. All we had to do was to wait for the new men.

The caravan that arrived the next evening needed an escort. We had begun work on a new camp and they used that. Archie took me to one side. When Sergeant Major Leonard had returned from his last escort the villagers at the oasis had said that they had beaten off an attack of some bandits who tried to take their animals. Archie said, "We will need to send out a patrol this time and ask them to scout around the oasis for a day or two."

"I will go, Sir."

"Are you sure, Griff?"

"Sir, I have had more than a couple of days off. I have slept in a bed and been wined and dined. I will lead it."

"Right, then take Atkinson and Wilson. They can get used to their new rank on the ride. Take Flynn and Foulkes from my section."

"When the new men arrive we will have to rearrange the sections, Sir. We can't have all the new men in the same section. I will sort it when they come. After all I am the adjutant and I have to earn the new pay."

I ensured that all my weapons were cleaned and loaded; my sword sharpened. I had plenty of ammunition and, as I turned in for the night, I found myself excited to be leading my men once more. The visit to Cairo had been both necessary and productive but it had shown me that, like my father, I was a soldier. He had been a soldier of the queen and I was a soldier of the king. I was a king's man and what I did was important. I knew, from speaking with him, that Horace knew he did not make a difference. As he had said to me, "If they could train up a monkey to salute then I would be redundant. I could not do what you do, Griff. If I led men into battle they would die and so would I. I learned what to do but as I have never had to do it, I have never been tested."

I knew, from the ball, that there were many officers such as Horace who served in Cairo. The army was a career and as they had not endured a war, they were the ones who oiled the wheels that enabled the train to keep moving.

We now had a good system worked out. Flynn and Foulkes were both excellent scouts and rode ahead. Atkinson brought up the rear with Wilson. Cartwright and I rode with the caravan master and Hunter and Bates rode to the left and right. We had discovered that the caravan masters were taciturn. Attacks on them had made them wary and they were as vigilant as we were. They carried guns but they were single shot weapons and knew that they relied on our firepower to protect them. The journey was uneventful but when we reached Abu Minqar we discovered that they had been attacked the previous day. A shepherd boy had been hurt and some goats and sheep had been taken.

Even though it was just a few hours before dark I did not hesitate. "Which way did they go?"

The headman pointed south and east, "That way, Effendi."

The animals would be taken closer to the river and sold. These bandits made a living by preying on small, isolated communities. They took whatever they could and moved on. In many ways our presence had made them change the way that they worked. They would still prey on caravans but the ones from Farafra were now protected. We followed the trail. It did not take a master scout to see it. The flock of animals had cut a swathe through the desert. We saw their dung and it was easy. Had we not been escorting the caravan then they might have succeeded. Our unexpected arrival meant that we had a chance to catch them for goats and sheep would not move quickly. We camped in a dried-up wadi. I did not want to lose them by trying to follow at night. I was not the callow officer who had first arrived in the desert. I now had confidence in both my men and me. We did not bother with a fire. For one thing it was not necessary and, for another, it might alert the bandits to our presence. The desert was like ice at night. Atkinson woke me for my duty at about three a.m. I think he let me sleep longer than I should have. Wilson and Flynn were with me. We checked the animals and then had a cold breakfast. As soon as we saw false dawn we woke the others and while they made water and breakfasted we went to saddle our camels. The three of us were mounted and examined the ground as the sun burst from the east. Its rays showed the path taken by the bandits. We might have missed it in the dark but the sun marked it clearly. It still headed south and east. The others quickly joined us.

It was a few hours into the day when we saw the dust cloud ahead. We knew what it meant. We had caught up with them. I halted. "Sergeant, take Flynn and Foulkes. Sweep to the left of

An Officer and a Gentleman

them. Wilson, take Hunter and Bates and sweep to the right. Cartwright and I will come at the rear. I want them surrounded. With luck they will cut their losses and run. All we want are the animals."

Atkinson said, "Sir, just you and Cartwright?"

I said, "You think we can't manage it, Sergeant?"

"No, Sir, but…"

"We will make a lot of noise and dust. I want their attention on us so that when they eventually see you they think there are more of us than there actually are."

He was not happy but he nodded, "Sir."

"Right, check your weapons and make sure there is one up the spout." Quick reactions were what was needed.

My two NCOs led their men off in a wide loop. We gave them five minutes start and then Cartwright and I set off. We rode with a ten-yard gap between us. A camel can get up to fast speeds but it takes more time to do so than on a horse. Cartwright was behind me to my right. He was trying to keep up with me but I had the fastest camel in the troop. It was exhilarating to be racing across the desert. When I saw the dust become close enough for me to make out the men at the rear, I began to whoop and shout. Cartwright joined in. It had been alien to him at first but now he was part of the troop. I knew that we would be making dust and while the two of us would be visible they would not know how many of us there were.

I saw three riders at the rear. Two had camels and one had a horse. They raised their rifles and fired. I knew from the cracks that they were Lee Metfords. They had been taken from British or Egyptian soldiers some time in the past. They were a good weapon and accurate but they were single shot. Another three camel riders joined them. I did not waste a bullet. They were still two hundred yards from us and although I had the range, the back of a racing camel was not a good platform for an accurate shot. A bullet whizzed over my head. It was close enough for me to be slightly worried. Luck could always play a part in such firefights. My camel could move me into the path of a bullet which might otherwise have missed me. Cartwright fired. He was not the greatest of shots but as he fired five shots in rapid succession it had an effect. The riders chambered and fired a last bullet before hurtling off. The horseman disappeared first. I heard the sound of Lee Enfields from the right and left. My men had arrived. Scheherazade was at full speed now and I began to overhaul the bandits. I left my rifle in its scabbard and drew my service revolver. I emptied it at the back of the nearest man. One of the bullets, more by luck than anything, slammed into him and I saw him leaning over the saddle. We passed the milling sheep and goats. They were panicked by the fleeing camels. I realised it would take some time to gather them and return them to their owners.

I watched as a bandit was plucked from his saddle. The bullet came from my left and that meant Sergeant Atkinson or one of his troopers had hit one. I holstered my service revolver and drew my father's Webley. I was close enough to one of them to shout for him to surrender. A prisoner might be useful. If we could learn where their lair lay we could destroy their nest. He turned and aimed his rifle at me. I fired three shots and this time hit him cleanly. He fell from the saddle. By now the other bandits were at full speed and there was little point in pursuing them. We could secure the flock and that was why we had come.

"Halt! Reform!"

Wally Wilson was close enough to hear and he repeated the command. For the first time it was his voice and not the bugle that did so. I reined in. As usual the first thing I did was to turn and see that Cartwright was unhurt. His face was flushed but he was smiling. "Well done, Cartwright."

The rest of the patrol arrived and I saw that none were injured. That was a relief. "Flynn, Foulkes, fetch the loose camels. Hunter and Bates, take the weapons from the dead. The rest of you let us try to gather up the animals."

It took two hours to manage to flock the sheep and goats and we rested and ate. We needed them to be calm. My men and I had accounted for three bandits. Another was wounded. They would not stop their attacks but would choose somewhere other than Abu Minqar. We could not make the whole of Egypt safe but we could make our part of it a little more peaceful. Our presence was necessary. If the Turks took over again then these people would suffer. The desert people liked the British. It was those who were packed into the cities who did not.

An Officer and a Gentleman

We camped that night in the wadi we had used when we had pursued the thieves. It was easier to manage the flock there. I knew that the lack of water for the sheep and goats would be a problem but that could not be helped. We used our water skins to let the animals, who were clearly pregnant, to be refreshed. It was not much but it helped. We cooked food and set sentries. Bates had a good singing voice and we knew that singing calmed animals. He sang to them and they settled down for the night. We now had enough officers to have one on duty with the sentry. It helped the others sleep more soundly.

It took the whole of the next day to reach Abu Minqar. I was pleased that we had not lost an animal but they were in poor shape by the time we arrived. They raced for the water of the oasis and we were welcomed like heroes by the villagers. There were some in England who thought that we oppressed the people in lands like Egypt. The reality was that without us they would have been much worse off. The villagers appreciated us. The headman told me that when the Turks had ruled them then they had both bandits and Turks to worry about. That steeled me for what lay ahead. We would have to take on the Turks or the people of Abu Minqar and Farafra would have a miserable existence once again.

We were dirty and weary when we reached the fort but I saw, as we neared it, that the new enclosure had been finished. There was also a wooden watch tower. That was a clever idea. As we dismounted I said, "Well done, men. We did good work out there." Their smiling faces told me I had said the right thing. "Cartwright, see to the camels. I will go and report."

"Sir."

Captain Dunn was leaning against the door to the office, "Problem? We expected you back a couple of days ago."

"Bandits stole some sheep and goats. We got them back."

"Burton, pot of tea."

A disembodied voice came back, "Already on it, Sir. Welcome back, Lieutenant."

Archie poured me a whisky and sat back, "Just give me the oral version and write the rest down at your leisure."

By the time we had drunk both the whisky and the tea I had finished the report. "Let us hope that you hurt them enough to discourage them."

"I hope so too. I saw the new camp. The watch tower is a good idea."

"Sergeant Major Leonard came up with it. We had enough wood and it means we can have two sentries there. They can cover the oasis and the camp."

"And now we wait for the replacements."

"Yes, I have given that some thought. Now that Atkinson is a sergeant we can move Shaw to my section. You can have Wilson."

I nodded. They were all good soldiers.

"Any thoughts where we can put the Maxim gun, Sir?"

"Over the main gate would seem the best place. Of course, if an enemy knows where it is then they can attack one of the other three walls."

"That means we can move more men to those walls. When we were attacked we had barely four or five men to a wall. With the reinforcements we will have twelve or thirteen. A Maxim is the equivalent firepower of a section."

"We will need to maintain our vigilance though, Griff. I am annoyed that they scouted us out and we knew nothing about it. Since you left I have had two men riding the wadi and the land around looking for signs."

"I got the impression that this German, if he is coming back here, is a clever chap. He was quite brazen at the ball. It was almost as though he was taunting me. He won't do the same thing next time."

"You said he had a duelling scar?" I nodded, "Then he is a Prussian Blue Blood. They think they are better than anyone else."

I thought back to Sandhurst. I knew what he meant.

Chapter 6

It was a week later when we spied the dust from the column of men and supplies as they headed to the fort. It was in the middle of the afternoon and I wondered if they had pushed on through the heat or camped. We normally expected caravans towards dusk. All the men were at the fort and there was interest from everyone. The cooks and the garrison were intrigued by the arrival of so many men. They were used to us and we all got on. That was not to say they wouldn't get on with the new men but change is always difficult. For the rest they were wondering how the new men would adapt to life at our fort. The captain and I had decided that we did not want to make everything too formal. The 1st Desert Group, by its very nature was informal. We waited in our uniforms but wearing keffiyeh.

The NCOs stood behind us. The rest just watched as the column rode in. I saw, immediately that we had a horse. The officer, I took him to be the doctor, rode a horse and not a camel. I wondered how that would work. The twenty men were less than I had expected. I turned to Archie, "Sorry, Sir, I was promised twenty-five men."

He smiled, "We have a doctor, a Maxim and ten more men than I expected us to be sent. This will do, Griff."

I saw that whilst we did not have the men we had expected we had an extra eight camels. They carried the supplies and tents and as there were no drivers to take them back then they were ours. Remounts were always needed.

They halted and the sergeant said, "Troop, dismount!"

They did so. I saw that the doctor did so gingerly as did about half of the troopers. That told me that not all of them were cavalrymen. We would have to divine their experience quickly.

One of the garrison ran over to take the reins of the doctor's horse. He walked stiffly towards and saluted, "Lieutenant Harold Quinn, Sir. I believe you sent for a doctor?" He smiled and I knew that we would get on. He was fresh faced and looked to be straight out of medical school. He must have served in the militia or else they had just given him the rank. The general and Horace had suggested that it might be hard to find a doctor. He was dark haired and not fair skinned. That would help in the furnace that was the desert. He was also slightly built. He looked as though a stiff breeze would knock him over. His Sam Brown and holster looked brand new. I doubted that he had even fired it.

Archie held out his hand, "Captain Archie Dunn and this is First Lieutenant Griff Roberts."

He shook our hands and smiled, "Then I am low man on the totem pole, eh?"

"Don't worry, we are fairly casual here. I take it you are unused to riding."

He ruefully rubbed his backside, "I am but I am just grateful they had a horse. I did not relish the thought of riding one of those beasts." He frowned for the first time, "Will I have to ride one, do you think?"

Archie shook his head, "You will be based here in the fort but we need you to train up a couple of troopers to be medical orderlies."

He looked relieved, "Then that is not a problem." Archie turned to look at the sergeant, "Sorry, Sergeant, we have kept you waiting in the sun."

The sergeant said, patiently, "Sir, Sergeant Ritchie reporting with the relief troopers, the doctor and the Maxim gun and crew."

He was an older soldier and I could tell that he was unsure of his role and duties. He had an accent albeit a slight one. While we had been talking to the doctor I saw him studying the fort and the garrison who were lounging around the sides.

Archie nodded and said, "Welcome one and all. Today is the time for you to settle into the fort. Troop Sergeant Shaw, see to the erection of the tents. Sergeant Hamed, see to the Maxim gun crew. Sergeant Major if you would join us in my office. Sergeant Ritchie, Doctor…"

I saw that the sergeant was torn. His charges were being taken away from him. Sergeant Major Leonard said, somewhat gruffly but with kindly intentions, "Look sharp, Sergeant, we don't stand in the sun when we don't have to."

Burton and Cartwright had anticipated everything and the two of them had a pot of tea and mugs as well as some honey cakes with dried fruit in them. The two could be like old women in

An Officer and a Gentleman

many ways but they worked well together and knew us. There were six chairs in the crowded little office but the desk had been cleared.

As the pot of tea, cakes, cups, sugar and milk were placed on the table Captain Dunn said, "You can leave us now. See that we are not disturbed and, thank you, this is appreciated." The two beamed and left. I saw the doctor studying us all. We were warriors and he was a healer. I knew it had to make a difference.

Sergeant Major Leonard said, "I shall be mother." He knew how we took our tea and added the milk and sugar for us.

He looked pointedly at the new sergeant who said, "Milk and four sugars, if that is alright. I have a sweet tooth."

Bob Leonard nodded, "Nothing wrong with that, son."

Archie and I sipped our tea and he said, "Eat the honey cakes. They are Burton's speciality and are delicious. If you have a sweet tooth, Sergeant, they will be right up your street."

I knew what Archie was doing. He was putting the new man at his ease. There were a dozen cakes and when he had finished one I saw the sergeant eyeing another one up. I smiled as I said, "Have as many as you like, Sergeant. Burton will be most upset if any are left."

Archie laughed, "Mind you that means the next time there will be eighteen."

Doctor Quinn said, "If it was in England I would say we needed the sugar, Sir, but here..."

Archie shook his head, "Here we need the sugar as much as in England. Doctor, tell us your tale and how you ended up here."

I was sat obliquely across the table and I studied his face as he spoke. I had learned, especially at Sandhurst, how to read people. His eyes flickered. What he was going to tell us was a version of the truth. His smile hid the lie in his eyes, "Well, Sir, I had been in the old Fencibles." He grinned, "An old-fashioned name but we in the county like it. When I finished and qualified I didn't fancy just treating old men for piles and their wives for flatulence. I thought I would see a bit of the world first."

"So you have never practised then?"

He said, defensively, "Well, no Sir, but I am qualified and..."

Archie held up his hands, "No criticism intended. In many ways that is a good thing. You have no preconceptions." The doctor looked relieved, "Oh and when we are in the office, you can dispense with the titles. I am Archie, this is Griff."

He looked relieved, "Thank you…Archie."

Archie looked at me and nodded. I turned to the sergeant who was next to me, "And now, Sergeant, what is your story? I am guessing that this is not your first appointment."

"No, Sir. I was in the 1st Royal Dragoons, where I was a corporal and we served in South Africa. We were on our way home and about to become a garrison regiment in England." We waited. There was more but, like the doctor, he seemed reluctant to speak.

I said, softly, "Sergeant this is a small post. We are more like a family than anything. Secrets can only hurt us." I saw the doctor flush a little confirming what I had thought.

He sighed, "Sir, I didn't get on with the troop sergeant." He could not help looking at Sergeant Major Leonard.

Bob nodded, "They can be nasty pieces of work. Carry on, Sergeant, I won't be offended by anything that you say."

The sergeant nodded, "I was a good soldier, Sir. I won a good conduct medal but the troop sergeant just took against me. I had no chance of promotion. When we were in Cairo, one of the officers, Lieutenant Bentinck, well he had a friend in Cairo, a Lieutenant Jamieson."

I could not help beaming, "Horace, I told you about him, Sir."

"I remember."

"Well he said they were looking for volunteers to join a mounted regiment and they needed a sergeant. As it was not the Royal Dragoons Lieutenant Bentinck suggested to his friend that if I was promoted I might suit." He gave a sad smile. "Not a pretty story, Sir, but the truth and no secrets." He looked relieved to have got it off his chest.

I said, "It shows character, Sergeant, and no one in this room will criticise you." I could not help but add, "I suspect you expected horses though."

He smiled, "Yes, Sir, the camels came as a shock but they are better than I thought they would be."

Bob said, "What is your first name, Sergeant?"

"John, Sergeant Major but everyone calls me Jack."

"Well, Jack, I am like you and was more used to horses but out here the camel can survive. More than that they are fast and can go further than a horse with less water. As you will discover water rules our life out here."

The sergeant nodded.

Archie became all business. "Right, the secrets are out of the way. Did you bring paperwork for the troopers?"

He took the leather satchel from around his neck and took out the paper. "Yes, Sir, but not on the Egyptians."

Bob said, "One was a corporal, Sir. I am guessing that Sergeant Hamed will have that information."

Archie handed me the sheet. "Right, Sergeant, tell me what you can about the men."

I looked at the typed sheet.

Corporal Michael Alexander
Trooper Angus McBride
Trooper Norman Thomas
Trooper Edward Gilmore
Trooper Herbert Dixon
Trooper Sidney Kent
Trooper Samuel Cave
Trooper Brian Foster
Trooper Henry Peters
Trooper William Pallister
Trooper Graham Allan
Trooper Ben Roberts
Trooper Geoffrey Robie
Trooper Joseph Garthwaite

We already had a Peters and there was another Roberts. I doubted that he would be a relative but it might cause problems when orders were shouted in the heat of battle.

"I only had them for four days, Sir. To be honest the doctor and I discovered more about them on the way here than back at the depot."

The doctor nodded, "Yes, Sir, they are a rum lot."

"Archie."

"Archie, sorry. Archie, do you mind if I smoke? I am afraid I am addicted to the weed."

"Of course, smoke away."

It was only when Sergeant Major Leonard took out his pipe that the sergeant did too. The doctor lit a long thin cheroot. He half closed his eyes as the smoke drifted up before him. He opened them and said, "I identified the malingerers straight away. They were the ones who complained all the time. Some were quiet chaps and a couple couldn't stop chattering. It was like travelling with a tiding of magpies."

Bob nodded, "We will rid them of that habit." He tamped down the tobacco and said to the sergeant, "Noise travels in the desert. We encourage silence."

Jack nodded and I could see that he was relaxing a little more. "Some of them have joined with the same motive as me, Sir. Corporal Alexander was a lance jack and he jumped at the chance of promotion. He has a wife and bairn at home." I recognised the accent now. He was from the north east of England. "The same is true of about half of the others but there are some, Sir, who have been dumped on us." He saw me take a pencil from the desk and he said, "Pallister. You will spot him straight away. Great big hulking brute with a broken nose and hands that are like hams. He has a record for fighting and drinking."

I made a mark on the list. I had my own code.

Bob said, "Well, there is nowt to drink out here and if he is handy with his fists…well there is company punishment, Sir."

Archie shook his head, "Let us see what we can do with him. Who knows, without the drink we may have a different soldier."

I saw the doctor nodding.

"Dixon. He is a thief. I heard his oppos were going to give him a good hiding for his thievery and so he volunteered."

"We will watch that one, Sir. We can't have a thief." Bob knew the way the men thought. They would protect one of their own but a thief in a barracks was a terrible prospect.

"Kent is the barrack room lawyer. Knows his rights and his duties."

I made a mark and said, "Then why did he volunteer?"

Jack looked perplexed, "You know, Sir, I spent the days riding across the desert trying to work that one out."

I said, "Secrets, eh?" I caught the quick glance that the doctor gave to me.

"The last two who are worth mentioning are Gilmore and Peters. They both came from the same regiment, the Engineers. Their sergeant sought me out in the bar one night and said to watch them. I asked him why and he just said, 'They are a pair of bad buggers and I wouldn't trust them as far as I could spit'." He took his pipe, which had gone out and lit a match to relight it. Between puffs he said, "Sorry, Sir, Lieutenant Jamieson said as how you needed every man we could get. I am afraid that beggars can't be choosers."

"Don't apologise, Jack," I noticed that Archie used the sergeant's first name to include him, "We are grateful for any men we can get. Right, Griff, I want you, the sergeant and the sergeant major to make up the three sections we shall be using. Doc, let you and I go and find you somewhere you can use as a medical room and you will need to let me know who you want as medical orderlies."

"Oh that is easy. Allan and Cave were in the St John's Ambulance Brigade. I chatted to them on the way here. Thoroughly nice chaps." I was impressed with the doctor. He had not wasted his time on the journey through the desert.

When the two had left us the three of us went through the list. My main contribution was to ensure that Archie and I had two of the villains, as Jack termed them, in our sections. Bob's was the smallest section and he would have to train up our new sergeant. Jack Ritchie had impressed me already but the sergeant major would give him better lessons in commanding in the desert than anyone. Bob just had Gilmore from the malcontents. I made sure to split up the two friends. The downside for the sergeant major and Sergeant Ritchie was that they had no medical orderly. It could not be helped.

When we had finished I said, "Until we send a patrol out, and that won't be until we have half trained the men your brought, you will all have to endure tents. When we have a patrol out, as it will be made of up at least one section and perhaps more, you can use the barracks in the fort."

The sergeant nodded.

Bob said, "And if you will excuse me, Sir, I have work to do," he nodded at the sergeant, "Jack and I need to get to know one another well."

"Of course, Sergeant Major and," I held out my hand, "Welcome Jack."

"Thank you, Sir." He shook my hand and said, "Lieutenant Jamieson said I would like you and he was right."

Left alone in the office I took a clean piece of paper and began to copy out my rough copy. The pristine one would go in the file. Burton and Carwright came in, "Can we clear, Lieutenant?"

"Of course."

Burton beamed. The cakes were all gone and the tea pot was empty. He said to Cartwright, "Next time more cakes and two pots of tea."

I had already worked out that we could not all eat in the mess and so I sought out Sergeant Shaw. "Troop Sergeant, have the mess tables and benches brought out in the square. We will eat outside tonight."

"Sir."

"I will arrange watches for tomorrow but I think it is important that we all dine together, eh?"

"Yes, Sir. It will be crowded but I don't mind. It means more men on patrol." He saluted and turned, "Corporal Higgins get the rest of our section."

I saw Sergeant Hamed approaching, "Sergeant, how are the new men?"

He looked pleased as he said, "They are good men and honoured to be chosen to fire the Maxim. I now have a corporal and he seems a good fellow."

"It might be useful to train others to fire the Maxim. Just in case."

"I have already thought of that, Sir."

"Tonight we will all eat out in the open. I will sort out watches so that the men can eat in two sittings. One night in the open is necessary but I would rather we ate within the mess."

"Of course, Sir. I will tell the cooks and the others."

"Are there enough supplies?"

The men who came with the gun told me that there is another caravan arriving in the next couple of weeks with ammunition and more food."

"Good."

An Officer and a Gentleman

I headed back to the office. I had more paperwork to do. I could not help but smile. My father hated paperwork and yet now he was a writer. I wrote out the watches and made a fair copy. I went outside and pinned it to the noticeboard. I returned inside to file the paperwork.

I heard the bugle sound for mess. Wilson still used it within the fort. I donned my cap and went out. The sun had gone down and we would not need the keffiyeh. The tables were crowded and men were seated closely together. Once I had arranged the rota then it would be much easier. Archie and I had planned on a short series of patrols and that meant the early patrol would breakfast first. The officers were sat at one end of one table and the NCOs at the bottom of the other.

Sergeant Major Leonard shouted, "Attention!" as Archie and the doctor emerged from their tour.

The captain took off his cap and so did I but he remained standing. He said, "Gentlemen, I welcome you to the fort and your new home. I hope you shall be happy here." He had clearly spoken to Sergeant Hamed for the men who would serve us food were poised. The sergeant came around and poured a tot of rum into the beakers before the men. I knew which one was Pallister. Even if he hadn't been the biggest man in the fort I would have recognised the licking of the lips. I wondered at the wisdom of the order. "This is the last of the rum ration until the next caravan arrives and I thought that this was a good opportunity to toast with it." Sergeant Hamed nodded. The captain raised his beaker and said, "I give you two toasts, the King and the 1st Desert Group."

Led by the original troop we all intoned, "The King and the 1st Desert Group." I saw that Pallister downed it in one. He might rue not savouring it.

"You may sit, Sergeant, the food."

With fresh supplies this would be the best meal until the next caravan. The original troop knew that but the new ones would not. I studied the men as I ate. The new ones had placed themselves together. Some of them were chatting to the original troop and I identified the malcontents and the quieter ones. When I had arranged the troops Jack had been able to tell me the solitary ones. Archie was right. It was better to try to change the ones who were not made of the right calibre of ammunition rather than reject them. Beggars could not be choosers. The two of us had discussed how to be more aggressive while we waited for the new men. We both knew that with Kitchener in India our support had gone. General Pemberton had only agreed to our request because of Lord Kitchener. The fact that he had not sent us either the numbers or the quality of troops confirmed that. We would have to show him that we could still achieve what Kitchener had wanted with the cloth that he had provided. Having said that the mood was, generally, a good one. Archie had been right to have us all dine together. The cooks had made a pudding. It was not an Egyptian one but a sponge pudding favoured by the troop. As it had suet in it, the pudding tended to last longer than otherwise. When it had been served and as the men finished it off I stood.

"Welcome to the new troopers. In case you didn't hear earlier on I am the adjutant. I have arranged the watches. I have pinned a notice up on the office wall. Tomorrow morning Section 1, Captain Dunn's men will breakfast in the mess at five thirty. Reveille here is at five." I heard a couple of groans from amongst the new men and saw the NCO's trying to identify them. "The patrol will breakfast first. Captain Dunn will then lead his section on a training patrol. The rest will remain here with me and I will conduct lessons in Arabic. We will also have rifle practice and I will go through the standing orders. Section 1 will be the first to dine tomorrow evening. The next day will be section 2's turn to patrol and so we will breakfast at five thirty. The day after will be Section 3. Two things to learn about the desert: water is vital and you need to take plenty of salt. Liberally dose your porridge with it. Dehydration can kill out here. Any questions?"

I knew who would ask the question and I was not disappointed, "Lieutenant Roberts, King's Regulations state that we are allowed a measure of alcohol each day. The captain said we have to wait until the next caravan. Is that right, Sir."

"And your name is?"

He hesitated. He did not like to be identified so early, "Trooper Kent, Sir."

"Well Trooper Kent, if you check your clearly well-thumbed copy of King's Regulations," I saw the NCO's smile, "you will see that there is a caveat," I had memorised it anticipating the question, "*'the supply of the alcohol in question will be determined by local circumstances. If there is no such supply then tea will be provided in its place'*." I smiled, "Does that answer your question, Trooper?"

"Yes, Sir."

Pallister had clearly not understood it in the first place. He frowned. I gathered he was not the brightest of lamps, "No drink, Sir?"

I shook my head, "No…?"

"Pallister, Sir, Trooper Pallister." He shook his head, "And no pubs?"

"This is a Moslem country, Pallister."

He shook his head, "That lying sergeant. He told me this billet was in the part of Egypt with plenty of pubs."

That made everyone, apart from the trooper burst out laughing. Even Kent smiled. Pallister was still confused. The trooper next to him said, "I will explain it to him, Sir."

Sergeant Major Leonard and the NCOs rose, "Right, lights out in ten minutes. We have a big day tomorrow. Thank you, Captain Dunn, Lieutenant Roberts, that was most interesting." They stiffened and nodded a sort of salute as they left. The new men would have another night under canvas. The original troopers would enjoy a roof. That was the only difference. The insects and the heat would be the same and they would all have to use the same piss pots that stood close to where they slept.

The doctor was still smoking his cheroot as we headed for our quarters, "Well that was illuminating. I can see that this is going to be more interesting than I anticipated."

As I went to my bedroom I reflected that I had not been sent a letter. Perhaps our mail was still in Alexandria. I was disappointed. I hoped that Lucinda would write but perhaps she had forgotten me already. I had been expecting a letter from my father and another from my aunt. They wrote whenever they could. Then I thought back to when I had been growing up. Letters to and from my father had been a rarity. I now wished that I had written to him more. It was a connection to home and I found myself missing England.

Chapter 7

The strident notes of the bugle woke me and that was unusual. I was normally awake before it sounded. I suppose I had been fretting about the lack of letters for it had taken some time to get to sleep. As Cartwright entered to help me dress, he would not take no for an answer, I looked in the mirror and, shaking my head, told myself to get a grip. To Cartwright I said, "And how was your first night sharing with Burton?"

"Not a problem, Sir, we get on well. Back in the big house I had to share a room with two under footmen and I did not get on with them at all! One of them was as flatulent as a well-fed cow." I found myself smiling at his expression.

I was in the mess just as Captain Dunn and his patrol were eating. I went to get a mug of tea and stood by him and Troop Sergeant Shaw. "All set, Sir?"

He nodded as he munched on a piece of toast. The cooks had learned he liked toast, even though it was not the sort of bread he was used to. His treat was a jar of marmalade. A generous man in every other way, Archie did not share his precious treat but it did not matter for I was not a fan. "I fear that today will be another hot one. I intend to ride to the wadi and then take a circle around the northern perimeter. We shall do no more than four miles and be back by noon."

"Then perhaps I could take my section out this afternoon, eh Sir?"

"Good idea."

The advantage of having just two officers was that we could change our minds and our orders.

"I will go and tell Atkinson."

I knew that new sergeant would be up. He had been recently promoted and seemed determined to prove that we had been right to elevate him. "Charlie, a change of orders. We will take our section out after the noon break. We will just ride a couple of miles to orientate the new men and to see what they are like on the backs of camels when they are not riding over a well-used trail."

He looked happy at the change of order, "Keep 'em busy, Sir. That'll stop them complaining."

"Complaining?"

"Oh yes, Sir, it is in the nature of soldiers to complain. If they didn't I should be worried."

"What do you make of them, Charlie?"

"They are, what is the word…" Charlie liked to read and was constantly trying to better his English. He had said he would buy my father's book when it was published. "Malleable, that is it." He looked pleased with himself. "There are the usual villains but no more than in any other unit. The difference is, Sir, that here there is nowhere to run and hide. There may be tears and tantrums from some but they will bend or…" his voice and face became a little more serious, "break."

I went to the gate to see the patrol off. I saw that Sergeant Hamed had begun work early. He had two of his cooks helping the Maxim gunners to set up the new weapon. One thing we had plenty of was sand and I saw them carry freshly filled bags to give even more protection to the gunners. I found myself excited at the prospect of seeing it used. When they had gone I said, "Close the gates, Private." There had been a time when we might have left them open. The attacks had stopped that and the two Egyptians closed and barred the gates. Some of the new men were walking to the mess and saw them as they were shut. They stared at them. This was not the cosy world of a barracks in Cairo. This was the front line.

The new ones who were already eating all stood when I entered. I waved them to their seats, "We are all in the same mess."

Atkinson and Wilson sat with me and I used the time to give my instructions, "When we go out this afternoon you take the rear, Wilson. Atkinson, you ride in the middle. Watch the new men. According to Sergeant Ritchie none of them have ridden camels before they came here. The ride from Faiyum will not have been fast. I intend to make them go a little faster this afternoon." I smiled, "We have a doctor now in case there are any bruises."

As if on cue the doctor came in, "My God it is hot out here. I thought Cairo was bad enough but…"

An Officer and a Gentleman

I pointed my knife at the cooks, "Help yourself to food. It is not fancy but it is filling."

"I am not sure I could."

"I know you are the doctor but take my advice, eat as much as you can when you can."

When he returned with porridge and tea I said, "I am taking my patrol out this afternoon. Cave will be with me so do some work with him this morning. You can have Allan this afternoon."

"Righto." He began to eat. "Will there be much work for me?"

I looked at Atkinson and Wilson. They remembered the soldiers who had been wounded. I said, "A feast or a famine. Men will get cuts, bruises, and the like but the real reason we need you is when we have to fight. Cuts and bullets will be the order of the day."

"Are we at war?"

"We are always at war with the desert but there is a belligerent German over the border. He has attacked archaeologists and this fort before now. We intend to stop him and here diplomacy doesn't work. We use the sharp end of a Lee Enfield."

He nodded, "Then I will have to study my medical book. I do not want to be caught short by a lack of knowledge."

The Arabic lessons, with the new men, proved to be good for some and a waste of time for others. I had expected nothing less. I made sure they could all understand basic commands and polite interactions. It made for a more harmonious time if they could converse with the Egyptian garrison. I identified the ones who were poor and was not surprised when all of them had been the ones identified by Sergeant Ritchie: Gilmore, Kent and Dixon.

When the patrol returned Doctor Quinn had his first patient. Pallister had fallen from his camel. In trying to save himself his arm had caught in the reins and he had put his shoulder out. It could be remedied but, as the doctor said to Captain Dunn when he led the man away, it would be incredibly painful.

"Will he need time to recuperate?"

The doctor smiled, "He is a fit man, just give him three or four days. He should be alright." The doctor's worth was proved already. We would not have been able to put the shoulder back in and Pallister might have been crippled for life.

I think that Pallister was a tough man and had endured injuries before for he bore the treatment stoically. The room we used for treatment was next to the office and I could hear the doctor's gentle voice as he spoke to the patient. Trooper Allan, who was being trained to be a medical orderly was in Pallister's section and he attended and helped the doctor. I could hear from his voice that he was a good choice.

"I am betting Bill, that you won't fall off a camel again."

"Took me by surprise, that is all."

"You are doing well, Pallister. Allan, make sure his arm doesn't move."

I heard Trooper Allan laugh a little, "It doesn't help that you are so big, Bill. Camels go down at the front first. You should lean back."

"Aye, well, I will, in future. Doc, any chance of some brandy to help the pain?"

I heard the doctor's smooth voice, "I am afraid that until the caravan arrives, Pallister it will have to be an opiate."

"A what, Doc?"

"Medicine."

I heard a strange creaking sort of sound as Pallister said, "No, thank you." There was a pause and I heard a gentle, "Ow."

"Well done, Pallister, now Allan here will bandage you up. The bandage will just be needed for a day or two and is more to prevent you from using your left hand and arm. You have light duties and no riding for five days."

"Thanks Doc."

Doctor Quinn was wiping his hands when he came into the office, "A gentle giant that one. Bore it all remarkably well."

I shook my head for I had read the reports Ritchie had brought with him, "Tell that to the four men he put in the hospital last month."

The doctor lit a cheroot, "I am betting it is the drink. If we can ensure he drinks in moderation then I think you have a soldier who will be an asset rather than a liability." He blew out a plume of smoke, "I am a doctor and not a real soldier but I think I know people."

An Officer and a Gentleman

Just then the two troopers passed the open door. Trooper Allan beamed, "Our first patient, Lieutenant. What do you think?"

I smiled, "I think you all did well. I was listening, Pallister. When you are healed I will show you how to mount and dismount from your camel. There is a knack."

"Thank you, Lieutenant."

Just then Cartwright appeared with my cloak and keffiyeh, "And now it is my turn to see if the men can mount and ride their camels without needing the ministrations of our good doctor here."

Atkinson and Wilson had the men ready when we emerged into the sun. It had passed noon but it was still hot. My two NCOs had lined the men up where they could benefit from the shade of one of the walls. It was marginally more bearable. I donned my keffiyeh. "Put on your keffiyeh and your cloaks."

All but Kent did so and he shook his head, "No, Sir. King's regulations say that we have to wear the cap and tunic but not this Arab nonsense."

Sergeant Atkinson took a step forward and growled, "The officer said…."

I held up my hand and smiled, "Trooper Kent is quite right. He has made his choice, Sergeant." I caught his eye and winked. "Just bring them with you, Kent."

Sergeant Atkinson smiled, "Yes, Sir."

"Now, although we aren't going far we are leaving the fort and that means we keep these," I held up my Lee Enfield, "loaded with one up the spout. We may not need them but if you are given the command then draw them and be ready to fire. Tomorrow the troop will have lessons in firing from the back of a camel. I hope we don't need to use our weapons today as there is an art to shooting from the back of a camel." I sheathed my rifle and lifted my water skin, "You do not drink until you are ordered to do so. Out here water is precious. When you are commanded then drink but just one swallow. Little and often is the rule." I looked at Kent, "That is not in King's Regulations, that is in Lieutenant Robert's wise words of wisdom." All but Kent smiled. "Now we mount. As Trooper Pallister discovered it is not just riding that has inherent problems, there is also the matter of mounting and dismounting. You have all seen your animals and the way they move. Adapt yourself to those movements. I will mount first. Watch how I do it. Then the older hands will mount. Learn from us."

By the time I had mounted and the original troopers the new men had good models and all managed to mount safely.

Sergeant Atkinson said, as I waved my arm forward, "Section, Ho."

We all had to duck beneath the gate and then we were on the track. Cartwright rode just behind my camel's rump. I waited until we had all left the fort and then set Scheherazade to trot. It was not the most comfortable of gaits but I wanted the men to get used to the one we would use the most. It was clear, from the noises they made, that they had not used that gait before. I led them not towards the wadi that Captain Dunn had explored with his section but took them north and east. Here the caravan trail was clearer and there were fewer obstacles. I had intended, until Pallister had been injured, to have them gallop but they were clearly not ready for such a command. We would trot. I turned in my saddle. Wilson had ensured that an experienced trooper rode next to a desert virgin. It helped me to see the contrast. The new men rode as though they were sacks of potatoes. Surprisingly the one who was riding the best was the barrack room lawyer. That might have been because he was riding next to Sergeant Atkinson.

We rode for an hour. I was ready for water and I knew that the men would be desperate for a drink. There was no shade but the sun was marginally less scorching. I held up my arm and Sergeant Atkinson said, "Section, halt."

I turned in my saddle, "Water break. Three short sips." I saw that Kent's face and neck were red already. I could see the sweat on his tunic, "Do you wish to don your keffiyeh and cloak, Kent?"

He looked at me defiantly and pride rule his brain, "No, Sir, I am fine."

"Of course you are." I waited until they had drunk and then pointedly took two drinks. I hung my skin and waved my arm.

"Section, ride."

An Officer and a Gentleman

We walked for twenty paces and then I set Scheherazade to trot once more. I had decided where we would turn but as I was about to make the turn I saw some vultures descending. One never ignored such things in the desert and although the birds were three hundred yards from the caravan trail I headed across the open desert to investigate. I slowed to a walk and drew my Lee Enfield. I heard Sergeant Atkinson order, "Draw rifles." I saw that there was a pile of rocks and the rocks hid whatever the birds were feasting upon.

I did not need to tell my seasoned troopers what to do. Even Cartwright would be scanning the horizon for other signs of danger. I made sure that Scheherazade took the safest path to the birds who were clearly feasting on something. As I neared them they rose squawking and complaining. The would fly a few dozen yards and wait to continue their feast. I saw that it was a man and he was dressed in Turkish uniform beneath a ubiquitous cloak. I halted but did not dismount. As the birds had been at the corpse then I did not think it was an ambush but one never knew.

"Corporal Wilson, skirmish line. Trooper Cave, Sergeant Atkinson, dismount. The rest of you, keep your eyes open."

I dismounted. I saw that even the new ones had their eyes scanning the land for danger. I walked over to the body. The eyes had gone already. The vultures used that as the point of entry if there was no wound. I looked at the body and saw no wound. I stood, "Cave, you are the medical orderly, see if you can find a wound."

"Yes, Sir."

I turned to Sergeant Atkinson, "Well?"

"There were more than just this one here, Sir." He pointed to the tracks, "It is hard to estimate numbers but it was more than a couple."

Just then Corporal Wilson shouted, "I have found where they took a dump, Sir."

The sergeant pointed, "And they had a fire. They camped." I had seen the fire already.

"So what was a Turkish patrol doing here?" I looked around. "These rocks would give cover. Perhaps they were waiting for a caravan either to or from Siwa."

"Makes sense, Sir. This is a good spot for an ambush. With their camels lying down, they wouldn't be seen. If they had good rifles they are close enough to shoot the caravan master and the one at the end." I nodded. A classic ambush.

"Snake bite, Sir."

We had forgotten Cave. He had removed the man's trousers and turned him over. The two puncture marks were clearly visible. Atkinson said, "Well spotted, Trooper. He must have had his trousers down and was close to the ground." He shuddered, "Awful way to go."

I said, "What made you remove his trousers, Cave?"

"They weren't done up, Sir. It looked strange and I wondered if he had a wound to his stomach. When I didn't see one I turned him over."

"Good work. Sergeant, have the body covered with rocks. He doesn't deserve to be a meal for those vultures."

"Sir."

I cupped my hands and shouted, "You can dismount and drink another three mouthfuls. We have a man to bury."

Cartwright dismounted and joined me. He had been close enough to hear everything, "The one thing I did not miss when we were in Cairo were the creepies, Sir." He shuddered, "It is a bit much when you cannot go to the toilet without worrying about getting a bite to your bum."

"And that is why we always check, don't we, Cartwright? This man made a mistake. A costly one but one that could have been avoided." As I drank I smiled for Kent was surreptitiously fitting his keffiyeh. I had won or, more likely, common sense had prevailed. He had not wished to heed my advice but saw the sense of it. I was learning about the man. When I saw him don his cloak I was a little happier.

We reached the fort two hours later. We had walked rather than trotted back. The dead body had been a good lesson for the new troopers. They had seen the dangers. As we neared the fort I saw the caravan at the oasis. That meant an escort duty the next day

I watched the men dismount and when they had done so safely I dismounted. "Well done, men. Tend to your camels and then enjoy the shade." I handed my reins to Cartwright as Wilson and Atkinson led the men to the stables and camel lines.

I shook my cloak and draped it over Scheherazade's saddle. I went into the office and saw Archie and the doctor enjoying a pot of tea. I shook my keffiyeh before I entered. Burton appeared with a mug of tea, "Here you are, Sir. Freshly made."

Archie said, "You saw the caravan?" I nodded and sipped the steaming brew. It was like the nectar of the gods. Burton made a good cup of tea. "I will escort it tomorrow and let Sergeant Major Leonard ride with his section."

"We found a dead Turk, Archie. Twelve miles or so north east of here." I saw Archie stiffen. "He had been bitten by a snake and left by his mates. We couldn't work out the numbers accurately but it was more than a couple of scouts."

"Burton."

The batman's head appeared in the doorway, "Have Sergeant Major Leonard join us."

The doctor made to rise, "I will be in the way…"

Archie shook his head, "No, Harry, it is important that you know what is going on. We have just three officers and you are one of them."

He lit a cheroot, "I can see that I chose an interesting billet."

"Sir?" Sergeant Major Leonard appeared.

I said, "We found a dead Turk north east of here."

"Tomorrow, Sarn't Major, ride fifteen miles north east and look for signs of enemy patrols."

I added, "The body was four hundred yards off the road by some rocks."

"Ambush then, Sir." I nodded. "Right then and who will be escorting the caravan, Sir?"

"I will."

The sergeant major looked at me, "Then you will stay close to the fort, Sir?"

He was like an old woman at times but he meant well. I sighed, "Yes, Mother, I won't venture out."

He nodded, "Jolly good, Sir. A man has only so much luck and it seems to me that you have used all of yours up already." He turned and left us.

The doctor smiled, "This is nothing like I expected, you know."

Archie said, "Men like Bob Leonard are the reason we have an Empire, Harry. He has given his life to being a soldier. In less than six months he will leave and try to make a life for himself in England."

"Surely that is a good thing, Archie."

"I don't know. Out here he has a purpose. He has respect. You have just come from England what do you think?"

Once more I saw the shadow of his past creep across his eyes as some memory sparked a change in his face, "You may be right, Sir." He had finished his cigar and he stood. "Well I shall go to my little chamber of horrors and see if anyone needs salve or a boil lancing."

When he had gone, I said, "He seems a good sort. I heard him with Pallister and he has a good way with him."

"You are right. We dropped lucky there." He became more serious, "The sergeant major was right in one respect, stay close to the fort, Griff. I had hoped that the last attack and the way we dealt with it might be the end of the matter but from what you said about this German and the evidence you found today, I don't think it is. I will write a report tonight in case the supplies arrive early. General Pemberton and the brass in Cairo need to know what is happening."

The mood at the meal was a little more sombre. The other sections ate first and it was just my section who occupied the mess. The other two would have an early night for they would be leaving well before dawn. Until the sergeant major returned I would be in sole command of the fort. I had done so before but Archie was right, the German had not forgotten us as we hoped he might.

Pallister was eating with us and he was struggling to do so one handed. I smiled as Cave helped him to break the bread. My medical orderly was very much like Graham Allan. He was gentle and thoughtful, "Don't worry, chum, a couple of days and the bandage will be off. You will be right as rain."

Pallister chewed on the bread and said, between chews, "What do I do, tomorrow, Sir?"

An Officer and a Gentleman

Kent could not help himself, "Just sit on your backside Pally, you are excused duty."

The giant shook his head, "I can't abide being idle, Kenty. I need something to do." He looked at me and said, revealingly, "When I am doing nowt I just want to drink."

I nodded, "You can use your right hand, eh?"

"Yes, Sir."

"Cartwright here can show you how to groom a camel. Trust me it will make your camel appreciate you more."

Paul smiled, "Mr Roberts is right, Pally. I never fell off a camel but I was terrified of them when I first came. I discovered that grooming them made them less scary and when we have done that there are other things I can teach you."

Pallister looked gratefully at the gentleman's gentleman, "You know, Cartwright, when you speak you sound as posh as an officer."

"And that is kind of you to say so but I am just like you, Pally, a soldier."

The giant laughed, "Oh no you aren't. I wish I was like you but I am a big, clumsy lump who only knows one thing, how to fight."

Paul said, "Then we shall change that, eh?"

The look on Pallister's face told me that he had been misjudged in the past. He was what the world had made him. His size made others wish to fight him and as drink had an adverse effect upon him then it was a recipe for disaster. Paul Cartwright had seen that. He could not change me but he could make a difference to Bill Pallister. We had changed one of our misfits and we had another four to go.

Chapter 8

I rose early to see off the two sections. As the gates were slammed shut I was pleased to see two of the Egyptian gunners manning the Maxim and traversing as the camels passed beneath them. They were alert. Sergeant Hamed had given them watches of four on and four off. He had rigged an awning over the top so that they could be sheltered from the worst of the sun. I had barely turned when I heard a scream from the tents of the new men.

"Open the gate." When the gate was wide enough for me to slip out I ran for the tents.

I heard Sergeant Atkinson and Cartwright behind me, "Hold on, Sir."

The ones who remained in the tents were my new men. They would all enjoy two nights in the fort after tonight while the captain was away. There was a gate to the compound with the tents but it was unmanned. The Egyptians had gone off duty when the two sections had left. They would be at breakfast. Even as we entered I wondered if we had made a mistake with our duty rota. When I reached the tents I saw the diminutive Dixon holding his hand. His mouth was bleeding. Pallister stood over him and the other men from my section, Kent, Peters and Foster were standing in a circle. I saw that Cave was reaching into his medical kit for a bandage. Pallister's right fist was bloody. It did not take a detective to work out what had happened. I thought that Pallister had turned a corner but I was clearly wrong.

"What is going on?"

They all looked at Pallister as Herbert Dixon said, "That great lump punched me and then crushed my fingers."

Pallister looked to lurch forward but I arrested him with a command, "Pallister, stop." I allowed a silence to fall and then said, quietly, so as not to inflame the situation, "Now, Trooper Pallister, tell me your side of this."

"Sir, I got up early. I needed a leak. I knew that the others had gone on patrol and I saw someone moving in Bones' tent."

"Bones?"

Cave looked up and said, "Trooper Allan, Sir. Bones is his nickname, you know, healing bones and the like. He helped fix Pally's shoulder."

I nodded, "Carry on with your story, Pallister."

"I found this little scumbag going through Bones' stuff and I smacked him."

"That's a lie."

Pallister lurched again but my raised hand worked. He said, "Look in his pocket."

I said, "Cave."

My medical orderly had finished with the bandage and he reached in. He took out a watch. I saw from Dixon's face that he had been caught red handed. He tried to bluster, "Its mine."

Cave opened it and read, "'*To Graham, from Mum and Dad.*'"

"Your name is Herbert is it not?" I saw him open his mouth with another lie and then decided that the game was up. He nodded. My next words were intended for all of them, not just Dixon, "You know, Dixon, that in the Roman Army they had a punishment for men who stole from their tentmates. He was beaten by all of them. I think you have got off lightly. Sergeant Atkinson, take Dixon and Pallister to the grain store. Dixon is on bread and water until the captain returns. As we can't afford a guard I am afraid that you, Pallister will have to be Dixon's gaoler. Can you manage that with one hand?"

He beamed, "Not a problem, Sir."

Atkinson was smiling, "Come on Tea Leaf. We have your card marked. Quick March."

Cave repacked his little bag and Cartwright said, quietly, "Tea Leaf, Sir?"

"Cockney rhyming slang, Tea Leaf, Thief. Trooper Dixon has a nickname now and one I don't think he will like." I turned to face Kent, "All done according to King's Regulations, Kent?"

He shook his head, "I think this is better than King's regulations, Sir."

"Come on then, breakfast and I think we shall enjoy a better one than Dixon."

As we headed back to the fort I spied a kind of hope for Kent and Pallister but I feared that Dixon was a lost cause. Anyone other than the gentle Allan would have given Dixon a far worse beating for stealing. We had a problem.

The doctor ate with me. Trooper Cave had told him of the incident and he had checked that the wound would heal. "I am afraid that he won't be able to use his right hand for some time. There is a chance he might be crippled for life. After breakfast I will set the bones. We had some plaster but I think that Pallister's actions, whilst justified, have cost the section a trooper."

"I am not sure that Dixon was ever meant to be in this troop. I am not prejudging but I think the captain will have little choice but to return him to his original unit. They knew what he was like and tried to dump him on us."

The doctor nodded, "We are a small unit for sure but it is like we are representative of the whole British Army."

I kept the men busy for the rest of the day. I took them out to the firing range and arranged the sand filled bully beef tins as targets. I had the whole section, minus Dixon, and we expended ten rounds each at the target. It was not ammunition wasted for Sergeant Atkinson and I identified weaknesses that we could eradicate. After the noon break I joined them to clean out the ditch and sharpen the sides.

Kent's belligerence returned, "This is work for the Egyptians, not us."

I was going to answer but Wally Wilson did it for me, "When the Turks came to take this fort, Kenty, it was this ditch and the thorns that we planted which kept them out. That and resolute men firing Lee Enfields. Now I don't know about you but I would rather toil in the sun and sand knowing that I have less chance of having my throat slit."

Kent said nothing. He looked around and saw that everyone, sergeant, corporal, officer, medical orderly and batman were all working. No one was having an easy time.

The sergeant major and his men rode in somewhat later than I had expected. It was a good hour after the noon break when I saw their dust as they approached. As they came near me I climbed from the ditch, "Problems, Sergeant Major?"

He nodded to Trooper Gilmore, "Trooper Gilmore reckoned he didn't like salt and has not been adding any to his food. He fell from his camel. Luckily he did not do a Pallister and landed on soft sand."

Gilmore said, "Sorry, Sir. Lesson learned."

"Good, we can't afford to lose any more men." The sergeant major cocked an eye and I said, "Sergeant Ritchie take the men into the fort I need to speak to the sergeant major."

When Gilmore took the reins of Sergeant Major Leonard's camel, my spirits rose. When we were out of earshot I told the sergeant major of the incident. "You did the right thing, Sir, isolating him. Soldiers cannot abide a thief. He will have to be sent back."

I nodded, glumly, "That is what I thought too." I shouted to the men, "I think we have sweated enough today. Back into the fort. The new troopers find your bunks for the night."

They were all eager to have a night inside the fort and the new men raced off followed, at a more leisurely pace, by the original troopers.

"Did you find anything, Sarn't Major?"

"Perhaps, we saw some tracks to the east of the road but then Gilmore passed out and we had no opportunity to examine them. Sorry, Sir."

"Don't apologise, Bob, the priority is training the men up. Your information is handy. I will take a watch tonight with the garrison."

"I will relieve you, Sir."

"Thanks."

When Cartwright heard he insisted upon joining me, "Cartwright, I don't need you."

"A little harsh, Sir, but nonetheless I am your batman and I will wake with you. That way I can ensure you have something hot in the night or I can guarantee it will be a cold one, eh, Sir?"

I had learned that I could not argue with Cartwright. I had Sergeant Hamed wake us at a quarter to twelve. It was the time when the sentries would begin to become sleepy. The Egyptian sergeant told me he would be happy to pull a double duty but I was adamant. If anyone had been watching the fort they would know that more than a third of the troop was escorting a caravan. If nothing else they might choose to scout us out. I took my rifle and cloak. Cartwright had been right. It was, as my father might have said, 'Baltic'.

I walked the walls and spoke to every sentry. There were just five and a corporal. The corporal was at the Maxim. One was in the tower and the other five each had a wall to patrol. Inevitably their patrol was predictable. Two opposite sides walked towards each other leaving almost a quarter of the fort unguarded. Much depended on the eyes of the man in the tower who had a good view of every wall. The two men who guarded the tents were in the wooden tower although with no men in the tents they were not really needed but the extra eyes kept one wall under surveillance.

I joined the corporal at the Maxim. One man could not fire the gun alone and so my presence meant that, if we had to we could. Cartwright brought me some coffee. It was black, the way I liked it with two spoonful's of sugar. He had thoughtfully brought one for the corporal. My servant stared out over the black desert, "How can you see anything sir? It all looks dark to me."

"You look for movement, Cartwright. Shadows should stay in the same place. There is no moon tonight. If a shadow moves it is an animal or a man."

"Ah."

We finished the coffee and Cartwright said, "I will wash these up. Do you fancy a sandwich, Sir?"

I knew my batman liked to stay busy and so I said, "Capital idea." I translated and asked, "Corporal, a sandwich?" He nodded eagerly. I had never known a soldier yet who refused food. "I will take a turn around the walls." When I reached the tower I climbed the ladder, "See anything?"

"No, Effendi, nothing moves." He pointed up at the sky. There were clouds. "No stars to watch tonight."

I nodded, "Stay alert then. Sergeant Major Leonard will be on duty in an hour or so." The Egyptians had learned to both fear and respect the sergeant major.

I stared out and tried to work out what the Turks, led by the scar faced Prussian were doing. I deduced that there must be two motives. The sergeant major had told me that the Germans were training the Turks and it might be training. There seemed, to me,

An Officer and a Gentleman

to be a second reason. The constant attacks were intended to weaken our resolve. Von Kleist was a clever man. When he was at the general's ball he would have picked up the lack of support from Cairo. If we were forced to give up Farafra as we had Siwa then west of Faiyum would be the Turks by default.

I reached the Maxim and placed my rifle against the gun. Suddenly the corporal's head darted to the side. "What is it?"

He relaxed, "Nothing, Effendi. Probably a fox."

We had foxes. They were attracted by the rats that sought food and scraps from the fort. No matter how vigilant we were there was always food that was discarded. I picked up my rifle. "Where?"

He pointed to the north west. I peered into the dark but kept my head still. I was rewarded, after a few minutes when the shadow moved. I raised my rifle and tracked the shadow. It stopped, for five minutes and then moved again. It was making its way to the tents. It could have been a fox but then again… When the shadow stopped again I fired three rounds. There was not only a cry but a ripple of bullets sent in return.

I shouted, "Stand to! Return fire."

The men in the tent compound fired and those on our wall did so too. The corporal said, "Do we use the Maxim, Effendi?"

As Cartwright, sandwiches and rifle in hand, raced up the stairs I said, "No. It would be a waste of ammunition and it will tell them we have the extra firepower." The parapet and sandbags effectively hid the machine gun from view. I had counted just six muzzle flashes. "Put the sandwiches on the wall and load your rifle, Cartwright."

"There is nothing to fire at, Sir."

"Fire at the muzzle flashes."

He lifted his rifle and fired three bullets. There was another cry.

Sergeant Major Leonard arrived, "I have sent the other four non-coms to the four walls and Sergeant Hamed to the compound." I nodded. "Is it an attack, Sir?"

"I don't think so. From the way the shadows were moving I think that they were heading for the tents. Perhaps they thought to slit a few throats." Our men were firing at the muzzle flashes. I saw that the enemy guns had ceased and I shouted, "Cease fire!" The sudden silence was almost deafening. The air was filled with the smell of gunfire. The silence was broken by the sound of hooves. They sounded like camels.

"I think, Sergeant Major, that they have fled."

"Should we go after them, Sir?"

"In the dark? I think not." I laid down my rifle and picked up a sandwich. "Sandwich, Sarn't Major?"

He looked at Cartwright, "Mustard?"

My servant almost snorted his reply, "It is the only way a gentleman can enjoy a corned beef sandwich, Sergeant Major."

Bob and I laughed. Cartwright never changed. Before I bit into the sandwich I shouted, "Sergeant Atkinson, stand the men down and thank you."

"Right, you heard the officer, back to bed my lucky lads."

I turned to Cartwright, "And if you wish to go to bed, too, then feel free."

He gave me such a look that I knew he would stay.

We watched until reveille and as the sun rose I went with the sergeant major and Cartwright, rifles at the ready to see what we could discover. We found where they had tethered their camels and then worked our way along to where I had seen the shadows. We found spent cartridge cases and, most tellingly, patches of blood, blackening as it dried.

Sergeant Atkinson joined us. "I have sent the lads to breakfast, Sir."

I nodded and slung my rifle over my shoulder. Soon the sun would warm the land but while it was still relatively cool I wanted to make sense of the incident. It was not an attack because we had not given them the chance. By the time we headed back to the fort we were agreed that there had been eight men with British rifles, for they had used .303 ammunition and that we had wounded two of them. From the blood Bob reckoned that one was serious. As we tucked into our breakfast I reflected that the lost night of sleep had been worth it.

I sat with the doctor and the NCOs, "Our vulnerable spot is clearly the tents and the compound."

Charlie Atkinson said, "Until Captain Dunn returns we could always abandon it."

I shook my head, "And the camels?"

The doctor said, "We could always bring them into the fort at night. It isn't as though we use the parade ground at night."

Charlie said, "Camel dung, Sir."

The doctor was not a soldier but he was clever, "If I am wrong then put me straight. Camel dung dries in the sun, does it not?" We all nodded. "And can be used as fuel."

"Yes but…"

"Griff, if we have to endure the stink of camel dung for a few hours surely that is better than losing camels."

Bob nodded, "He is right, Sir." He chuckled, "And Dixon can shovel it with one hand. He is having too easy a time of it in my opinion."

And so it was decided. Both the doctor and the sergeant major were in agreement. They also both demanded that I go to bed. I tried to argue but I was exhausted and when Cartwright led me to my bed I did not argue. While I slept they emptied the camp of everything except for the tents. If there was a raid at night, not that I thought there would be, then they would find nothing. I rose when the bugle called men to the mess. When the sun dipped below the horizon the camels were brought in and whilst it was crowded for them, they were safe.

As neither of them had lost much sleep Sergeant Atkinson and Sergeant Ritchie took the night watch but all was quiet. The next morning I had both sections ready to ride. Pallister was put in charge of Dixon and the prisoner was given the dung shifting duty. As we mounted I could not help but smile at Kent's reactions. He was torn. The barrack room lawyer in him objected to the indignity that Dixon was subjected to but he did not like a thief. I watched him wrestling with the dilemma.

"Sergeant Major, you take your section to the north west and I will ride to the north east. Ride for fifteen miles and then return. You know what you are looking for."

"Yes, Sir. Section Three, let us ride."

I let them leave first, "Sergeant Hamed, bar the gate and keep a good watch."

He saluted, "Sir."

We left and used the same formation we had on our first patrol. The night attack had woken the new men to the reality of the desert and an undeclared war. Cairo had closed its eyes to the actions of the Ottomans but we had a reality to face and to deal with. Before we had left I had asked Hunter and Bates to get to know the new men. In the mess the troopers mixed with the men they knew and it was still old hands and newcomers. I needed a team that could work together. As we headed across the desert I glanced back and saw that Hunter and Bates were chatting to Cave and Foster. It was a start.

That day saw the first sandstorm in a long while. The old hands had endured them before but to the new men it came as a shock. I had been in the desert long enough to see the signs and I pointed to some rocks, "Follow me and fast." We galloped. Fortunately all of them hung on and Cave's skills were not needed. "Dismount and make a circle."

I could see the new men wondering what their young officer was doing. They hesitated. Charlie barked, "Just obey the orders, laddie."

"Do as I do, exactly!"

The camels lowered themselves and were a barrier. I sat with my back to my camel and I pulled my keffiyeh to cover my face. I lowered my goggles. When my old hands all copied me so did the new men and it was not a moment too soon. The sand I had seen whipping across the desert struck us hard. If we had been trying to ride then we would have been blinded. Within minutes the section would have been dispersed and men would have been lost. As I had told Horace in the general's palatial home, we had a war against the desert first and human enemies came second. The sand was so thick that I could barely see Wilson who was opposite me. I tried, as much as possible, to keep my head down but I did glance up every now and then to check on the men. The camels would endure the vicious storm but the new men would be, quite rightly, terrified. Even with the goggles and the keffiyeh the sand insinuated itself beneath our clothes. It would be an irritant when we rode again. Sandstorms normally last minutes but this one raged for at least forty-five minutes. Our patrol would be prematurely ended. Even though the camels had afforded some protection there was still sand covering us all. When I decided that it had passed I stood and shook the sand from me. The men rose and the new ones looked dazed.

They looked around and Trooper Foster said, "The desert has changed, Sir! How do we get back to the fort? It all looks different now." He looked around in a panic.

I took out my compass and held it up, "We use a compass and we navigate. The desert is often compared with the sea and it is a good comparison. Like the sea it all looks the same. You will have a better chance of survival out here if you learn to navigate. Have a couple of swallows of water and then mount. We will head back to the fort."

Foster was right in one respect. The landmarks we had used on the way out were now covered by sand and new ones had risen, when the sand that had covered them had been moved. If there had been Ottoman scouts out in the desert then they would have endured the same storm. As we neared the fort I reflected that all things being equal, the captain would be back the next day. I would be happier then.

The fort had endured the storm too but its high walls had kept most of the sand outside. The ditches had been filled and that would give us a job to do the next day. Sergeant Major Leonard arrived back shortly after we did. He dismounted and shook his head, "When I retire I will not miss those sandstorms." He handed his reins to a trooper, "We saw nothing, Lieutenant Roberts."

"Neither did we. We will have to clear the sand from the ditches tomorrow."

"I will sort that out, Sir." He looked south and added, "If the captain was caught in that…"

"I know, his return will be delayed. Carry on, Sergeant Major."

When I reached the office door I heard Cartwright, "I have the kettle on, Sir. Won't be a jiffy."

I had taken off my keffiyeh and cloak outside and shook them. I hung them on the hook just inside. Sand still trickled to the floor. Someone, probably Cartwright, would have to sweep it. I sat down and Harry came in. He sat in the chair, "Do those storm things happen often?"

"Often enough."

He shook his head, "Never seen the like. I was on my way across the parade ground and it was like being pelted with hail stones. What it must have been like in the desert I cannot imagine."

"We just hunker down and sit it out. You cannot move in a sandstorm."

He nodded and took out a cheroot. Cartwright entered. My resourceful servant had brought a cup for the doctor. "Sorry, Doctor, no cakes. There might be some tomorrow," he looked at me, "unless we are on patrol again."

"Not tomorrow, Cartwright. There is a ditch to clear of sand."

He smiled, "Then there will be cakes."

"A handy fellow, what."

I nodded, "When I was first given a batman I couldn't see how I would need one. Now I can't do without him." I sat back and enjoyed the hot sweet tea, "And you, Harry, how are you settling in?"

He blew out smoke and sipped his own tea, "It is an interesting billet. I daresay if we have a little action I might be busier. I spent today with my two patients. They are both much improved. Pallister has remarkable healing qualities. I took off his bandage today and his shoulder appears healed. He must be one of those chaps whose bodies can take punishment easier than others." He sighed, "I spent the rest of the day organising my medical supplies. Never been so organised."

"Do you regret volunteering?"

He gave me the same guarded look I had seen when he had first reported. He smiled, "What is it that the chaps say? A volunteer is someone who didn't understand the question."

I drank my tea and watched him. He said nothing more. I took a chance, "Harry, the desert is not a place to hide. Out here whatever is in your mind grows. It is like the sandstorm. One day whatever demons you are hiding will rise up and consume you from within. Here there are no distractions."

He gave a wry laugh, "I say, Griff, you are some sort of mind doctor, what."

"I am just saying that if you need to talk then I am here and I am a good listener and discreet."

He nodded, "I can see that and when I have my mind in some sort of order I will have a chat but…not yet, eh?"

I emptied my cup, "Just so long as you know," he nodded, "and now the grind of my daily report. The captain will want to know what we have been doing in his absence."

Chapter 9

The captain did not arrive back until late in the afternoon the next day. He and his men looked weary. Cartwright had made honey cakes with sultanas and he brought a pot of tea to the office when Captain Dunn entered. He smiled, "Just what I was looking forward to."

Cartwright said, "Good to have you back, Captain. If you need anything just give me a shout. I shall be with Bill."

I couldn't help smiling. The two servants were like a pair of old women. The would natter and fiddle on. They both kept busy but they liked to chatter.

The captain drank from the cup and closed his eyes to savour it. He opened his eyes and said, "While I enjoy this nectar of the gods, fill me in on what has happened and then I will tell you my tale."

I had an ordered mind but I needed prompts. I took my report and gave the highlights in chronological order. The smile on the captain's face disappeared when I told him about Dixon and then the incident in the night. When I reached the part about the sandstorm he spoke, "Yes, that hit us too. Shaw had spotted a trail and we were following it. We barely had time to hunker down before it hit and the trail was lost."

"Trail, Archie?"

He nodded, "Not bandits and probably Turks. It is why we weren't back sooner. The trail came from the south and west. Shaw has good eyes. I don't like this." He poured more tea into his cup. "Right, first things first. Dixon, you were right to confine him. You wrote up a report?" I held up the sheet of paper. "Good, then when the relief caravan arrives I will send him back to Cairo. His home unit can deal with him."

"I think they are in England."

He shrugged, "Then he will be Cairo's problem. As for the new men...what do you think, Griff? You have seen more of them than I have. The four I have were all angels. You had the villains here."

"I think they have settled in well. Even Kent has modified his attitude. Keeping Peters and Gilmore apart has worked too. They are still raw but they are riding better. Of course, the one who has not had the chance to improve his skills is Pallister but I am of the opinion that it was the drink that made him the monster. We can control that here."

He nodded, "Good. And the doctor?"

I leaned forward, "He is settled in too but he still has his secrets. I gave him the opportunity to chat but he said he wasn't ready."

"Good." He sipped his tea and nibbled on a cake. "These are good." When it was gone he dabbed the crumbs from his lips and said, "And you, Griff?"

"Me, Archie?"

"Are you still pining for the lovely Lucinda?"

I flushed and was about to deny it but remembered how I had wanted Harry to open up to me. I nodded, "I will be happier when I get a reply to my letter, Archie. Did I read too much into our conversations?"

Archie nodded, "Yes, we could all do with letters but no, I do not think you misread anything."

Silence followed. I saw Archie's eyes go to the map. "The Turks, probably prompted by this Prussian, are up to something. I don't want to be caught with our trousers down again. I want two sections ready to ride the day after tomorrow, Griff. We will leave Sergeant Major Leonard here. Let us choose the men to stay." I stood and went with my lists to stand next to the captain. He jabbed a finger, "Robie and Garthwaite struggled on the ride. They are both good chaps but they need a rest. We leave Gilmore and Kent. Perhaps the sergeant major can shape them into something. You think Pallister is fit to ride?"

"The doctor seems to think so and I think it would do him good."

"Then I will have Ritchie and Alexander with me along with McBride and Thomas. You have Bentinck, Dale and Foulkes." I nodded and he stood, "We will head west. I want us to be two pincers. We ride with five miles between us. We will take food and camp." He turned, "We need to be of one mind, Griff. We ride for twenty miles and camp. We rise at dawn the next day and ride for ten miles. That should take us close enough to the border to see if they are up to anything."

"We are leaving the fort a little short-handed."

He shook his head, "We have far more men here than when they tried to take it before besides I think I have the Prussian's game. He knows we are looking to the north and west. The trail Shaw found told me that he is likely to be coming from the west. He will have explored the trail. I hope to catch him heading for us." He smiled, "Don't worry, Griff, I will write all of this down before we leave. It is my responsibility."

"Don't worry about me, Archie. I trust you."

We handed over the watching of Dixon to the Egyptians. They were scornful of all thieves. As the sergeant said to me, "We would have cut off his hand and not merely crushed it." Dixon would not have an easy time of it.

Sergeant Major Leonard was not happy to be left behind but Captain Dunn pointed out that with the two officers gone we needed someone to command and that was the sergeant major. "And if any caravans pass through, Sir?"

"I am sorry but they will have to fend for themselves."

"Sir, just so I know."

We had decided against tents. It was summer and while the nights would be chillier we could wrap up in cloaks and blankets. Those of us with extra weapons took them. We had all learned that you could never have too many guns. I took my sword although I had yet to use it. I would hang it from my saddle and, if nothing else, I could use it to cut thorn bushes. Each section had a cooking pot. We collected the food we would need for the two or, more likely, three days we would be away from the fort. I went, with the sergeant major to examine all the camels. We had spares and we would only take the best.

That night we ate in two sittings. With Dixon absent and with a slightly different attitude from Kent and especially Pallister, there was a lighter mood to the meal. The patrols and duties had made the old and the new men a little tighter and there was even some banter. That was all to the good.

As we ate Archie and I went through the patrol and the timings once more. We would not be relying on the bugle. We only had one and we needed to communicate with one another. We decided that the signal for one to come to the aid of the other would be three bullets fired in quick succession. Maps were an

An Officer and a Gentleman

irrelevancy in the desert and with few landmarks we would have to rely on our watches and the pace we rode at. We intended to trot. Breaks were also included in our timings. There was a margin of error but it was important that we kept roughly in line with one another. Archie had just one more man than I did but as I had the more experienced men it evened itself out.

As I had three more men and they knew the ropes I was able to use them to ride two hundred yards to our right. As Archie and his section were to the left of us I was increasing what we could see. Breakfast was a frenetic affair. We had two sections to feed and to get out before the sun made the desert into an oven. We mounted our camels and headed out of the fort. We diverged almost immediately. We remained within sight for close to half an hour. Then the increasing heat of the desert and the accompanying haze made them disappear. The sandstorm had taught my new men, the benefits of a keffiyeh and goggles. The cloaks also shaded us from the sun. I reflected that we looked more like Arabs than British soldiers. It was no wonder that men like General Pemberton disapproved.

I was acutely aware both of the pace we were keeping and the time. I referred to my watch regularly. It was a good one and had been a gift from my father. I had to constantly force myself to concentrate on the job in hand. Whenever I thought of the watch I thought of my father and that made me think of home. Now, home also meant Lucinda, and she was a distraction. I studied the desert. Like my non-commissioned officers I looked for signs in the desert of other travellers. The caravans kept to the well used caravan trails. I was using a compass to plot a course which, large obstacles not withstanding, would be as straight as I could make it. Thus far we had not seen a hoof or footprint. There were no signs of fires. Rocks had not been arranged to make improvised seats. The desert was empty. We saw signs of animals: the serpentine tracks of snakes, the holes of the desert rats and the distinctive marks of scorpions. The new men did not see them. To them they were just odd marks in the sand. They would rely on me and my officers to ensure that we read the signs correctly. It was a sobering thought that their lives lay in my hands.

We halted at 11.45. Archie and I had agreed on the time. We would rest for two hours while the sun was at its height. We were lucky for we found a tumble of rocks and even better we found a small pool of water that lay beneath an overhanging rock. We let the camels drink and then used our cloaks to rig shelters between the rocks so that we could rest safely. We drank sparingly and ate from our rations. In my case I chose the dates we had been given by the last caravan master. Cartwright lit a fire, he had brought kindling, he would make tea using the pot. He was making work for himself for he would have to use sand to clean the pot out later on. The section would not appreciate having tea flavoured food. He had brought a tin of milk and sugar. I confess that when it was brewed it was refreshing. The whole section had a cup. I think Cartwright had made it just for the two of us but he resigned himself to just the one cup. That single cup of tea made us all feel better and when the time came to move there was no grumbling and even smiles.

Foster said, "Thanks, Posh, that was a lovely cup of tea."

As we rode I turned to Cartwright, "Posh?"

He shrugged, "The new lads think I sound posh. They have given me a nickname. I think it came from Pally. I take no offence, Sir."

Cartwright was an easy-going chap and I was lucky to have him as my servant.

I kept to the schedule and stopped at the times agreed with the captain. When we camped for the night we were close to more rocks. This time we searched them for reptiles and other creatures. The fate of the Turkish soldier was still fresh. We lit a fire and the men arranged their beds. We were all hungry. The handful of dates I had eaten at lunchtime had not been enough. We had flatbreads we had brought from the camp. They had been fresh when we left but they were already getting stale. We added bouillon cubes to the water and then put in the sliced vegetable, barley and chunks of corned beef that made up our meal. When the corned beef can was washed out, the water was added to the stew. Nothing was wasted. It would be a hearty stew and the stale bread would mop up all the juices. We had cans of fruit and that would be our dessert. The empty corned beef tin was used to boil the water for the tea. Cartwright was less than happy but no one seemed to mind the slightly meaty taste to the tea we drank. The smokers smoked and the rest of us just lounged on our blankets. We had a rota for duty. Wilson, Shaw and I would each stand a watch. Two would be of two hours and the last one of four. It would even itself over the next three nights and I had the four-hour dawn watch with Foulkes and Cartwright.

    I enjoyed watching the sun rise over the desert. It began as an almost purple hue before becoming a blue line that was like the Atlantic and then it changed to the lighter blue of the Mediterranean. I had lit the fire and I turned to the east to watch the blue become the red and pink of dawn. It was as though God himself was painting the sky and just watching the sun rise made me feel peaceful. Foulkes checked on the camels while Cartwright busied himself with the tea and the breakfast. It would not be porridge but the last of the flatbreads toasted on the fire and filled with honey and dried fruit. I knew that the men yearned for bacon or ham but this was the desert.

    I looked at my watch as the men finished off their food and swilled it down with the tea. "Ten minutes."

    The older hands knew what that meant: make water and empty their bowels. The new men, even our lawyer, followed suit. I was mounted and looking at my watch by the time they had all finished. I waved my arm and led them on the ride north. We would not travel as far this day. Archie had argued that any further north might take us over the border and that would not be a wise move.

    It was at 10 30, I know because I had just checked my watch, when we heard the sound of gunfire. Then I heard the three distinctive cracks from our left. Even without them I knew that the section was in trouble. If Archie had spotted the enemy he would have fired the three shots first.

    "At the gallop. The captain needs us."

    I wheeled my camel and urged her to run faster. I knew that Wilson, at the rear would wait with any of my men who fell off. This was the first time any of them had ridden a camel at anything like full speed. It was both exhilarating and terrifying in equal measure. As soon as we had begun to gallop I listened for the sound of more guns. There was a slight delay but that was all. Then I heard the crackling of gunfire. I recognised the Lee Enfield and the cracks of Lee Metfords but there were other weapons whose sounds I did not recognise. I drew my rifle. I would not command the new men yet for they would need both hands to control their camels. My officers and experienced men, Cartwright apart, would draw their guns. The five miles between us was approximate but at the speed we were travelling we ate up the ground. I saw, not the captain and his section, but the backs of Turkish soldiers. It looked to be four or five troops. I estimated seventy men. They were in the rocks and using them for cover. Ten men were acting as horse holders. The noise of the gunfight was such that they did not hear us. There were just thirteen of us. I used my rifle to point to the left and right. My experienced men knew what that meant and as they went into a skirmish line the new men followed suit. The Turks were half a mile from us and still had no idea that we were attacking. I had told the men, before we had left the fort, that they were only to fire when I did so. I hoped they could remember the order. I saw beyond the Turks, Captain Dunn and his beleaguered section were using some rocks and their camels for protection. I saw the puffs of smoke from their rifles. I hoped that Archie could see us. If he did then he could order a mad minute and send a hundred and forty bullets at the enemy. If nothing else it would keep their heads down.

Timing was everything. There was no point in having my men waste bullets firing at the gallop. I was ahead of the rest; Scheherazade was the fastest and the best. I reined in and shouted, "Halt!" The others slid into a loose line and finally one of the Turks turned around. I shouted, "Rapid fire!" I raised my Lee Enfield and fired as quickly as I could. When one magazine was empty I loaded another. All around me were the barks and cracks of rifles. Through the smoke I saw men falling. I also saw a European wearing a grey uniform. It was von Kleist. He had an automatic pistol and he was firing at me. It was a mistake on his part as my rifle was more accurate. I turned and fired at him. I was a good shot but luck played a part. A Turk ran between us and my bullet hit him. When I looked again the German had gone and I heard the Turkish bugle. They were pulling out. We kept firing as the survivors mounted and fled.

Sergeant Shaw shouted, "Do we chase them, Sir?"

"Let us see if the others are safe first. Corporal Wilson, take Foulkes and make sure the ones who are still on the field cannot use their weapons and secure any animals."

"Sir."

"The rest of you, with me but watch out for any playing dead."

I counted twelve dead Turks. As we neared our men I saw Archie stand and wave. His arm looked bloody. I saw Bones tending to a man who lay on the ground. There was another man lying on the ground with Pallister standing over him. I reined in, "Cave, give Allan a hand. The captain is wounded."

"Sir."

I walked over to Archie and saw Jack Ritchie putting a cloak over a body. We had lost a man. I waited until Trooper Cave had his medical kit and was attending to Archie before I spoke, "What happened, Sir?"

"Ambush. Peters got it in the first volley. He was on his own to the right. We were lucky that they only had single shot weapons and they fired prematurely. It gave us the chance to take cover and I knew that you would get here. Thanks."

I pointed my rifle to the north west, "Do you want me to give chase?"

For once Archie was indecisive. He chewed his lip and winced as Cave dabbed his arm, "Sorry, Sir."

Perhaps the pain decided him, "Get after him and follow him to the border. Leave the medics, and Cartwright. Take the rest."

"Yes, Sir."

"Cartwright, Cave, Allan and Burton, stay here with the captain. The rest of you mount." I was already reloading and I slipped my fully loaded weapon into my scabbard. "Column of twos. Wilson, stay at the rear with Higgins."

"Sir."

The border was not marked by a line. We just knew, roughly, where it lay. I suspected that the enemy would slow once they came to the border. They would wish to tempt us across. Whilst they had crossed and raided we dare not. Cairo would not brook such contempt for international boundaries. They had the advantage that their animals had been rested. We had ridden hard and galloped for five miles. I glanced around and saw that some of the newer men were flagging. We were no longer galloping but cantering at the ground eating pace that was keeping pace with the dust that marked the Turks. We were in a column of twos but their order was gone and it was a mob. The German would be at the front. I had seen that he wore a different uniform and, as I watched the cloud a sudden image of a second European in a different uniform flashed across my mind. It all made sense. The German would have an aide, a servant perhaps, and that explained the different calibres being used. It would not change what was going to happen but I had an ordered mind and I liked answers.

The cloud appeared to be getting closer. I glanced from left to right to look for any signs that might tell me if we were close to the border. There were none. I began to slow a little. Atkinson appeared on my right, "Something wrong with Scheherazade, Sir?"

I shook my head, "No, Sergeant Atkinson but…"

The ripples of muzzle flashes told me that the enemy had halted to fire a volley from the dust cloud. Had I not slowed then we would have ploughed into the wall of lead. The rest of my men had, like Atkinson, also slowed.

"Return fire!"

I used Scheherazade's back to rest my forearm and waited until I saw a muzzle flash. I fired. I heard cries from my left and right. Men were being hit. I gave an order, "Mad minute!"

I knew that the older ones would understand and I hoped the new ones would copy them. I fired as quickly as I could and when my rifle was empty sheathed it and, drawing my Webley, emptied that gun too.

"Cease Fire!"

The dust cloud had moved and I saw, ahead, two bodies lying on the ground and a wounded camel trying to catch up with the enemy who had ambushed and fled. I turned and saw that Bates and Robie were both wounded, nicked by wildly fired bullets from the dust cloud, "Sergeant Atkinson, see to the wounded men."

"Sir."

"Sergeant Ritchie, take two men and see if those Turks need assistance."

"Let the buggers die."

"Corporal Higgins, we are soldiers of the king and we behave like soldiers."

"Sorry, Sir."

The wounds were not life threatening but the sooner we got back to the others the better. The two Turks were dead. As we were close to the border, perhaps we had even crossed it, I left the dead for their comrades to bury. I led us back to Captain Dunn. It was four in the afternoon when we reached them. I saw that they had a fire going. There was a crude cross that marked where they had buried Trooper Peters. Burton and Cartwright were at the pot and the two orderlies were talking to the captain and their patients. I was relieved that no one else had died.

Allan and Cave saw the blood and raced over to help the two troopers from the backs of their camels. I dismounted and handed my reins to Sergeant Atkinson. I walked over to Archie. He looked up. I saw that his arm was in a sling but he also had bloody trousers. He had suffered two wounds. "Well?"

"We caught up with them, it must have been close to the border and they tried another ambush. Bates and Robie were hit. We killed another two. I decided it was prudent to return."

He nodded, "The right decision." He looked over to the grave, "In the grand scheme of things we have come off best." He used his good hand to point to the pile of cloak covered bodies that marked the Turkish dead, "But it does not sit well."

"Your wounds, Archie..."

"The arm is a clean wound; the bullet passed through and missed the bone and artery. Bones is a good man with a needle. The leg was hit by a splinter of rock. It just hurts."

I nodded, "Then we camp here tonight and head back in the morning or do we..."

I got no further, "We are not crossing the border, as much as I might want to. When we get back to the fort we will write a joint report and I will request Cairo's permission to cross the border should they repeat this."

Cartwright brought me a cup of tea, "Here you are, Sir. Get that down you and we will have food ready in a jiffy."

"Thank you, Cartwright, just what the doctor ordered." I drank some of the tea and felt my thirst slaked slightly, "I saw two men in uniforms that were not Turkish and I recognised the German, von Kleist. I had him in my sights."

"We put that in our report. The name helps give credibility to our action."

"Surely Cairo must act."

He shook his head, "From what you told me we were only sent the men and the Maxim because of Kitchener. He is now in India. We are an inconvenience. Cairo and, I dare say Horse Guards, is only interested in the Suez Canal. They will keep a firm grip on the Nile but the rest?" He shrugged, "A few caravans that are taken will not bother them."

"What about the archaeologists?"

"You can bet that Cairo will not give permission for any more such expeditions." He stared morosely at the ground, "You know I thought we would make a difference. I spied an opportunity to change the way the army worked in the desert." He raised his head, "Your father was ahead of his time. You and the others are an example of how we can fight and act in the desert but Whitehall and Cairo does not like khaki covered soldiers who dress like Arabs. They like red uniforms and men who stand in line to fight. Do you know what Garnet Wolsey said after Rorke's Drift?" I did but I said nothing. "Your father told me. The general said that the eleven men who had been given the VC did not deserve the medals as they hid behind mealie bags." He gestured towards the men who were busy making camp and just getting on with their job, "Even the worst of these chaps is a hundred times more useful that the general staff who still want to fight a war the way we did when we had the Duke of Wellington in command. That is why the Boers almost won their war in the south. Trust me, Griff, this von Kleist is the future. The Prussians won't play by the rules. Our generals think this is a game of cricket and you wait for your turn to bat."

Burton came over, "Here you are, Captain, have another cup of tea. It will make you feel better."

I saw a change come over Archie that day. It was like an hourglass. Up until that moment he was half full but soon the sand would tip to the bottom and he would become half empty.

He took the tea and smiled but I knew that the tea could not heal the hurt in his head. "Thank you, Burton." He sipped it, "Could you arrange the watches, Lieutenant?" He had his composure back.

"Of course, Sir."

Chapter 10

It took two long days to reach the fort. The wounds were not life threatening but the loss of blood had weakened the troopers and there was no need to rush and risk aggravating the wounds. We had burned the Turkish bodies before we left. The spiralling smoke could be seen until the heat haze made it vanish. The new men, Kent apart, appeared to have gained from the encounter. Pallister was a different man. He laughed, joked and bantered with the others. Wally Wilson was next to me and he smiled, "Falling from the camel was the best thing that could have happened to that one, Sir. If we can make sure he doesn't get daft with drink I reckon we have a good soldier."

I nodded, "They all did well."

"You are right, Sir. They are smiling." He shook his head, "They didn't know Peters, the older hands did and that is why there are fewer smiles amongst them, but this is a good thing for the troop. Once we get rid of Dixon we just have Kenty to change."

"I think we just leave him alone and let him work things out for himself, eh? He looks the thoughtful sort and I think he is clever. When we fought he was firing and fighting just as hard as the rest. Everything else is up here," I tapped the side of my head. "That is a battle he has to fight himself."

The fort looked as welcoming as ever when we neared it in the late afternoon. I caught the glint of sunlight from binoculars and knew that Sergeant Major Leonard was watching us and counting the camels. We were at least one day late and I knew that the old soldier would have worried. I had largely led on the way back. I was unwounded and I did not mind taking some of the burden from Archie's shoulders.

As we rode through the gate Doctor Quinn, seeing the bandages, shouted, "Allan and Cave, bring the patients into the hospital."

"Sir!"

I smiled; the hospital had been a place where oil had been stored until the doctor arrived.

"Sergeant Atkinson, have the animals stabled. I am afraid that we will have to use the compound again. We are all back in the fort."

Someone muttered, "Well so long as the Tea Leaf is still banged up we are alright."

No one reprimanded the man who voiced the opinion of everyone in the troop.

Bob Leonard strode over to me as the captain was led by the doctor into the cool of the accommodation. "Bad, Sir?"

I nodded, "Come into the office and we can chat."

Cartwright said, from behind me, "I will have a brew on, Sir, just as soon as I have seen to Scheherazade."

Pallister strode over and took the reins of both Cartwright's camel and Scheherazade, "You go and make the lieutenant a brew, Posh, I can deal with these."

As the sergeant major and I headed into the office Bob said, "Well, there's a sea change and that's no error."

He sat and listened as I spoke. The spiralling smoke from his pipe made me think of my father. Cartwright came in halfway through along with Archie. I vacated the chair for the captain and sat next to Bob. The sergeant major put his pipe on the ashtray and gave us his report. One caravan had come through and had to head south without an escort. Apart from that it had been quiet.

"No relief column then?" He shook his head, "We used a lot of ammo in that little firefight. We shall have to husband the rest until we are resupplied. Take your section out tomorrow, Sergeant Major and head to Abu Minqar. Make sure the caravan reached there and ask them if they have had any trouble."

"Right, Sir." He nodded towards the sling, "The arm?"

"Itchy. The doc was pleased with the work that Bones did. If nothing else we now have better medical treatment."

"From what the lieutenant told me we have done more than that, Sir. The troop did well."

"Sergeant Major, we lost a man."

"And that is sad, Sir, but he was a soldier of the king and we all know that a bullet can come from anywhere at any time. A soldier who does not think that is a fool, Sir."

Archie drank more of his tea and when he put it down he said, firmly, "And as soon as we are given permission, we cross the border and give this von Kleist a taste of his own medicine."

I looked at Bob. Neither of us said anything but I knew we would try to dissuade him from such an action. It would mean the end of his career.

Archie forced a smile, "But you are right in one respect, Sergeant Major, the troop did well and you both deserve credit for that."

Doctor Quinn entered. He was smoking a cigar, "Well, we either have a feast or a famine. A week of doing nothing and then a flock of patients."

I asked, "How are they, Harry?"

"Allan and Cave are both good chaps. Trooper Allan managed to clean out the pieces of cloth from your leg, Captain. If they had not then you might have lost the leg or worse."

For the first time Archie looked surprised, "But it was just a rock fragment."

"That drove fibres of cloth into your leg. You had been in the desert for days and your trousers were filthy. It is often the infection that kills and not the wound. Graham Allan knows his stuff and he and Sam Cave cleaned out every piece of stone and cloth."

Archie shook his head, "I wondered why they were with me longer than the troopers. They didn't say anything."

There was silence and Archie said, "There must be some of the general's whisky left. I think this is the moment to drink it. Open it Griff."

I walked over to the cupboard next to the map and took out the bottle. There looked to be enough for four decent sized drinks.

Burton and Cartwright must have been listening at the door for they entered. Cartwright had four freshly polished glasses and Burton had a tray with a handful of cream crackers. Burton said, "I have been saving these crackers in the hope that we might get some cheese. I have spread some corned beef and Worcester Sauce."

It was a thoughtful gesture and Archie said, "Thank you both, very thoughtful."

I poured the whisky and emptied the bottle. Cartwright took it and the two batmen, grinning like schoolboys left us. Archie raised his glass, "Here's to the 1st Desert Group."

Bob added, "The finest troop in the British Army!"

We each clinked our glasses and then took a mouthful. We were not Pallister. I rolled the whisky around my mouth. It could have done with a splash of water to soften the harshness but despite that it made me feel content. I swallowed and smiled.

Harry Quinn grinned and waved his arm around, "Farafra Fort, the Savoy Grill of the desert." His words made us all smile and we tucked into the improvised hors d'oeuvres. We sat and chatted until the bugle sounded for mess.

Burton entered, "Sergeant Shaw has arranged the eating, Sir. You gentlemen are on the first sitting and the sergeants and corporals will be on the second."

I saw Bob Leonard nod approvingly. His non-commissioned officers were well trained.

The sergeant major took his patrol out the next day. Our impromptu party meant that Archie and I did not write our reports until the next day, I thought that was a good thing, Archie had not been in the right frame of mind the previous day. When I wrote mine I was careful to use non emotive language and used the facts. I mentioned von Kleist by name for I had recognised him and I described the uniform. I thought it was German but I did not say so in the report. I would let others read my words and come to their own conclusion.

The patrol returned four days later and reported that the caravan had reached Abu Minqar unharmed and the headman said that all was peaceful. We were relieved. We limited our patrols to a circuit of ten miles from the fort. Until Archie's arm healed then the patrols were led by me and the three sergeants. We had two out each day; one in the morning and one in the afternoon. It kept the men active and yet did not tire out either animals or men.

It was almost the end of June when the relief column arrived. They were Egyptians although the officer was English. We had more food, ammunition and, best of all, mail. The late arrival told Archie and me that we were low down on the pecking order. We were not a priority. What we did not have was a further intake of troopers. There was also a sealed envelope from General Pemberton. While I entertained Lieutenant Fiennes, the officer in charge of the column, Archie read the report. When he joined us his face was as black as thunder but he said nothing. The lieutenant was merely the messenger. He dined with us and Archie said, "We have a prisoner for you to take back with you. Trooper Herbert Dixon, a thief. There is a report to give to your superiors."

"Righto, Sir." He placed his knife and fork on his plate, "What is it like out here, Sir? I mean how do you stop going crazy? Just the journey across the desert was bad enough but to live out here…it does not bear thinking about."

Archie was still morose and I said, brightly, "One gets used to it and, in the main, the chaps we have here are all good soldiers. We serve the king."

"But doing what? I mean who wants anything in this godforsaken land?"

Archie roused himself, "There are people here who try to make a living. There are others who try to take from them. We are here to protect them."

"But they are not English!"

Archie shook his head, "We took this land and when we did so we took on the duty of care for these people. I know that we make a difference, Lieutenant."

Harry nodded to the fresh-faced lieutenant, "I was a little bit like you when I first came, but in the short time I have been here I have seen the need for a garrison."

"Well, better you than me. If you don't mind, Sir, I would like to retire. My sergeant says he wants to leave at four o'clock in the morning. The chap seems to know his business."

"Of course." He left us and Archie said, "He was not a bad fellow but his attitude shows you what we are up against. I wish that Kitchener still commanded here."

I had no letter from Lucinda, and that upset me, but I had two from my family. It was small compensation. Aunt Sarah's was full of family news and I enjoyed it but it was the one from my father that I left until I had read hers.

April

An Officer and a Gentleman

Son, I know not when you will receive this letter and how you will be faring. I know the situation and it is interesting to see it now from this side of the English Channel. I now know what your Aunt Sarah went through.

We had a visit from a delightful young lady. Lucinda called in with her guardian on their way north to Lancaster. She gave me your letter. It was more than kind of her, she could have just posted it. They both told us of your courage. I had the impression that you and the young lady had exchanged more than a few words. I am pleased. Your Aunt Sarah was most impressed by her. She is such a clever young woman. I liked her courage. She lost her father but did not go to pieces. She has invited us to stay with them in their home. Your Aunt Sarah is keen but I am not sure. We shall see. You must write to me and tell me what your intentions are, Griff. I know you are an officer and a gentleman and that you will behave well.

I now have my first book with the publisher. I am not sure it will make me a fortune but 'Soldier of the Queen' was written to honour my comrades and not to make me rich. I am content and my pension, allied to my brother's investments keep us comfortable.

I know that being given leave will be difficult but if you can get home you should know that we are all desperate to see you. I know that Aunt Sarah will have told you about your cousins and aunt. I will write more in my next letter and hope that I have one from you.

Your father,
Jack

I read and reread the letter. I wondered why Lucinda had not written to me and then realised that there could have been a dozen or so reasons. I looked at the envelope. My father knew the ways of the army and the address had ensured it would get to me. Lucinda did not know such things. For the first time in a long time I wanted to go home. I needed a leave. Even as the thought entered my head I knew that Archie needed it even more; the last patrol had stretched him to breaking point. I had enjoyed a break in Cairo. He had been stuck here for longer than me. It would not take much to drive him over the edge. The line between sanity and madness, out here in the desert, was a fine one.

Surprisingly even though none of us had seen much of Dixon, his absence lightened the mood of the fort. We now had rum but as we were all aware of Pallister's problem it was kept under lock and key. Archie had been a midshipman in a previous life and he used naval tradition to ease the situation. He put Sergeant Shaw in charge of the rum and he asked Wilson and his bugle to call 'up spirits.' The men were given a measure each. I saw Pallister throw down the first ration and then realise what he had done as the rest savoured it. The next day he sipped his. It was the start of a change.

Over the next weeks we fell into a routine. We escorted caravans, patrolled and cleared the sand from the ditch. We were also counting down the time until Sergeant Major Leonard retired. He was not looking forward to the event. As he had told us he thought we were the best troop in the army and he took pride in the fact that he had helped to create it. He and Stan Shaw got on well and when Bob left it would be a seamless transition. Once Archie healed then we were able to have more time off. Each of us had three patrols every four days. Of course, when we had a caravan to escort that upset the rhythm a little. July and August were the hottest months and our patrols were earlier in the morning and later in the afternoon. The caravan escort duties became the worst.

At the end of August we had another relief column who brought more supplies. It was a different lieutenant who came.

He handed a manilla envelope to Archie. There was a long message for the captain and he asked me to stay in the office while he read it. I had seen the pile of mail on the desk and recognised a woman's hand. I had a letter from Lucinda. I was only half listening to Archie for I was desperate to read the letter.

Archie slammed down the letter angrily and reached for the whisky bottle. He took two glasses and poured a more than generous measure into each one. "Damned fools! They have read our reports and we have been reprimanded for killing Turkish soldiers. They ambushed us. In Egypt!" He downed half of the whisky. I sipped mine and waited. The outburst was not over. "We are told to restrict our activities to escorting caravans." He shook his head, "And there will be no further replacements. It was my fault we lost Peters and now we are being punished for my mistake."

I shook my head, "There was no mistake, Sir. It was a good plan. We killed more of them than we lost and we chased them back over the border. By anyone's estimate we won."

He shook his head, "You don't see it, Griff, do you? He knew we were coming. That he didn't anticipate your arrival is immaterial. He had a good ambush set up and he had numbers. He cannot have known our intentions but he planned. This German is clever. He is paying a game with us and learning how to beat us."

"I don't understand."

He poured himself more whisky and said, "I am not sure you attended his class at Sandhurst but there was a chap there who spoke about a Prussian game, Kriegsspiel. Some Prussian invented it and it allowed officers to fight battles without losing men to try out strategies. I think thus von Kleist is using those lessons. It is like chess but without the strictures of a board. He is not done with us yet. He will do something else and I am not clever enough to work out what."

I could see what he meant but, like Archie, I could not see how to thwart him. I sipped more of the whisky and said, "Anything about leave?"

He picked up the letter and read, "*'At the discretion of the commanding officer.'* Do you want a leave?"

I did but it did not seem prudent to say so, "Perhaps in a month or so but…"

He snorted, as he drained his glass, "Well I had better stay here. If I went to Cairo then I might say something that would end my career." He gave a wry laugh. "Perhaps that is not a bad idea."

I said, "I was thinking more of a leave back to England."

He glanced over at the mail and smiled, "Ah, the archaeologist's daughter. If you wish to go then you have my permission. God knows you have earned it a dozen times over." He pushed the letters to me, "Here you are, adjutant." I stood and he saw that I had barely taken two sips of the whisky, "Your drink…"

I shook my head, "A bit early for me, Archie."

He took the glass and poured it into his, "Waste not, want not."

I went to the mess and shouted out the name of each man as I handed him his letter. There were only four. Most of the men had no communication with home. The troop was their life and they seemed content. Even Kent did not complain so much. He was teaching Pallister how to improve his reading. I think that Trooper Kent had missed his vocation. He was a natural teacher.

I went to my quarters. Cartwright saw me and the letter in my hand. He beamed, "I will bring you a nice cup of tea, Sir."

"Thank you, Cartwright." I slit open the letter with my knife. It smelled slightly perfumed; I think it was lavender. I was sniffing it when Cartwright returned. He said, "I will see that you are not disturbed, Sir. They brought some cream crackers, Sir, and cheese. The cheese is a bit smelly for the trip did it no good. Still, it was thoughtful of someone to think of us. We shall serve it tonight."

When he had gone I opened the letter.

Lancaster

April

Dearest Griff,

We have just reached our new home and I have put pen to paper to write, as I promised.

On the way from the ship to our home we called in to deliver your letter. What a delightful family you have. I so admire your Aunt Sarah. Your Aunt Bet was kindness itself but the greatest pleasure I had was meeting your father. He is a hero of Rorke's Drift and a writer. You must be so proud of him. I know that he was almost bursting with pride when he spoke of you. I confess that I became a little tearful as he spoke for I knew that I would never have the chance to speak again to my dear father. You must get home to see your father as soon as you can.

My guardian has a position at Lancaster College, teaching archaeology. It is a small college with few students but it is employment. I am to be his assistant. We will be able to use my family home at Grasmere from time to time as my guardian plans to take his students to Ambleside and excavate the Roman Fort there. It will keep my mind occupied.

I think of you often and that is strange for until I met you I had little interest in young men. My father, before we left for Egypt, had tried to introduce me to eligible young men but they seemed shallow and lacking spirit. I find myself thinking of our words on the journey to Faiyum. I should like to continue our correspondence and when you return home I would be honoured if you and your father could visit with us at my home. I have included both addresses. The house we rent in Lancaster serves a purpose but it is not home. The college terms are just ten weeks in length. I know you are a clever fellow and will work out which address is the best one to use.

I pray that you and your troopers are safe. Give my regards to Trooper Cartwright. He is one of the most delightful men I have ever met and you are lucky to have him as a servant.

All my love, Lucinda
I hope I am not too bold with my salutation

I kissed the letter. I read it again and again. I know not how long I studied it but the half-drunk tea was cold. Cartwright knocked on the door, "Everything alright, Lieutenant?"

"Perfect, Cartwright, and Miss Lucinda sends her best wishes to you."

"That is kind. Sorry to bother you, Sir, but Captain Dunn wishes a word about the report to Cairo."

I nodded and folding the letter I stood, "I shall come." I was back in the world of the troop but my heart was in England and I would ask Archie for permission to travel home as soon as I was able.

Archie had spoken to the lieutenant and told him he had a report to send back. The lieutenant had planned on leaving in the early morning and so it meant we had to write quickly. We sat in the office and wrote a new report. The one we had already written covered what had happened but Archie wanted to respond to the new orders. I tried to tone down his anger by suggesting milder words but he wrote it all. He made it clear that we would do everything in our power to protect the caravan trail. He bordered on the line that was close to insubordination. The next column would return in two months, I feared that by the time October came there would be an order for Captain Dunn to return to Cairo. It was only as the lieutenant left that I realised Sergeant Major Leonard would be returning to England with the next column. I decided to wait until then to ask for a leave. I could not abandon the troop. Lucinda and my father would have to wait.

Once September arrived there was a marginal lowering of the temperature and an increase in the number of caravans. We were forced to curtail our local patrols to just one a day. We often had a caravan to escort to Siwa and a second one to Abu Minqar. We knew the caravan masters who travelled to Abu Minqar but the ones who went to Siwa were new to us. We soon got used to them. As the ones to Siwa went no further they had the luxury of an escort both going and returning.

The Egyptian garrison at Siwa had gone and the oasis was a little wilder. The caravan master was glad to have my section

An Officer and a Gentleman

with him. Cairo had been short sighted in not replacing the poor officer who had destroyed the garrison. My first patrol was to escort a caravan to Siwa. I did not know the caravan master but he was a thoroughly nice man. He insisted that I ride next to him. He was an older man. I guessed that he was older than my father. He cracked open pistachio nuts as we rode and offered some to me. He spoke of the desert as we rode. He was more like Archie than any trader I had ever met. He viewed the desert like a sea. He knew its moods and he knew its dark side. Ismail had been travelling the caravan routes for fifty years since he had been a boy. He was a grandfather and had many children. He described his home. It sounded palatial and I asked him why he did not stay there and enjoy the comfort of a life made rich by toil.

He smiled, "Effendi, I know from other merchants that you are good at what you do. You are hard working. I began riding these lands when I had seen little more than ten summers and had to cling to the camel like unwanted baggage. I am used to hard work. I take but one day a week off and that is to honour Allah. I have a duty to my family to continue to trade. I ride this route because my sons travel to Abu Minqar and Mut. They work as hard as I do. I cannot stop." He tapped his chest, "In here, my heart makes me go on, for my family."

I enjoyed his company and his men clearly adored him. One was his grandson who was learning to become a caravan master. I saw the old man teaching him with a word here, a suggestion there, a look of disapproval or a nod. I had no children. I was not sure if I ever would have them but Ismail was a good model to follow. I had been denied my father when I had been growing up. He had been a good teacher when he was home but I had more contact with Aunt Sarah. There was nothing wrong with that but a boy needed his father. How would I be there for my son?

As we neared Siwa, Ismail became serious, "This is a nest of vipers, Effendi. They were bad enough when your soldiers were here but now that they are gone I fear that your men will need to be night guards along with my men. They are thieves and cutthroats. They do not follow the ways of God."

I saw what he meant from the moment we arrived. The smiles on men's faces were not in their eyes. I watched them eyeing up my men's weapons and the camels that we rode. While Ismail and his men set up their wares I beckoned to Atkinson and Wilson, "We need to keep a good watch on everything here. Tell the men to keep their weapons close to hand. Use the slings for the rifles. Hobble the camels. Make a thorn fence around both the caravan and our camels. We will have three shifts tonight."

"These aren't like the people at Abu Minqar then, Sir?"

"No, Wilson, they are not. Ismail seems a canny bloke and he docs not trust them. I know it is a hard duty but it will be safer this way." They nodded and I pointed west, "And the border is not that far away. I know we bloodied the Turks' noses but…"

Sergeant Atkinson nodded, "You are right, Sir. We will warn the lads."

Ismail's men had levelled and loaded guns as they traded. By the time darkness fell half the goods had been sold. I saw the old man nod approvingly when he saw my curtain of thorns and my vigilant men.

"We will feed you this night, Effendi. Your men will watch?"

I nodded, "I will watch."

He beamed, "You are a good man, Effendi, and I will pray that Allah watches over you."

The men ate with the caravan guards. We had no tents but we shared the food and the fire of the caravan master. It was spicier than we were used to but we all seemed to enjoy it.

The grumpy Kent came over to me as I went to make water, "This is not proper food, Mr Roberts. You can't tell what it is." He sniffed the plate handed to him by the driver and wrinkled his nose.

Charlie was nearby and he said, "It is likely to be lamb or goat, Kenty. There will be fruit in it and nuts as well as spices."

"Fruit? And lamb?"

I shook my head, "Don't you have apple sauce with pork?"

"Well yes sir but…"

"And mint sauce with lamb?"

"Yes but…"

"There is mint in here and I am betting that the mint sauce you had was sweetened. Give it a try. If you don't like it then there is always corned beef and flatbread."

An Officer and a Gentleman

It was the sight of the others gobbling the food and wiping up the juices with their bread that won the day. I think he enjoyed it but he was not the kind of man to admit it.

As I had the middle watch, I had eaten with Ismail while Wilson, along with Kent and two other troopers, stood guard. The food was good. It was spicy but I was used to that. The fruit in it made it sweet. I knew that my tastes had changed. I still looked forward to the English food I would enjoy when I was back in England but I knew that I would yearn for something spicier.

His men made coffee after the meal but I took the tea made by Cartwright. I needed some sleep and the coffee would keep me awake. When I explained Ismail was not offended. "We are similar, you and me. Although I am old and an Egyptian I can see that we both do our best. We try to do the right thing. Sometimes that is not enough. It is a wise man who knows how to take those setbacks and learn from them."

I wondered if Archie had learned from the ambush or was he allowing it to seep into his soul and poison his mind?

"Do you have a woman in mind to be your wife?" I almost choked on my tea. He smiled, "I am sorry, Lieutenant Roberts," my name sounded strange when he said the unfamiliar words, "it is just that you seem to me a personable and attractive young man. I would have expected there to be a young woman in your life."

I looked down, "There may be but she is in England and there is no prospect of my return, any time soon."

He sipped his coffee and nodded, "There are many paths our feet take us. You know that from the desert. When the sand blows and covers the trail we find another route. You are clever and you will find your way."

When I was woken to take over from Wilson I thought about Ismail's words. He was wise. Like my father he had spent a great deal of time away from his family yet he had been successful. I would find a way. My decision to stand watch was a good one. As I stood with Cartwright and Sam Cave while Bates stood by the camels, I saw a shadow move towards the thorn fence. We were stationary and standing next to a stand of trees. I gestured for the others to stay where they were and drawing my Webley I moved silently towards the shadow. There were two shadows and they were men trying to get at the pile of unsold goods by Ismail's tent. I saw knives in their hands. I think the knives were to cut open the bundles and steal them but they were weapons and I would have to be careful. They were so intent on reaching the goods that they did not notice me moving behind them.

I pressed the Webley into the back of the head of one of them and hissed, "I think you know what the punishment is for theft. Perhaps a bullet in the back of the head might be kinder." Their heads whipped around. The Webley was not a big gun but to the two men it would have appeared like a cannon. "Drop your knives and stand."

Ismail emerged from his tent. I saw that he had drawn his sword and was bare headed. He might be old but he looked like a man who knew how to handle a sword. The two men looked from me to him and then dropped their weapons.

"Walk." I headed towards the oasis. Cartwright and Cave had levelled rifles and the two men reached the end of the thorn fence. "Spread the word. From now on we shoot first and ask questions later. Do you understand?"

The man whose head had felt the Webley nodded and said, shakily, "Yes, Effendi."

I walked back to Ismail who had sheathed his sword. He handed me the knives, "Souvenirs perhaps?" He smiled, "We are both good at our jobs."

When we reached Farafra Ismail gave me some dates and said, "When next I pass through I will bring a gift for you."

"You have no need, Sir, I am just doing my duty."

He frowned, "A man can choose to give a gift and I choose to give one to you." He smiled, "I like you and I wish to thank you. But for you we might have lost goods. I think that the next time we are at Siwa they will not try to steal."

I nodded, "Forgive me, Ismail, I did not wish to sound ungracious. I would be honoured to take a gift from you."

Chapter 11

I had two days back in the fort where I took short patrols out. The next time I had a caravan to escort was at the start of October when I escorted a caravan to Abu Minqar. It was one of Ismail's sons, Mohammed, and, like his father, insisted that I ride with him. He told me how much I had impressed the old man. "My father is the head of a large family. When he passed seventy summers, last year, we all gathered to honour him. With his sons, daughters and grandchildren there were seventy of us." I knew that Arabs liked numbers and I could see the significance of the age and the number of guests. "It was a special occasion and we are lucky to have such a man as the head of our family. When you are at Faiyum we would be honoured for you to be our guest."

"I did not know your father was seventy. He looks and acts younger."

"He works hard and his body is lean. I shall try to be like him but I fear that I am a shadow of the man." I could hear the admiration in his voice.

I enjoyed the ride not least because it felt safer than the ride to Siwa and the border. We had hit the bandits hard when we had first come and now they avoided the route. I doubted that we needed to escort the caravans but I knew that the first time we did not would end in disaster. We left Mohammed at Abu Minqar and headed back. I rode next to Kent. The other so-called villains had all changed since they had arrived. I was proud of that for it showed we were a good troop and perhaps their bad behaviour, Dixon apart, had been because of their original units. Kent was still a work in progress.

"So, Trooper Kent, have you taken to life in the desert yet?"

He was always suspicious and said, "Why do you ask, Sir? Have I done something wrong?"

I changed my tack, "Why did you volunteer?"

He gave a wry laugh, "Let us say, Sir, that I was pushed. My officers and the sergeants didn't like me. I was told to volunteer or my life would be hell."

"Then why did you join up at all?"

"My dad was a soldier. I was brought up in a town filled with soldiers. The other lads all joined up when they were old enough."

I stabbed in the dark, "But you wanted to carry on with your schooling."

For the first time his guard dropped, "How…"

"You are clever and I have seen the books you read. Listen Kent, I don't want an unhappy man. I can arrange for a transfer to another regiment. Perhaps one based in England. You could be a clerk or…" I shook my head, "look I am not sure what but I am certain that there are things you could do in the army."

He looked ahead and then said, "Sir, you are a good officer, I can see that, so I would rather stay here than risk going to another regiment where I might find myself in bother." He shook his head, "I know I moan a lot and I can be an awkward so and so but I quite like this posting. There are no distractions and I can think and read."

"Well, if you change your mind, I have a few contacts and…"

"Thank you, Sir. I appreciate it."

I sensed a change. I was not sure he would ever fit in as well as the others but he had made a start and from that conversation on he smiled a little more and complained a little less.

Captain Dunn took Ismail on the next patrol to Siwa. I knew that the old man was disappointed but he was a gentleman and was gracious. That night, as they camped at our oasis, one of his men came for me. I went to the camp and Ismail handed me a velvet bag. "The gift I promised you, Lieutenant Roberts."

I opened it and inside was an exquisite ring. There was a small ruby in the middle surrounded by seven diamonds, tiny ones admittedly but diamonds, nonetheless. "I cannot accept this. It is too valuable."

He smiled, "You have forgotten my words already." He folded my hands around the bag and the ring, "It is a gift and it is given. When you are ready to take a bride then you can give this to the young lady. Tell her how you came to have it." I nodded. He smiled, "Lieutenant Roberts, Griff, it pleases me to do this and I will sleep happier knowing that I have given it to you. My wife died last year and this was her ring. I have too many daughters and it would have caused arguments if I had given it to any of them. This is better."

After they had left I looked at the ring. Was this a sign?

Archie was drinking more heavily these days and I was glad that the ride to Siwa and back would prevent him from doing so. Ismail would chat to him and Archie would not wish to offend the old man. I was left in command of the fort. When Mohammed returned a day or so before the captain was due to return I gave the escort duty to Abu Minqar to Bob. It would be his last such duty. We expected the relief column in a fortnight and this would give him the chance to sort out what he was going to take back to England and to say his goodbyes. He had become close to the new men. He and Sergeant Ritchie had got on well.

The fort seemed empty without two thirds of the troop. I took my men to clear the ditch. They complained, of course, but it kept them occupied. As we were expecting more ammunition I allowed them, as a reward, to fire the Maxim. Even Kent enjoyed it. I let them fire fifty bullets each at corned beef cans filled with sand. The gun had only been fired once, the first day the gunners had set it up. When we finished they were all like giddy girls who had enjoyed their first kiss. The Egyptian gunners then had their own practice and showed my troopers how the gun should be fired. The gunners impressed my men. I had not done it for that reason but I was pleased with the result.

Ismail and Lieutenant Dunn arrived back the next day. Ismail came into the fort. Archie said, "Ismail will be returning immediately from Farafra. Siwa, it seems, is growing and they need more goods."

Ismail beamed, "It is good for us and good for Siwa. Perhaps you will escort me the next time, Lieutenant Roberts."

"I would be honoured."

After he had gone Archie said, "I know he will make money from the trade but I do not like the men of Siwa."

"I know what you mean but a profit is a profit."

Bob returned from his last patrol and seemed more than a little sad. "I shall miss all this you know. Here I can make a difference. Back in England…"

We waited for the relief column. It was overdue. When the two Egyptian riders rode in late one afternoon we knew that something was amiss. They were, it seemed, relief for two of the garrison who had been granted a leave. They handed a letter to Archie, "But where is the column? Where are the supplies?" The two troopers looked blank. It was not their fault. Archie read the letter and shook his head, "Things are going from bad to worse. The commander at Faiyum has not enough men to escort the supplies. They are waiting for us but we have to fetch them." He dismissed the two men and said to me, as he poured himself a whisky. "They want us gone and this is the start."

"I will take my section, Sir. Sergeant Major Leonard can come back with me, eh?"

"Good idea."

It was an impromptu party but sometimes they are the best. It was hurriedly arranged and we allowed a double tot for the men. Pallister was most restrained. We had changed him. I was touched by the affection my men showed the old sergeant major. Normally such men as the sergeant major were feared, largely hated, but Bob was different and even Kent and Pallister who had come to hate the rank seemed sad to see him go.

I said my goodbyes that night for we would be leaving early. "Bob, it has been a pleasure to serve with you."

"We have the ride to Faiyum to chat, Sir."

"Griff."

"Griff."

"This is the time for goodbyes, Bob. I have learned a lot from you."

"No, Griff, you needed no lessons from me. Your dad taught you well. I should like to have met him. Talking to the lads who served with him I can tell that we would have got on."

"Then call and see him back in England."

"I couldn't do that, Griff. Land uninvited."

"I will give you a couple of letters Bob. They will be your invite."

He visibly brightened, "Well that would be a treat. Thank you, Griff. You know, you would have made a good sergeant."

Many people might have been insulted but I was honoured. I left him to continue with the party and wrote two letters. One

An Officer and a Gentleman

was for my father and one for Lucinda. I slept well that night. For my troop it was exciting to be going to Faiyum. For one thing it was the nearest thing we had to a town and for another it was not the usual duty. It was a journey that necessitated a couple of stops and, at the second, we found ourselves camped close to Ismail who was on his way back to Siwa. He shared his food with us. The sergeant major had not met him but the two got on. Ismail was interested in the man who had no family and was leaving the world he had known to go back to a new one. I let the two chat, I would have more opportunities to speak to Ismail. In fact, I relished the prospect for the old man was wise.

We parted the next day as we headed for the last part of our journey. Bob said, "I should like to have talked to him a little more."

"I know what you mean. When you have lived as long as he has then you learn a great deal. I feel like I have a better view of the world."

He nodded, "And I feel like a young man in comparison. You know, I have been looking at this through the wrong end of a telescope. I should be more like your father and Ismail. When your father retired he didn't sit and bemoan the fact that he had lost the use of a limb. He started something new. Ismail just keeps on doing what he is best at. I don't know what I shall do but I have a long train ride to the sea, a longer sea voyage and then a train to visit with your father. I shall buy plenty of tobacco in Cairo and think things out."

I was sad to leave Bob at the station. He shook hands with all the men and after shaking my hand gave me a salute. I felt honoured. I had given him my letters and he strode off to catch the train. My good feelings evaporated when I went to the supply depot. There were more than enough men to have escorted our supplies. The second lieutenant was clearly embarrassed when I pointed it out to him. Eventually he gave me the real reason, "Orders, Sir. General Pemberton said that we could not afford to leave Faiyum unguarded. Sorry, Lieutenant, the major's hands were tied."

I knew that from the major's absence. He had not wanted to explain it to me and left it to the second lieutenant. By the time we had checked all the supplies and taken them and our animals to the camp we would use, it was too late to leave. "We will make camp here. Sergeant Atkinson, take charge, Cartwright, Pallister, Kent and Cave, come with me. We shall buy some treats for the men."

They were pleased to be going into a town. Their pay was in the chest that Atkinson and Wilson were watching but they still had the money they had been paid when the last column had arrived. They could make purchases. I was confident that they would not be able to buy alcohol. This was a Moslem country. We went to the town and bartered for tobacco. I bought dates and figs. When I had bought all that I needed I gave then fifteen minutes to buy goods for themselves. I said to Cave, "Sam, keep an eye on Pallister, you know what I mean."

"Don't worry, Sir, having tamed the bear none of the lads want to risk him reverting."

Cartwright and I went to an Indian who sold tea and coffee. I knew that Cartwright and Burton prided themselves on their tea. The tea sent in the supply train was adequate but no more. We invested in some good tea and coffee for the officers. I thought that we deserved the treat.

When we rejoined the others I saw that they had all made purchases. Pallister shook his head, "Not a proper town, this, Sir, no boozers."

Kent sighed, "Pally, how many times have I told you, the people in this land do not drink. They take hashish but don't drink."

Pallister shook his head, "No booze and all this sand. I feel sorry for the poor buggers. Sorry, Sir."

"Right, let us head to the garrison."

Kent asked, "Why, Sir? We have the supplies."

I nodded, "We have the supplies the army has sent but we can buy from the commissariat some things that they don't send us."

I headed to the commissariat office. They were about to close up but seeing an officer the old soldier who ran it smiled and said, "Yes, Lieutenant, what can I do for you?"

"I need half a dozen bottles of whisky and two dozen bottles of beer."

He looked around as though he did not want to be overheard, "Is this sanctioned by Major Howard, Sir?"

I slipped a guinea across the counter, "What do you think?"

He grinned, "Would you be Lieutenant Roberts, Sir?"

"Yes, how did you know?"

"Well, for one thing, I was told you were coming and for another you look like your dad. I was with him in Wales. We were young soldiers together. I stayed on at this billet when my time was up. How is Jack?"

All the time he was talking he was gathering what we had ordered.

"Enjoying life. He is a writer now."

"Well, I'll be. Who'd a thought. He always had something about him. Tell him that Dai Jones was asking after him."

"Jones? You don't sound Welsh."

"Welsh Dad and an English mother. As we lived in Gloucestershire I grew up with an English accent. I can still sing though." He pushed the items over and gave me the price. I paid him and he pushed the guinea back, "Wouldn't do to take money from the son of a butty. Good luck in the desert, Sir."

As the troopers carried the whisky and beer from the building I said, "The beer, Pallister, is a treat for the troop. There are two bottles each. One for tonight and one for tomorrow night. Is that clear?"

I could not see his face but I heard the smile in his voice, "Right, Sir, Christmas has come early!"

The food was already cooking when we arrived back. I secured the whisky with the payroll and then sat around the fire with the others. It was getting colder at night. Pallister had been right; Christmas was just around the corner and I would have another Christmas far from home. I had done the maths and there was one spare beer. As I didn't drink mine either that meant two spares. We had two more nights of camping. That meant on the last night I could let three men have an extra beer. There was a good spirit amongst the men.

Charlie was next to me and he said, quietly, "Good shout, that, Sir. A bottle of beer is not much but to the lads it is a real treat."

I nodded, "Christmas for the new lads will be hard in the desert, Charlie."

"Aye, Sir, that it will."

The journey back was slower. We had camels that were heavily laden. Only four had been supplied. Had I known I would have brought some of our spares. We had to spread the load amongst all the camels. I thought Kent might have objected but he didn't. We took it steady and rested for longer at noon. There was no rush. Better to get back with no injuries to our camels than race and risk an injury. I gave the bonus beers to Pallister, Hunter and Foster. Without knowing there would be a reward, they had all worked harder than anyone. Their delight made me smile.

We were in good humour when we reached the fort. I saw that the tented compound was empty. That meant the patrol to Siwa had not yet returned. Sergeant Ritchie would be enjoying his first real solo command. I was looking forward to talking to Ismail again. While the camels were unpacked we took the letter from Faiyum for Captain Dunn, the whisky and payroll to the office. Although there was nothing to spend it on, the men would be looking forward to having pay in their pockets. Archie and I went through the books and counted out each man's money. We wrote the names on the envelopes provided by the paymaster and sealed them. Sergeant Atkinson had our men line up and they took their pay. We did the same for the Egyptians and then the money for the patrol in the desert was locked in the chest. That done Archie opened a bottle of whisky. It was late afternoon and the sun was over the yard arm somewhere so I joined him. We had given the letters out to the men when we had paid them. There were only a couple and I guessed they were leftovers from the last delivery. Perhaps they had been left behind. The report from Cairo remained unopened. I think Archie dreaded opening it.

I pointedly glanced at my watch. "Might as well open them, Archie? Get it over with."

When he did I saw that it was a single sheet of paper. That did not bode well. Two pips fell from it. Archie read it and tossed it to me. While I read it he downed the whisky and poured himself another one.

The orders were stark. The British Garrison was to return to Cairo on the 1st of January. Egyptian Camel Corps would replace us and Sergeant Hamed was promoted to lieutenant to be garrison commander. The men were to be returned to their units. I turned it over, "It does not say anything about us, Archie?"

"Us?"

"You, me, Shaw, Atkinson, you know, the ones who are 1st Desert Group." Just then we heard the bugle for mess and we stood.

He snorted, "Perhaps they are hoping that we will resign. Dammit I might just do that."

"You are too good an officer for that. They will have something else in mind." I looked at the letter again, "Good news for Sergeant Hamed, though."

Archie smiled, "Yes, he deserves it. We will tell him about the promotion but let us wait until Ritchie returns with the patrol until we tell the others." We were near the mess and we heard the laughter, "Let us not spoil the good mood, eh?"

We both smiled as we entered and the men cheered. Archie said, "Sergeant Hamed." He was with the cooks and wore an apron. He would be serving the food.

He came over, looking slightly nervous. "Yes, Sir."

Archie held out his hand and said, "Congratulations, Lieutenant Hamed. You have been promoted." He dropped the pips in his hand. The whole mess erupted. He was popular with the troop and the garrison.

He looked stunned, "An officer, I never thought…"

Archie shook his hand, "You deserve it. You had better make your corporal a sergeant, eh? Good news for everyone."

We sat at the head of the table. There was a buzz of excitement around it. I saw Pallister telling Graham Allan about the beer. Kent was also animated as he spoke to Simon Flynn. The two got on. I had seen them playing chess. I suddenly thought back. It was when Flynn had brought out the chess set that the sea change had begun with Kent. He had something other than King's Regulations to interest him.

Cartwright and Burton brought our food and we began to eat. Archie said, "A damned shame. We have just got these chaps where we want them and they are going to be disbanded."

"Look on the positive side, though, their home units will all benefit from what they have learned."

Archie snorted, "Pah! I am sorry, Griff, but they will be like square pegs in round holes. We are a fine unit but good for one thing and we are doing it here. Do you think these lads can go back to standing in lines and fighting in the way they did in the last century? Our way of fighting is the future and Cairo and General Pemberton has just put it back fifty years." He poured himself another whisky, "You know, I think I shall resign my commission. I have had enough of this nonsense!"

Chapter 12

The caravan had not arrived by the next day. I was concerned but Archie was philosophical about it, "They might have stayed an extra night, Griff. They were well laden when they left. Old Ismail said that it would make their fortune. If they are not back by tomorrow then you can take some men and look for them."

The letter from Cairo had ripped the heart from Archie Dunn.

I had just finished my breakfast when I heard the sound of a shout from the walls. I raced out into the parade ground. I looked up at the fighting platform. One of the Egyptians shouted, "Lieutenant Roberts, three men are heading here. They look to be hurt."

I turned and shouted, "Stand to! Doctor, incoming wounded." I could not see Harry but I knew he would be in earshot.

Archie emerged. His eyes were red, "What's up?"

"Three riders. It looks like Number Three Section." I ran to the stables and saddled Scheherazade. I did not bother with asking for help. If the sentry saw a problem then speed was needed. "Open the gates."

Men were racing to the walls, rifles at the ready, as I galloped through the open gate. I spied the three men and saw what the sentry had meant. One of the camels was limping and two of the riders were slumped over the saddles. I recognised Corporal Alexander leading them but the two others were hidden by their keffiyeh and cloaks. My camel was fast and as I wheeled her around to ride next to the corporal, he said, "Thomas and Foulkes are in a bad way, Sir."

I looked and saw that his leg was bleeding, "And you are wounded." He looked down as though he was surprised. I looked up and saw Allan and Cave, along with Sergeant Shaw and Corporal Wilson approaching. They had wasted no time. "Don't worry, boys, help is on the way."

The two orderlies each took a patient and my two NCOs took the reins. I heard Sam Cave say, "Now then Thommo, what have you been up to."

I said to Alexander, "What happened?"

He sighed and, as he began to speak, I heard his voice start to break, "The Turks, Sir. They came at night. The bastards in Siwa helped them. We were set up. They were all friendly, like, when we arrived and brought us food. Ismail was delighted at the money he was making. Jack, Sergeant Ritchie, set the guards," he shook his head. "The Turks must have been hiding in the houses. The first we knew was when they shot Ben Bentinck. They were all over us. They hit Jack and then started firing at the men asleep. They had no chance."

"And you, where were you?"

"I was with Thomas, Sir, at the camels. They were moving as though there was an animal close by. I know now that Turks had deliberately spooked them to draw us. I saw them when they shot Thomas but we managed to drop the three of them. I suppose that was when they hit me. We were running back when Jack was hit again. He shouted for me to get the survivors away. By then there was just old Ismail, Gilmore and Foulkes. If it had not been nighttime we wouldn't have escaped. As it was Gilmore and the old man were both wounded." He gave a sad smile, "The old man took out three with his sword. I shouted for him to get to the camels. The three of us got away and we headed for home."

We passed through the gate and while the others helped Foulkes and Thomas from their camels Harry and I lowered the corporal to the ground. Harry said, "Can you walk?"

"A little."

"Get him to the sick bay. These two look in a bad way."

I let Alexander lean on me and Cartwright appeared to support the other side, "What you need, Corporal, is a nice cup of tea. I shall make you one once we are inside."

Harry had anticipated blood. Oilskins covered the tables. Alexander climbed on one and when Cartwright left us I took my knife and cut open his trousers. The bullet had scored a long line along his thigh and there had been bleeding but the artery and bones had been missed.

"What happened next?"

Archie appeared in the doorway. He had a glass of whisky. He handed the glass to the corporal who drank it in one, "Thank you, Sir, I needed that."

I said to Archie, "The men of Siwa conspired with the Turks. The section and the caravan were attacked, "Go on, Alexander."

"The five of us headed across the desert. There was a moon and we took the caravan trail." He shook his head, "On reflection, Sir, that might have been a mistake. They knew where we were going."

Archie said, "Even if you had gone across the desert they would have known where you were going."

He nodded, "I dropped to the back with old Ismail." He smiled, "He was a game bugger, Sir. He had a bullet in him, I saw the blood but he kept the sword in his hand. He kept saying as how if the lieutenant had been there we would have beaten them. He thought a lot of you, Sir."

I dreaded hearing the rest. Ismail and Gilmore were not with the survivors. That meant they were either dead or prisoners.

"It was dawn when they caught us. Gilmore was the least injured of the others. I told Bentinck and Foulkes to keep going. I drew my rifle and so did Gilmore. I asked the old man to join the other two and he said," he shook his head, "*'They have killed my grandson and now they will pay. Tell my son that I died well.'* I couldn't stop him, Sir. He wheeled his camel and charged the Turks. Gilmore and I emptied four magazines and we hit half a dozen. The old man killed another four before that German shot him. He emptied his pistol into his head. I tried to get Gilmore out of there. We turned and headed for the other two. I didn't see Gilmore fall but I heard the bullets. His camel appeared next to me and when I turned I saw him sprawled on the ground. Even as he tried to rise they shot him. I chased after the other two." He looked almost in tears, "I did my best, Sir."

Harry came in, "Right, out you go, you two. This man needs to be treated. You can finish your questioning afterwards. It isn't as though you can change what has happened, can you?"

We left the sickbay. I saw the other two being carried on a stretcher to the sleeping quarters. Four men carried each stretcher in silence. We were all stunned. Burton had a pot of tea ready and the bottle of whisky was on the table. Archie sat down and poured whisky in the tea. He drank some and then said, "I got the end part. Tell me the rest."

I went through it as dispassionately as I could and when I finished I began to drink my tea. Archie stood and went to the map. "Hindsight, Griff, is always perfect. I should have been suspicious when the men of Siwa said that they wanted more goods. They planned this after your visit. That was the first time in a long time Ismail had taken a caravan to Siwa. They must have planned it with that German. He learned from his first ambush. This was easier. He knew exactly how many men would be with the caravan and he had the complicity of the Siwans. From what Alexander told you our men gave a good account of themselves but it is hard to see how they could have stopped the Turks."

"We will have to tell Ismail's family. His grandson was killed."

He nodded. Then he turned and poured whisky in his cup, "And we will punish them."

I shook my head, "Sir, no one wants that more than me but we are risking a war here. Cairo will not support us. They will hide this atrocity like they did when the archaeologists were attacked."

"I know Griff, and that is why I am going to leave you in command of the fort when I leave. I will take only volunteers. No blame will be attached to you."

I stood and I was angry. My knuckles were white, "I am insulted, Archie. Do you think I will sit here and let my men follow you into this disaster? They will all want to go. I am begging you, as a friend, cool down and think about this."

"Think about what, Griff? I have no career. This troop was the brainchild of Lord Kitchener but I was the one charged with creating it. You helped me. I cannot simply sit by and not do something about the men who died."

I sat, "You cannot bring them back and this way more men will die."

"Volunteers, Griff, and if no one comes with me then so be it. I will go alone."

I shook my head, "I am sorry, Sir, but I do not see you as a Don Quixote and besides every man jack will volunteer."

"My mind is made up."

"Sleep on it, Sir."

He shook his head, "When we have eaten then I will ask for volunteers. I will also write my final report so that the blame will all be laid at my door. I am prepared for that." He smiled, "I might rejoin the navy."

The only one to whom I could talk was the doctor. "How are the men, Harry?"

"Alexander will recover. Foulkes will take some time and Thomas…I had to take his hand. It is his left one but…" He shook his head and lit a cheroot, "As for their mental state. That is anybody's guess."

I took a chance, "The troop is being disbanded, Harry. Cairo is getting rid of it."

He nodded, "Sad but I can see why. This little incident will probably confirm their view."

"Archie wants to lead a raid and attack the Turks."

For the first time since I had known him I had shaken Harry. "What? Madness. More men will die and…you must stop him, Griff."

"I have tried. He is going to ask for volunteers."

"Perhaps it is his mental state that is the problem."

Archie did not wait for the meal to be ended nor did he wait for Harry and me to join him. As I walked in he was saying, "So if any of you wish to volunteer, we will be leaving after breakfast."

I saw the men look at each other and then, beginning with Pallister, one by one they stood and said, "I will volunteer." It became a sort of echoing approval to the raid.

Cartwright looked at me and said, "You, Sir?"

Harry grabbed my arm, "Griff, no…"

I gave him a sad smile, "I don't have much choice do I, Harry? I think it is a mistake but these are my men. Half of the ones going are in my section. Atkinson and Shaw served with my father. I have to go."

Cartwright said, "Then I shall go with you, Sir."

We had just begun to eat, although I was in no mood for food, when we heard a cry from the gate, "Riders!"

Perhaps we would not have to go to the Turks to get revenge, they were coming here.

147

"Stand to. Allan and Cave stay with the doctor, you may be needed."

By the time we reached the wall I saw that it was a false alarm. It was another caravan, for Abu Minqar this time. I shouted, "Open the gate."

When I recognised Mohammed I knew that the horrors of the day were not over. We had bad news to break. Mohammed clearly had no idea what was about to befall him. He dismounted and came to us with a smile on his face, "Good to see you. Has my father returned from Siwa yet?"

Archie said, "Come into the office. I will speak with you."

I spoke to the caravan guards, "Use the compound by the oasis. Your master will join you there soon."

"Thank you, Effendi."

I heard the cry from the office before I had even opened the door. He turned as I entered, "Is this true, Lieutenant, or a cruel joke?"

"I fear that it is true but your father wanted you to know he died well."

Harry had followed me and I asked, "Doc?" Alexander was his patient and it was up to the doctor to sanction this.

He nodded, "Come with me."

Alexander could speak Arabic but not well and I went with the two of them. Alexander spoke and I translated. I saw Mohammed taking in that the corporal was wounded. "Thank you."

When we emerged he said, "I will bring men with me when you go for vengeance."

I cursed Archie. He should have said nothing. The fort would be left with just the Egyptians, Doctor Quinn, three wounded men and the four camel drivers who would not be coming with Mohammed. I worried that von Kleist might be clever enough to anticipate what we would do and attack the fort while we were absent. His men had not pursued Alexander and the others when they could have done. If they had chased and taken them then we would have been blind.

The next morning, as we ate, I voiced the fears that had filled my head during my nightmare filled sleep. Archie had been blinded by the attack and would not listen. "If you are so afraid then stay here."

"I am not afraid, Archie."

"Then trust in me and all will be well."

We left the fort silently before dawn. Mohammed and four of his men were with us. I insisted on being the vanguard. I did so because I feared that Archie's judgement was clouded. I had Charlie Atkinson and Cartwright with me. Charlie had good eyes and I knew that Cartwright would fret if he was with the main column.

The sergeant said, "Sir, are you worried that we might be ambushed?"

"I am, Sergeant. This is well thought out and Alexander and the other two were allowed to return to the fort. Why?" I saw him thinking. "Keep sharp, both of you." We were riding two hundred yards ahead of the column. The men were in twos with two flank sentries on each side. As I was leading I was choosing the route. I knew the land relatively well and I took us on a route which sometimes avoided the caravan trail. There were places where the caravan trail passed through rocks where an ambush could take place. I rode around those places, adding to the length of our journey but ensuring that we were not attacked there.

When we stopped at noon Archie took me to one side, "Griff, this is taking too long. Keep to the caravan route."

"No, Sir. That is a recipe for disaster. What is the hurry?"

"We have to catch them before…"

His voice tailed off and I said, "Before he gets back over the border?" He said nothing, "If you are right and that is what he has done then he will be safe inside his fort and our journey will be wasted. We cannot attack a fort."

He was silent for a while before he said, "They might stay in Siwa."

"Do you really think he will be at Siwa, Sir?

"They might fortify it."

He was clutching at straws. The drinking and the deaths had taken their toll. Externally Archie Dunn was still the same leader I had happily followed to the desert but inside he was broken. "And if they do then we will bleed to death attacking it. The people of Siwa might have conspired with the Turks but they would not be seen to oppose us. Let me lead you on this goose chase, Sir. I will keep us as safe as I can for as long as I can."

I found us a relatively safe place to camp that night although we reached it somewhat later than we normally would. I had Sergeant Shaw set sentries and we enjoyed hot food but there was a sombre mood. We had lost friends. Bentinck had been popular. Wally Wilson and he had been close. As I walked the perimeter I reflected the irony of Sergeant Major Leonard's departure. He would have been with the patrol and I was not sure that he would have been taken in as Ritchie was. Jack Ritchie had been a good soldier but he had been new to the desert. As we had crossed the desert I had thought of such things. Bob Leonard might have been suspicious. From what Alexander had said they were given food by the men of Siwa. We had all spoken of the Siwans before and none of us trusted them. Ritchie had been taken in.

I took the watch before dawn. I saw and heard nothing but there was a prickle at the back of my neck that made me suspicious. We left at dawn and Archie said, "I will lead today, Lieutenant. You have taken enough chances. You stay with the column. I will use Mohammed and his men. They have good eyes." I began to speak. He held up his hand and I could smell the whisky on his breath, "That is an order."

"Sir."

"Burton."

"Sir. See you later Paul."

"You be careful out there."

"It can't be that hard, you did it yesterday." The two bantered as they always did.

As we mounted my batman said, "Mr Dunn is not himself, Sir. Perhaps the doctor should have stopped him from leaving the fort."

"I don't think he would have listened." I turned, "Sergeant Shaw, put Atkinson with the flank guards to the north of us and Wilson to the south. I want eyes and ears there too. Have Higgins at the rear. He is dependable. Make sure that everyone has a bullet up the spout and listen for my orders."

"Sir." He paused, "You think there might be an attack before we get to Siwa?"

"This German seems to me a very clever chap. He has outwitted us every step of the way. We rode our luck a couple of times and poor Ritchie and Ismail ran out of it. I expect trouble before we get to Siwa, yes."

Archie pushed harder than I had done. We kept to the caravan trail and I got the impression that he and Mohammed were racing to get to Siwa before the day was out. It was impossible, of course. If we achieved that feat it would cost us camels and men. The pace began to tell on us. The column was strung out even more than it had been. I was glad that Higgins was at the back. If anything happened he would hold the men there together. If he was at the front he might try to go to the aid of the captain.

It was when the captain, Burton and the scouts galloped hard that I knew there was trouble. Instead of charging after them I shouted, "Stand to!"

Cartwright said, "Sir, what about the captain?"

"This may be a trap." I peered around the desert. I saw that Atkinson and Wilson were doing the same. They were my men and were well trained. They wanted vengeance too but they were professional. I saw, ahead, mounds of sand close to the road and ahead of where the captain and Mohammed were racing. I took out my binoculars and focussed on both the sandy humps and the road. I saw what looked like markers next to the road. Even as they came into focus I saw Mohammed and the captain dismount. I saw that Burton remained mounted and had his rifle levelled. They were not markers, they were stakes and I saw Ismail's head, his was distinctive because of his beard and another three I took to be my men.

I shouted, "It is an ambush. Skirmish line twenty paces between each man. Higgins, Kent and the two medics, stay at the rear."

I heard the chorus of "Yes, Sir."

"At the trot." I did not pull out my rifle. I would use my pistols. We had a long line of men and we were well spaced out. I peered at the humps and saw, to my horror, that the lumps rose and Turkish soldiers appeared. They opened fire at Archie and the others. There were men on both sides and the six of them stood no chance. Burton managed to empty a magazine before I saw him plucked from his camel.

There were too few Turks for this to be the real ambush. There were just twelve or so. I heard Wilson shout, "Ambush!" He and the other two flank guards wheeled their camels and I saw them open fire at an, as yet, hidden enemy. I shouted, "Atkinson, hold your position. The rest, wheel left and follow me."

The wheeling meant that I was on the right of our line. I heard the gunfire and saw Corporal Wilson leading the other two back to us. There were clearly superior numbers coming at us. I saw the line of Turks charging after Wally and his flankers. Once again their single shot weapons had saved us from greater losses but I saw Peters clutch at his arm. He had been hit.

I shouted, "Fire when you have a target." I knew that most of them would wait until we were within a hundred yards of the Turks. Even then it was only my most experienced men who might achieve a hit. As I had learned, luck always played a major part in such encounters. I knew that Cartwright was angry. He had seen his best friend butchered and he was firing as fast as he could reload. He was not the best shot in the world but luck favoured him and I saw a Turk fall from his camel. Many of my men were firing now but I held my pistol until I could be sure I would hit one. Cartwright's shot had hit the man on the extreme left of the Turkish line and so I guided Scheherazade to go obliquely at the charging soldiers. I began to slow to give myself a better platform. I saw an officer whose attention was at the fore. Like me he had a pistol in his hand and was firing as quickly as he could. I fired three bullets and he fell. I switched my target to the bugler next to him and emptied the Webley into him. I drew my rifle as Cartwright and I ploughed into the Turks. Shaw was in the centre and he was a tower of strength. He was one of the best shots in the troop and I heard his Lee Enfield, along with the others, rattling out death. The Turks had numbers but we had the firepower of the Lee Enfield. It began to tell. I emptied the rifle and reloaded. It was not quite a mad minute but, combined with those around me, it began to have an effect and I saw the two grey uniforms at the rear begin to shout out orders. When the Turks began to turn I heard my men cheer.

They thought it was over. I became cold. We had to hurt them. "Hold and empty as many saddles as you can. No pursuit!"

An Officer and a Gentleman

With our camels halted and the accuracy of the Lee Enfield, we had plenty of time to hit as many of them as we could before they were out of range. Sergeant Shaw hit the last of them. It was a fine shot at a range of more than five hundred yards. I reloaded and shouted, "Sergeant Shaw, take your section and collect any stray animals."

"Sir."

"Higgins, stay with the wounded."

"Sir."

"The rest of you, with me." I did not want Higgins to see his dead officer first. As we raced across the desert we saw the Turks who had hidden in the sand as they headed for the bodies and the camels. They must have thought that we were too far away and battling to bother them. Scheherazade raced ahead of the others and one of the Turks saw us and turned. He realised his dilemma, pointed his rifle and fired. It was too far from me and missed but it alerted the others. They turned and ran back to their camels, all thoughts of ransacking and despoiling the bodies driven from their minds. The one shot cost the Turk his life. Scheherazade's speed was such that in the time it took for him to chamber another bullet and aim his gun we were one hundred yards closer. The range was not too far, especially as I fired five bullets in rapid succession. He was hit and spun around. Two others fell before the rest managed to escape. We reined in and I ran to the bodies. They were, as I expected, all dead but we had stopped any violations of the bodies.

"Cartwright, cover the bodies."

"Sir."

I turned and saw that Pallister had stopped close to us too. "Give him a hand, Pallister."

"Sir."

I walked to the heads. I saw that it was Bentinck, Ritchie and Gilmore whose heads were also on the stakes. I walked over to them. I first took Ismail's head. He looked surprisingly peaceful, "I am sorry I was not here to protect you."

I heard a voice behind me. It was Shaw, "Let me do that, Sir."

I shook my head, "We will both do it." I saw that the Turks had keffiyeh. "Take the keffiyeh and wrap the heads in them. We can bury them back at the fort."

By the time the rest joined us the bodies were covered and the heads hidden. I knew that I had to keep hold of myself for the sake of the men. I forced my voice to be calm and measured. "Put the bodies on the camels. We will take them back to the fort. They deserve that. Shaw, have men take the weapons from the Turks."

"Sir."

Higgins and the medical orderlies arrived with six wounded men. We had lost not a man and none of the wounds were life threatening. That was a mercy.

"Shaw."

"Mount."

"Lead them off, Sergeant Shaw, I will stay at the rear with Higgins."

"Sir."

"Ride until dark, I want to be as far away from the border as we can."

"Sir." Before he rode off he said, "You did all that you could, Lieutenant. But for you we might all have been killed. I am sorry about the captain, but…"

"Thank you, Sergeant."

Both Cartwright and Higgins kept looking back at the four stakes which looked vaguely like the crosses from Golgotha. I said, "Face ahead and the future. Put their deaths from your minds. You cannot change what happened as much as you might want to."

There was silence as they faced the front once more. Higgins said, "What now, Sir?"

I knew what he meant. Archie had not wished to tell them of the disbandment of the troop but now seemed a good time. If I told the two of them then Higgins would be prepared and it would help me when I spoke to the troop at the camp.

"The troop is to be disbanded in January, although I have the feeling that after this it may be sooner."

Cartwright sighed, "So it has all been a waste then, Sir?"

"It depends on your point of view. We kept many caravans safe. Think of the lives we saved while we held the fort. We stopped the fort from being overrun and in terms of numbers while our losses will hurt us they are nothing compared with the ones we punished for their actions."

Higgins snapped, "They don't mean anything to me, Sir. I just want Captain Dunn back. He was a good bloke."

"He was and believe me, Higgins, I am mourning him as much as any but we are soldiers. There is a time for grief and for mourning. It is not yet that time. We have wounded men to get to safety and burials to be arranged."

"Sorry, Sir, I should have known. You two were closer than any."

He was right but in the last days he had changed. It had all begun when he made one tiny mistake and Peters had died. It was like a pebble falling from a mountain. It could have just trickled down and been forgotten but, instead, an avalanche had ensued.

At the camp I kept the men busy. Having told Higgins I had to tell them all the news. Leaving Cartwright and Higgins on watch I gathered them around and told them of the disbandment. The reaction of Kent surprised me, "Sir, that is not right. We did nothing wrong. This is a good troop, Sir. We are well led and, if you don't mind me saying so, Sir, we are bloody good at our job."

Pallister clapped him on the back, "You are right, Kenty."

I nodded, "You are right but I have to tell you, Trooper Kent, that the writing was on the wall before you new men were recruited. There were officers in Cairo who did not like the idea of an independent group who did not conform to their idea of an army. I am just pleased that we achieved so much in such a short space of time."

Stan Shaw asked, in a quiet voice, "What happens to us, Sir?"

"The men who were recruited from other units will be given the chance to return to them."

Kent snorted, "Not me! They got rid of me once and I am not going back with my tail between my legs."

"As I said they will be given the chance to return to their regiments." I emphasised the word, *'chance'*. "However, as some of you have not served in any other regiment I am guessing that arrangements will have to be made. I will ensure that you all retain your rank and the Camel Corps is always desperate for new men. You NCO's could transfer to the Egyptian Army."

Pallister looked at Kent, "That sounds alright, eh, Kenty. I am used to camels now but it won't be the same, Sir, not without you and Captain Dunn."

"No, you are right." I turned to Shaw, "Sergeant, arrange sentries. Change them every two hours. This is no time to be caught napping…again."

It was the nearest I came to criticising Archie.

When we arrived back with the laden camels it cast a pallor over the fort. I know that Harry had feared the worst but Lieutenant Hamed was clearly shocked not only with the deaths but the news that the troop was being disbanded. I consoled him, "I think that is why they promoted you, my friend. The border is now your responsibility. The first thing we need to do is to bury the dead." I turned to the camel drivers, "You will need to take your dead back to Faiyum."

The senior driver, an old man of an age with Ismail, nodded, "Thank you, Effendi. I know that you did all that you could. We will leave in the morning but this will mean a blood feud with the men of Siwa. They will have to pay." I knew I could not dissuade him or the family but it would make life harder for Lieutenant Hamed.

We buried our dead in our small cemetery. When Wilson played, 'The Last Post' I saw men weeping. I held it together as best as I could. That night I wrote a report that I would send with the drivers to Faiyum. The letters to the families of the dead would have to wait. I knew I could not rush them.

I knew that a response would soon be forthcoming from Cairo. We did all that we could to make the fort more secure. In addition, we made mud walls around the cemetery. Lieutenant Hamed told me that so long as there was a garrison at Fort Farafra then the cemetery would be safe. I reflected that once there had been Romans here. Who guarded their graves? I made a gift of my Lee Enfield to the lieutenant. He had always admired it and I could not see me needing it again. I gave the rifles from the dead and Archie's pistol to him too. He could distribute them to his men. We all knew the value of weapons out here, at the frontier. Archie's sword I would send to his

An Officer and a Gentleman

family along with the letter that I knew I had to write. I kept his compass. The wounded were all fit to travel and it was almost a relief when a week after our return the two riders arrived with our orders. A letter addressed to me told me to present myself at a court of enquiry in Cairo along with Doctor Quinn. We were the surviving officers.

That night we held a party. I gave the last two bottles of whisky to the mess and told Sergeant Shaw to break out the rum. I knew it was a risk with Pallister but the troop was dying and deserved a wake. Surprisingly enough while Pallister drank a lot he did not get into any fights and seemed almost paternal as he helped those who had drunk too much to go to bed. Before the end they sang sentimental songs and swore undying friendship. I knew it was well meant but was ill fated. They would be split up and the golden memory of Fort Farafra would be just that, a memory.

Harry and I sat apart and watched. He was in a reflective mood, "You know, Griff, I dreaded coming here but needed to escape. Now it feels like home. I have not been here long, barely a moment in the grand scheme of things, but I have been happy. We must keep in touch."

I sighed, "And as much as I might like that, Harry, we both know it is unlikely." He nodded and blew out a long plume of smoke. "Tell me, Harry, what is the secret you brought here?"

He sighed, "I knew you knew. I could see it in your eyes. You are a perceptive chap, Griff." He stubbed out the cheroot and took another from his case. He shook his head, "Just four left, still I can buy more in Faiyum." He lit it, "The usual, a woman. I was engaged to Helena. She was the love of my life but a week before the wedding she ran off with my best friend." He shook his head, "That was not the worst of it. Everyone, it seemed, knew about it but kept it from me. I thought everyone was laughing at me and I ran here to hide." He laughed, "Only now can I see that in the greater picture it means nothing. I lost a faithless woman. Poor Archie, Burton, Ismail and Peters lost their lives. I shall resign my commission and become a country doctor. I will treat people with headaches and bad stomachs and deliver babies. I am sure there is another woman out there for me. And this time I might be lucky and find one that is not faithless. And you?"

"I fear that with Archie dead they will be looking for a scapegoat. My military career may be ended and I am not happy about that."

"Surely not. You did everything you could and I shall say so at the enquiry."

I shook my head, "What do you think? They will vilify a dead man?"

"But the Turks! The German!"

"Will be ignored. The information will be stored and used diplomatically but they will not risk a war over the death of a couple of soldiers and an old Egyptian."

He thought about my words and shook his head, "It is not right."

"Of course it isn't but that is the world in which we live."

Part Two

Half Pay

Chapter 13

It was the same lieutenant I had met the last time who greeted us when we reached the base at Faiyum. It was fortunate that we had said our goodbyes on the journey across the desert for the two of us, along with Cartwright, were given our orders. He handed me an envelope. "There is a train for you gentlemen and your servant at four o'clock this afternoon." I glanced at my watch, it was twelve, noon. "Your men will be housed here until their future is decided."

That was not good enough for me. "Lieutenant, these men have served their country and they are to be treated well. Listen to what they want, do you here? I don't give a damn what pompous General Pemberton wants or does not want. If I find that these men have been misused in any way shape or form then you will have me to deal with." I had no idea if I would have any power but whatever I had would be used for the men.

The lieutenant recoiled, "Sir, I agree, and the major has charged me with dealing with them. I can assure you that their wishes will be taken into account."

I smiled, "Sorry, for that, Lieutenant, it has been a difficult time."

He leaned in to speak so that only Harry and I could hear, "Sir, I have read the reports and in my view you and these men deserve medals and not a court of enquiry."

"Thank you." He stepped back, "Well men, it appears this is where we say goodbye. We three are taking a train this afternoon. The lieutenant has promised me to look after you as though you were his own." They were not his words but I saw him nod as I addressed them. "I do not know if we shall meet again but know that it has been a privilege to lead you. I know that Captain Dunn felt the same way." I saw a few of them straighten as I said the words that came from my heart. "I include all of you in those words. The 1st Desert Group had a short life but I was proud to have served in it." I snapped my feet together as did Harry and Cartwright. I saluted. "Thank you!"

Almost as though it had been rehearsed, which I knew it had not, they all came to attention and their hands came up in the smartest salute I have ever seen. I could see the emotion on the faces of the older hands. Suddenly Pallister belted out in a voice of which Sergeant Leonard would have been proud, "Three cheers for the best officer in the British Army. Hip, Hip, Hooray!" I found myself welling up but forced myself to hold it together.

When my hand came down I managed to croak, "Thank you, 1st Desert Group, and thank you, Pally." I turned and impulsively handed him the reins of Scheherazade. "And try riding this one. She might suit you."

"Thank you, Sir."

I stroked her nose, "Farewell. Be gentle with this one and he will be a good master, won't you, Pallister?"

"Sir, you know I will and when I ride her I shall think of you."

I dared not risk breaking down and I hefted one of my bags on my shoulder and turned. Cartwright had his bag and a smaller one of mine. We walked in silence towards the station. We didn't say a word and we did not look back. The memory of that farewell stayed with me for a long time and, even now, when I feel at all down or depressed I think back to that poignant farewell.

We reached the station at two o'clock as we had visited the tobacconists and bought Harry's cigars and went to the waiting room where there was a buffet. Cartwright went to buy us tea. He frowned when he returned with it. "They put the milk in second!" He was appalled.

We chatted inconsequentially for a short time. We were just filling the silence. The silence made me, and I dare say the others, remember and the wound was too raw for remembrance.

When the four Egyptians entered I recognised one of them as being one of the caravan masters. They walked purposefully towards us. I smiled as I saw some of the European passengers move away. The four had daggers on their belts. The older of the four said, "Lieutenant Roberts."

I found myself smiling. He had said my name in the same way that Old Ismail had. "Yes?"

"I am Ismail ibn Ismail. I am now the head of the family. My brother and our sons wished to come here to say goodbye. We heard you were leaving and when you were seen in the town we came as soon as we could. That our father died is a tragedy but that he died in the company of brave men gives the family comfort. Take this as a token of our esteem and our thanks. My father liked you."

The youngest of the four handed me a beautifully carved cedar box. It looked like it could hold, perhaps, four cigars. I opened it and inside was a pendant with a ruby hanging from it. The ruby was the same colour and cut as the ring I had been given.

"We know that my father gave you a ring and this goes with it." He smiled, "He told us that he planned to give you this when you brought your young lady to Egypt. Sadly they will never meet but take this as a token."

"I am honoured and touched." He was about to leave but I could not help but add, "I know anger and hatred burn in your hearts but you have lost three of your family. If you seek vengeance how many more will die?"

He said, simply, "We are men and we will do what we must do."

They bowed and left.

The doctor looked at the jewel, "That must be worth a small fortune."

I gave a sad shake of my head, "It is worth more than that, Harry, for it is a gift from beyond the grave."

When we were on the train I opened the envelope we had been given. I saw that we were to be put up in a good hotel. I knew it was not the best but it was not the worst either. The letter told me that we would be picked up by a carriage, the following day, and taken to the residency. They were wasting no time. When we reached the hotel I was pleased that everything was organised but disturbed when the manager said, "We have two good rooms for you, Effendi. You will be here for three nights, I believe."

As the three of us sat in the bar I told them my fears. "The enquiry begins tomorrow and they think that we will be done by the end of three days. It sounds to me as though this is a foregone conclusion." I shook my head, "I bet the conclusion is written already."

Cartwright nodded, "When I was talking to the concierge he told me that our passage back to England was already booked. We leave Egypt in five days."

I downed my drink in one, "Then I have nothing to lose. I shall speak the truth and shame the devil."

"Sir, your career."

I laughed, "I have no career, Cartwright. It looks like you shall be back to being a gentleman's gentleman."

He shook his head, "I have a gentleman already, Sir, and he suits me. I shall not seek another."

His words made me stop drinking. I needed a clear head. That night he took my best uniform and found somewhere he could press it. There appeared to be a sort of brotherhood of servants which transcended race, creed and language. When he returned he polished my boots until you could see my face in them.

"I shall rise early, Sir, and run you a bath. Your hair needs cutting and now that we no longer need a beard then a good shave will do the trick."

I said, sincerely, "Thank you, Cartwright, I don't know what I would do without you."

He merely smiled and left.

It had been the truth and yet when I was at Sandhurst the last thing I expected was to enjoy having a servant. Having seen how the blue bloods acted, I wondered that any servant would suffer such abuses.

I slept remarkably well considering I knew that my career was ended. Aunt Sarah would be pleased and my dad? I honestly did not know. I think he would be angry with senior officers and disappointed that the army had changed so little. It was as Cartwright was shaving me that the thought I had kept hidden in the dark recesses of my mind came to the fore. Lucinda. How could she countenance a relationship with a cashiered and disgraced officer? Any chance of courting her would end with the court of enquiry. That depressed me more than anything.

Cartwright was also wearing his number ones and when we met the doctor to take the carriage poor Harry shook his head, "It seems I am the pauper at the feast. You two look so smart."

"I am sorry, Doctor Quinn, I should have thought. I could have pressed your uniform too." I could see that Cartwright was already berating himself.

"Gentlemen, your carriage." The smartly dressed corporal ended any discussion about our state of dress. As we clip clopped down the Cairo street, it felt to me like a tumbril taking me to the guillotine. There were armed sentries outside the residency. Seeing the carriage and our uniforms they snapped to attention as we passed. For some reason it seemed to please Cartwright. The driver said, "I will wait here, Sir, to take you back when you are finished."

Once inside we were greeted by Horace Jamieson who was also dressed in his number ones. He held out his hand to me, "Good to see you, Griff, sorry it is under these circumstances." He was smooth and silky. He was the aide once more. He smiled at Cartwright, "Cartwright."

"Sir."

"And you must be Doctor Quinn. I am Lieutenant Jamieson, Horace. If you gentlemen would follow me." He led us from the hall. I noticed that the floor was marble and our boots echoed on it. The high ceilings also looked like marble but I knew that sometimes they used, as the Romans had done, plaster painted to look like marble. I saw double doors at the end of the corridor but Horace took us into a side room some yards from it. There were comfortable chairs and a low informal table. "Take a seat, gentlemen. Refreshments will be forthcoming." He paused and it was the kind of pause someone takes before they deliver bad or awkward news. "Now, first, this is not a court martial, it…"

I said, rather more sharply than I intended, "I never thought for one moment that it was a court martial. A court martial would imply that orders were disobeyed and that was not the case."

Horace shook his head, "Griff, Lieutenant Roberts, calm yourself I beg of you. I was going to say that this is a court of enquiry to establish the facts after the incident by the border. That is all. There will be no blemish on anyone's record as a result of this."

Harry lit a cheroot, not bothering to ask permission, "For my part, it does not matter as I have my letter of resignation here," he patted his tunic pocket. "I am done with the army."

I think he took Horace by surprise. Certainly the aide said nothing for a moment or two. "Trooper Cartwright, you will not be called to answer any questions. You are here to support Lieutenant Roberts."

Cartwright nodded, "Ah, I am not an officer, my word does not count, I see."

We now had the officer flustered, "No, that is…" he shook his head and sighed. "If you would remain here until you are called. I will fetch you." He looked at the doctor, "You may smoke, Doctor."

Harry beamed, "Dashed kind of you, old boy!" He did not talk like that normally and I knew he was mocking Horace.

Almost as soon as he had gone a pair of servants entered with two trays. They spoke perfect English, without a trace of an accent. "We have tea and coffee. Would you like us to pour?"

Cartwright stood, "No, thank you, I can manage." They left and closed the door.

We sat in silence. Had we done anything wrong then we might have gone over our stories to make sure they matched but everything had been done as it should have been. What I had decided was that I would not sully Archie's name. I knew he had sought vengeance above all else but no one else did and no one would. At the end of the day I knew that Bill Burton would have followed Archie to the gates of hell and beyond. Bill would not have wanted his officer's name dragged through the mud.

Not surprisingly it was Harry who was called first. As he left his cheroot to slowly die on the ashtray he patted his pocket. "I shall tell them all and a few things more and then deliver this broadside, eh? A pleasant sea voyage and back to England."

He left and I said, "Cartwright, now that we are alone, what are your plans?"

He was calmness itself as he poured me some tea, "Sir, I am your batman and until you leave the service I will continue to serve you."

"And if I am not an officer?"

He put his cup down and looked me in the eye, "Sir, you are not Doctor Quinn and you will have no intention of resigning your commission. To cashier you they need a court martial." He waved an airy hand around the room, "This is a place to hide that which they intend what they wish kept hidden. The general has probably already written his report. The whole thing will be covered up. When we stayed with the general I spoke to the servants. General Pemberton has lofty ambitions. He sees this post as a step to the general staff and Horse Guards. His wife and daughter hate Cairo and they will do all that they can to leave. I think that this is his chance. No, Sir, you will not be cashiered and wherever you are posted I shall be your servant."

He was an astute man and I saw that he was right. The casual use of Kitchener's first name, the ball for his daughter, the grand house, all of them pointed to an ambitious man.

The doctor was away longer than I had expected and when he came back he was grinning as Horace said, "Lieutenant."

Harry said, cheerily, "Well that upset the old general and no mistake."

Horace led me down the corridor and hissed in my ear, "The doctor was clearly a poor choice to be sent to the desert. He is clearly unhinged…some of the things he said…" he shook his head, "Thank goodness you are a sensible fellow, eh? Play a straight bat and you will be alright."

We entered the room and there were just two officers with General Pemberton and a secretary who was taking notes. The two officers were captains and young. He would be grooming them. They would agree to whatever he said and they would be rewarded afterwards. General Pemberton's face looked flushed.

The general waved a hand towards the chair that faced the table. He smiled but it was just with his mouth. His eyes were like two blocks of ice and they stared at me as though trying to divine my thoughts. The words and tone he used were those one might use to a child who has been a disappointment.

An Officer and a Gentleman

"I had hoped, Lieutenant Roberts, after our last meeting that your posting would prove to be a safer one. Sadly, that was not meant to be. Can I put on record now," he nodded to the secretary, "that I disagreed with Lord Kitchener when he ordered me to increase the garrison at Farafra, in my view it should have been handed over to the Egyptians long ago." I saw the two officers nodding agreement. "Now, Lieutenant, this will not take long and then you can enjoy a couple of days leave in Cairo before you return to England." The outcome was decided, no matter what I said. "Now, first, the incident with the bandits and the attack on the caravan. Tell me what you know of this."

"It was not bandits, Sir. It was a troop of Turks led by two Germans."

The general shook his head and held up a piece of paper, "I have this from the Turkish military attaché. He categorically states that no Turkish soldier crossed the border and that they had a shipment of uniforms stolen by bandits." He turned to the two officers, "It makes more sense for bandits to attack a caravan." They nodded.

"But they were led by a German. I recognised him."

For the first time a shadow fell across the general's face. This play had gone off script, "Recognised?"

"It was Oberst von Kleist." I paused, "He attended your daughter's birthday party."

The smile left his face and his eyes narrowed, "I think you are mistaken, Lieutenant."

"I am not General Pemberton."

"I say that you are mistaken and that is what will be recorded."

"But…"

"Moving on, when the news of the bandit raid was delivered, what did Captain Dunn do?"

I knew now that the report was written and I was doomed but I would do all in my power to save the name of Archie Dunn and the 1st Desert Group. "He immediately ordered us to leave the fort, where those wounded by the Turkish soldiers could be tended. Ismail's son and some of his men came with us."

"And you went to attack the men of Siwa."

I adopted an innocent look, "General Pemberton, there were British soldiers and an important Egyptian and his people lying in the desert. Captain Dunn went to Siwa to recover the bodies so that we could give them a decent burial."

"But you went armed!"

I smiled, "General, in the desert you are always armed and, in the event it was a wise decision for we were ambushed by Oberst von Kleist and the Turkish soldiers that he commanded."

"You mean the bandits masquerading as this so-called German and the Turks."

"I recognised the German, Sir. He had a duelling scar on his face."

I watched the secretary begin to write but the general's hand stopped her and when she looked at him he shook his head.

"Lieutenant Roberts, I understand that you have been placed under a great deal of strain. You are a young officer who once had the prospects of a good career. Sadly, the influence of Captain Dunn has made you misjudge events. Captain Dunn was motivated by a need for glory and he paid the price." I opened my mouth and he held up his hand. "Just answer the questions of this board. I will not have wild speculation tarnish the name of the British Army and I will not risk a diplomatic incident with either the Turkish Empire or Germany. How did the captain, his batman and Ismail ibn Ismail, along with the other Egyptians, die?"

This was easy, "The Turkish soldiers had placed the heads of some of our dead and Ismail on stakes driven into the ground. The captain was acting as part of the scouting party for he was the most skilled navigator I ever knew." I waited until the secretary had written that down before I continued. I wanted it on the record.

"And? Get on with it, Lieutenant Roberts, we do not have all day."

I said, quietly, "Why the rush, General? The dead are dead and this enquiry is to bring out the truth, is it not?"

For the first time the two officers cast questioning glances at the general and he became a little flustered, "Of course we want the truth but you are taking a long time getting there."

"The men who died were serving the king, Sir, they deserve to have their story heard." I paused and he waved his hand. "The Turks…"

"The bandits disguised as Turkish soldiers…"

"Rose from beneath the sand and opened fire at point blank range. The six men stood no chance. Before we could go to their aid we were attacked."

"By more bandits."

"By Turks led by the two Germans. Thanks to our superior weapons we drove them off and were able to recover the bodies."

General Pemberton smacked the table in triumph, "And there you have it. The lieutenant has admitted that the men who attacked had poorer weapons. That proves it was bandits." He beamed, "Thank you for your testimony, Lieutenant. Lieutenant Jamieson has your orders. Your ship sails in a couple of days and I hope that the sea voyage brings you back to the real world. It would do you no good to spread scurrilous stories about German led Turkish troops when it is quite clear that it was bandits who attacked the caravan. Lieutenant Hamed has been given orders to rid the border of these bandits. You are dismissed."

I sat. I had not expected much but I was being called a liar or a deluded fool. I shook my head, "General, I am not deluded and I spoke the truth."

His smile came back. "You gave us what you thought was the truth but the letter from the military attaché proves otherwise. Lieutenant Jamieson…"

Horace took my shoulders to raise me to my feet, "Lieutenant," I turned to look at him and he gave a sad shake of his head, "come with me, eh? It is for the best."

I stood. No one was wearing a hat and so I did not have to salute. How could I salute the man who was whitewashing what had happened?"

Once outside I snapped, "Horace, I spoke the truth."

He nodded, "I know."

"Then…"

"I believe that you and Captain Dunn acted for the best. It cost him his life. You are lucky and you live."

"How can you serve such a man?"

He sighed, "Because, Griff, I am not like you, I am not a proper soldier. I am a diplomat in uniform. Like it or not I am tied to the general. I am to be promoted to captain when we return in January to England."

"You have been bought cheaply."

"It means I shall have a bigger pension when I leave the army."

I felt sick and all I wanted to do was to get out of the building. "What happens now?"

"You are to be placed on half pay and the reserve list. You will need to let me know the address in England where you will be residing so that we can send your pay and recall you to the army should that be necessary."

"I am being thrown out of the army?"

He smiled, "No, no, no. You will be needed at some time in the future and Cartwright will be paid as your servant by the army until you do rejoin. You have back pay waiting for you and half pay means that you can live quite comfortably. I envy you."

"But then you are not me, are you?" I shook my head, "Get out of my way, you pathetic excuse for a man."

He recoiled as my hand moved towards him. When I reached the waiting room I opened it and said, "Let us leave this cesspool of vipers and carrion. I would breathe fresher air."

I said nothing until we reached the hotel. The driver handed us an envelope, "Your tickets and travel warrants, Sir, for the train and the ship. I hope you have a pleasant voyage." He paused and then stood to attention, saluting, "Heard what you did in the desert, Sir, well done. It was the talk of the mess. Sorry it had to end this way."

"Thank you, Corporal. Tell your mess that the 1st Desert Group are real soldiers."

I turned and we went into the hotel. We sat in the bar and I told them what had been said. Harry was annoyed, "Half pay? Can you manage?"

"I have not spent much of my pay so yes but what do I do? Live with my father and become a recluse? And poor Cartwright here, lumbered with me in a little house in suburbia."

"Sir, I am delighted and I know that something will turn up. You are too good an officer for that not to happen. Let us enjoy the journey home. You were overdue a leave and I believe you hoped to be home by January in any case. You can see your family and then there is always Miss Lucinda."

I stared at Cartwright. How could I face Lucinda after this? He was right in one respect. I was due a leave and I would enjoy the time with my family. Perhaps my father could make sense of it.

I smiled, "And the three of us will be together. I take comfort from that."

Chapter 14

It was a pleasant voyage and the two of them tried to cheer me up for the whole journey but I was not in a good frame of mind when we docked, not at Liverpool, as I had hoped, but Southampton. When I knew that, I had sent a telegram from the ship to warn my family that I would be arriving, I gave a rough date, and there would be another guest who would be staying for a while. I had worried about everyone's reaction to the news. I felt as though I had failed. It was the last week in November and the weather in England was bleak. Surprisingly there was a driver waiting for us when we docked. The three of us had been looking for a hackney carriage to take us to the station but a corporal was waiting at the foot of the gangplank as we went ashore. "Lieutenant Roberts? Doctor Quinn?"

"Yes, Corporal."

"Brigadier General Dickenson wondered if Doctor Quinn needed a lift to the station."

Harry looked at me, totally confused, "Well this is jolly nice but who the hell is Brigadier Dickenson and why offer me a lift," he looked at the horseless carriage, "in this contraption?"

I smiled, "He is the chap who helped to set up the Desert Group with Lord Kitchener and I am guessing, Corporal, that you are here to take me to meet with him."

He looked relieved and smiled, "Yes, Sir, you have it in one. I am to drive you to Windsor. He is based there now."

I looked at Harry, "The station then?"

He said, "Windsor station is just as good. There is a regular service there to London. I thought to have a couple of days there before I headed home."

I knew that home was in North Yorkshire; the village of Kildale. "There you are, Corporal, just one drive."

"Right, Sirs, if you would get in I will load the cases."

"And I will help you." Cartwright's motives were simple. He did not wish the luggage to be damaged.

Cartwright sat in the front and chatted to the driver. I saw the corporal put on goggles. He handed a pair to Cartwright. The wind would hit them and shelter us. Harry and I were able to converse in the back, despite the noise from the engine. The seats were upholstered although I was not sure how they would stand up to the British weather. "What does a brigadier general want with an officer on half pay? Perhaps he is going to offer you a job." Harry did not know the brigadier. I was suspicious of any meeting now with a senior officer.

That thought had occurred to me but I did not want to get my hopes up. I shrugged, "I am not sure but as it saves us having to find a train I am happy about that." I shivered, "It is a while since I have been in England. It is bloody cold."

Harry smiled, "That it is. I shan't miss the heat and I will never complain about the British summer."

I leaned forward, "Corporal, we are a little chilly here. We have been in Egypt for quite a while."

"There are a couple of blankets back there, Sir. It is a little fresh today. This is a nice piece of machinery but the roof only keeps off the rain. It does not stop the cold."

There was a barracks in Windsor but it was not far from the station. Harry and I had exchanged addresses and we shook hands. Harry did not smile, he just said, "Take care, old chap, and remember *nils desperandum*. You are a damned good officer and I would hate to think that this has poisoned your mind. Archie let that happen to him and… well."

"Don't worry, Harry. We will get this little meeting over and then Cartwright and I will soon be safe at the family home. What I need is sage words from my hero, my father."

He nodded and shook hands with Cartwright, "And you, Paul, make the best cup of tea I have ever enjoyed. Never change."

"Don't worry, Sir, I never will."

We watched him head towards the station and turned to rejoin the driver. He said, "It is just around the corner. We will be just two ticks."

Victoria barracks was the place the guards for the king's castle were housed. Being a short walk from the castle it added a little pomp and majesty to the small town that was often home to the royal family. I wondered if Brigadier General Dickenson was now attached to the household infantry.

The car was allowed to enter the barracks and we were driven to an unassuming office that I took to be a sort of guard room.

An Officer and a Gentleman

The corporal said, "Your chap can stay with me, Sir, and your luggage in the car. The brigadier said that this would be a short meeting."

The corporal was a confident young man and I found myself intrigued by this little meeting which felt more clandestine with each passing moment. I entered the office and found myself in a tiny room filled by a desk and a rather large sergeant. He smiled, "You must be Lieutenant Roberts. Hang on and I will see if the brigadier is ready for you."

He stood and went down a very short corridor. I heard his knock but his words were muffled. He returned, "The brigadier will see you now. Cup of tea, Sir?"

"Yes please, three sugars."

"Righto."

I walked down the corridor, knocked on the door and when I heard, "Come." I entered.

I had last seen the brigadier at Sandhurst and then he had been a colonel. He now had the red collar that marked him as even more important than he had been. He beamed and held out his hand, "Congratulations on the promotion. From what I have read it was thoroughly deserved. Take a seat."

I did so and said, "Thank you, Sir." I was in strange territory. Why had we been picked up? That this was a short meeting was clear from the driver's words. That the brigadier had read about my time in the desert was also slightly disconcerting.

"How is your father?"

"I don't know, Sir. As you know letters take some time to reach us and I may well have passed my letters on the voyage here. The last I heard his first book was about to be published and he seemed content."

"Good, good."

The sergeant brough the tea and a small plate of shortbread. "Thought the lieutenant might like a little snack, Sir."

"Thoughtful, Barker." I sipped my tea and waited. General Pemberton had made me wary of senior officers, even one who I had always thought of as a friend. "This business near the border... you must know I think that the general handled it badly."

"Sir, how do you know? We were a small outpost on the backside of the Empire."

"You are a good officer, Griff. You have a sharp mind. I read everything that I deem to be important. My role has changed over the years. I no longer deal with units like the now defunct 1st Desert Group. I have a different remit. For the time being that is all I can tell you but I asked you here because I was interested in the reports you and Captain Dunn first sent. I was lucky enough to read a copy of them, sent to me, well let us say that not all of General Pemberton's officers agreed with what he did. Your original report about the last attack has disappeared, it seems." He patted an envelope on his desk. "This arrived just a week ago. Mail ships are slightly quicker than troopships."

I thought I recognised the handwriting on the envelope that was addressed to Senior Officer, Egyptian affairs. "Horace!"

He held up his hand. "Better that I just say it was sent to England by an officer who likes you and that it found its way to my desk because someone in the Egyptian office knew of my interest."

"Then, Sir..."

He held up his hand and then took out his pipe, "Tell me the whole story from the first time you went to Farafra. After that I will answer, within reason, any questions you may have."

I took a good drink from the tea and then began. All the reports I had written helped me. I had a mind that seemed to be compartmentalised. He took notes, in pencil on a notepad. When I came to the German he paused, pencil in mid-air and asked, "Now this German, you are sure of his name?"

I nodded, "He was announced at the birthday party for General Pemberton's daughter."

"And you would know him again, if you saw him?"

"I could pick him out from a regiment of Prussians, Sir. I had him in my sights."

He smiled, "And I know from your Sandhurst record that you are a skilled marksman. Carry on."

When I had finished he relit his pipe and then folded his arms. I finished my tea and then took a biscuit. Breakfast had been a long time ago.

An Officer and a Gentleman

He looked at his notes again and then said, "You have questions, I believe."

"General Pemberton was wrong and yet he got away with it, why?"

"Friends in high places. Our General Pemberton likes to cultivate important people. It won't do you any good but you should know that most people in Whitehall disagreed with his decision. I could understand why he handled it with kid gloves. The Turks and the Germans are belligerent. The Kaiser, especially, seems to think that as he is related to the late queen he too can rule an empire. Between you and me, Griff, I think that Archie had the right idea. If we had made a show of force, a regiment of camels and not a small troop, then they might have been discouraged." He leaned back and shook his head, "Water under the bridge now and we can do nothing."

"What about the men, Sir, the ones in the troop?"

He smiled, "As soon as I received the report I sent a telegram. They are to be held at Faiyum and they will all be offered the chance to become a discrete troop in the Camel Corps. I made the point to the powers that be that their expertise would be lost otherwise."

I smiled for I was relieved, "Thank you, Sir. That takes a load off my mind."

He said, thoughtfully, "You are so like your father. He was always considerate about his men. The apple does not fall far from the tree."

He shouted, "Barker, more tea."

A voice came back, "Righto, Sir, on the way."

He looked at me, "And in all this you have not said a word about you and your position. Just like your father but I am guessing you are not happy."

"No, Sir, I am a soldier and an officer. It does not sit well for me to be on half pay doing nothing to earn it. Perhaps I should resign my commission and…"

He banged his hand on the desk, "No, Griff! That is the wrong decision. I want you in the army. Listen to me."

The door opened and Barker came in with more biscuits and two fresh mugs of tea. He said, as he put them down and took the used ones away, "I made sure your chap and the corporal had something. It is Baltic out there and as you have just come from Egypt…"

When the sergeant left he continued, "As I was saying I want you in the army. I have something in mind which might suit your talents but I need to put more things in place. Go back to your father. Enjoy Christmas. See your young lady and…"

"My young lady!"

He smiled, "Sorry, I read the other report. When the girl and her guardian were in Alexandria they were interviewed, not by me, you understand, but by someone in the diplomatic service. I read the report and Miss Cowley seemed quite taken by you. I believe she is working not far from you."

I was stunned. I had, it seems, no secrets.

"So, Corporal Reed will drive you home. With luck you might make it back before midnight, if not he has the authority to find accommodation in a hotel. I know where you are. Regard this as leave. By the time I have sorted out my plans it will be spring and you might be getting a little restless. Trust me, Griff."

I nodded, "I am afraid that General Pemberton has slightly soured my view of senior officers."

"I know what you mean. Kitchener was an exception. There are more men like Garnet Wolsey than him but things are changing. It just takes time for the British Army does not like change." He saw that I had finished my tea and stood, "Better make time while we can. It might be cold but the weather has yet to make the roads too dangerous." He held out his hand, "I will thank you for your service in Egypt, Griff. I know the ones who should have will not and remember this, Archie Dunn is not forgotten. What he did will bear fruit in the future."

As we passed the office the sergeant stood. He had a hamper. "I had a picnic made up, Sir, and a flask of tea. It will save you from having to stop. You will want to get home, I expect."

"Thank you, Sergeant Barker."

"Not a problem, Sir, we have to look after the men who have served the king, don't we?"

When I reached the car the engine was running. "Have a good journey and drive safely, Corporal Reed."

"Yes, Sir."

I waited until we were on an A road before I spoke, "I don't like putting you out like this, Corporal. We could take a train."

He laughed, "You are doing me a favour, Sir. I come from Leigh and that isn't far from Liverpool. I have a four-day leave. The brigadier is a good chap."

I nodded, "That he is."

Cartwright was in the back with me and he opened the hamper, "Very nice. Pork pie, sandwiches, boiled eggs and sausage rolls. This will just fit the bill, Sir. George here said there is a nice spot we can stop for lunch at the side of the road close to Burton on Trent."

"George?"

"The corporal, Sir. We have had a nice little chat. From what I learned your brigadier friend is a nice chap too. I have a good feeling about the changes, Sir."

It proved to be a pleasant journey. My mind was more at ease as I knew the troop were looked after and I also knew that others knew about General Pemberton. It was a start. I had never been in what was called an automobile before. This one was not particularly comfortable and, as Reed told me, it had a tendency to break down. George was a genius at all things mechanical. It had just, so George told me, a two-speed gearbox. It was not particularly fast on hills but we had few to negotiate. He had wisely brought his own petrol as he could not guarantee supplies on the road. I was not convinced about the viability of such vehicles but when we stopped to fill with petrol and I mentioned my feelings, George was adamant. "This is the future, Sir. The brigadier thinks so too. He loves it."

"Then why has he let me use it?"

"Well, he can use the train back to London, Sir, but I think he likes you and he feels bad about the incident in Egypt."

"You know about that?"

"Me, him and the sergeant are a close team, Sir. We have shared the information. I hope you don't mind."

"Of course not. I am just surprised. Tell me, what does the brigadier do exactly?"

Until that point the corporal had chattered away easily but he just said, "You would have to ask him, Sir."

It was almost midnight when we neared the house. There had been another breakdown. By my reckoning there had been at least five, although as one of them appeared to be when we stopped for a picnic I may have been wrong. Before we got out of the car I said, "Will you be alright on your own, Corporal? What if you break down again?"

"I have only a few miles to go and I shall strip the beastie down at my dad's house. He likes all things mechanical and, to be truthful, he is looking forward to seeing an internal combustion engine. The Asquith will be the first one he has seen." We got out and he said, cheerily, "I daresay we will meet again, I am looking forward to it. The brigadier is right, you are a good bloke."

The noisy vehicle pulled away and I saw lights appear in the window. A face appeared but I could not make out who it was. We headed up the path to the front door. My Uncle Billy had bought the biggest house he could afford and now it would be stretched to the limit.

The door opened and my father, in his dressing gown and with a candle in hand, beamed, "You made it! What was the awful noise I just heard?"

"An internal combustion engine."

I heard Aunt Sarah from within, "Who on earth is disturbing the street at this ungodly hour?"

"Come in! Come in! You are letting in the cold." He held the door open for us.

I said, "This is Paul Cartwright. He will be staying with us for a while."

"Welcome, welcome, any friend of Griff's…"

"I am your son's batman, Sir, although I would be honoured if he thought of me as a friend."

Aunt Sarah appeared at the top of the stairs. The stern look was replaced by a beaming smile when she saw me. "Our little boy is home."

Her shriek woke the whole house. Cartwright was superb. He sought the kitchen and while we all hugged and said hello, he went into the kitchen and made a pot of tea. Aunt Sarah said, as he went back to the kitchen for more cups, "Who is he?"

My dad said, "He is Griff's servant. All officers have them. He will be staying with us but what Griff hasn't told me yet is how long is the leave?"

"It is not a leave, Dad, I am on half pay until I am recalled." I left the part about Brigadier Dickenson for another time.

Rather than being disappointed, as I had expected, my father was delighted, "Wonderful news. This will be the best Christmas, ever!" He gave me a sad smile, "Senior officers are often like spiders, Griff. They weave webs that few can see unless they, too, are a spider. You are better off away from that world."

Poor Cartwright was out on his feet by the time we all retired to bed. His room was what we called the box room. It was big enough for a single bed, a wardrobe, a chest of drawers and a bedside table. He was delighted with it. The room he had shared with the under footman had been the same size. As I went to my room my father put his good arm around me, "Good to have you home. We shall talk in the morning but you have made us all very happy."

I thought coming home in what amounted to disgrace was a bad thing. I now saw that it all depended on your perspective. Aunt Sarah and Aunt Bet did not care why I was home, just that I was home.

I slept soundly. It was my old bed but any bed, after the cot at the fort and the cabin on the sea tossed ship, would have seemed like heaven. I woke early. That, I think was my nature. On the voyage back, with no real reason I had risen at five a.m. I slept until six and it felt like a lie in. Poor Paul was still asleep and, after dressing in the clothes I had not seen for a couple of years, sneaked past his bedroom to walk down the stairs, using only those that did not creak. I was, of course, not the first one up. Dad was there drinking his tea and looking at the notes for his latest book.

He nodded, "I see the clothes still fit."

"You know Army food. You are never going to get fat in the desert."

He nodded, remembering, "Tea or are you now a coffee man?"

I smiled, "I like your tea, Dad."

"Sit down and I will pour you one." I sat and looked at the newspaper. I pushed it to one side. I did not need news. "Porridge alright?"

"Of course."

He stirred the pan and then brought me my tea. I nodded at the notes, "How is the book coming?"

"It is easier than the first and I think better. I can see mistakes now that I made in the first. I can't change them now, not until the second edition. I will have to live with them."

"Is Aunt Bet still enjoying the typing?"

He smiled, "She is and I pay her. She didn't want to be paid but it is only right." He smiled as he stirred the porridge once more. "I have yet to see much of the royalties but I dare say they will come."

I nodded, "Like Army pay. I have back salary due. Before I forget, I will pay my way. You and the family will not be out of pocket because of us."

"Thanks to Billy's shares we are comfortably off. The dividend grows year on year and Aunt Sarah does a little bookwork for a couple of local companies."

"Dad, I will pay."

He said nothing but nodded and ladled porridge into the bowls. The tin of golden syrup was already open. The steam rose from the dish and I took a spoon and did as I had done when I had been a boy, I made a pattern in the white oats with the golden syrup. I waited as I always had done for the edges to meld into the oats before stirring it. Neither of us spoke until the porridge was gone. I picked up the bowls and went to the sink. "You smoke your pipe and I will do pan bash."

Just then Cartwright appeared, "Sir, you should have woken me. What are you doing?"

I smiled, "The dishes. Now sit and have a cup of tea. I am in my home now and, believe it or not, I quite enjoy doing the dishes... occasionally."

"Aye, Paul, and as the novelty wears off, probably by this evening, let us enjoy the sight of Griff working while you and I get to know one another." He nodded and poured himself some tea. "Griff says you worked in a large house with servants."

"Yes, Sir."

My father took the pipe from his mouth and shaking his head said, "In this house I am Jack. I was in the army such a short length of time that I did not get used to the title."

"You had a servant…Jack?"

"I did. Ged Adams. He died at Omdurman. He was an old soldier." My father said no more. I know that the death of the old man had affected him almost as much as the loss of his arm. As Paul sipped his tea my father relit his pipe and when it was going said, "You know I write." Paul nodded, "Well, some time I would like to pick your brains about such places. I like to make my stories as realistic as possible. That is what I write stories about, war and the army. It is what I know. I can write about family life but posh folks in big houses…well it is out of my league." I saw Paul smile and Dad asked, "Why the smile? What did I say?"

I had washed the bowls and was dealing with the pan. Without turning I said, "The lads in the troop gave Paul the nickname, Posh."

"I can see that. Well, Paul, will you help me with the research?"

"Of course, Jack, I would be honoured but I think you will find it dull."

"Leave that to me and you, Griff, we need to sit down so that I can make better notes on what you did."

I turned as I began to dry the dishes, "You are going to make that into a story?"

"Of course, too good not to. Of course I will change the names and some of the characters. I knew Stan and Charlie, of course, but the others will end up being men I knew when I was a soldier."

"Is that how writers work, Jack?" Paul appeared genuinely interested.

"It is how this writer works. I use people that I have met and know. I understand how they will react."

"Fascinating."

I topped up my tea and my father's, "Help yourself to food, Paul. The pantry is yours. I know you are dying to explore it."

"Yes, Sir but I will not abuse the privilege."

"I never thought for one moment that you would."

I sat at the table and stirred the sugar in the tea. I was home and the pace of my life would change. I would have to do nothing. My time was my own and I could go and do whatever I wanted, whenever I wanted. Dad's pipe had gone out and he put it on the ashtray. He asked, quietly, "And Lucinda, what about her?"

I looked up. It was as though he had been reading my mind, joining the dots and coming to the conclusion that I would have, in time. "I suppose I will write to her and tell her I am home."

"You could go and see her."

I laughed, "It is not as though I have access to the brigadier's internal combustion engine. I would have to get there."

"There are trains and we are close enough to the station to easily get there."

"She will be in Grasmere and that is not as easy to get to."

"You are deliberately putting obstacles in your way. Why?"

I was silent.

My father knew me. He had not been home much when I had been growing up but in the times he was on leave and after he had lost his hand he had more than made up for it. We had walked in the woods, hunted and drank in the pub. We were alike too. "She won't think any the less of you because of what happened. I only met her the once but I could tell what she was like, instantly." He stood; I knew that it was past the time he normally began to write. He said, "Write to her. Tell you what, invite her down here for Christmas."

I looked up, almost startled, "The house is full as it is."

He laughed, "You can bunk either with me or young Jack."

"What about her guardian?"

"The same. Just write to her and invite her. She can say no and then you can work out how to go and see her. I bet she is wondering why she has had no letters from you."

"But I wrote to her…"

"When?"

"The same time I wrote to you." I thought back. The last letters I could remember sending had been sent when the new troopers had arrived. That had been June. Then I remembered I had given letters to Bob. She would have had that one about a week ago. He was right. It was better to get it over with. At least this way I might have a reply within a week. I nodded, "Very well." I saw that Paul had made himself some toast. "I will go and write this letter and then you and I, Paul, will go into Liverpool. I have Christmas presents to buy."

He nodded and asked, a little sheepishly, "Would it be alright if I had some marmalade? I have missed it in the desert and…"

"Of course you can. Treat this as your home Mr Cartwright." We all turned as Aunt Sarah appeared in the doorway. "And I will make us both a fresh pot and we can chat."

The smile that I saw on my batman's face was reassuring. I had not seen him smile since we had buried Bill Burton. He had lost his only friend. Aunt Sarah was a warm woman and she would help to heal the hurt in her own inimitable style.

Chapter 15

Perhaps it was the presence of my father, writing down his story, that helped me to write the letter to Lucinda. He had the harder task as he had to engage his readers and keep their interest. All I had to do was to tell the woman with whom I was infatuated, that I was home and would like to invite her and her guardian to spend Christmas in the Liverpool suburbs. I was fairly certain that she would refuse, for a whole raft of reasons, but she might invite me up to their home. This would be the vacation time for the college and they would be free.

I sealed the envelope and wrote the address. I went into the kitchen where I could hear the chatter of not only Paul and Aunt Sarah but also Aunt Bet, Jack and Victoria. There was laughter and they all appeared to be getting on well. "Are you ready Paul, or…"

Aunt Sarah asked, "Where are you going?"

"I need to post this letter and I thought to do some shopping in Liverpool."

"It will be a nightmare, Griff. The streets are always crowded at this time of year."

Jack said, "Vicky and I have to get to work. Come with us. There is an omnibus stop at the end of the road now. We will be there in two shakes."

Paul's face lit up, "An omnibus? I have never travelled on one."

I laughed, "That settles it. Get your coat."

I suddenly realised that Paul was wearing his uniform. That was all he had. I think Aunt Bet saw it too. She suddenly said, "Billy's old clothes are still in the wardrobe." She gave me a sad look, "I was going to donate them to charity but… I am sure they would fit."

"Oh no. I couldn't."

Aunt Bet took it the wrong way, "Oh I am sorry. I have offended you. Fancy offering you second hand clothes."

"It is not that, Miss Elizabeth, but I am just a servant."

Aunt Sarah snorted, "Nonsense! We will have none of that in this house. You are our guest. Off you go and when you return I want to see you in civilian clothes. The army is a bad memory."

I felt a sense of relief when the letter was posted and then Paul and I walked around English shops. Egypt had its souks and there you bartered in the open trying to find shade when you could. Here you sought shelter in the warmth of shops and paid the clearly marked price. Despite what Aunt Sarah had said Cartwright still felt like a servant and he carried my purchases.

We were home by lunchtime and walked into a house that smelled of Christmas already. After putting my purchases in my room and taking off the many layers we had worn we went to the kitchen. I saw a pot bubbling away and asked, "What is going on?"

Aunt Sarah and Aunt Bet were both wearing pinafores and were at the table where I saw flour and dried fruits as well as a bottle of brandy. Aunt Sarah looked flushed but happy, "We had prepared for your arrival, Griff, but our Jack says that you invited your young lady and her guardian for Christmas. We need to do a little more. We have made a Christmas pudding. It could do with longer to mature but we made up for that with more brandy. We have made a Christmas cake already but we are going to do a second. It is bad luck not to have Christmas cake ready for first footing."

I sighed with exasperation, "She is not my young lady and they may not even come!"

Aunt Bet smiled, "Griff, we met her and whether you think so or not, she is your young lady. She was smitten by you and, I think, you by her. She will come."

Everyone in the house seemed certain. As I waited for a letter, listening for the sound of the postman, my life fell into a pattern. Once the postman had visited and there was nothing from the Lake District, Paul and I would don outdoor clothing and we would head to the woods to tramp the trails where I had hunted with Old Joe. The old man had died the last winter but his voice came back to me as we walked through the woods. We would arrive back for lunch and then while Paul helped my father with research I read through his manuscripts looking for spelling and grammatical errors. There were few of them but I enjoyed reading the story. Before we ate my father and I would go to the pub where we enjoyed a pint of beer and he smoked his pipe. Paul stayed in the house where he helped my two aunts to prepare the food. He loved it.

The letter arrived on the fifteenth of December. I recognised the writing. My father said, "Well then, open it."

"What if she says she can't come?"

He sighed, "Then you will know, won't you? You have been like a nettled hen these last days. Read it!"

It was almost like a command and I opened it.

Grasmere

December

Dearest Griff,

I was so pleased to receive your letter and know that you are safe and you are home.

I was even more delighted that you invited me to spend Christmas with your wonderful family. It is a most wonderful happenstance as my guardian had planned on taking us to Oxford where some archaeologists were going to spend Christmas at some country house to discuss some new excavations in the Middle East. As much as I like archaeology I do not enjoy the company of desiccated old men rambling on. My guardian will give me the highlights after Christmas.

I will travel with him to the station at Manchester on December the 20th. He will continue to Birmingham where he will change trains. I believe I can catch a train from there to Liverpool. My train reaches Manchester at twelve noon. If you are not there to meet me in Liverpool then I will take a hackney cab to your house.

I am so happy about this that I feel like a giddy girl. This is not like me at all, Griff, I can assure you. It must be the time of year.

All my love

Lucinda.

An Officer and a Gentleman

My father grinned, "She is coming then?"

"Yes, but without her guardian."

"See, I told you."

I saw the reaction of the rest of my family and Paul. They were all clearly delighted and I did not know why.

I was at the station at twelve. I went alone despite Paul asking to accompany me. I wanted nothing to spoil the meeting and whilst Paul would not exactly spoil it he would be a distraction and I wanted her all to myself. That way I knew I could not miss her. Snow began to fall that morning as I ate my breakfast. By the time I headed to the station it was lying on the ground. It looked very Christmassy but I would rather have had clear weather. Once Lucinda was in my home then it could blow a blizzard for all that I cared. As soon as I reached the station I went to ask what time the train would be arriving. I was told 12.45. I said, "What about the snow?"

The man smiled, "Snow does not stop our trains, Sir. It will be on time."

I went immediately to the hackney cabs. The horses all wore a blanket even though they were covered by the station roof. I went to the one at the end of the line and engaged him to take us both home. A half a crown secured him. I did not care if it cost me a guinea.

I had gloves and my army greatcoat but I wore a civilian hat. I stood and stamped as I watched the great steam trains come into the busy station. Faiyum had two trains a day, Cairo had more but I watched eight trains arrive in the hour that I waited. As the noon train hissed and puffed into the station, right on time I noticed, I found that I was as excited as I had ever been. I watched the doors opening and when I saw the conductor carrying a passenger's luggage I ran down the platform. Most of those who were arriving looked to have no luggage. I saw Lucinda step from the train. She looked like some sort of snow princess. Her fur hat perfectly framed her face and I could see her glowing pink cheeks. She had a muff covering her hands and I saw the conductor shout to a porter.

I reached them in three strides and said, "I can carry that." I handed the man a shilling and said, "Thank you."

I took the bag and then looked at Lucinda. Our eyes met and she said, "On time! I knew you would be." She linked my left arm and I carried the bag in my right. As I passed him I saw the envious look on the conductor's face.

"I have a cab waiting and my family are so excited to see you."

"And I them. Is Cartwright with you?"

"He is."

"He is a good fellow. And Captain Dunn, is he home too?"

I stopped and turned, "Archie Dunn died in the desert. Sorry to have to break the news like this."

She squeezed my arm, "You poor dear. You were close. It must have hit you hard."

I nodded and we continued walking. Before I could answer her the driver had jumped down and said, "Here y'are, Sir, I will take that from you." I helped her into the back and sat next to her. The driver draped a blanket across our knees. "Now you two young people settle back. I can't promise a quick journey. This snow is treacherous but Marie is a good horse and we will get you there for the agreed price, Sir."

We set off and she took my hands beneath the blanket. Impulsively, I kissed her and immediately regretted my action. "Sorry!"

She laughed and said "Whatever for? I have dreamt of that since we first met." She kissed me back, hard and long. When we came apart she said, "I am no wanton, Griff, but each night since we parted I have dreamt of you. I could not say in my letters what I meant to. This kiss is the measure of my feelings."

I said, "I too dreamed but I thought you too far above me."

"Too far?"

"You are the daughter of a professor and I am from humble stock."

She laughed, "Griff Roberts, you are a goose and I can see that I have my work cut out for me but I can tell you that I am prepared. I believe that you and I are meant to be together. I did not need to see your face at the station to remind me of that but when I saw you running down the slippery platform my heart soared with elation."

I shook my head, "You should slap me."

"Why?"

"For I am sure that I am dreaming."

"No, my sweet, this is a delicious reality and I, for one, pray that it does not end."

I almost resented my family as my father and aunts crowded around her to greet her. I wanted her all to myself. She was taken away to the bedroom she would share with my cousin Victoria. Aunt Sarah said it was for the best. She thought that if Lucinda slept alone we might be tempted to behave inappropriately.

I waited in the parlour with my father. Cartwright was humming happily as he made a pot of tea to go with the cakes and scones that my aunts had baked. I saw my father viewing me curiously. "What?"

He shook his head, "I was thinking about your mother. She would have loved Lucinda. I never got the chance to really court your mother." He began to fill his pipe, "My fault I know, but I have always felt guilty about the way I… Water under the bridge and the past is done. You cannot change it but you can learn from it. Treat her well, Griff. You are a good lad and your Aunt Sarah has done a good job with you. I am proud of you but…"

"Don't worry. I won't make a mess of this."

He had just struck a match when the three entered the room. He hurriedly put the pipe down. Lucinda put her hand on his, "Do not desist because of me, Mr Roberts. It reminds me of my father."

Aunt Sarah said, "Jack can smoke later. The smell will not help the cakes."

My father held his hands up, "I surrender. Sarah is quite right."

Lucinda told us how long she could stay. She was almost apologetic. "My guardian will be in Oxford until the 3rd of January. I hope I shall not be a bother." We all protested that she could stay as long as she liked and she laughed. "He said he will come here to pick me up when he returns. I hope that those arrangements will suit."

"Of course."

And so began the most wonderful Christmas I had ever spent. We did behave and Aunt Sarah insisted when we went walking, in the woods, that Cartwright should accompany us as some sort of chaperone. That said we managed many a furtive kiss. When we were away from the house we held hands and Cartwright pretended not to notice. When we were in company we laughed for the house seemed to be filled with laughter and gaiety. I discovered that she did drink but in moderation. She liked a drink called gin and tonic. It appeared her father and guardian had come to like the drink when they had been excavating in Turkey before the Ottomans forbade English archaeologists. She loved the food that was prepared and often helped in the kitchen. When she, Aunt Bet and Vicky were stacking the dried dishes after Christmas Aunt Sarah, her face flushed from one glass of port too many, sat next to me and said, "This is the one for you, Griff, and if you let her go then you are a fool and I know you are not that." She gave me a porty kiss on the cheek.

"She has a guardian and is not yet twenty-one, Aunt Sarah."

"Pish! Lucinda knows her own mind and her guardian will go along with whatever she says. Speak to her before she leaves." She wagged a finger, "That is an order, Lieutenant Roberts, and I outrank any officer save for your father!"

The moment I chose came about almost inadvertently because, for the first time since I had known Cartwright, he over imbibed and told us, whilst in his cups, that his birthday was January 2nd and that he had rarely celebrated it. The next day the four women of the house set about planning a party. I was excluded because of my sex but I was delighted with the way the four of them got on so well with each other. My father and I, along with Jack, took Paul for a walk and then the pub while they plotted and planned. My batman was a little embarrassed by his apparent fall from grace. In truth he had just been a little giggly. He had just a pint of shandy whilst we had a couple of pints each.

The days leading up to New Year's Eve were always quiet. In the north we tended to celebrate the New Year almost as much as Christmas with a whole host of traditions. Someone with dark hair would stand outside the front door to await the chiming of the church bells that would announce midnight. He would carry a lump of coal which he would give to whoever opened the door. It was normally Aunt Sarah. She would give him a coin, a glass of whisky and a piece of Christmas cake. He would receive a kiss and after he had finished the cake and drink go to the back door to let out the old year. We would then celebrate in earnest. My father told me that growing up in St Helens men would often visit a number of houses to let in the New Year. For those who had small families it ensured good fortune for the following year.

I had let in the New Year before now but it was decided that we would let Paul Cartwright let in the New Year. He was both delighted and apprehensive. He did not want to bring bad luck. It all went off swimmingly. Aunt Sarah kissed him and made him blush. Aunt Bet kissed him and then Lucinda and Vicky. I think he was taken aback and then we shook hands. He was determined to do it all right and he downed the whisky after he had eaten the cake. I saw the relief on his face when the old year was sent packing. As we celebrated he said, "You know…" he still had a hard time calling me Griff but my father had insisted, "Griff, you are the luckiest man in the world. I have never met such a wonderful and caring family. I envy you more than I can say. You need to make Miss Lucinda your wife. You are perfect together."

As luck would have it Lucinda had been talking to Vicky and the conversation had ended. She heard, 'your wife' and turned, "You have a wife, Paul?"

He was flustered and said, "No, Miss Lucinda, I just said that the lieutenant ought to make you his wife."

The room fell silent in an instant. Until that moment I had spoken to my whole family about it but I had not plucked up the courage to ask her. Lucinda had enjoyed two gin and tonics and was flushed. She said, "Well as he hasn't asked me yet it is a moot point."

The silence was almost unbearable and every eye was on me. I looked up into Lucinda's eyes and I saw only encouragement. I glanced to the side and saw my father nod. I dropped to one knee. No one said a word but I saw Vicky put her hand to her mouth to stop herself from screaming. "Lucinda Cowley, would you do me the honour to be my wife. I have little to offer you except…"

She grabbed my hands and raised me to my feet, "Of course, you silly goose. I have been waiting for the last week for the proposal." She kissed me hard and I kissed her back. It was then that the room erupted.

Poor Cartwright stood silently and after the other men had shaken my hand and the women kissed me said, "I am mortified, Sir. I spoke out of turn."

Lucinda grabbed him and hugged him, "You are my hero, Paul Cartwright. Had you not spoken I doubt that this officer who can charge a squadron of Turks feared to ask me for my hand."

I reached into my pocket. I had kept it close since Ismail had given it to me. I held the ring and said, sheepishly, "If it does not fit then…"

Aunt Sarah burst into tears, "Griff Roberts, you are nothing like your father for you are a romantic."

Lucinda put it on her ring finger and it fitted. Whilst it might be a little loose in the cold weather of England Lucinda would wear gloves. "It is perfect."

I decided to keep the gift of the locket for our wedding day. Perhaps Aunt Sarah was right.

It was late when we went to bed. I sat on the settee with Lucinda and we did not let go of one another's hands.

The next day was something of a hiatus for how could we top the proposal? It was Aunt Sarah who secretly reminded the others that we had a party to plan. My father and I took Paul out again for Jack and Victoria were back at work. In the pub my father said, "It is one thing to ask Lucinda but you have a guardian to persuade now."

"Lucinda says that will not be a problem. He regards me as a perfectly acceptable officer." I looked from one to the other, "But should I be an officer? I could resign my commission and…" My voice tailed off lamely.

"And do what?"

My father was right, I knew nothing else. As I was on half pay that did not matter. Of course Lucinda had a job, of sorts. "I suppose I will have to live with them in Lancaster, at least during term time."

"It is good that you are thinking of these things, Son, but let us just take one step at a time. Once you have spoken to Mr Bannerman-Castle then we have a wedding to plan. I am guessing that as there is no other family we could hold it here. You need to ask Lucinda if that would suit."

We stayed out more than long enough for the cake to be iced and hidden so that when we returned we ate dinner and retired to bed.

There were cards and presents for Cartwright and he was overawed. That evening when the cake was brought out he looked close to tears. It was a lovely way to end the holiday.

We awaited the arrival, the next day, of Lucinda's guardian. We had no idea of the time he would be arriving. He had told Lucinda that they would leave for Lancaster almost immediately. Lucinda had decided, already that would not happen. I moved from my room to share with Jack and it was prepared for the guardian.

My father said, "He will wish to stay. This is meant to be, Griff."

It was late in the afternoon when he arrived. He was clearly flustered. He ran to the door although we had seen the cab arrive and opened it already, "Lucinda, is she packed? I missed my connection. If we are to make the Lancaster train we must take this hackney back to the station."

My father put an arm around the archaeologist, "Griff, go and pay the cab. Mr Bannerman-Castle, you can stay the night and leave in the morning. We have much to talk about."

He looked stunned, "We do?"

Just then Lucinda appeared and grabbed him, "I am so glad you are here. I was worried. Come inside. Aunt Sarah has put the kettle on."

I paid the driver and gave him a good tip. I hefted his bag and headed into the house. I carried the bag upstairs to my room. By the time I was downstairs once more I could see from the faces that turned to me that the news had been broken. John Bannerman-Castle smiled and held out his hand, "Thank you, Lieutenant. I think that my ward has made a wise choice and you have my permission."

Lucinda threw herself at me and we kissed.

Cartwright insisted upon serving us at dinner, he thought it was important for the family to be together. My father nodded, "Just this once, Paul."

An Officer and a Gentleman

The archaeologist seemed distracted by something other than the wedding although he allowed the women to plan a date and a place. We would be married in the church that was close to the house and we would have a small reception at the house. It was when the date was mentioned that the archaeologist became animated, "The fourteenth of February, you say?"

My aunt misunderstood, "If you think that Valentine's Day is inappropriate then…"

"The date is immaterial as is the venue but I have some news which concerns Lucinda." We all looked at my wife-to-be and my heart sank. This sounded ominous. "When we were in Oxford we were talking about a dig at a few miles from Petra, the ancient city that lies close to the Holy Land. It is newly discovered and the temples look to be Roman rather than Nabatean. It seems that the Romans wished their own temples close to the place where Moses was supposed to have made water appear. It is nowhere as large as Petra and much was damaged in an earthquake but there is a temple." That meant nothing to me but Lucinda nodded. "We have heard that thieves had been stealing from the tomb and we wanted to save as much as we could. Of course there are problems with the Turks but Professor Wingate said he had a contact in the government and he and Professor Teal went to London for the day. It must have worked for he came back, not with an official but a soldier. He came in a car, would you believe! He listened to us all for an hour or so and then announced that he would get us permission to dig and try to find us some sort of protection. He was a splendid fellow. We hope to be there by February and the dig will go on until the start of June. After that it will be too hot." He smiled, "Not only that but at the end of May it is Hajj. There will be many pilgrims heading to Mecca and the last thing we need is to upset them," He turned to Lucinda, "So you see, Lucinda, this is a load off my mind for you will be looked after and the paper that we will write should ensure that I can gain a place at a more prestigious university."

"But I would love to excavate a Roman site; especially one that is undiscovered, I am still an archaeologist." She grabbed my hand, "And as Griff is on half-pay, he can come with us. He speaks Arabic. Perhaps he could be paid as a translator."

I said, for I had a feeling of icy dread come over me, "This officer, his name wasn't Brigadier Dickenson was it?"

When the archaeologist beamed and said, "That is amazing, it was his name, do you know him?" I saw my father's face. He saw the work of a spider, a spider with a red tab on his collar. My family was being manipulated once more.

"Yes we do and I am guessing that the protection will consist of my batman and me." Lucinda's face, when she turned, was almost white as she realised what that meant. I smiled, "When the letter comes then I will be pleased to accept for being my wife's protector will be a pleasure."

This was not the time to talk about the situation, Mr Bannerman-Castle was too excited about this dig and the wedding. It was decided that they would return to Lancaster the following day. They had to tell the college that they would both have to give a fortnight's notice. "It is a small college and they have just six students." I felt sorry for the students. "We will close up the Grasmere house and then return here before the wedding."

Aunt Sarah said, firmly, "At least a week before the ceremony."

"What? Oh quite."

As they all left to pack there were just the three of us in the lounge. Cartwright said, "Do you think the brigadier knew about this when he spoke to you, Sir."

This was army and it would be, sir, again. "I think so. He knew about Lucinda and he said himself that he had a contact in the Foreign Office." I shook my head, "Why could he not have been honest with me?"

My father tapped the ash from his pipe, "He did not have all his ducks in a row, Griff. He needed the archaeologists to come to him. You can bet he had his contact plant the seed with the professor."

It suddenly struck me, "Then this is not about protecting the archaeologists? It is his world?"

"Oh there will be men to protect the diggers but you will be there for another purpose. It is Brigadier Dickenson's way. You are now repaying him for Sandhurst."

I looked at Paul, "Listen, Paul, this could be dangerous. If you wish to stay in England I am sure …"

"Sir, I now have not only you to watch over but Miss Lucinda too. I know my duty and I shall do it."

I went with them to the station. I could see that the gloss had been taken from both the wedding and the dig by the news about my involvement. She was not blaming me but I could tell she was not happy. We might be beginning our married life with a cloud hanging over us.

Brigadier Dickenson arrived the day after they had left. He came with Sergeant Barker. Neither was in uniform and that made me wary from the off. As I let them in I said, "No Asquith this time?"

The brigadier shook his head, "Damned thing keeps breaking down. It is fine for short journeys. Reed is at Windsor trying to mend it."

Paul made tea. I knew that Aunt Sarah did not like any of this and Aunt Bet persuaded her to go with her to town to buy things for the wedding. It was a wise decision. Aunt Sarah could be terrifying when she was angry.

We sat at the kitchen table. The sergeant said, affably, "Nice house this. You must be comfortable here, Sir."

He was addressing my father who nodded, "It is, Sergeant, and what regiment were you in?"

"Northumberland Fusiliers, Sir, but the corporal and I have been seconded, like."

I had listened but I was becoming annoyed. The brigadier said nothing. He looked at me as though daring me to speak first. I obliged him. "I am not happy about this Brigadier. I get the feeling that all of this has been orchestrated."

Sergeant Barker stared into his tea as though he was trying to read a message there. My father smoked his pipe and the brigadier sipped his tea. "It was not me who had you put on half-pay, Griff. You should know that I sent a telegram to General Pemberton objecting to what amounts to a punishment. I confess, however, that when I was approached by Professor Teal I saw an opportunity. If Mr Bannerman-Castle had not asked to go on the expedition then I would still have wanted you in the region."

"Why?" He looked at the door as though it might overhear what was said.

My father jabbed the stem of his pipe in the brigadier's direction, "You chose this as your meeting place, Brigadier, live with it."

He nodded, "You have skills, Griff. Your father had skills too but yours are on a different level. You showed that you are a thinker and a keen observer. The Kaiser has sent many of his officers to work with the Turks. They are allies. As you saw in Egypt part of their remit is to destabilise the region. The area with the temples is close to Jerusalem and that city is always on the brink of unrest. However, the most dangerous development is the building of the Hejaz Railway from Damascus to Medina. The British government has objected to the line they wished to build to Aqaba and the French prevented them from building to Jerusalem." He paused to finish his tea, "Petra is just fourteen miles from the railway. Your task, Lieutenant Roberts, is to gather as much information as you can about the railway line."

I asked, "Why? What difference does it make if the Turks are building a railway line?"

He looked at my father, "Ask your father about the work he did in Persia."

I saw the look of confusion on Dad's face and then realisation dawned. I had not made the connection but he had, "Oil."

"Oil indeed. The Royal Navy needs oil for the new battleships that will soon be launched. We will have to protect that oil and we need to know the threat the line represents. The defence of the realm may be at stake. If these new ships we are building do not have oil then our fleet, the steel walls which guard our island, may become useless." He smiled, "Excellent tea, Cartwright, another cup?"

"Sir."

When it was poured he continued, "We need all the information we can about units in the area. How are they officered? Are there any von Kleists amongst them? We are in the dark at the moment and all our attempts to get men close have ended in failure. This gives us our best chance. It will be for just a few months and you will be back by June."

"And then?"

Barker stared not at his tea but me as the brigadier said, slowly, "Your unique talents should not be wasted in some regiment that drills in Aldershot and parades just for the king. You should serve the king as a soldier. You would work for me."

"I would be a spy."

He shook his head, "No, for you would wear your uniform."

I laughed, "And as we would be in the desert and wearing keffiyeh and cloaks how would we look any different from the locals?"

"Quite."

There was silence. This was my decision. I was caught in a trap and it was a clever one. Lucinda loved me, I knew that but she also loved archaeology. I could not forbid her to go and I could not let her go alone. I would be going.

"There would, of course, be a promotion. You would be paid as a captain and that pay would begin immediately. If you were working for me then you would not be on half pay." He smiled, "Surely, if you were to resign your commission it would be better to do so as a captain."

I saw Cartwright pouring more tea for my father. "And Paul, here?"

"It is up to him, Griff, but if he chose to be your servant we would make his pay that of a corporal."

Paul stood erect and said, "You do not need to bribe me, Brigadier. I will go with Lieutenant Roberts wherever he serves."

"Then you will be raised in rank and pay. So, Griff, Captain Roberts, what do you say? The archaeologists will be going and there will be protection for them but I would be happier if you were involved."

I looked at my father who shrugged and then nodded. In truth, I had already decided. I said, "Then I agree but know this, Brigadier Dickenson, this has only confirmed my opinion of senior officers."

The brigadier nodded, "And mine too but I do what I do for my king and my country. You are a warrior, Griff, and I am the one who decides what those warriors will do. I do not like what I do but I know my duty."

When they had gone the three of us sat and spoke of it all. My father was able to give me perspective. "You could do nothing else and this way you will be there, along with Paul here, to watch over Lucinda. It is for six months and then, as he said you can resign your commission."

"Do I tell Lucinda?"

"Tell her?"

"About the way we have been manipulated."

"It is up to you but I would say no. Do not take the sparkle away from doing that which she loves. This may get the idea of living in the desert from her mind. I travelled that part of Arabia and it is brutal. It makes the Sudan and Egypt seem like Southport beach."

I nodded, "And you, Paul, your mind is made up?"

"It is, Sir. The pay and the rank do not interest me but I now have two people to look after."

"Then we just need to tell Aunt Sarah."

Dad smiled, "And plan a wedding. Do not forget that."

Part Three

The Spy

Chapter 16

The next weeks were like a blur. When I was not helping to plan the wedding I was preparing for the trip. I did not see the brigadier again but letters, sent by special delivery arrived with instructions and information. My dress uniform arrived but I would not take that with me. I could not foresee an occasion where I would need to dress up. The dig would all be about being a soldier. The tropical outfitters in Liverpool had been informed that Captain Griff Roberts now had an account and Cartwright and I were kitted out there. As the day of the wedding loomed so did the amount of information increase. As the dig had the backing not only of the college in Oxford but the British government, not to mention Lord Clifford who was interested in ancient cultures, then we would be travelling in a specially commissioned small steamship. It would begin its journey in Liverpool before travelling to Southampton to pick up the rest of the archaeologists, the soldiers and the equipment. I had been told, before the brigadier left, that although the men who would guard the dig were ex-soldiers, they would be under my command and obey all my orders. I made sure that by the time I was to be married, all the preparations had been made for our new life together. It was not the way I had expected it to be but when I had buried our dead at Farafra I had not expected to be married within a few months.

My father also received news that his second book, the one about Omdurman, would be published in June. I was pleased for it meant I would be home in time me to read it. His third one was already half written.

Thanks to the women in my life the wedding was immaculately planned and executed. It was cold when we wed but the skies were blue and the weather did not seem to matter.

My aunts wept and I saw the envy in Victoria's eyes. She had a beau but he had not yet proposed. I wondered if our marriage would accelerate that decision.

Our wedding night was not in the family home but in the Midland Adelphi next to the station in Liverpool. It was a luxury but Lucinda was worth it. When we arrived I took the pendant in its velvet lined box and handed it to her, "A wedding present." Her eyes welled up. She put the box down, threw her arms around my neck and kissed me passionately. The pendant could wait as could the story of how I was given it.

That night, as we lay in each other's arms, I was as happy as it was possible to be but I lay awake long after Lucinda slept in the crook of my arm as I pondered the next months. We would not reach our destination until the end of the first week in March. It would be their spring but still hotter than an English summer. If thieves had been stealing from the dig then the men I would lead would have to work hard from the moment we got there. Despite my orders from the brigadier, the protection of my wife would be my priority.

I was still awake before Lucinda. After we had dressed we enjoyed a breakfast that would keep me going all day. I paid the bill and we took a hackney cab back to the house. The SS Chester Castle would be docking on the sixteenth. We would have one night at home and then depart. I arranged for the cab and another one to return the next morning to take us and our luggage to the ship. We were welcomed as though we had been abroad already and yet it had just been one night apart. My aunts and Victoria were very close to my wife and I knew that the parting, the next day would be a hard one.

I spent most of the day with my father while the women sat in the kitchen and chattered and giggled. Victoria had been given the day off work and the wedding was discussed and dissected in minute detail. Aunt Sarah had never married and this was as near to her own wedding as she could imagine. Victoria was already planning hers.

Sitting in the parlour, we heard the laughter and my father smiled, "Lucinda is good for them all, Griff. She is a blessing."

I nodded. Cartwright and I spent the day being taught by my father, what to expect. He had worked with men who were not regular soldiers anymore. His experience had been a good one but he warned me about the possibility of a rogue one. I smiled and looked at Cartwright who said, "I wouldn't worry about the captain. He dealt with some men who others thought were beyond salvation. They were not."

The meal that night was prepared by all four women and we enjoyed wine with it. Once we left the ship it would be like Fort Farafra all over again. Tea would be the drink of choice. Lucinda and I slept in my bed but there was no lovemaking. We both wanted to but it did not seem right. This was not our home.

There were tears. Victoria and Lucinda both wept when my cousin left for work. When the cabs arrived and while we loaded them she and my aunts wept once more. Just when I thought there was no more salt left Aunt Sarah and Aunt Bet kissed, hugged and wept over me. It was a relief to sit in the cab with Lucinda. My father and Paul were in the second one.

John Bannerman-Castle was already at the quayside with another of the archaeologists. Nick Fields was from Victoria University, Manchester and was a friend of Lucinda's former guardian. The Chester Castle was not as big as the Carnic had been but she looked to be fast. What I feared was a spring storm before we reached the Med but I concealed those fears. Captain Jennings was younger than I expected. He had a neatly trimmed beard that made him look like the picture of Drake I had once seen. He made a great fuss of Lucinda who would be the only woman on the ship. They hugged and I saw that poor Lucinda was on the brink of tears. Cartwright, the captain and the chief steward took her to the cabin while my father and I supervised the loading of the cases and bags.

"Weapons?"

"I have my Webley and your pistol. The brigadier said there would be a Lee Enfield for me and for Cartwright at Southampton. I have a couple of knives and I do not think I will need a sword. Everything else will be with the men."

"Let us hope they are well chosen."

"I have the names and their service records. They all served either in India or Egypt. We shall see."

The captain was anxious to leave as the weather was set fair and mid-February was not the time to waste such benefits. I shook hands with my father.

He nodded at my new uniform, "I am proud of you, Griff. You now that and I am glad that we had the wedding we all wanted. It made up for…well never mind that. Watch out for yourself. You are in murky waters out there and despite what Dickenson said it is not worth your life or Paul's. Come back safe." He stepped back and saluted, "Captain Roberts."

I stepped aboard as the gangplank was removed. "I will try to write but…"

He shook his head, "You would be home before any letter reached us. We will think of you and I know you will think of us. That will be enough, eh?"

The sound of the ship's horn drowned out any more words and we were left to wave. Lucinda raced up on deck and blew a kiss at my father as we headed out to sea, passing the New Brighton ferry as we did so. The passengers there waved and we waved back. Lucinda cuddled closer to me, "I should have said a longer goodbye to your father. It did not seem right racing off like that."

"What and risk more tears? No, he said his goodbyes last night. He knows what we are going to have to do better than anyone." She shivered, "Do you want to go below deck?"

She shook her head, "No, I would like to watch England as we leave."

Suddenly Cartwright appeared and draped her coat around her shoulders, "Here you, are, Miss Lucinda. It is a little chilly."

"What would we do without you, Paul."

He smiled and tapped his stripes, "It is corporal now."

She shook her head, "You will always be Paul to me."

We had a good voyage down to Southampton and with just five passengers it felt as though we had our own private yacht. I had wondered if Lucinda would want to talk all things ancient with the two archaeologists but she stayed by my side. Paul gave us space when we needed it and attended to the two other passengers. Our cabin was the best one. I think that the captain had known we had just married and arranged it. As John

Bannerman-Castle had been the first to arrive at the ship that made sense.

When we pulled into Southampton I suddenly remembered troop ships and men going to war. I could not help but think of Archie, Bill Burton and all the other men who had fallen. I also knew that our idyll would change. I would become the officer once more. I would have to command and I had a short time to see the calibre of the men I would be leading.

When we docked I saw the soldiers, huddled under oil skins for it was raining, waiting to board. There were cases and bags also protected from the rain. They wore forage caps and their greatcoats, army issue, were pulled tightly up around their collar. Until they came aboard I would be blind. Once we were tied up the First Mate waved them to the forrard hold where a crane was rigged to help move the cargo. The archaeologists hurried up the gangplank as soon as it was fitted. Lucinda, Cartwright and I stood under the shelter of the bridge and allowed Nick and John to greet them. When I saw a man struggling up with bags I knew he was a servant. Cartwright said, "I will go and give that poor chap a hand, Sir."

We were both wearing our greatcoats and he jammed his hat upon his head.

John Bannerman-Castle led the party down to us. We were away from the worst of the rain. "This is my ward, Mrs Lucinda Roberts and her husband Captain Griff Roberts."

It was the first time anyone had used my wife's name and I liked it. I clicked my heels, "Pleased to meet you all."

Lucinda held her hand for them to kiss.

"This is Algernon Wingate."

The eldest looking chap with white hair and a fine beard kissed her hand.

"Delighted and congratulations on your marriage although a honeymoon with relics like us…"

"Will be a delight." My wife knew what to say.

"Thomas Teal."

He was middle aged and had sharp eyes and a nose that resembled a beak. He kissed Lucinda's hand but addressed me, "And you, I believe, are our security."

"Yes, Sir."

An Officer and a Gentleman

"You look a little young for that, if you don't mind me saying so."

I felt Lucinda's hand tighten on my arm. John Bannerman-Castle said, "You could not be more wrong, Tom, this young man was the one who save my ward and I at Siwa."

His mouth opened and closed like a fish, "You are the fellow. I apologise, Sir, and know that we are in safe hands."

The last one was Peter Potts. Although clearly younger than Algernon he was a forgetful man who acted older than his years. As I came to realise, however, he knew the Middle East better than anyone.

Lucinda said, "Come let us go into the lounge out of the rain. My husband will wish to greet his men alone."

She swept away like a queen with her courtiers behind them. She might be the least qualified of all of them but Lucinda was not going to be intimidated by them.

Cartwright and the servant appeared. They were dripping wet. "This is the last of it, Sir. Captain Roberts this is Alfred Tantor." He shook his head, "Fancy only bringing one servant."

Alfred was in his fifties but he had a permanent smile on his face, "I can cope, Mr Cartwright. Looking forward to this. My old bones will appreciate a bit of sun on them."

"I will pop back, Sir, when I have Alfred settled. Come along, Alfred and it is Paul, I told you."

I smiled. They would get along.

The seven men I would command headed up the gangplank. Each carried a kitbag over his shoulder and I saw that they all carried Lee Enfields. I waited to greet them. They had their heads down against the rain and when they lifted them, in the lee of the bridge, I recognised one of them. "Corporal Reed! This is a surprise."

He tapped his greatcoat and I saw the three stripes there, "Sergeant Reed now, Sir."

I nodded as a precocious wind suddenly swept around us. "Let us save the other introductions for later. Follow me. I will take you to your berths."

There were two classes aboard the steam ship, 1st and 2nd. We had the 1st Class cabins on the promenade deck. The others would have the 2nd class on the deck below. The advantage was that they each had their own cabin. For soldiers that was a luxury. On the voyage from Liverpool I had familiarised myself with the ship and I led them unerringly through what, to them, would appear a maze to their cabins.

I pointed at the eight cabins, four on each side, that we had been allocated, "There you are, Sergeant Reed, I will let you decide who sleeps where. We have one spare cabin and you can use that for your bags and guns if you like."

He was business like, "I will have this one." He slung his bag into the first cabin. "Tupper, this one." He gave him the one opposite and then moved down. "Ransome, here."

"Sarge."

"McTeer here."

"Righto, boss."

"Boyce and Pendle, here and here."

"Sergeant."

"Williams choose from the last three."

I said, "If you will dump your bags and follow me I will take you to the mess we will be using. After that you are free. I think today is a time for a recce of the ship."

"Good idea. Right lads, follow the captain."

The second-class lounge and dining room was on this deck. There were scuttles to allow in light and as it could accommodate twenty guests it was roomy. I pointed to the dining room before taking them into the lounge and its attendant bar.

"Take a seat and smoke if you wish."

I watched as they all looked to Sergeant Reed. He nodded. He was clearly in charge and I liked that.

"I am Captain Griff Roberts and like Sergeant Reed, a serving soldier. I have seen your records and know that you all served in the British Army at some point." I smiled, "I would be interested in why you took on this commission but we have two weeks or so to get to know one another. You should know that I recently married and my wife is one of the archaeologists we will be protecting." Just then Cartwright came in, "And this is Corporal Cartwright, my batman, and he is also a serving soldier."

I could see everyone, except Sergeant Reed and me, sizing up the others. They might make assumptions about Cartwright and me. Thomas Teal had. He had seen an officer with a servant and thought I was a blue blood. If they did then that was their mistake. I knew what I had to do and with Lucinda to protect I would do it.

"I won't be dining with you every night. I don't want to impose on you. Sergeant Reed is the one who will command you both here and in Transjordan. I will give the pep talk when we are closer to our destination but know that this will not be easy. My father was a soldier and he was charged with protecting oil prospectors not far from where we will be." I paused. "He buried some of his men out there." I let that sink in. "Anyway, get yourselves settled in and we will get to know each other as the voyage progresses."

As I passed him Sergeant Reed said, quietly, "Just the job, Sir. The right tone and all that."

I nodded, "Come up with me to the bar. I need a chat about you and your presence."

"Upstairs is it, Sir?"

"It is."

"I will join you there. I will just let them know what they can and can't do."

Paul and I headed up the stairs to the slightly more palatial 1st Class. "Well, Sir, this should be interesting."

"Indeed it will."

Lucinda and the archaeologists were seated around a table in the lounge and enjoying drinks served by the steward with the help of Tantor. I went over and said, "I am not being rude but I need to speak to my sergeant over there. I hope you don't mind."

It was clear to me that Thomas Teal was the leader for he smiled and said, "Of course not, Captain, and besides, we have your lovely wife to entertain us."

Her eyes met mine and I knew that she would rather be talking to me but she knew the rules of this sort of thing.

"What are you having, Sir?"

"I think that as we are starting something new it will be a whisky." He nodded, "And Cartwright, bring one for yourself."

He smiled and shook his head, "Oh, no, Sir. This is not your home and I am back to being your gentleman. I am happy just to serve."

I sighed. I thought Aunt Bet's home had changed him. It had not.

When the sergeant appeared Cartwright had just brought me my whisky. "Sergeant, a drink, perhaps?"

"A beer, Corporal, and thanks."

"So, Sergeant, why you?"

He sighed, "The brigadier thought that you might need another serving soldier, Sir. I mean Cartwright is alright but…"

"He is tougher than he looks, you know."

"I don't doubt it, Sir, but…" he leaned forward to speak conspiratorially, "look, Sir, I think you need to know everything. You are not the first officer that the brigadier has used like this. He had one in Gibraltar last year. He was worried about the German presence there. There was a German boat going from the Rock to Africa and we couldn't work out why. Lieutenant Carruthers was found dead in the harbour. His throat had been cut. The brigadier thought that you would be a little, well, wiser, Sir. I mean you survived in the desert and spotted that Prussian. I am just letting you know, Sir, that the men are to look after the archaeologists and I am to look after you."

Cartwright brought the beer. It was chilled and whilst that might not be necessary yet it boded well for the voyage and the heat we would encounter, "Just the job."

Cartwright joined us and we chatted about the men. I only half listened as I was distracted for I now had a clearer idea of the dangers involved. I had thought the dangers would come from the desert, the reptiles and the tomb raiders. Now we had enemy agents to add to the mix.

Dinner was a lively affair but I was the most silent around the table in the 1st Class lounge. Cartwright was eating with the others in the 2nd Class lounge, he had wished to serve us but the chief steward was appalled at the suggestion that a passenger should wait on tables. If Lucinda had not been there then no one would have noticed that I was largely silent. The archaeologists were full of chatter about the dig of a temple that had been barely explored. Would it prove to be another Petra? Even distracted I learned things. The land around the temples and Petra had been the home of the Nabataeans, a desert people who had fought off all invaders until the Romans. I learned that they traded and that gave them their wealth. There was a lively debate about the reason for the decline of the place. Lucinda quoted a passage she had read about an earthquake partly destroying the city. It was as we sat, the others drinking coffee, that Lucinda said, quietly, "What is bothering you, Griff? Was the conversation at dinner, dull? If it was I am sorry but…"

"The conversation was fine and I enjoyed it. There are things on my mind." I squeezed her hand. "We will talk in the room, eh? I shall sit and be the boring soldier."

She squeezed my hand back, "You are anything but that, my sweet."

That night we undressed and she lay in my arms. I decided that honesty was the only way forward. Secrets could only hurt us. I did not tell her of the agent who had his throat cut but I did say that there would be danger from more than just tomb raiders and that even in Gibraltar we would have to be guarded. "Fortunately we just take on coal at Gibraltar and fresh supplies. We shall not be there long but once we reach the Holy Land and travel through Turkish occupied land then we will need to be wary."

She cuddled me and then rose, "Thank you for your honesty and now I shall be honest. I confess that I did not like to have secrets from you." She went to her handbag and brought out a pistol. I saw that it was just a .22. It would have no stopping power at all but it was a weapon.

I held my hand out for it. It was an air pistol and fired one bullet at a time. Technically Lucinda needed a licence for it. It was easy to cock and fire but firing just one bullet Lucinda would have to be close to her target to hit it and she would not be able to stop an attacker. "Where did you get this?"

"Uncle John bought it in Cairo when we were on our way home. I used it in Grasmere. I am quite a good shot, Griff. I killed a rabbit that was eating the lettuce."

I handed the weapon back to her, "You might be but using this might be more dangerous than simply swinging a heavy handbag at his head. I will see if I can get you a proper gun and I will teach you how to use it."

She looked disappointed, "It is not a real gun?"

"It is a toy. The rifle version can kill a hare but that is all."

She replaced the gun and climbed back into bed, "Then I am still in danger?"

"It is not like Siwa. There are nine of us to protect you and the others. You had none at Siwa and you were surprised. One thing I must ascertain is what weapons the rest of the men have."

"Uncle John has a pistol, a real one and I think that Thomas Teal has a shot gun."

"I will ask. We have a pleasant voyage to Gib to discover all that there is to know and I can get used to my men."

I met the men the next day and I was impressed. All had served and been honourably discharged. None of them had families. There were many reasons but they had all found that civilian life did not suit and when they saw the advertisement they jumped at the opportunity it afforded. George told me that they had twenty applicants but these were the best. Any who were dubious they had rejected. None had served in what I would call real desert. Alec had been in South Africa and Reg had been based on the Nile. The other drawback was that none of them were camel riders. They had all ridden a horse but Cartwright and I were the only ones who knew how to ride a camel.

Even George was worried about riding a camel, "I thought we might ride horses, Sir."

I shook my head, "I don't think that Petra will be as bad as the Sahara or the Great Arabian desert but a camel means that we can be sure they will cope with the conditions. They also give you a better view, isn't that right, Cartwright?"

He smiled, "Listen, lads, if I can ride a camel then you will have no problem. The hard thing to learn is getting the beast to rise and then sit. The captain and I saw many troopers fall when trying to do that."

I had them all clean their weapons. George and I checked that they had everything that they would need. They had been equipped in Southampton but we inspected every man's kit. They all had a hundred rounds of ammunition. I said to the sergeant, "That won't be enough."

He nodded, "I have a chit from the brigadier and we can get as much as we like from the Rock."

An Officer and a Gentleman

"I know we will have to carry it but another five hundred rounds might be needed. I hope it won't but better to have it and not use it than not have it and need it." They all had goggles but no keffiyeh. George did not have one either. I said, "A keffiyeh is essential in the desert. We will buy them when we dock in Haifa." The sergeant had given me a report from the brigadier when he had boarded and while the sergeant and Cartwright drilled the men I sat on the promenade deck and read the report.

What became clear was that it was the presence of men like von Kleist that worried the brigadier. There was a German messianic cult called the Templers. They had settled in the Holy Land, especially around Haifa, and while they appeared to have peaceful intentions, there were so many of them that there could be agents hiding in plain sight. How would I discriminate between a genuine German who was following his beliefs and an agent of the Kaiser seeking to undermine Britain and France? By the time I had finished the report, which mentioned the dead Lieutenant Carruthers, I was relieved. I was pleased that George had told me for it meant I could trust him. I went to our cabin where I secreted the report in the bottom of my bag. I also used the time to clean and service my weapons.

Two days from Gibraltar our pleasant sea voyage ended as an Atlantic storm smashed into us. We were all confined below decks although I did venture out once to go to the bridge to speak to the captain. He frowned when I appeared, "Captain Roberts, whilst you command your men I command this ship and I confined everyone below decks."

"I know, Captain, but I need to know how this storm will affect us. We have a short time to complete our work."

He took his pipe from his mouth and pointed out at the huge waves that rose like grey walls, "See there, that lump of wood?"

I peered out and saw what he meant, "A log from a ship?"

"That was a Spanish ship. We watched it pounded to pieces two hours since. We had to view the crew as they drowned. We are made of steel but we have suffered damage. The crane that was used to hoist aboard your supplies was torn from us this morning. There is other damage too. Each time our stern leaves the water then the screws are in danger of damaging the prop shaft. I do not know how this will affect us but we shall have to spend longer in Gibraltar than an hour or so. There will be repairs that need to be made. In addition, the storm will affect when we arrive." He smiled, "We will not sink and you and the passengers will be safe. Stay below decks and let us do our job, eh, Captain?"

"Yes, Captain."

When I reached our cabin I was soaked and had to change.

Lucinda and the archaeologists were in the lounge and I was able to change and reflect on the captain's words. If we were stuck in Gibraltar then there would be danger. My men and I would begin work sooner than we had expected. I told them all of the potential delay.

Chapter 17

We did not limp into Gibraltar but neither did we race in. The ship had been damaged. We looked like someone who had been in a fight. We were still standing but bore the marks of damage. One of the hatches on the hold had been torn off. The captain told me that would necessitate an overnight stay but we would leave as soon as was possible. The crane would also need to be replaced. I gathered my men around me as the ship was tied up.

"The passengers will wish to go ashore. As the sergeant and I need to acquire more ammunition that means that you will all be called upon as bodyguards. I am afraid we cannot have you carry your rifles for you are not in uniform." I did not mention that it would alert the spies who proliferated on the island. Lieutenant Carruthers was still on my mind.

Alf Tupper grinned, "Don't worry, Captain Roberts, we all have other weapons."

I cocked an eye and frowned, "Really?"

He sighed, "Look, Sir, we knew when we took on this job that there might be danger. We are all being paid twice what we would have earned as a soldier of the king. We have knives, knuckle dusters and saps. We can look after ourselves. Even if they all go off on their own we have enough to watch them."

Sergeant Reed said, "He is right, Sir."

"Very well." I did not like this enforced delay. "I shall be happier when we are at sea once more."

I told Lucinda that she would either have to stay on board the ship or come with the sergeant, Cartwright and me. She chose the latter. I also tried to dissuade the others from going ashore but they all had their own reasons for stepping from the ship. We had not even reached the land of the Turks and there would be danger.

As we stepped from the ship I was keenly aware that we were being observed. Some of it was natural curiosity. I saw men looking to see how they could make money from us and others who wondered at the three British soldiers with the pretty woman. Then there were the normal thieves who inhabited such places and would look for an opportunity to profit. The greatest threat, however lay in the two German ships which were tied up and I knew that we would be identified not least because we wore uniforms. If the brigadier was right then they would most definitely be interested in us. I was armed with my Webley and I had given Cartwright my father's pistol. The two of us flanked my wife. Sergeant Reed had his own pistol and he watched our backs.

The armoury was not close to the harbour but was in the complex known as the Rock. There was a garrison here that protected the most valuable of British assets. The Suez Canal had made it even more important. However, I was a lowly captain and of little importance to the officers of the garrison. The brigadier's letter gained us access to the quartermaster who did as all such warrant officers would do in the same situation. He frowned and shook his head, "This is a lot of ammunition, Sir, and it will take time to assemble."

I nodded, "Well, Sergeant, when it is ready could you have it taken to the SS Chester Castle?"

He shook his head and said, "More than my job is worth, Sir. You will have to take it with you."

Lucinda put her hand on the sergeant's, "Sergeant, I would like to see a little of Gibraltar. Do you think you could have it ready in, say an hour or so and have some of your men take it with us? It would be a help and we would be ever so grateful."

I saw the effect it had. He took in the ring and said, "Of course, Mrs Roberts. An hour it is."

Once in the sunshine she beamed, "There, I knew I could be useful."

I could see that Sergeant Reed was torn between waiting for the ammunition and protecting us. I made it easy for him, "Sergeant, come with us and do not fret about the ammunition. We do not sail until the morning in any case."

He looked relieved, "Righto, Sir."

We spent money and enjoyed the strange mixture of the British, African and Spanish cultures of Gibraltar. We spent money buying gifts for those at home. Lucinda wanted to thank Sarah, Bet and Victoria. I found a good pipe and bought that for my father. I would get him some tobacco when we landed. There would be more choice there. I was, however, distracted as I saw

An Officer and a Gentleman

that we were being followed. I saw at least four men. One was a blond European, one an Arab and two looked to be African. They seemed very interested in all of us. They could have been thieves looking for an easy theft or they could have been people with more serious intent. I thought it more likely to be the latter. By the time we returned for the ammunition I was glad that the warrant officer had made us return. We had four soldiers to carry the boxes to the ship. As they all carried Lee Enfields our safety was guaranteed. They carried the boxes aboard and although we offered them a drink they declined. They were fearful of their sergeant smelling alcohol on their breath. I stood, with Sergeant Reed, at the gangplank watching for the other passengers and I did not relax until they were all aboard.

I had just turned to head for the lounge when a messenger came from the captain, "Sir, a message from England."

"Thank the captain. Will we be ready for sea by the morrow?"

"Oh, yes, Sir, all shipshape and Bristol fashion."

Left alone I unfolded the telegram. It was a brief but sinister message. The brigadier said that German agents had been seen close to both Haifa and Petra. There would be danger. I wondered how he knew.

We had eaten well thus far on the voyage but the access to fresh fruit, vegetables and meat meant that the meal was even better than we had yet experienced. The archaeologists had also stocked up on local wine which they had bought, they said, for coppers. They all drank well but I drank in moderation. While we were in port I would be wary.

Cartwright, Lucinda and I, along with Alfred helped the gentlemen to bed. They had all enjoyed the food and drunk at least six bottles of their wine. Alfred and Paul went to the 2nd class and we entered our cabin.

Lucinda had enjoyed a couple of glasses of wine and it showed. She kissed me hard when the door to our cabin was closed, "That was a lovely night, Griff. I have not seen John in such good humour, well, not since before Siwa. He took my father's death hard."

I had seen many men die and knew that the memory never totally left. The drink would have masked it, that was all. John

Bannerman-Castle would still have his demons. Archie had his and, I suppose, Archie's death lay heavily on me. I had told myself that I had done all that I could but had I? If we had been closer to him might we have been able to prevent his death? I knew that by stirring those demons I was giving myself less chance of a good night of sleep.

We lay in the bed. I took the door side. I suppose it was the officer in me for if there was a problem I could reach the door first.

"We should all make the most of the good life before we reach the desert. Alcohol and the desert do not mix. Dehydration can kill." At the back of my mind was the thought that Archie's end had been hastened by alcohol. In his case it was not dehydration but impairment of judgement.

"Then there will not be many more nights such as this, will there?"

"No, I do not believe that the Mediterranean will be as threatening as the Atlantic."

We kissed and she lay with her head in the crook of my arm. I usually stayed awake long enough for her to fall asleep and then slipped my arm out. When she was breathing deeply I moved my arm and then turned to face the door. The memory of Archie's death had been triggered and sleep would not come. My eyes were still open and I saw a shadow in the corridor. Normally I might have ignored it but the men who had followed us had made me suspicious. Who would be sneaking around the ship's corridor at night? I slid from the bed and listened. I heard heavy breathing outside the door. Someone was there. Even before I could seek a weapon the door opened and a half naked man slipped in. The light from the corridor, dim though it was, showed the shape of my wife beneath the blankets. I saw the dagger in his hand. I watched him raise it to strike down at the bed. I had one hand around his neck and the other holding his hand in an instant but he was strong. I still do not know why I did not shout out but I did not. I was too intent, I think, on preventing either Lucinda or I coming to harm. He hooked his foot behind mine and pushed. I lost my balance and we crashed to the ground.

My wife murmured, as she stirred "What is it?"

I could not speak for the fall had winded me. The man used his elbow to hit me in the ribs and that hurt too. We rolled around and it was he who was on top. My grip was weakened and he was gradually turning me. I still held the knife but his head was now above me and he used two hands to push the wicked dagger towards my throat. I was trying to stop him but the winding had given him the edge. In such encounters it was often tiny details that determined the outcome. I saw, in his eyes, that he saw victory and he used his feet to push his body down to me. The pop from the .22 was inconsequential but the pellet had hit the man in the neck. A tendril of blood dripped down. I saw Lucinda standing just six feet from him. He turned his head and in that moment I was able to turn the dagger so that it was not pointing at me but at his stomach. He turned and pushed down, not realising what he had done. It was his own bodyweight that drove the dagger into his own body and when he went still I knew he was dead. I closed my eyes.

Lucinda said, "Is he…?"

I said, "Yes."

"Did I kill him?"

I smiled, "No, but you saved my life." I pushed the body from me. My pyjamas were covered in blood but the carpet on the cabin floor was saved from damage. I saw that it was one of the men who had followed us, one of the Africans. I had to think. I said, "I need to go and get some help. Come with me."

"Why?"

"I am not leaving you here with a dead body."

She nodded and slipped her dressing gown on. I hurried down to the deck below and knocked on Cartwright's cabin, "Paul, look after Mrs Roberts."

His eyes widened when he saw the blood, "Sir! Are you…"

"It is not mine, Paul. Keep her here and keep her safe. Use your gun."

"Sir."

I hurried to George's cabin and knocked on it. He opened it and I saw that, behind his back he had a pistol. "Sir!"

"Not mine, Sergeant. A man came into my cabin and tried to kill me. I think he was one of the four men I saw following us. There may be more. Rouse the men and search the ship but do so silently without disturbing the other passengers or alerting any more potential killers. Have one of them go to my cabin and watch the body."

"Mrs Roberts?"

"Is safe and with the corporal." I smiled, "She saved my life. I will go and find the captain."

I went to the bridge and the First Mate who was on duty looked horrified at my pyjamas. I saw he was alone. We were in port and tied up to the quay. There was no helmsman or watchkeeper. That was a good thing but also told me how the killer had got aboard. Before he could say anything I said, "Where is the captain?"

"In his cabin, asleep." He saw the blood and my face, "Follow me and I will take you to him."

I think sea captains must be like soldiers. They are never really off duty and he was awake in an instant. I quickly told him what had happened. "I have my men searching for any accomplices."

I watched his mind at work. He said to the First Mate, "Wake the chief engineer. I want to leave as soon as he can get steam up."

"But, Captain, the dead man."

"Mr Balfour, obey the order and leave the rest to Captain Roberts and me." When he had gone he said, "I wondered if something like this might happen. Brigadier Dickenson told me a little of the possible danger." He shook his head, "I should have kept a watch on the gangplank! Hindsight eh? Brigadier Dickenson wanted me prepared and, it seems he was prescient and I was remiss. We will get under way as soon as we are able. There are spare cabins in 2nd Class. Have your men move the body to one of them. Try to avoid blood on the carpet, eh? The owners would not like it. Tomorrow night, when we are at sea, we will dispose of the body. I will speak to Mr Balfour and ensure he is silent. The man wants promotion." He saw my questioning look and said, "First of all if we involve the police then it will delay our departure. Secondly, it will upset the academic gentlemen. I know that your soldiers can cope but the others…"

"You may be right and there is a third reason."

"Yes."

"When the man fails to return they will not know if he has succeeded or not. At least not for a while. We have enemies out there, Captain, and we need them to be in the dark."

He nodded to the pyjamas, "And change out of those, Captain. They can go overboard with the body. We don't need our dhobi wallers asking awkward questions."

I went directly to the cabin. Bill Pendle was watching the body. He saw my pyjamas and said, "You were lucky, Sir, this man was a professional."

"I know, Bill. Go to the empty cabin on your deck and bring me the sheet from it."

He hurried off and I dressed. Sleep would be impossible. I took the dagger and washed it in the bowl of water on the night stand. I would keep it. It would not be a souvenir but it might tell me about the man so that I could identify another if I saw them. Pendle came back and we wrapped the body. I could hear the throb of the engines as the chief engineer slowly brought them to life. A steam ship took time to be ready to sail. I peered out of the door and the corridor was empty. I knew that the cabins were occupied by the archaeologists and their servant. I nodded for Pendle to pick up his end of the bundle and we moved out into the corridor. I dreaded one of the doors opening but the drink they had consumed ensured that they would only wake if there was an explosion. Getting the body down the stairs was not easy but Pendle was strong and we managed it. We laid it on the bed and covered the body with more blankets. I had noticed that there was no blood coming from the body. The dagger must have killed instantly. The purser would have to write off the loss of the sheet. I wondered how the captain would explain it. That was his problem.

We locked the door and I pocketed the key. We went on deck. The sergeant said, "Keep in the shadows, Captain Roberts, best you stay hidden." I obeyed. "There was no one else aboard, Sir, but look." He pointed to a building just beyond the dock. I saw a light and a head moved. "Someone was watching. They will be wondering what happened. That was why I said to hide. If they tried to kill you then let them think they have succeeded."

"Well done, Sergeant. The captain is taking us to sea. Pendle and I have locked the body in the empty cabin on your deck. We will dispose of the killer tomorrow night when we are at sea. Until then you and the others make sure that no one else comes aboard."

"Right, Sir." He paused, "What exactly happened, Sir, and how did Mrs Roberts save you?"

I told him and watched him smile, "She is a game 'un, Sir. A .22 you say?" I nodded, "I have some spare weapons. One is a bit small for the lads to use, it is a .38. Should fit the bill. I didn't know your wife was Annie Oakley."

"Neither did I. However, Sergeant, if it had been anything bigger than a .22 then I would be dead too. At a range of six feet even a .38 would go through the killer and me!"

I waited until we had steam up and the ship pulled away from the quay before I went to Cartwright's cabin. The door was locked and Paul had a gun pointed at me when he opened it. "You can put that away, Paul. We are heading to sea." Lucinda threw her arms around me and said, "I thought he was going to kill you."

"And that was his intent. Are you alright to go back to our cabin?"

She nodded and said, "Of course." Then she added, "The body…"

"Is not there. Thank you, Cartwright."

"Sir, if you want me to sleep outside your door…"

"That will not be necessary but thank you for the offer."

Lucinda managed to get to sleep. It was three a.m. when she did so but that allowed me to slip out of the room and head to the bridge. The captain took me to the flying bridge where the helmsman could not overhear us. I told him what we had done and the captain nodded. I said, "What did you tell the port authorities?"

"That with the repairs done we had to make up for lost time. They were happy to have the berth. We should be safe until Haifa but then…" He took out his pipe and began to fill it, "You know that while it might take your enemies a couple of days to realise that their killer is dead and not you they will know and will send a telegram. There could well be men waiting for you."

"I know, Captain, but to be fair, we always expected danger there. We will be armed and we will have systems in place. One thing this has shown me is the calibre of my men."

He had the pipe going and as he blew out a plume of smoke he said, "And their officer, too, not to mention his resourceful wife."

If Lucinda was a little quiet at breakfast none of the archaeologists noticed. They were all nursing hangovers. They did not even comment on the fact that we had moved in the night. After breakfast Professor Teal decided to hold a planning meeting to decide what their priorities would be once we landed. I went to join my men at the after promenade. There were deck chairs there and we sat. I know the crew thought we were just enjoying the sun but the truth was that we now knew the scale of the problem.

"From now on we treat every day as though there is going to be some sort of battle." They all nodded. "While on the ship we cannot carry our Lee Enfields but I want you all armed. Sergeant Reed has some handguns. Get used to wearing them. If any of the crew notice or say anything then blame me and say I want you prepared for dangers ahead." I turned to Sergeant Reed, "Now let us assume that our enemies know they have failed and are waiting for us. I don't think they will try anything in Haifa. Too many witnesses."

"I agree, Sir. The brigadier and I thought that they might try something closer to the temple site and blame it on tomb raiders."

I smiled, "It seems we are all of the same mind then. I do not intend to take any men from Haifa with us nor spend too long there. The Germans have too much influence. If we hire diggers, and I assume we will, then we will use local people. I will go ashore first and select the camels we will be using. The brigadier has arranged that already?"

"Yes, Sir, there is a camel dealer at the port and he has been paid already. We just select the twenty camels we want."

"Then Pendle and Tupper, you will come with me when we pick them. They will try to give us old and tatty ones. We will be armed. Cartwright, from now on you stay as close to my wife as is humanly possible. It should be me who is there but I think I will be a magnet for bullets and blades. I have a task to perform in the desert and I will do that alone. I want the rest to be safe."

"Yes, Sir, I have to agree and I intend to practise each day with the pistol." We had secured enough ammunition. Cartwright had a steely determination in his eyes I had not seen before. He was protective of Lucinda.

I smiled, "We are a small team but last night showed me that it is a good one. There will be no medals, lads, but…"

Alf Tupper grinned, "Sir, with due respect, we would rather have the money than the medals. We were all given plenty but in civvy street they mean bugger all." He looked at the others, "Sir, one thing… me and the lads have been talking. If we do have to fight then can we keep anything that we take?"

"Of course, there are only three of us paid as soldiers."

His grin became wider, "Thank you Sir, that was all we needed to know." The British soldier was always self-reliant, when he was allowed to be.

"One more thing, we will leave Haifa as soon as we have camels. I want to give our enemies no chance to make another attempt. We ride hard that first day and from then on make well defended camps."

They nodded. Cartwright and I would be the experts. We had made many such camps in the desert.

It was midnight when I left Lucinda to dispose of the body. "If you want to lock the door I will understand."

She smiled, "I am not afraid of the bogey man. Just do what you have to do and come back to bed. You had no sleep last night and you must be exhausted."

The captain had ensured that there was no one on duty apart from the First Mate on the wheel and himself. The lookouts had been sent below to make cocoa and George, Paul and I hurried to take the body to the stern. When the lookouts returned they would look to the bridge and the bows and not the stern. George and I held the body and I mouthed, "One, two," and on "three" we hurled it astern. It was not out of consideration for the assassin but we did not want the propellors fouled by the sheet and my pyjamas. Any further delay would be disastrous. We saw that the body floated for a while and it was then tugged and pulled. The sea would dispose of the assassin.

The captain smiled, "And now we can all get some sleep, eh?"

Chapter 18

We reached the port not long after dawn. The captain had made good time. It was the end of the first week in March. Haifa was not Gibraltar but it was growing in size. There were half a dozen ships being unloaded. I wondered if that was the result of the Germans settling there. While our baggage and supplies were brought ashore and guarded by my men I went with Cartwright, Pendle and Tupper. The three carried rifles. This time I did not care if people saw that we were armed. We headed out of the port to the enclosure just beyond it. My nose would have found the camel trader even if I had not been given directions. The camels were in the open and I saw, immediately, the ones I would not want in a month of Sundays. I knew camels and while I could not hope to find another Scheherazade I wanted good ones. I saw that some were mangy and others were thin. Those camels would not last the journey we had to make.

The greasy looking trader spoke English to me. I answered him in Arabic and I saw the doubt on his face immediately. If he thought I was a naïve British officer he was wrong. I showed him my authorisation but while he could speak English I doubted that he could read it. I think my uniform was enough for him. He waved an arm and led me to the camels he wished me to have. They were the poor ones and even as we approached them and he was singing their praises, I said, "Not those which are fit only for the feeding of my neighbour's dog. Let us look over there and I will choose."

The smile which he had worn since he had greeted me had been fading and now disappeared altogether, "Those are for another client."

I tapped the paper, "I have a contract here and I will choose my twenty camels."

His face now became angry and he waved over two men shouting at them to arm themselves. He had clearly forgotten I spoke his language. "Cock your weapons."

The sound of the three bolts on the Lee Enfields was enough for him to hold up his hand and arrest the movement of his men. Their single shot weapons would not be a match for three British rifles. He waved a hand in surrender, "Choose your camels. You will reduce me to sending my family to beg on the streets."

I chose them and sent Cartwright and the other two to fetch the saddles. To mollify the man and stop him from trying to steal them back I said, "When we return, before high summer, I will sell the animals back to you."

He gave a half smile, "If you survive." I think he realised he had said that which he should not. "I mean who knows what the next months may bring. I pray that Allah watches over you."

It was a warning. Did he know of tomb raiders or Germans? It seemed to me that he was in the pay of Germans. He worked in Haifa and would come across them every day.

We did not ride them back but led them. I had chosen Lucinda's as soon as I had picked the beasts we would have and mine too. Mine looked to be the leader and she needed a good rider to control her. The best camel rider would be me. Lucinda's was an older camel. She would be gentler. By the time we had loaded the camels and I had managed to secure keffiyehs, it was noon. While I would not risk riding in the desert at noon, we were close to the coast and the air was cooler. I wanted to be away sooner rather than later. We might have left an hour earlier but Algernon Wingate was not a camel rider and while the other novices soon picked it up he struggled. In the end I attached a halter and decided that I would lead him. Sergeant Reed rode at the back with Pendle and Tupper leading the pack animals. The other four spread themselves between the archaeologists. I rode at the fore with Lucinda next to me and Cartwright on the other. I knew she could ride a camel and Cartwright was there with his rifle to protect her. We headed from the port to take the road down the coast and then east to the road to the mountain. We had two hundred miles to go and while my troop and I could have made that journey in four days, it would take at least a week for us and that worried me. It meant six nights where we would have to make a defensive camp. My men would be exhausted before we got there. My men obeyed what amounted to an order and wore the keffiyeh. John Bannerman-Castle apart, the archaeologists did not.

I was not as worried about the first night's camp for we were close to a town. Jaffa was a port and whilst not as big as Haifa would allow us to find somewhere safe to sleep. The breeze not only kept us cool it also kept the insects from us. The result was that after a half day of riding we were not in a bad way. They all had sore backsides and that included the soldiers but they were not distressed. We bought food in the port for I did not want us to begin to eat into the supplies we would need at the Roman temple. I set guards and Cartwright and Tantor, aided by Lucinda, cooked the food.

Thomas Teal was like Harry Quinn; he liked his cigars. He lit one and walked with me as I inspected the perimeter. "We have made a good start, Captain."

"Better than I could have hoped but once we leave the coast and head inland it will be harder."

"You have been to this part of the desert before?"

I shook my head, "No, but I did my research and I know that the road will be a hard one. It climbs up through the mountains. It was built by the Romans and so is straight but I don't think the Ottomans did anything to improve it."

"You have done well to have done so much planning, Captain. I was, however, disappointed that we left Haifa so quickly that we had no time to find diggers. Before we leave tomorrow, we will hire some."

"No, Professor Teal, we will not and for a number of reasons. One, we need to move as quickly as we can. Two, we cannot afford to feed diggers on a slower journey to the site and thirdly, we do not know the motives of men around here. From my research I learned that around the temple site are just Bedouins who are caravan drivers or goat herders. Their families eke out a living in the desert. They will be grateful for the income."

He frowned, "You are our security and I am the one in command."

I sighed, "Professor, do you really need diggers? From what I was told the main temple and tombs are above ground anyway. We are there a short time. If you discover new tombs you are doing the work for the tomb raiders. Surely it is better for you to record what you see and gather information about what may be there. When the time is right you could return, perhaps over the winter months when it will be easier to dig. We only have until June, Professor. We will just be touching the surface of the dig."

An Officer and a Gentleman

He had finished his cigar and he threw the stub into the fire. "You are a clever young man and your argument is a cogent one. We pass through Beersheba do we not?"

"Yes, Professor. The Turks, so I read in the report, have built a new town a mile or so away from the one named in the Bible."

"Then we will make our decision there. I agree we should make all haste but Beersheba is just two days from this new site. It is close enough so that the Nabateans who ruled Petra were able to raid Beersheba." He smiled, "I have also done my research. You may be right, Captain, but the decision to hire diggers is an archaeological one and not a military one."

I had the second night watch and I rolled under the blankets with Lucinda. She had witnessed the discussion and she asked, "What was all that about?"

I told her. "I think that the professor will consult with you archaeologists."

She cuddled in tighter, "And I will support your view, Griff. You are right. We do not want to expose more graves for the tomb raiders to rob. Nick Fields has brought a camera and he intends to record what we find for posterity." I was relieved.

We bought food in every town we passed. It was cheap enough and our cans of food and dried goods stayed wrapped up. Once we turned inland to head to Beersheba then it would become harder to buy food. We still managed it but the food was of poorer quality. I thought back to Abu Minqar. Often we had bought a kid from the oasis dwellers. I hoped we could do the same. Here they did not live in oases but villages that had been here since the time of the Old Testament. Like the Egyptians the people who dwelt here learned to live with the land.

The twenty miles from the coast to Beersheba gave everyone the chance to realise how much harder it would be once we passed the town. We could see the rocky peaks beyond. As mountain ranges go it was not particularly high but the climb would tax the academics. My men had learned to ride the camels and even to like them. Cartwright had helped there. He remembered his own problems and the advice he gave them was sage. I was not sure they had respected the gentle man when they had first met him but now they did. Some of the academics were also suffering from the sun. On the third day they had seen the advantage of the keffiyehs and had worn them but by then the sun had done its damage. The red skin was blistered and would heal, in time, but I think they learned to heed my advice.

I led the line of camels not to the Ottoman town but the old village. There were few people there but they were desert dwellers. They had endured Romans, Byzantines, Crusaders and Turks. Their way of life had endured for centuries and would continue when the Ottoman Empire, as all empires do, crumbled. We stopped in the middle and while Sergeant Reed organised the camp I went to find the head man. Thanks to my time in Egypt I could now converse easily. I had an accent and there were some local words I did not know but speaking to locals in their native tongue brought smiles rather than scowls.

The headman was seated beneath an awning where he was drinking coffee and children were playing close by. I saw a couple of goat herders driving the small flock into a pen. They knew the desert and its predators both human and animal. They would protect them at night. The Bedouin, for I recognised his clothes, stood and bowed his head slightly, "Welcome to the village of Beersheba. I am Talal al-Askari and I am the head man here, Effendi, what brings so many visitors to my humble home?"

"I am Captain Griff Roberts and I am escorting these men to Petra." He frowned and I said, "You may know it as Wadi Musa."

He smiled, "The home of the Nabateans who preyed so much on my ancestors." They never forgot. "They wish to see the ancient tombs?"

"They intend to explore some new ones and record what they say so that people across the sea may know of their wonder."

He shrugged, "The past is gone and we concern ourselves with the living."

I nodded. The people who lived in the desert had a different view of the past from academics who could indulge their fascination. "I wondered if you had a kid you could sell to us."

He beamed, "Of course." He leaned in and pointed a bony finger towards the new town. "The Turks like to take. They never pay. Come, we will choose a good one. Would you like milk for your tea?"

I nodded, "That would be good."

He chuckled, "I never know why Englishmen spoil coffee and tea by putting in milk. Milk is to make cheese and to feed the young." He called over one of the goat herders, "Abdullah, we need a kid."

The young man nodded and glanced at me. He had not heard me speak and assumed, I think, that I did not speak his language, "I shall pick a sickly one."

Talal snapped, "Do not embarrass me. Captain Roberts speaks our language and he is paying. A good one."

"Sorry, Grandfather."

When it was selected I paid and Abdullah slit its throat for me. The blood was drained into a pot. It would be used by these people to enrich a stew. I had seen the same thing in Egypt. Desert dwellers wasted nothing. I said to Talal, "You are more than welcome to join us."

"Thank you, Captain, you are a most civilised young man but I will dine with my family." I nodded. "A word of advice, my people will not harm you or try to take from you but the Turks? They are a different matter. Hobble your camels." He shook his head, "They have a garrison of twenty men but the officer is more of a bandit than a gentleman like you."

"Thank you for your advice."

I handed the goat to Pendle who would skin and butcher it, "We eat fresh meat. Keep the bones and boil them up."

"Aye, Sir. Almost like a shoulder of lamb at home, eh?"

After giving the milk to Lucinda, I waved over George Reed. "Hobble the camels and ginger up the sentries. The old man reckons the Turks might try to steal them. I will take the first watch tonight."

"Right, Sir."

I wandered to the fire. The nights were still a little chilly and the professors were huddled around it. Tom Teal said, "We have been talking, Captain. Your wife is very persuasive and made a good case. If we need diggers then we will hire them in Wadi Musa."

"Good."

"I saw you talking to the old man. Did you learn anything?"

"That the Turks are very unpopular and he thinks they might try to steal our camels."

He raised his eyebrows, "I would have thought we were in more danger from the Bedouins."

"In my experience if you make an enemy of an Arab then you are in trouble, but if they are your friend then they are as loyal as anyone. I trust the old man."

Alf Tupper and I were the night guards. I used my trusty cloak. It kept me warm and made me almost invisible as I sheltered next to the wall. Tupper was wearing his greatcoat and the flickering firelight reflected from his buttons and his white face. He was on the far side of the herd. The camp was asleep. Cartwright and Alfred Tantor had made their beds so that anyone trying to get to Lucinda would have tripped over them.

I sensed rather than saw the movement. Men were coming around the herd. I could not tell their numbers at first but I drew my pistol. It was clear that they were avoiding Tupper. They thought he was the solitary sentry. I saw that there were three of them and although they wore cloaks I spied military breeches. They were young soldiers. Talal had implied that the officer was a thief. Was he sending young men to steal our camels? I did not move and by keeping still I remained invisible. I waited until they were just ten feet from me and had removed their knives to cut the hobbles from the camels. I levelled the Webley and said, "If you try to cut the hobbles then I will shoot you."

They whirled. Clearly they had not seen me. My words brought Tupper over and he covered them with his rifle. He said, in English, "How did they get past me?"

"The light shone from your buttons." I turned back to the three, "Drop your knives." They hesitated and I said, "I do not want to harm you but I will. Now obey my command." They did so. "Any more weapons?" They shook their heads but I did not believe them. I holstered my pistol and said, "Cover them." Tupper was annoyed that they had got past him and he glared at the three. I patted them down. One was a young officer and he had a pistol and holster. I removed them.

"You cannot do that."

"I already have. Now slink back to your camp but know this, next time we open fire and ask questions later."

"Captain Kukuk will not be happy."

I smiled, "Then that should be an interesting conversation tomorrow, eh?"

I woke not just George Reed but Ransom and McTeer. I told them what had happened. "I don't think they will be back but tomorrow, when this Turkish officer comes, I want the men and their guns hidden."

Sergeant Reed nodded, "Good idea, Sir."

The rest of the night was untroubled but as I was stirring the pot of porridge the Turkish captain and six men rode up. They were on horses. I studied them as they approached. The officer looked arrogant. His uniform was immaculate and I recognised the German pistol in his holster. He was another who was German trained. My men, Cartwright apart, were all hidden. Lucinda and the archaeologists gathered together for the Turks were deliberately intimidating.

The officer said, "You took weapons from my men. I wish them returned."

I saw that the three men were not with him. I smiled, "Then they came here to steal our camels with your permission, Captain Kukuk."

He looked non plussed, "Of course not. Their weapons."

"If you did not send them I assume they will be punished. If they were my soldiers they would be."

"Do not presume to tell me how to command my men." He held up his hand and said, "Sergeant!"

His men levelled their single shot carbines. I did not say a word but the sound of eight Lee Enfield bolts being pulled back was ominous. Cartwright's was aimed at the captain. I walked closer to his horse and, holding the bridle, said quietly, "Captain we are here with the permission of your government and I have no intention of returning weapons that might be used against us. Now if you are foolish enough to risk a firefight then you should know that these eight rifles can send eighty bullets into you and your men before they raise theirs and fire their one bullet."

I stepped back and I saw the anger flaring on his face. He snapped, "Sergeant!" and waved his arm. The carbines were lowered. "It is a long way to Petra, Captain Roberts."

He whirled his horse around and they galloped back to the town. My men came over and Sergeant Reed said, "Remind me never to play cards with you, Captain." He saw my face and said, "What is up, Sir?"

"He knows my name and the direction we are taking. They were waiting for us to come here. The only good thing is that he thinks we are going to Petra and we are not going there. I think that we are now on a war footing, Sergeant. Our men are going to earn every penny of their pay."

The sergeant shook his head, "The brigadier had to have known that they knew what he planned. You are bait, Sir."

"Perhaps but that does not mean that I have any intention of being devoured, Sergeant. Believe it or not I feel quite at home in the desert. When I scout out the railway that is my element. These Turks and their German officers are not natural desert warriors. The old man, Talal, he is, as are his children and grandchildren. They know how to adapt to the desert like the fox who lives in Egypt and has enormous ears to hear his prey. When I ride the desert alone then any who seek my life had better be prepared to pay with their own. I have no intention of making my wife a widow." I smiled, "I do not think that she suits black."

The archaeologists were shaken by the encounter. They did not understand all the words but the carbines and rifles had frightened them. I put their minds at ease before we left. "Gentlemen, we knew that the Turks would not be happy about our presence. My men and I are not afraid of this Captain Kukuk. For a start he only has twenty men and they are riding horses. If they follow us we will know. We make all speed to the Roman temples. I hope to be there by tomorrow night. I intend two long hard days of riding. The terrain will hurt but we can then make a camp and protect ourselves from any threat. The sooner we get to the dig site the sooner you can begin to record what you need to."

Lucinda rode as close to me as she could as we wound our way through the passes to Transjordan. "The Turks could cause us trouble, Griff."

"Lucinda, they knew my name. We were bound to have trouble with the Turks the moment their attempt to kill me failed.

Don't worry, when we are at this temple complex in the desert we can make it defensible."

"I wish we had never come."

"As do I but we are here and I have a job to do. Trust me, my love. I will do it."

Chapter 19

I pushed them hard. I let George lead and I rode two hundred yards behind the last man but I did not let them slow or stop too frequently. I wanted to be at the rear to watch for pursuit. I think we caught the Turkish officer unawares. Our speedy departure meant he must have been tardy to follow. When we did have a halt, at a conveniently overhanding rock at the bend of the road, I used my binoculars. I had seen the dust and the glasses brought them into focus. The Turkish captain had brought all his men. That would please the headman. They looked to be five or six miles behind us. It would be hard on us but harder for the horsemen who would need to water their horses more frequently than we did and they would be playing catch up. If they did catch up with us before we camped then they would be in no condition to do anything.

At our noon stop I saw that they were still six miles or so behind us. They were not drawing any closer. Thomas Teal came over to me as I walked my camel to the place George Reed had picked to water the camels. "Captain, you are pushing us hard."

"Yes and that is deliberate. Professor Teal, I did not choose to excavate these Roman temples, you did. It must be clear to you, by now, that we are not welcome. The longer we spend on the road the more danger we are in. It is my understanding that there is one entrance to this temple complex." Professor Teal had shown me the maps and the written report from the traveller who had found the hitherto unknown Roman temples. They were in a hidden dry valley that was surrounded by cliffs and protected by a ridge. The only way in or out appeared to be either over a tricky trail through the ridge or through a narrow gorge paved with a Roman road.

"So, I believe."

"Then that gives us the best chance to make everyone safe. We will fortify the entrance and you and your archaeologists can excavate to your hearts content but you will be secure. When we camp tonight my men and I will lose sleep. We can do that for a limited time but tired men make mistakes and out here mistakes can be fatal."

"You make a good case, Captain. I will speak to my people." He smiled, "The one I need to address is the one who still looks fresh, your remarkable wife."

He was right. I had seen her strength after Siwa but she seemed to have grown stronger since then. We camped an hour before dark. I might have pushed on but Sergeant Reed was of the opinion that the academics could ride no further. Corporal Cartwright confirmed it when he spoke of some of the camels struggling. I heeded his words for I had taken the best camel and he was the worst yardstick to use. When we made camp I said to my wife and George, "Don't wait for me to eat and don't worry if I am away some time. I want to see where the Turks are."

"Be careful." Lucinda kissed me.

"I will."

I took my rifle and walked back down the road to a place I could watch for the Turks. George had picked a flat place with some greenery. I think Cartwright had suggested that they might find water and they had done. I used the rocks at the side of the road to seek a rock behind which I could wait. I took out the binoculars. I knew that the setting sun would reflect off them but that could not be helped. Besides, they knew where we were. I saw them. They were still six miles away but they were strung out. Two of the horses had become detached. I tracked them as they wound in and out of sight as they passed twists and turns in the roads. The Romans liked to build straight roads but nature sometimes made life hard for them. There were fewer turns on this road than the ones in rural England.

I wondered if the Turkish captain would push his men to catch us. Just before the sun dropped below the horizon in the west I saw him wave his arm and the men circled. They would camp. I waited until I saw the flicker of firelight before I headed back up the road to the camp.

Ransome appeared from behind a rock, his rifle cradled in the crook of his arm. "Sergeant Reed asked me to keep an eye on you, Sir."

I nodded, "They are five miles down the road and camped. If we make a start before dawn we should increase our lead."

We walked back together. Everyone but the two of us was eating. McTeer and Tupper were sitting on a rock and watching

An Officer and a Gentleman

the camels but they were eating. Lucinda brought me a bowl of food. "You must be starving." She led me to the two saddles that had been placed to make seats. Later on they would help to make a bower for our beds. We said nothing but ate. That is to say Lucinda ate and I devoured the food. She was right, I was hungry.

Cartwright had made a pot of tea and he brought me some. He smiled, "I never thought I would actually like goat's milk, Sir, but it is better than tinned milk. We have enough for another day and then it is back to the tins."

"It's a hard life, Cartwright. With luck there will be goat herders where we are going and we can buy some more."

He wandered off allowing Lucinda and I to have what passed for a little privacy out here in the desolate emptiness of the hills and mountains. "Do you regret coming?"

She laughed, "Of course, not. I mean there are parts I could have done without but from what I have read we are going to see what amounts to an ancient wonder. It is less than ten years since it was discovered and few men have examined it. It was the discovery of the Roman road that led to travellers finding it. I feel privileged."

I nodded, "And when this is over and we go back to England, what then?"

She stopped, her cup almost at her lips, "You mean us?"

"I mean archaeology and you."

She sipped her tea, "I had not given that as much thought as I should. I would like to be an archaeologist but it doesn't pay very much. When we return I will put down on paper our discoveries and take a leaf out of your father's book, literally. I will write a book. I can still keep house."

I had not thought of that. "You can do that anywhere?" It was a question.

"Of course. Wherever you are posted I can be with you."

I remained silent for it suddenly occurred to me that Brigadier Dickenson might have plans for me. What if this was my future? What if I was to be a spy? After I had walked the lines and given my orders, I lay down with Lucinda and ran through what might happen. Rather than be a spy I would resign my commission. There were other things that I could do. I could not think of one of them for the moment but I had months to work them out. The last night had been without rest and I soon fell into an exhausted sleep.

George woke me at two and after making water I wandered to the place I had watched the previous evening. I saw the glow of their fires and, in the shadows it cast, saw the sentry. They were still there.

I roused the men two hours before dawn. I knew I was tiring them out but we had to make the most of our advantage. They prepared the camels and food. I woke the archaeologists an hour before dawn. We set off before the sun had risen when the air was chilly and the academics complained about the cold, their joints and the lack of sleep. I did not say that if it had just been my men and me we would have left an hour before dawn. Once more I rode at the back. It became easier from the off because we were dropping down to the valley of the Dead Sea. That patch of Biblical salty water lay to the north of us but it meant our camels could make better speed. Of course we would have a climb towards the end when we ascended the valley sides to Petra and then the new site but that was at the end of the journey.

As we headed towards the other side of the valley I looked back and saw the Turkish horsemen. They had stopped not far from where we had camped. I scanned them with my binoculars and saw that two of the horses were being led and not ridden. I waited and, eventually, they turned around and headed back the way that they had come. I did not think they were done with us but by the time they returned we would be ready for them.

We passed Petra and I thought that looked magnificent. We carried on towards the new site. I used my map and compass. It was just three miles away. We followed the Roman road and our going became much easier. When we passed through the rocky entrance to what was, in effect, a hidden city, we were all exhausted. I saw ruined temples and buildings that must have had a purpose other than religion. It was much smaller than Petra. It was, after all, an imitation. I glanced up and saw, on the ridge above, what looked like a ruined watch tower. The other thing I noticed, in the darkening gloom, was the magnificent columns of the temple but then my nose smelled camel dung burning. There were people here.

An Officer and a Gentleman

"Sergeant, make a camp. Put two men at the entrance. Tupper and Ransome, come with me."

I dismounted and led my camel. She had carried me enough. I followed my nose and we passed through what must have been, some time in the past, a good place to live. I heard the goats before I saw them. We passed a building that had clearly been damaged by an earthquake in the past and I saw the tents of the desert dwellers. I had been worried that these might be tomb raiders but the goats and the tents were reassuring.

Six men stood, almost barring our way, ancient rifles held across their bodies. I handed my reins to Tupper and with palms out walked towards them, "I mean no harm. We are men sent by the government who have come to inspect these ruins."

There was a fire and in its glow I saw that there were about twenty people altogether. The women had their arms around the younger children and the older ones stared at us.

One of the men came forward. I think my use of his language was reassuring and we were not Turks. He was not as old as Talal but he was clearly the leader. He said, "I am Tarif al-Takari and I am the leader of this clan. If you come in peace then you are welcome. This place has grazing and water. More importantly few people know of it and it suits us to spend the winter here. How many are you?"

"Fifteen men and one woman. We are English and my name is Captain Roberts."

He smiled, "Good, you are not Turks."

I nodded to the goats, "If you have any to spare we would buy milk from you and, perhaps, any animals that you wish to sell us. We have food but…"

He smiled and I saw that many of his teeth were missing, "We are always happy to be of service. You would pay with gold?"

"We would pay with gold."

"Then you are welcome, Captain Roberts." When he said my name I could not help but smile for he sounded it the way old Ismail had.

I pointed, "Our camp is over yonder. We will have men guarding the entrance but we will not bar the way. We have heard that there are tomb raiders."

He spat, "They are not men, they are jackals and they desecrate the spirits of the past. When we see them we chase them. They are not men. They run rather than fight."

That was welcome news. I had feared we might have to fend off such men.

He continued, "We will be moving our flock in three days. We seek better grazing but we will return."

"We are only here until the days are as long as they will ever be."

"Then we will not be back here by then. This place has good grass in the winter but in the summer we seek other pastures."

He sent one of the boys with us carrying an earthenware pot with the milk. We would decant it and I would pay them. We were promised an old goat the next day. Not as tender as a kid it would need longer cooking. We now had the time.

With two men on the entrance I was able to relax a little more. I told the others what had been said and like me they were relieved that we would not have a battle with the tomb raiders. Thomas Teal said, "But no diggers."

"No diggers but when Tarif comes the next day I will ask him where the nearest village is to be found." I guessed it was Wadi Musa which I had heard mentioned but I did not know.

Tarif confirmed that there was a village just couple of miles away. He said that the tribe who lived there were the Liyathnah. They lived in houses made of mud and they farmed. According to Tarif the water came from the spring created in the past by Moses. His words, when I translated them made the archaeologists sit up and take notice. He mentioned a tomb that was reputed to be that of Moses' brother Aaron. It more than made up for the journey. They had more grist for the academic mill. I was sceptical for Lucinda had said there was a similar story about the spring at Petra. I guessed that water was so rare here that ascribing it to a miracle made some sort of sense.

While they all explored the temple complex we set up the camp. By the time our new neighbours had gone we were as prepared for problems as was possible. We watched them pass by and head through the gorge and along the Roman road. They lived life to a pattern and were a happy people. It mattered not who controlled the land, Nabateans, Romans, Crusaders, Turks, they continued life in the same measured manner.

I rode with Sergeant Reed and Thomas Teal the day after the goat herders left and we rode to Wadi Musa. To the archaeologist's delight they were more than happy to supply diggers. They were happy for the coins they would be paid and it meant that the work could move on apace. It was decided that we would not need them for a week or so as the archaeologists needed to assess the place first and prioritise the digging. That suited the men of Wadi Musa.

That night I sat with Sergeant Reed, "And tomorrow, I will be leaving you. I intend to do what the brigadier wants me to do, see how far they are with the railway."

"I should come with you, Sir. I am supposed to protect you."

"I would rather you stay here. If the Turks come in my absence then I need you to take charge."

He glanced over at the six men we had brought. They were good men but none was a leader. "How long will you be gone, Sir?"

"How long is a piece of string? I hope less than a week and certainly not as long as ten days."

"Mrs Roberts will not be happy, Sir."

I smiled, "I know."

I would be camping alone and I would be in a place I did not know. I made sure that I had plenty of water. The Roman site was well supplied thanks to the spring. I took food that did not need to be cooked. Tarif's wife had sold me some cheese and Cartwright had made me flatbreads. Like the sergeant he was unhappy that I was going alone but he was torn. Mrs Roberts needed his protection more. Surprisingly, when I rose early to leave and Lucinda rose with me she seemed to be philosophical about the whole matter. She seemed resigned to my absence and had accepted it. "You are good at what you do. I know that when someone has skill you must trust that skill. I do not like that you are alone but I think that might make you safer and harder to spot." She kissed me hard, "Come back safe. While you are gone, I will throw myself into my work. When this is over I shall have much to occupy my mind."

An Officer and a Gentleman

I mounted the camel. I had named her Sarah for the trader had not given her a name and she seemed to have the same attitude as my Aunt Sarah. After leaving the site I turned and headed into the rim of light that presaged dawn. It was cold and that was good, it meant we could move better until the sun began to rise and to burn the land to a crisp. The railway ran north, from Damascus to Medina in the south. All I had to do was to head east and I would find it. We plodded steadily south and east and I was treated to a most magnificent sunrise. The sky changed colours before my eyes and bathed the land in the most beautiful light. I knew from the maps my father had given to me that the caravan trails were to the south and north of me. I could have taken the ancient one that had made Petra so rich in the ancient world but I did not want to run into Turks or Germans. We had permission to be in this part of the Ottoman Empire but I thought that they would take a dim view of someone looking at their pride and joy, the Hejaz railway.

I had learned in Egypt that the desert is not as featureless as one thinks at first, but it did change. As I descended from the high ground to the sea of sand I sought out features that I could mark on my map. Archie Dunn had drummed that skill into me. When I saw rocks I marked them and used my own unique nomenclature: sheep's head, dragon's mouth, Tarif's teeth. The Hejaz lay well to the south of Aqaba and the land there was even less well known than where I was but, as Brigadier Dickenson had told me, the Turks prevented any westerner from map making in their empire. I was adding to my father's and they would be as valuable as gold if there was ever a war between the two empires. There was a town to the south of me and while I was heading closer to it I had no intention of risking finding a desert patrol. Ma'an had a fort and a garrison. The railway, we assumed, passed through it. As such they would patrol the land around it. I would avoid that. There would be traders heading there now for when the pilgrims came they would need animals and food. The town was a honey trap.

I made good progress that first day especially as I was not using the caravan trails. I travelled twenty miles. When I spied the tiny patch of green surrounded by a crown of rocks, I headed to it. It was a slight depression in this desolate land and water gathered there. The rocks afforded some protection from the sun and life had sprung up there. Some seeds had been taken there. Perhaps a bird had taken them or they had fallen from the coat of a camel but there were stunted trees and a couple of bushes. It was not much but it was a place I could use, a refuge. I filled one of my skins before I let Sarah drink. I examined my camp for reptiles, scorpions and spiders and found none. I climbed to the top of the highest rock and used my glasses to scan the horizon. I saw no movement and I decided to risk a fire.

    I tethered Sarah and she grazed on some of the greenery. Her grazing would encourage more growth as would the dung she deposited. I lit the fire and while the water began to boil and in the last light of the day I added to the map. I called this place Village Green. I made the tea. I used the pot I had boiled the water in as a teapot and ate flatbread, cheese and some bully beef. My dessert was a handful of dates. That done I made my bed as darkness enfolded me. I fed the fire before I turned in although I knew it would be out by morning.

    The next morning I was more cautious. I knew that I would be coming upon the railway sooner rather than later. It was the sight of the smoke in the north that told me I was close. I made Sarah sit and then hid behind her. I heard the train as it hissed and lumbered south. I used my binoculars. As I was facing north I hoped that there would be no reflection from the sun. I saw that the train was about a mile north of me. I tracked it as it came south. There must have been a slight incline for it seemed to be struggling a little. This was not a work engine pulling sleepers and workers to the rail head. The train had carriages for passengers as well as two flatbed cars with wood on them. I also saw Turkish soldiers. The railway was open, at least as far as Ma'an and as this was not yet Hajj season, then the presence of passengers suggested it might be open almost as far as Medina. As I tracked it south I knew I could go back immediately for we had the news that Brigadier Dickenson sought but I was a thorough officer. I would inspect the rails myself.

    I waited until the train had disappeared from view and then mounted my camel. We rode due east and I saw that it was a single-track railway. That was good news. It meant there must be some passing places. I would have to find them. I also saw that while most of the sleepers were wooden, as in England, one in five were made of metal. That was curious. I did not want to go south as I was unsure how close Ma'an was. I rode north up the railway line. I stopped at noon and watered my camel from the water taken at the Village Green and I drank from the other. I had a canteen, too, in which I had poured the last of the tea. I would savour that luxury at my evening repast. I was not sure that I would be able to light a fire.

I was wondering if there was a passing place as the sun began to dip in the west but then I spied, using my glasses, a pair of buildings and what looked like a small tower. They looked to be made of wood. I focussed my binoculars on the buildings. There was a Turkish flag flying but that was all that I could tell. I would need to get closer to inspect it and that meant using the night. I found a depression just off to the north and went there to eat a cold meal. The tea, whilst it was cold, somehow revived me. When it was dark I walked along the side of the railway line. The one train I had seen had been the only one. I had not seen any travelling north. I felt safe. When I heard voices I stopped and dismounted. This was not Scheherazade and I could not trust Sarah to stay. I hobbled her. I drew my pistol and headed, not along the line, but to the north. I would approach the buildings from that direction.

There were two buildings and both were made of wood. I saw that the tower was a water tower. I heard voices and froze as a door opened and in its light I saw a Turkish soldier in his off-duty fatigues. He turned to shout, "Leave some for me!" before he closed the door and walked into the dark. I had my pistol ready but when I heard the hiss and splash I knew he was just making water.

I waited until he had re-entered before I continued around the back of the building. The water tower was there to keep the men in the building supplied. Why were they there? I found, just a few yards to the northwest, a wooden shed. It was not locked and when I inspected it found tools. That explained the soldiers. They were here to maintain the line. I headed for the line and it was there I found the passing place. The train I had seen pulled three carriages, two flat cars and a guard's van. As I walked down the passing place I deduced that they could accommodate a

An Officer and a Gentleman

train twice that length. I smelled Sarah and crossed the line to retrieve my camel. I walked her to the west, away from the line. My work was done and I could return to the archaeologists and our camp. Before I did so I would find somewhere to watch the line. A day spent in the sun studying the line could only add to the information I was taking back.

I did not find water but I found some rocks where we could hide. There was a little vegetation and Sarah grazed. The water I had taken from Village Green was enough to keep her happy. As I added to my map I reflected that I would have to head back to the water when I headed home.

I heard the train heading north at about eleven. I should have checked my watch but I was too busy trying to focus on the train. I wanted to see if it would halt at the huts. This time there were two more carriages and no flatbeds. There was a Turkish flag and I saw soldiers on board. It halted at the stop which was a mile away. I saw officers descend and the men from the hut came out and saluted. It was when I saw one of the officers suddenly turn that I knew I had made a mistake. Even though I lowered the glasses instantly I knew that I had been seen. The light from the sun in the south east had reflected from them. Sarah was sitting down and I was behind the rock so they would not know who I was but I knew from Egypt that the flash of light from the desert meant only one thing, soldiers. I lay still and waited. I risked looking out and saw that six soldiers were making their way to my place of concealment. I made a decision and I mounted Sarah and set off to the west. The six cracks from the rifles told me I had been seen. I did not turn. They would see, not a British officer, but an Arab riding a camel. I knew that the desert dwellers did not like the Turks and I hoped that they would dismiss me as an accidental watcher and not a spy but the binoculars were a mistake. The next shots came long enough after the first to tell me that they were single shot rifles. I dropped down into another depression and risked a glance over my shoulder. There was no sign of the soldiers and I slowed down my flight.

I had to think. I had not seen a telegraph line and that meant news of my presence would have to wait until the train reached a station. I stopped and consulted my map. It would either be

Hasa, a tiny village, or Al-Qatrana. Hasa was closer. I shook my water skin. It was half full if you were an optimist. The desert was filled with the bones of such optimists. I knew that I might be able to reach our camp by dark but I could not guarantee it. The Village Green was a couple of hours away. I chose that option.

    I reached it just before dark. Sarah needed the water but I filled her skin first and then the pot for tea. It was only then that I allowed her to drink. I lit a fire. I needed hot tea and I would toast the stale flatbreads. I had finished the cheese already and my meal would be bully beef, toasted flatbreads and dates. In the light of the fire I added a few more details to my map. After hobbling Sarah I went to sleep.

    When I woke I knew that I had about twenty odd miles back to the camp at the new Roman site. I saddled and mounted my camel and set off north and west. I slipped my map case around my neck and my water skin. It was a hot day already and that meant we would have to travel more slowly. I kept scanning the horizon with my glasses although the heat haze limited what I could see. At noon I guessed that I was fifteen or so miles from what I hoped was our camp and it was then that disaster struck. I was looking north and I saw, less than two miles away, six riders. It was not a caravan. It was Turkish soldiers and they could cut me off from the camp at the Roman site and Petra. Even as I turned my camel I saw them begin to gallop towards me. I had been found.

Chapter 20

I knew that luck, good and bad was part of every soldier's life. Thus far I had enjoyed good luck but that day my life was riddled with bad luck. Sarah was struggling and I was travelling over uneven ground. I kept glancing over my shoulder and saw that the Turks were well mounted and as they were covering flatter ground were gaining on me. I leaned over and stroked her, "Come on sweetheart, you can do this." She tried to respond but was flagging. Scheherazade would, even weakened, have left the Turks for dead. I glanced behind and saw that the Turks were within three quarters of a mile. Looking ahead I saw the ground rising and whilst there were rocks that I could use for cover, they would catch me before I could reach them. The sun was incredibly hot. Had I not been pursued I would have stopped to find shade but if I stopped then I would be a prisoner. I cursed my luck and my single mistake. There had to have been a garrison at Hasa and the officers had sent them to find me.

It was as Sarah struggled to negotiate a steep section that my ride ended. The Turks were a long way off but they saw their chance and the guns all fired. One was a lucky shot or, from my perspective, an unlucky one. Sarah stumbled as the bullet slammed into her leg and she stopped. Sometimes you have to make quick decisions. I grabbed my Lee Enfield from its scabbard and dismounted. Sarah would go no further. I levelled the rifle and used her neck for support. I aimed at the Turkish camels and fired five bullets in quick succession. I was a good shot and the Lee Enfield was more accurate than their weapons. They were stopping even as one of the Turks clutched his arm. They dismounted and opened fire. I ran. I heard Sarah give a cry as she was hit again. I did not look back for I was concentrating on avoiding a fall but I heard her body as it crashed to the ground. It would take them time to mount and follow. I searched ahead and saw the rocks that would give me a chance. I made them and slamming another magazine into the rifle sought a target.

The one I had wounded was following the other five who had remounted and were galloping up the rocky slope. I aimed at

An Officer and a Gentleman

their camels and emptied my magazine. I reloaded and kept firing. The fates decided that I had endured sufficient bad luck and I hit two camels. It made them stop. The last thing they needed was to be afoot in the desert. I reloaded and took in the situation. The sixth man joined them and I saw them speaking. I looked at the sky. It would be dark within the hour. I needed to hold them off for an hour and then try to slip away in the dark. Would they give me an hour?

I watched their debate and kept my gun levelled at them. I saw them bandaging the wounded man. All the time, one of them had his rifle aimed at me or, more likely, the place that had seen the puff of smoke. I knew that I was hidden well with my rifle in the cleft of the rocks. I was happy to let them debate. The longer they did so then the better my chances of escape for darkness was my friend and was coming to my aid. I had water and a few dates in my tunic pocket. I had my canteen with the remains of the cold tea and I had a skin of water. I was twenty miles from safety. By moving through the night I might survive. The next, I looked at my watch and then glanced at the sun, forty-five minutes would determine that.

I knew, from their movements, that they had decided on their plans. They left the wounded man to watch the animals and the rest spread out in a semi-circle. I aimed at the man who had given orders. I took him to be a sergeant. There were too few for it to be an officer. They came in a crouched manner. One man fired and the other four scurried and zig zagged up the slope. They stopped and another aimed at the rocks. It was classic light infantry tactics. As long as I did not fire they would not know exactly where I was. I would have to choose my moment well. I aimed at the sergeant. My bullet was well aimed and slammed into his leg. They all dropped to the ground and fired a fusillade at my smoke. My head was down and I was rolling to my right. I raised my head and aimed at another man. This time I hit his arm. Once more they responded but there were just three rifles this time and the bullets pinged from the rocks at my first position. I rolled to the right and then began to crawl up the slope to where I had spied, in the setting sun, my next strong point.

The three men who were unwounded were brave and they spread out in a wider half circle to charge the rocks which I had

An Officer and a Gentleman

just evacuated. I aimed my gun but did not fire. I saw them searching the rocks and one lifted up some spent cartridges. He shouted, ".303."

I had the one who had shouted in my sights when the sergeant called out, "We will track him in the morning. He cannot get far and if he is a British soldier will not survive the desert. We will take his corpse back to Captain Schmidt."

That was good news and more intelligence for me to take back. There was another German officer. I waited until the sun had set before I moved. I moved across the slope, still hidden by the rocks until I could see a route that would take me west. I ran crouched and watched, in the dark, for any shadow that might be a hole or a reptile. When I had travelled far enough; in my mind I estimated a mile, I stopped and drank some tea and ate two dates. They would have to sustain me. After reloading it I slung the rifle diagonally across my back and set off. I could not see my map and besides it would not help me. None of the landmarks I had seen on the way south and east would be visible. I had to rely on my compass and my in-built sense of direction. I set myself visible targets in the dark. My compass gave me the direction and I headed to the place I had selected. It was a slow but steady journey and each step took me further from my pursuers. I stopped each hour to drink and eat one date. I had enough to last the night and then I would have to go hungry. I hoped that dawn would find me close enough to the camp for it not to matter. My legs were unused to such marching across rough terrain and I found it hard. On the uphill sections I found my lungs bursting but when dawn came I looked and saw that I had climbed the worst and it was now downhill. I could not see either Petra or the new Roman site but I had landmarks in my head and I thought I recognised one. I finished off the tea and devoured my last date. From now on it would be water. After two hours I recognised a rock. I was to the north of where I needed to be. It explained why I had not recognised anything before. There was a bush growing with the hard tough leaves that meant it could survive without much water. I chose that moment to not only make water but empty my bowels. The dates had worked. I used the coarse leaves. The sun had risen even higher

An Officer and a Gentleman

and was beginning to beat down. I needed to reach the camp before noon.

Knowing where the camp lay made me hurry and that was almost my undoing. I spied the building that we had found on the first day. It was an ancient tower overlooking the city. Romans built well but the earthquake had almost destroyed it. The part that remained was like a sort of coronet. If there had been danger then the sergeant and I had decided it would make a good place for a sentry. I headed for it and as I did so I spied movement on the ground below. There were Turkish soldiers wriggling like snakes along the ground to the edge of the ridge that overlooked the camp. These could not be the same ones who had chased me, I would have heard their camels and besides there were too many of them. These were others and they were up to no good. I caught a movement and thought I saw a grey uniform but in the shadows it was hard to be certain. I reckoned I could make the ruined watch tower. I had a plan but it was a risky one and might mean my death. I had been so confident that by guarding the single entrance we would be secure. I had forgotten that the ridge could be used. I had to warn the camp of impending disaster but that warning might cost me my life.

I had to keep low and move obliquely across the slope. I was slightly above the crawling men but I would have to drop and then climb towards the tower. Would I make it in time? I would be helped by their serpentine approach. They were moving steadily so as not to attract attention. I made the bottom of the slope, unseen, and then climbed up to the old watch tower. I could not see the Turks any longer as I was on the far side of the ancient monument. When I reached the top I slipped over the stone and unslung my rifle. I was given a good view of the old city and our camp. It would have made a good place to watch. I saw the tents and the fire. Tantor was stirring something. Ransome and Tupper were at the entrance and I saw McTeer watching the camels. I could not see all of the archaeologists nor the rest of my men but I suspected that the Turks would have a view of them when they reached the crest. The only safe place would be in the temple itself but that would mean that they were trapped.

An Officer and a Gentleman

I levelled my rifle and aimed at the back of a sergeant I could see. I was about to squeeze the trigger when my conscience took over. If I killed the sergeant then it would be me who initiated the attack. I could not bring myself to do so and, instead, fired a single shot at the rock close to Tupper. I aimed ten feet above his head and prayed that no flying chips would harm him. The sound of the shot echoed around the cavern that was the old Roman temple site. Immediately, the Turks, thinking that one of their own had fired, began to shoot. My single bullet had been enough warning. Tantor dropped behind the pot. Ransome and Tupper took shelter behind the rocks and McTeer hid behind the camels.

I heard Sergeant Reed shout, "Alfred, get to safety. The rest open fire." The servant raced to the safety of the camp. The three men I could see began to fire. It gave me the chance to ascertain the strength of the enemy before us. I counted twenty. I recognised the officer. It was Captain Kukuk. When Ransome was hit in the arm I knew I had to take a part. I aimed at the sergeant. My target was the fleshy part of the leg. He was hit and rolled over. Such was the noise from the enemy weapons that I remained hidden and, more importantly, undiscovered. I next aimed at the captain who was looking down at his sergeant. My bullet hit his right hand. A .303 is a big bullet and it drove through his hand, smashing the handle of the gun. He did not look up but ducked beneath the ridge. Many of his men followed suit. I saw Boyce run to Ransome. He was followed by Bert Williams. As the Welshman fastened a dressing around the wound, Williams emptied a magazine at the ridge. I prayed that they would not fire at the muzzle flashes from the tower. When Williams turned and began firing at the entrance to the city I knew that this was a two-pronged attack and men were coming to attack the men guarding the gate. I had to risk everything. I raised myself and began to methodically move along the men on the ridge, I fired to wound. It was not entirely out of a sense of mercy. Wounded men would need to be tended. A dead man would encourage his friends to seek revenge. I hit four of them before I had to reload and I was seen.

I heard Captain Kukuk roar, "There are men in the tower, get them."

An Officer and a Gentleman

I fired at the first soldier who responded and, as I hit him saw Ransome point at me and say something to Boyce. Pendle and Reed ran to the entrance. If they used a mad minute then the narrowness of the gorge that led to these temples might save them. I was not sure it would save me. I was firing as fast as I had ever done but the Turks were moving quickly and I missed more than I hit. I had done all that I could in the tower and I went to the far side and rolled over the broken wall. I slung my rifle as I did so. I would have to use my Webley. I had needed my hands to climb up and now I needed them to stop myself from tumbling over as I ran down the rock-strewn trail. As I reached the bottom I opened the flap on my holster and was just drawing it when a Turk came around the side. He raised his rifle as I drew and fired. I was only saved because it took longer to raise his weapon that it did for my Webley to clear my holster. I fired two bullets and they knocked him over. I ran as bullets zipped around my head. The gunshots echoed from the walls and the hills. It was hard to know the direction the bullets were being fired from. The Turkish guns gave off more smoke and there was a sort of foggy haze.

    I was now living on my wits. I knew that there was a path, of sorts, that led to the main part of the ancient complex of temples. It was a steep one and I risked falling. The trouble was I was being followed. The bullet that pinged off the wall to my left was just a little higher than my head. I whirled and fired from the hip. I unslung the rifle, dropped to one knee and then sent a shower of bullets up the trail. I dropped the empty rifle and emptied the last bullets from my Webley. I picked up my weapons and ran knowing I had bought myself moments only. As soon as I saw a bend I turned and holstered my pistol. I loaded a fresh magazine and peered at the trail. The two Turks who raced along it must have thought I had kept running for they were running full tilt. I fired four bullets at their legs and one fell immediately. The other clutched his leg. Both men dropped their weapons and I ran. I had to watch the rocks for a fall now would be disastrous. When I saw the start of buildings with good stonework I knew I was close to the place the archaeologists were working.

An Officer and a Gentleman

I turned the corner and found myself looking down the business end of a Lee Enfield. Cartwright gasped, "Captain! I almost shot you."

I turned and said, "The next men who come down you can shoot." The man who appeared with his rifle at the ready was hit by a bullet from me in the leg but the two from Cartwright blew a large hole in his chest.

"Mr Potts has been wounded. The rest are in the main temple, Sir." He smiled, "Mrs Roberts is unhurt and tending to him."

I shook my head, "They will be coming down this path. You and I need to discourage them."

I saw a movement and fired. The bullet pinged off a rock and ricocheted. I knew from the fighting in Egypt that bullets and rocks made a fearful combination, especially in a confined space. I could hear the sounds of many bullets being fired and they appeared to be coming from the entrance. They might need our help but if I left this back door open then we were in trouble. I changed magazines as I was unsure how many bullets I had fired. When there was another lull I would reload my Webley.

I had just snapped home the magazine when Cartwright fired three bullets in rapid succession. I smiled, "You have become a proper soldier, Cartwright."

He gave a sheepish grin, "Must be the stripes, Sir, or watching you."

I had not taken my eyes off the trail and when I saw the barrel of a gun I fired, not at the rifle but the rock on the opposite side. I was rewarded by a cry when a rock splinter hit the rifleman. I heard a shout from up the trail. I understood half of the words for the man was speaking them with a German accent. The gist was that they were ordered to withdraw.

I reloaded my Webley as I heard the footsteps receding up the trail. "Cartwright, stay here. I will have you relieved." I ran crouching around the corner to what must have been a busy ancient thoroughfare. I noticed that the firing from the entrance had diminished a little. I ran there.

Sergeant Reed looked around and grinned, "I thought it had to be you, Sir. Thanks."

I nodded, "What is the situation here, Sergeant?"

An Officer and a Gentleman

"When we were pinned down on the hillside, Sir, we started to make a defensive position here. That was when they sent men down the gorge." He pointed to the top of the gorge, "They had men up there and it was touch and go for a while. There were too many men and we had too few defenders. Then we began to pick off the ones at the top of the gorge." He explained, "They had to lean over to fire and as they have single shot weapons we had the advantage. We sent bullets down the gorge and the ricochets keep them busy."

I nodded, "Pendle and Williams, go and relieve Cartwright, send him here. He is covering the back trail into the site."

"Sir." They both picked up their rifles and ran zig zagging as they did so. Bullets came down from the ridge but they were soon in the lee of the temple and safe.

"McTeer and Tupper, go back to the temple and make a defensive position there. Take Ransome with you."

"I can fight, Sir."

"And you can do that just as easily from inside the shade of the temple. I am still in command. Now go."

"Sir."

"Wait until the sergeant and I give you some covering fire. Sergeant, give them a mad minute down the gorge and I will keep their heads down on the ridge."

"Sir."

"Right, then, on three. One, Two, Three." I turned and aiming my gun at the ridge methodically moved down the ridge firing as fast as I could. The two men helped Ransome and they hurried off. We both reloaded. I would soon need more magazines. There was a flurry of bullets from the ridge and Cartwright appeared. I said, "How is it?"

He smiled, "I used your technique, Sir, and kept hitting rocks. They have learned to be wary."

I nodded, "I want you to go back to the temple and take command. I want a wall made of whatever you can. Once it becomes dark then we are vulnerable here."

"Sir."

I smiled, "Let us see what you learned from Doctor Quinn and the orderlies eh?"

"Sir."

An Officer and a Gentleman

"Ready again, Sergeant?"

"Sir."

"One, Two, Three."

We opened fire and the echoing noise was deafening. Cartwright made it back to the temple. We reloaded and I told the sergeant what had happened. "This attack has nothing to do with my scouting. I recognised Captain Kukuk. This is all to do with our presence here. Istanbul might have sanctioned the dig but not the local military. There has to be at least half a company here."

"So it looks like we are up a sand creek without a paddle, Sir."

"Not quite. We have two wounded men but they have many more. Cartwright killed one and I accounted for at least half of the men who were up there. I think they would have left already but for the German officer."

"German officer?"

"I caught a glimpse of a grey uniform and heard orders given in an accent."

"So, Sir, you sent the others back to the temple, what is the plan?"

I took a deep breath. "My father told me about Rorke's Drift. They were outnumbered but they held off forty times their number by making a defensive wall. I intend to do that but we have an added problem, the camels. We cannot afford to lose them." I glanced at my watch; it was almost noon and soon the sun would bake the men on the ridge as well as those at the top of the gorge. The only ones who would be safe from the glare would be in the gorge itself. "They have not fired for some time and I am guessing they are planning what to do. We use that time." I pointed to the camels. We had tethered them in the shade of the temple down a jumble of fallen masonry created by the earthquake. "We will get to the camels and you and I will take them to the temple."

"Put them inside, Sir?" I heard the shock in his voice. "What about the ruins?"

"Sergeant, the dig is immaterial now. We have a wounded archaeologist and the excavation has been compromised. I just want to get as many out alive as we can."

An Officer and a Gentleman

"Sir."

I slung my rifle over my shoulder and shouted, "Cartwright, when we move give us covering fire."

"Sir."

We had one advantage. The Turks on the ridge would expect us to run to the temple over the killing ground. They would have seen the others run across it but the sergeant and I had deterred them. When we moved we would be vulnerable.

"Go!" We ran, keeping as low as we could. It took a moment or two but the ridge erupted. They fired at the path to the temple and it took them seconds to realise what we were doing and readjust. By that time we were hidden by the temple and buildings. Of course we had left the front door open so to speak and as soon as the men in the gorge realised that it was undefended then they would surge towards us.

I was more of an expert with camels than the sergeant but he was a quick learner. He saw how I tethered them in a long line and copied me. When I heard the bullets firing from the temple I knew that men were coming up the gorge.

"Ready!"

"I suppose so."

"Then run. Hai! Hai!"

The camels were to my left and protected me but we had lost my camel already. We could not afford to lose many more. The men on the ridge had no target and the fire, directed by Cartwright, kept the ones coming out of the gorge more intent on survival than anything.

I shouted, "Clear a space. Coming through!"

Getting the camels up the steps was the hard part but we managed it just because of the bullets zipping around us like horseflies. They encouraged the camels to run. As soon as we entered the gloom of the temple I smacked the rear of the leading camel who wandered off into the partly excavated site.

I turned and saw a grinning Sergeant Reed, "Life is exciting with you, Captain."

I saw Lucinda tending to Professor Potts. Ransome was bandaged and was firing at the gorge. I waved at her. "And now I need to extract Pendle and Williams."

"Sir, let me go."

255

"Sergeant, I gave the order and, besides, I know the route to take. I did it once before. Now give me covering fire."

"Yes, Sir," he nodded. "On my command make the entrance a death trap. Captain Roberts is going for the other two."

I handed my rifle to Cartwright who said, "Take care, Sir. I don't think Mrs Roberts is ready for black yet."

I drew my Webley and nodded to the sergeant.

"Rapid fire! Commence! Commence! Commence!"

I hurtled the boxes that protected the riflemen and their bullets cracked and pinged off the walls. I ran along the side of the temple. I shouted, "Officer, coming in."

When I reached the two men I saw that they were unwounded. I peered around and saw a second body lying next to the one slain by Cartwright. Bert Williams grinned, "Getting a bit naughty here Sir."

"Don't worry. We are leaving soon. Now this will be tricky. We have abandoned the entrance to the gorge but we are safe from the ridge. Williams, I want you to empty your gun along with me down the trail. When that is done the three of us run as fast as we can for the temple. Pendle, keep your gun loaded and fire from the hip when we run."

They both nodded.

"On Three. One, Two, Three."

I fired three bullets down the trail while Williams emptied his gun. We turned and I followed Williams and Pendle. Pendle's gun barked quickly as he fired and chambered a fresh round. The rocks and the masonry made the bullets' flight unpredictable. I sent the last bullets from my pistol towards the entrance. I thought we had made it when I felt a bee sting in my leg. I was wondering where the bees came from when my right leg gave way and I stumbled. I had been hit. I hit the ground and that saved me as bullets flew over my head. I half rose and stumbled towards the temple. Hands pulled me over the boxes and I heard Sergeant Reed shout, "Cartwright! The captain is wounded."

I was bundled deeper into the temple. "I am fine, get back to the boxes and keep their heads down."

Cartwright and Lucinda appeared above me, "Where are you hit, Sir?"

"The right leg I think."

An Officer and a Gentleman

Lucinda poured a cup of cold tea and held it to my lips. I realised that the last drink I had enjoyed had been just before I had seen the Turks. That was six hours ago. She shook her head, "Why you, Griff? Have you always to be the hero?"

I shrugged, "It comes with the rank."

"Then resign the rank. I want the man and not the uniform."

Chapter 21

I was lucky, the bullet had passed through the fleshy part of the leg. We had enough dressings and medicine to ensure that Cartwright could eliminate any infection. The bee sting now began to hurt. Lucinda brought over the bottle of whisky and topped up the tea. I shook my head, "I need to be alert."

She pushed the cup to my mouth, "I am the senior officer here, Captain Roberts, now drink." I sipped it and felt its warmth course through my body. "The sergeant knows what he is doing and as you have had no sleep and no food you are in no condition to be in command. Not yet anyway."

She was right and as she rolled up my cloak and keffiyeh to make a pillow I lay back. I was fighting sleep but I guessed that they had put something else in the tea apart from whisky for I began to feel sleepy. Perhaps she was right and I had gone too long without sleep. Darkness took me. It was a troubled sleep for the faces of the dead flashed before me, Archie, Burton, Ismail and the dead assassin. The last face I saw was that of Lucinda! I woke with a start.

When I opened my eyes the others were eating. Lucinda put her hand on my arm and said, "Feel better?" I shuddered because of the last image. I tried to stand but pain shot through my leg, "You are wounded. Remember?"

I nodded, "What is happening?"

"At the moment we are eating. Professor Potts is awake now, too. Tupper and Pendle are on duty watching the gorge but the afternoon has been quiet."

I nodded, "Where is the sergeant?"

A voice came from behind me, "Here, Sir. You needed the sleep."

"But now I am awake and if they have been quiet this afternoon then you can bet they intend something tonight. When the men have eaten have the ones who will watch tonight, get to bed."

"I had already worked that out, Sir. It will be me, Boyce and Williams." He nodded over to where the archaeologists were eating and talking. It looked like a heated debate. "Professor Teal is less than happy, Sir. He wanted to wake you." He chuckled, "He learned that your wife has a sharp edge to her tongue. I am guessing he will be over now that you are awake."

"And the ammo, is that holding out?"

"Yes, Sir, but no more mad minutes. We have no idea how long we have to hold on for. I have told them to be careful."

Cartwright brought me a bowl of food. "Well, you look a lot better, Sir. Here you are. Get this down you and I will check the dressing."

I smiled as I took the bowl. I was ravenous. I saw the archaeologists had finished their food and were looking over at me. I continued to eat. It was a typical Cartwright stew. It was the sort of food we would have eaten most nights on patrol. A stew made with bouillon, corned beef and whatever cereals were to hand. The only thing lacking was the flatbread. They had all gone and with no locals to provide more we would have to do without.

"Lucinda, did we get diggers from Wadi Musa?"

She looked around as though the answer might be on the painted walls, "Now you come to mention it, no. I mean, we have not needed them yet. We have spent all our time recording and interpreting what we have seen. I don't think we will need them for a week or so."

Cartwright still hovered close by, "Is it important, Sir?"

"I was just thinking about the bread and the milk they promised. If they haven't come then there is a reason and I think the Turks might be that reason. It tells me that they have been here for at least a day longer than I thought. This Captain Kukuk, or perhaps the German with them, was careful to line up all their ducks before they opened fire."

Cartwright nodded, "Luckily you were there to spoil the party, Sir. If you hadn't pre-empted the attack…"

I saw Lucinda's face as she took in our words. It would have been Siwa all over again. A sudden swift attack with people killed quickly. I handed the bowl to Cartwright, "Delicious."

It was almost as though Professor Teal was waiting for me to finish for he suddenly raced over, "Captain Roberts, this madness has to end. I want you to speak to these people. We have the right to be here but it seems that your actions have

An Officer and a Gentleman

created a dangerous situation." I saw Sergeant Reed sidling over. He pointed to the camels, "And these animals are unacceptable. We are destroying an ancient treasure."

Lucinda said, "Thomas, that is nonsense. My husband saved us from disaster. We might be dead or worse by now."

"Worse!" He could not keep the incredulity from his voice, "What is worse than death or this?"

"Slavery, Professor."

He laughed, "Captain Roberts, you are deluded and I put it down to the medication. I am in command and I order you to speak to these people."

I waited to ensure that my voice was calm and that I was not shouting, as the professor was, "These men want us dead, Professor Teal. Tonight they will come from the ridge and the gorge and they will assault us. When they do they will slaughter us. We will just disappear. When the British government and your backers investigate they will be told that it was bandits. We will all be forgotten."

"Ridiculous."

I sighed as I explained, "Britain does not want a war. The South African War is too raw yet and we did not emerge well from it. The Turks and the Germans know this and they are pushing as much as they can. Corporal Cartwright and I saw that in the desert. Why do you think the diggers did not come from Wadi Musa? They would have sold us food and earned money. These people are not so well off that they can afford to spurn such opportunities. They were ordered not to come and they will be ordered to back up the official version of events here. So, no, I will not speak to them but what I will do is prepare our defences so that when they come tonight it is they who will die and not us."

I saw the professor's mouth open but before he could speak Sergeant Reed said, "Why do you think Brigadier Dickenson sent men to protect you, Sir? He thought this might happen. Captain Roberts saved us this morning, make no mistake about that. The two sentries at the gorge would have been shot and the entrance attacked. With men on the ridge they could have picked us off at will." He turned to me, "Sir, are you fit enough to…"

"I shall have to be. We need to strengthen the front of the temple. What else have we got that will make a barrier and slow down a bullet?"

"Saddles, Sir."

"An excellent idea, Cartwright."

George Reed put his arm around my batman's shoulders, "When I first met you, Corporal, I thought you would be a passenger. You are anything but. Right lads, shift those saddles."

Lucinda turned, "Are you still here, Thomas? Shouldn't you be slinking back to your rat hole."

"You realise, Mrs Roberts, that this is the end of your archaeological career?"

She laughed, "My, but you are full of your own self-importance aren't you? I have learned enough from the time spent here and the time we will spend when my husband saves us, to write my own paper."

He was appalled, "You cannot do that! I will have my name on the paper and my colleagues will be listed as associates."

"But my paper will have my name." He turned and stormed off. Lucinda turned to me, "And you will stay here. You are in no condition to fight."

I sighed, "Your tone may work with Thomas Teal but not me. I know my own body better than anyone. I am the most experienced man in this temple when it comes to night fighting and as I will not have to move the wound to my leg will not be a problem. I will be with my men."

I saw her debate whether or not it was worth a fight. She decided not to. "And I shall be next to you." She patted the holster. "And before you argue you do not have enough men to spurn the offer of another weapon."

My men had been busy building the barricade while we had been speaking. Cartwright helped me to my feet and I limped, gingerly, over to the saddles. I went to the middle. My batman said, "I will get you your rifle, ammo and waterskin, Sir."

Lucinda nestled next to me. I said, "Keep your head down and shoot here," I pointed to the arch of the saddle. "That way you will be protected from their fire."

She nodded, "And this won't be like Siwa. We will not be sitting ducks."

Just then John Bannerman-Castle came over, "Mind if I join you?" He held up his own revolver. He smiled at Lucinda, "Thomas Teal is a self-centred arrogant fool. I believe you are right, Griff." He found himself a place next to Lucinda.

Cartwright came back and handed me my rifle. He lay down next to me.

Sergeant Reed said, "I have all the lads in position, Sir. I will be at yon end." He pointed to the right. "Alf Tupper is a solid chap and he is at t'other."

"Wait until I fire and remind the men to fire only when they have a target."

"Sir."

I peered into the dark. While we had a clear field of fire and we were above any attackers there was no moon and we would be watching shadows once more. I tried to listen for the sound of a footfall or a disturbed rock but there was too much noise. The archaeologists were chattering away. I shouted, "Either help us defend or shut up. Your incessant chatter is unhelpful."

I heard Teal said, "Well of all the…"

Alfred Tantor's voice cut through, "I think it is a good idea, Professor. We can get our heads down. We will be safe from any flying bullets eh?"

I heard him mumble, "This is nonsense. There will be no attack." But silence followed. Soon the only sound was that of the camels but they were far enough at the back of the complex so as not to intrude too much.

I kept my head still and slowly moved my eyes from right to left. It was getting close to midnight and I expected them before dawn. The chatter of the archaeologists would have carried outside and any soldier worth his salt would wait until there was silence that suggested sleep. They had seen men wounded and knew our numbers. Although we had hurt them they would have confidence in their superior numbers. My Lee Enfield rested on the saddle. I could reach it in an instant. It was the sound of the solitary rock slithering from the side that alerted me. I hissed, "Stand by!"

Knowing that someone was coming helped for when I saw a shadow that moved I knew it was a man. I wanted to hit as many in the first fusillade as we could. Their captain was wounded as was their sergeant. The leader would be the German. He would be wearing grey and in the dark would be as close to invisible as it was possible to be. I saw more shadows moving. I realised some were slithering across the ground as I had seen them that morning on the ridge above the temple complex. That was clever. It would be harder for us to hit them.

I put the rifle to my shoulder and peered down the sight. I was taking a slight risk as my head was a little above the saddle but it was an easier position for me. I could rest on my good knee and I would be able to hit the crawling men. I chose the one I would fire at. He was the closest. I worked out where his head would be and aimed at it. I knew the rifle would kick up a little but by aiming there I had a good chance of hitting his back. I waited until he was less than thirty yards away.

Lucinda whispered, "I can see them!"

I squeezed the trigger. The crack of the bullet echoed off the walls of the gorge and the flare of the muzzle lit up the night. My men were all ready and their Lee Enfields barked. The two pistols sounded too. I moved my rifle as men stood to rush us. My men were heeding my orders and the bullets were fired singly. The Turkish rifles cracked and spat bullets at us. I heard one gun that appeared to be firing quicker. That had to be a pistol and it suggested the German officer. The attackers were being hit but when I heard a cry from my left I knew that we were not having it all our own way.

"Tupper's hit."

"Corporal, go and see to him." Cartwright would have to be the doctor.

"Sir."

We had lost almost twenty percent of our firepower. Worse it was two Lee Enfields that were no longer firing. Lucinda and her guardian were firing as fast as they were able but neither were soldiers. When the figure rose just six feet away and fired his rifle I barely managed to hit him. He flew backwards but Sergeant Reed shouted, "Boyce has bought it, Sir!"

Another rifleman down. When Lucinda said, "My gun has jammed."

I said, "Take my Webley." I slipped the lanyard from around my neck.

An Officer and a Gentleman

In that instant as my rifle no longer fired they rushed us. There were at least a dozen. I fired as quickly as I could. The rest of my rifles did the same and Lucinda and her guardian did all that they could but there were simply too many. When my rifle was empty I used it like a club and swung it at the first Turk who lunged at me with his sword. The butt smacked into his jaw but behind him I saw the grey of a German officer and he had a sword. He was coming for me. I shouted, "Lucinda, get back."

I held up the rifle as the sword swept down. We were in danger of being overrun and it was hand to hand fighting now. The sound of gunfire had ceased. I heard John Bannerman-Castle shout, "The captain is right, Lucinda, let us get to the rear."

Somehow the thought that my wife might be safe gave me confidence. The sword bit into the stock of my rifle and stuck a little but the German was above me and he pushed down. My good leg gave way and when I crashed to the ground I felt a shock of pain race through my wounded leg. As I fell I put my hand out to slow me down. It meant the German was able to force his sword closer to my head. Luckily, he caught his own leg on the saddle and as my hand touched the ground felt the hilt of the dagger I had taken from the assassin on the ship. I pulled it out and even as the German sword scored a long cut along my forehead I slashed at his arm. The assassin's knife was sharp and it tore through the uniform and into flesh. I felt the blood pouring from the wound in my head but I knew it was not a mortal one. I would, however, have to end this fight sooner, rather than later.

Lucinda and her guardian might have retreated deeper into the temple but I could hear their guns still firing. They were the only ones. Lucinda, I knew it was her, was trying to help me. She was firing at the German and it was one of her bullets zipping over his head that distracted him, albeit momentarily. I lunged with the dagger and it tore into his side. He swore in German and pulled his sword free from the stock of my rifle. As it came down there was the sound of two pistols being emptied and one of them managed to hit the hilt of the sword. The weapon fell and the German shouted, in Turkish, "Out."

The Turks, the ones who were able, rose and fled. My men were angry and they fired at the fleeing men. I shouted, "Cease fire and reload."

An Officer and a Gentleman

Lucinda raced over with a dressing in one hand and the still smoking pistol in the other. "You are wounded, again."

"A flesh wound. It looks worse than it is."

"Paul! I need you. The captain needs you."

I shouted, "Sergeant, throw the enemy dead out. See if there are any injuries?"

"Right, Sir."

I reloaded my Lee Enfield as Cartwright wiped away the blood. I took the Webley from Lucinda's hand and began loading it. "You are Annie Oakley. That was fine shooting and you distracted the German just long enough for me to hurt him."

"I thought you were dead."

I laughed, "It takes more than a couple of wounds to hurt a Roberts, ask my dad."

Sergeant Reed appeared, "Alec McTeer is wounded."

"Paul, Mrs Roberts can see to me. Go and tend to Pendle."

"Sir."

"Bill Pendle is dead."

"Damn, a third of our men are dead and another third are wounded. If they come back...."

As Lucinda fastened a bandage around my head the sergeant said, "I doubt it, Sir. There were fifteen bodies we had to shift and there were others who were wounded."

I was doubtful but we could do nothing in any case.

By the morning the stink from the camels was becoming overpowering. Sergeant Reed and Alf Tupper went out to reconnoitre. It left just three of us. Thomas Teal apart, the archaeologists seemed keen to help and they cooked breakfast. Alfred Tantor took it upon himself to take out the camel dung.

I was getting worried when my two scouts had not reappeared by eleven. When they did they were moving so casually that I relaxed. I hobbled out to the steps.

"Where are you going?"

"To speak to the sergeant away from the others." I saw the bodies. My men had covered them as best they could and laid them out.

Sergeant Reed said, "They are gone, Sir. Not a sign of them. We went up to the ridge and the bodies are gone from there, too."

An Officer and a Gentleman

I nodded, "You two bring the camels out. Get Williams to help you. I want you and Tupper to ride to Wadi Musa. Find out what you can."

The sergeant frowned, "Sir, my Arabic is not that good."

"Then if Cartwright is done with his doctoring take him."

"Sir. What happens next?"

"That is a good question. I have no intention of risking wounded men on the road. We stay here and do what we came for. We let the archaeologists explore this complex and leave in June."

"Right, Sir."

By the early afternoon the inside of the temple was smelling better. Between them Tantor, Williams and Tupper had buried the bodies and we had marked each grave with the name of the soldier using the information to hand.

Cartwright and Reed arrived back in the late afternoon. The men of Wadi Musa were less than happy about the intervention of the Turks, whom they seemed to hate. They had been told not to help us and a pair of armed sentries had been left there to ensure that they stayed out of it. They had heard the gunfire. The two men returned with flatbread, milk and cheese that they had bought in the village. Ransome and McTeer insisted on standing a duty. I think they realised how lucky they were. Two of their comrades were dead and my wounds were far more incapacitating than theirs.

A sheepish Professor Teal came to speak to me after we had eaten. Out in the open the atmosphere appeared less claustrophobic than in the temple. "Captain Roberts, it appears I owe you an apology. Your strategy appears to have worked. I am in your hands now. What do you suggest?"

"You continue to do that which was planned. You dig this site and use the men of Wadi Musa to help you."

He looked at my bandaged head, "But you are wounded, as are two of your men."

"And we can still do our duty. The Turks may well return and I cannot predict when that will be. Work as hard and fast as you can and leave the Turks to us."

Over the next two weeks I healed. The bandage was taken from my head and I just had an angry scar that would turn white

An Officer and a Gentleman

eventually. My leg began to support my weight although I was dreading having to ride a camel. The dig went on from dusk until dawn. The diggers were paid each day and that pleased them.

At the start of the third week I felt fit enough to ride. I needed to check for myself that we were safe. My men and my wife would not let me travel alone and Sergeant Reed said that as he had to stay and command the camp in my absence, Corporal Cartwright was more than capable of being my bodyguard. I rode back along the route I had walked after my camel had been shot. I found her body. The Turks had clearly cut hunks from her and the vultures had done the rest. There were bones, some skin and pieces of flesh. By the end of the summer there would be nothing. I rode to a place where, by using my binoculars, I could see the railway. Having been there I knew what to look for. I would not have to get close. What I was looking for was a sign that they had increased their patrols. It was as I lowered towards the southern end of the line that I saw the camels. They now had men patrolling. We headed back to the Roman site. I had information for Brigadier Dickenson.

It was the fourteenth of April, two months since we had left England that the column of Turkish horsemen appeared. Bert Williams had spotted them and we were ready with weapons to hand. There was no German with them and they rode towards us as though it was a pleasant day for a ride and they were visiting.

Once through the gorge, the officer dismounted and the sergeant told his men to dismount. I saw that he was a major and I saluted. He smiled and said, "I am Major al-Masri and you, I take it, are Captain Roberts?"

"Yes, Sir, I am."

He smiled, "I am here to escort you and the archaeologists back to Haifa where a ship will soon arrive to take you back to England." He reached into his satchel and brought out a folded telegram. "This is from your commander, a Brigadier Dickenson." I nodded and read the telegram which confirmed the major's words. "It is brief but it orders you home. I have my orders from Damascus. I show you the telegram as a courtesy. I will accompany you home." He leaned in, "You have managed to upset some people. I do not say that this was wrong but they may take matters into their own hands unless you have protection. Better for all I think if my men and I are with you."

"Yes, Sir."

"Especially as you have your wife with you." He wiped the dust from his cloak, "We will stay the night and leave first thing. I would be honoured if you would introduce me to your wife and the others."

"Of course." I pointed to the graves, "We buried the men who died over there. We tried to mark the graves with their names but…"

"Thank you for that. It shows that you have honour. They will be reburied but not by me. Now lead on, Captain, and I look forward to an entertaining ride back to Haifa." I could see him choosing his next words carefully, "And we shall hunt down those bandits who attacked you and caused such terrible injuries to our brave soldiers. I believe that Captain Kukuk will lose his hand. You were lucky, were you not, Captain Roberts?"

I had been right and the whole incident was being expunged from the record.

The archaeologists were happy to be going home. The site was far from excavated but they all had enough information to write a paper and as we would be home before the heat of summer they were pleased. Professor Teal was still distant with both Lucinda and me but poor John Bannerman-Castle was also included. All the wounds were healed except for the memory of the two lost comrades. Before we left we went to their graves, marked with their names on crosses, and we fired a salute over them. The last look we had was of the graves as we went through the gorge.

The major was a gentleman. He was from the Kurdish Sanjak and regarded himself as a warrior. He despised men like Lieutenant Kukuk and told us so in quite bald terms. He was also disparaging about the Germans. "They are everywhere and even if Istanbul cannot see it I can. They seek to use us for their own ends."

By the time we reached Haifa and the ship I felt as though we were friends.

We sold the camels back to the trader. He made money and we bought gifts at the market before boarding the steamship that

An Officer and a Gentleman

had been chartered to take us home. It was the end of April when we set sail. We left when the weather was getting hot but we all knew that England would be chilly. The voyage back was more pleasant than the outward one had been mainly because there was no attempt on my life and we had no storm. Lucinda and I spent more time with my men than the archaeologists. I told them I would make sure that the two dead men's families received the full pay due to them. All of them would be paid for the full contract. I think that they had decided not to continue life as mercenaries. The pay they had received would help to make their pensions go further. The last night we held a party and it was a better end to the trip than we could have hoped for.

Epilogue

Brigadier Dickenson, Sergeant Barker and a civil servant from the Foreign Office were waiting for us all at Southampton. I knew the meeting and debrief were inevitable but Lucinda and I just wanted to get home. We were taken by hackney cabs to the hotel next to the station, The Midland. It was a grand hotel and the brigadier or perhaps the Foreign Office, had taken over a function room. The civil servant took down the archaeologists' comments about the expedition. We had a debrief with the brigadier. He did not keep the men too long. Sergeant Barker handed them their pay, with a bonus as well as a travel warrant.

They seemed reluctant to leave us. Alf Tupper said, "I am not sure if we will meet again, Captain Roberts, and that is a shame for me and the lads would do so again. You are a good officer and," he glanced at the brigadier, "you know what you are doing. Say goodbye to Mrs Roberts for us will you as ..."

He got no further as Lucinda had been waiting for her turn to speak to the official and she came over. "That will not do Mr Tupper, you can say goodbye in person and give me a hug."

Poor Alf flushed and then said, "It has been a pleasure, Mrs Roberts, for you are a real lady." They hugged and Lucinda repeated it for all of them.

"Mrs Roberts..." the civil servant snapped impatiently.

"Coming," she gave a curtsy, "and you are all gentlemen. Thank you."

After the men had gone the five of us went to the bar. "Didn't turn out quite the way I had hoped but," the brigadier held up the written report I gave when we docked, "from a quick glance at this, it was worth it."

"Not for Boyce and Pendle it wasn't."

He looked at me, "You have to learn to look at the bigger picture, Griff. Anyway, you have benefitted from this. You and your wife can go back home and enjoy some time there until I need you again."

Cartwright's mouth dropped open. The brigadier's two soldiers dropped their heads, not wanting to meet my gaze. I said, "You need me, Sir? But I thought I would go back to the regular army."

He smiled, "In the fullness of time we can arrange that but the incident in the desert not to mention the complaint made by the Turkish government means that, for the time being, at least, you will be attached to my office. That means full pay and the work will be a little more interesting." He smiled, "Another drink before you catch your train?"

Sergeant Reed seemed to want to stay but the brigadier clearly wanted him to leave. The sergeant saluted and I held out my hand. When he shook it I noticed that he had a firm grip. "I learned a lot from you, Captain Roberts. I was sent to protect you," he glanced at the brigadier, "but I reckon you were the one who did the protecting. Like the lads, I would serve with you any time."

"Come along, Reed. This is no time for sentiment." The difference between real soldiers and senior officers was encapsulated in that comment.

When Lucinda came into the bar, half an hour later, we had finished our second drinks and there was just Cartwright and I there. She beamed, "Good, we can go home. You know, Griff, for the first time in my life I feel like I am going home and yet it is your home, strange is it not?" I decided to keep my news until a more suitable time.

Cartwright smiled, "And they are kind people there, too, Mrs Roberts. They are people you know you can trust." He looked at the door through which the brigadier had departed, "There are others who smile but you wouldn't trust them an inch."

I could see that she did not understand. I stood and took her arm. "Let us go and find a porter. I think we shall let someone else carry our cases, eh, Cartwright?"

"Yes, Sir. I shall go and get one."

He scurried ahead and Lucinda squeezed my arm and said, "And Paul is also part of the family."

"That he is."

We headed for the door that led to the platform. The journey north would wipe the memory of the brigadier from my mind, at least for a while, until he summoned me again.

The End

Glossary

Bevvy - a drink (slang)
Butty (pl butties) - 19th-century slang for close friends
en banderole - worn diagonally across the body
Cataracts - rapids and rocks that impede the passage of boats
Dhobi (n) - washing (from the Indian) dhobying (v)
Fellah - an Egyptian soldier, the equivalent of a private in a British regiment
Hajj - annual pilgrimage to Mecca
Half a crown - two shillings and sixpence (20 shillings to the pound, 12 pennies to a shilling)
Laager - an improvised fort made of wagons
Jibbah - short white blouse worn by the Mahdists
Lunger - nickname for the sword bayonet
Nabob - someone from India who has made a fortune
Peaching - informing
Puggaree - a cloth tied around a helmet
Sanjak - an administrative region of the Ottoman Empire ruled by a Bey
Souk - market

Historical Background

This book is about life as a soldier, an ordinary soldier. The soldiers of the queen did not care who they were fighting, they just knew they were fighting for their queen and country. That idea may seem a little old-fashioned now, but I am not rewriting history, I am trying to show what it might have been like to live in 19th Century Britain. The British Army saluted with their left hand until the First World War. The weapons used are, according to my research (see book list), the ones used in the period.

Anyone who has researched their family history in the nineteenth century and looked at the census records will know how even relatively well-off factory workers rented or boarded. Four and five to a bed was the norm. We take so much for granted today but even in the 1950s life was hard and had a pattern. With coal fires, no bathroom, an outside toilet, no carpets and little money for food it was closer to life in the 1870s. Offal was often on the menu and you ate what was there. Nothing was wasted. Drinking beer and smoking were not considered unhealthy pastimes. There was a teetotal movement but it was only in the latter part of the nineteenth century that the water the people drank became healthy. Until then it was small beer that was drunk.

One reason why the attempt to relieve Khartoum failed, apart from the usual vacillations of the politicians, was that the main army travelled by boats which had to be unloaded and carried over the cataracts and the smaller, allegedly faster relief force led by General Stewart, marched in square and took ten days to cover one hundred miles.

The British NCOs who were recruited to retrain the Egyptian army were the Sergeant Whatsisnames made famous by Kipling. They did a good job. Every officer who volunteered was given the rank of major so that no Egyptian officer could give them orders.

The use of the border patrols is factual but I have made up the incidents. There were bandits who came from what is now Libya as well as regular and irregular Ottoman soldiers. The British presence was resented. Further south the French had similar problems. The two nations had built the canal and would do all that they could to keep it safe.

I made up the Roman ruins but my recent trip to Pompeii showed me that there may well be many such ruins out there yet to be discovered and as that part of the world is a little dangerous for a research trip you will have to forgive my fertile imagination.

This series will continue but unlike my British Ace Series and my WW2 one, I will not be working my way through wars. I intend to look at how British soldiers served this country and how their lives changed as Britain changed.

Books used in the research:

- The Oxford Illustrated History of the British Army - David Chandler
- The Thin Red Line - Fosten and Fosten
- The Zulu War - Angus McBride
- Rorke's Drift - Michael Glover
- British Forces in Zululand 1879 - Knight and Scollins
- The Sudan Campaign 1881-1898 - Wilkinson-Lathom
- Onwards to Desert War - Keith Surridge
- Desert War - Donald Featherstone
- The Arab Revolt 1916-18 - Murphy and Dennis
- Lawrence and the Arab Revolts - Nicolle and Hook

Griff Hosker
2025

An Officer and a Gentleman

Other books by Griff Hosker

If you enjoyed reading this book, then why not read another one by the author?

Ancient History

Roman Rebellion
(The Roman Republic 100 BC-60 BC)
Legionary

The Sword of Cartimandua Series
(Germania and Britannia 50 A.D. – 128 A.D.)
Ulpius Felix- Roman Warrior (prequel)
The Sword of Cartimandua
The Horse Warriors
Invasion Caledonia
Roman Retreat
Revolt of the Red Witch
Druid's Gold
Trajan's Hunters
The Last Frontier
Hero of Rome
Roman Hawk
Roman Treachery
Roman Wall
Roman Courage

The Wolf Brethren series
*(*Britain in the late 6th Century)
Saxon Dawn
Saxon Revenge
Saxon England
Saxon Blood
Saxon Slayer
Saxon Slaughter
Saxon Bane
Saxon Fall: Rise of the Warlord

An Officer and a Gentleman

Saxon Throne
Saxon Sword

Medieval History

The Dragon Heart Series
Viking Slave *
Viking Warrior *
Viking Jarl *
Viking Kingdom *
Viking Wolf *
Viking War*
Viking Sword
Viking Wrath
Viking Raid
Viking Legend
Viking Vengeance
Viking Dragon
Viking Treasure
Viking Enemy
Viking Witch
Viking Blood
Viking Weregeld
Viking Storm
Viking Warband
Viking Shadow
Viking Legacy
Viking Clan
Viking Bravery

Norseman
Norse Warrior

The Norman Genesis Series
Hrolf the Viking *
Horseman *
The Battle for a Home *
Revenge of the Franks *
The Land of the Northmen

An Officer and a Gentleman

Ragnvald Hrolfsson
Brothers in Blood
Lord of Rouen
Drekar in the Seine
Duke of Normandy
The Duke and the King

Danelaw
(England and Denmark in the 11th Century)
Dragon Sword *
Oathsword *
Bloodsword *
Danish Sword*
The Sword of Cnut*

New World Series
Blood on the Blade *
Across the Seas *
The Savage Wilderness *
The Bear and the Wolf *
Erik The Navigator *
Erik's Clan *
The Last Viking*
The Vengeance Trail *

The Conquest Series
(Normandy and England 1050-1100)
Hastings*
Conquest*
Rebellion

The Aelfraed Series
(Britain and Byzantium 1050 A.D. - 1085 A.D.)
Housecarl *
Outlaw *
Varangian *

The Reconquista Chronicles
(Spain in the 11th Century)

An Officer and a Gentleman

Castilian Knight *
El Campeador *
The Lord of Valencia *

The Anarchy Series
(England 1120-1180)
English Knight *
Knight of the Empress *
Northern Knight *
Baron of the North *
Earl *
King Henry's Champion *
The King is Dead *
Warlord of the North*
Enemy at the Gate*
The Fallen Crown*
Warlord's War*
Kingmaker*
Henry II
Crusader
The Welsh Marches
Irish War
Poisonous Plots
The Princes' Revolt
Earl Marshal
The Perfect Knight

Border Knight
(1182-1300)
Sword for Hire *
Return of the Knight *
Baron's War *
Magna Carta *
Welsh Wars *
Henry III *
The Bloody Border *
Baron's Crusade*
Sentinel of the North*
War in the West*

An Officer and a Gentleman

Debt of Honour
The Blood of the Warlord
The Fettered King
de Montfort's Crown
The Ripples of Rebellion

Sir John Hawkwood Series
(France and Italy 1339- 1387)
Crécy: The Age of the Archer *
Man At Arms *
The White Company *
Leader of Men *
Tuscan Warlord *
Condottiere*
Legacy

Lord Edward's Archer
Lord Edward's Archer *
King in Waiting *
An Archer's Crusade *
Targets of Treachery *
The Great Cause *
Wallace's War *
The Hunt*
The Prince and the Archer

Struggle for a Crown
(1360- 1485)
Blood on the Crown *
To Murder a King *
The Throne *
King Henry IV *
The Road to Agincourt *
St Crispin's Day *
The Battle for France *
The Last Knight *
Queen's Knight *
The Knight's Tale *

An Officer and a Gentleman

Tales from the Sword I
(*Short stories from the Medieval period*)

Tudor Warrior series
(*England and Scotland in the late 15th and early 16th century*)
Tudor Warrior *
Tudor Spy *
Flodden*

Conquistador
(*England and America in the 16th Century*)
Conquistador *
The English Adventurer *

English Mercenary
(*The 30 Years War and the English Civil War*)
Horse and Pistol*
Captain of Horse

Modern History

East Indiaman Saga
East Indiaman
The Tiger and the Thief

The Napoleonic Horseman Series
Chasseur à Cheval
Napoleon's Guard
British Light Dragoon
Soldier Spy
1808: The Road to Coruña
Talavera
The Lines of Torres Vedras
Bloody Badajoz
The Road to France
Waterloo

The Lucky Jack American Civil War series
Rebel Raiders

An Officer and a Gentleman

Confederate Rangers
The Road to Gettysburg

Soldier of the Queen series
Soldier of the Queen*
Redcoat's Rifle*
Omdurman*
Desert War
An Officer and a Gentleman

The British Ace Series
(World War 1)
1914
1915 Fokker Scourge
1916 Angels over the Somme
1917 Eagles Fall
1918 We will remember them
From Arctic Snow to Desert Sand
Wings over Persia

Combined Operations series
(1940-1951)
Commando *
Raider *
Behind Enemy Lines
Dieppe
Toehold in Europe
Sword Beach
Breakout
The Battle for Antwerp
King Tiger
Beyond the Rhine
Korea
Korean Winter

Tales from the Sword II
(Short stories from the Modern period)

Books marked thus *, are also available in the audio format.

An Officer and a Gentleman

For more information on all of the books then please visit the author's website at www.griffhosker.com where there is a link to contact him or visit his Facebook page: Griff Hosker at Sword Books or follow him on Twitter: @HoskerGriff or Sword @swordbooksltd
If you wish to be on the mailing list then contact the author through his website: Griff Hosker.com